Blood Family

Blood Family

Graeme Hampton

hera

First published in the United Kingdom in 2020 by Hera Books

This edition published in the United Kingdom in 2022 by

Hera Books
Unit 9 (Canelo), 5th Floor
Cargo Works, 1–2 Hatfields
London, SE1 9PG
United Kingdom

A CIP catalogue record for this book is available from the British Library.

Print ISBN 978 1 80032 852 5
Ebook ISBN 978 1 912973 21 7

This book is a work of fiction. Names, characters, businesses, organizations, places and events are either the product of the author's imagination or are used fictitiously. Any resemblance to actual persons, living or dead, events or locales is entirely coincidental.

Look for more great books at www.herabooks.com

Printed and bound in Great Britain by Clays Ltd, Elcograf S.p.A.

1

For Gary

Prologue

There was blood on the floor. Lots of blood.

She tried to look away. Focus on something else. Anything else. But all she could see was the blood. It pooled on the floor and ran in rivulets along the gaps between the tiles, turning the grouting red.

He was dead, and nothing would change that.

They should call the police. They would be in trouble but at least it would be over with.

She closed her eyes, hoping the scene would have disappeared when she opened them. Except it hadn't. It was still there. Red. So much red...

Chapter One

A cool breeze blew along the street. It ruffled the leaves on the trees that lined the road and caused an empty crisp packet to scud across the pavement and slap against the side of a wheelie bin.

Detective Inspector Matthew Denning sighed as he surveyed the dismal scene. It was too early in the morning to be dealing with this kind of thing, he thought. A coffee and a Danish, then ease yourself into the day. That was his preferred start to a morning. Today, however, fate had decided to deal him a different hand.

Gibney Road was a typical London street in the north-east corner of Islington, just before it runs into Hackney.

A long row of Victorian terraces ran down one side, while solid, red-bricked villas dominated the other. There was nothing remarkable about the street, except for the blue and white police tape that flapped across the frontage of number forty-two.

The house was one of the large villas on the south side of the street, many of which, Denning guessed, had been divided into flats. Number forty-two, however, was a house. Or rather, what was left of one.

A couple of LFB fire appliances took up most of the available space in front of the house, and beyond them a solitary squad car sat half on the pavement and half on the road, its blue light still strobing.

Within the outer cordon, fire officers could be seen bustling around the appliances, or entering and leaving the property. A long, thick hose snaked across the garden, disappearing into the dark void beyond the gap where the front door used to be.

He showed his ID to the young constable standing sentry next to the outer cordon.

'Morning, sir.' The officer glanced at Denning's ID and pointed to a white-clad SOCO standing near one of the fire appliances. Denning nodded his thanks and headed over to join the group of forensic officers waiting beside the taped-off inner cordon.

Seeing him approach, one of the SOCOs smiled and raised her hand in acknowledgement. 'DI Denning. What brings a nice boy like you to a gory show like this?'

Sheila Gorton was the crime scene manager. She spoke with a faint trace of a Canadian accent and smiled a lot when she spoke. They had worked together before. He admired her professionalism and efficiency, while she seemed to like the fact he was young, bright and going places, or so someone back at the nick had told him.

Denning was with East London MIT – one of the Met's eighteen Major Investigation Teams. They formed part of Homicide and Serious Crime Command, and as such they didn't usually bother themselves with anything as mundane as a house fire, unless there was something suspicious to prod their interest. This, apparently, was suspicious.

'We got a call from the brigade. Seems they have some concerns about the fire's cause.' He kept his voice cool, professional. 'As there are suspected fatalities, it falls within the remit of MIT.'

Denning had got into the office early that morning, intending to catch up with paperwork and prepare a fellow detective for an upcoming promotion, when one of the uniformed officers attending the scene had called it in, stressing the presence of casualties. He'd informed his DCI of the situation and put in a formal request for a forensic team to get there ASAP. And here they all were, standing around like extras on a film set, waiting for their cue.

'Nothing's been confirmed as yet,' Gorton said. 'We only got here ourselves a few minutes ago. But from what I've managed to overhear, the speed at which the fire spread certainly seems to suggest the possibility of arson.' Next to where they were standing, her team were either climbing into their plastic coveralls, or already wearing them and awaiting the instruction from Gorton to get the show on the road.

Denning sympathised; he was keen to find out what the deal was himself, and whether he was going to have to get his team down here to make things official.

'Any chance they'll let us in there sometime soon?' Denning asked, nodding at the gutted building. He didn't fancy wasting his morning making small talk with SOCOs.

Gorton shrugged. 'They're still trying to make the place safe, apparently.' She looked over at the burnt-out house. 'There was a real fear the roof was going to collapse at one point. They can't take any risks.' She offered him a dry smile. 'It's all about health and safety these days.'

'In the meantime,' said Denning, 'we're stuck out here scratching our backsides.'

'Speak for yourself, Inspector.' She waved at one of the fire officers, beckoning him over and then introducing him to Denning. 'This is Tom Keeble, he's the Incident Commander.'

Keeble removed his helmet and shook Denning's hand. He was in his mid-to-late forties, thick set with broad shoulders and a thinning salt and pepper on top. His face was glistening with sweat and his eyes were red and liberally smudged with black soot, like badly applied mascara.

'Detective Inspector Denning is keen for us to get inside and have a poke around,' Gorton said, with a slight twinkle in her eye. 'Any chance?'

Keeble eyed Denning as though challenging him to question his authority. The rules governing the specific responsibility for a suspicious fire were very strict: only when the Incident Commander had deemed a building safe would they officially hand control over to the police, and only then after the signing of the relevant paperwork. Like a dog marking its territory, Keeble wanted to remind Denning that this was his call until such time as he said otherwise.

'My team have almost finished in there,' he said. 'We're just securing the building now. The fire's out and the structural integrity is being checked as we speak.' He glanced back at the house. 'We've just sent a hydrocarbon detector dog in along with its handler.'

He noted the puzzled look on Denning's face.

'It's trained to detect the presence of any residual amounts of ignitable liquids that may still be present,' Keeble explained. 'You don't want the place going up again the minute we leave, do you?'

Denning nodded his agreement. 'Can you say at this stage what caused the fire?'

Keeble sighed and scratched his chin. 'Seat of the fire would appear to have been the living room. We initially thought it might have been caused by an electrical fault, or a candle left burning. You'd be surprised how often that happens.'

'But you now think otherwise?'

There was a momentary silence. 'That's why the fire investigator called you in.' He looked at Denning, then at Sheila Gorton. 'I don't think this was an accident.'

'So, we are talking arson?' Gorton asked.

'I'm sure your mob will be able to confirm it,' Keeble said, nodding at Gorton. 'But the fire investigator found what we suspect are trace elements of some kind of accelerant. He can't say for sure at the moment, but the clever money's on petrol.' He glanced back at the house. 'It would explain a lot. According to neighbours, the house went up like a Roman candle. Poor sods in there didn't stand a chance.'

Denning winced, remembering there were casualties; knowing that if the fire investigator was right, then they were talking probable murder. Manslaughter, at the very least. 'How many bodies?' he asked.

There was a pause before Keeble answered. 'Five.' He scratched at his chin again. 'Including a child.'

Gorton muttered something that sounded like *Jesus Christ*.

Before anyone else had a chance to respond, Keeble added, 'If it's any consolation, I think they likely died from smoke inhalation.'

It was scant comfort. Being suffocated was marginally preferable to being burned alive, but it still wouldn't have been pleasant. Denning could imagine the fear and rising panic, knowing they weren't going to get out alive.

Denning was about to ask Keeble a further question when one of the firefighters wandered over. A young man in his twenties, sweating and red-faced like Keeble, he lightly touched Keeble on the elbow to attract his attention. Keeble introduced the younger fire officer as Jamie Beck. 'It's all clear now, boss,' Beck said. 'We've had to put a support truss in to make the roof safe but it's secure now. The hydrocarbon detector dog found faint traces of accelerant, probably what was used to start the fire, but it's been safely extinguished now, so it's OK for forensics to enter.' Denning watched as a black and white spaniel was led out of the building by its handler. The dog was wearing what looked like little red booties to protect its feet.

Keeble nodded at Sheila Gorton, who pulled on her hood and face mask, and shouted over to her officers. Denning watched as Gorton led her white-suited team past the inner police cordon and into the burnt-out house, brushing past the occasional fire officer who was still exiting the building.

Beck turned to Denning, no doubt correctly guessing he was police. 'We've left the bodies in situ,' he said. His voice sounded gritty, like a car crunching on gravel.

'Where were they found?' Denning asked.

'That's the weird bit.' Beck looked from Denning to Keeble, as though waiting for the senior officer's permission before answering. Keeble nodded. 'They were all found in different rooms. One in the kitchen at the rear of the property, another two in what I guess was the living room at the front of the house.' He paused. 'And it looks like an adult and the child were in an upstairs bedroom.'

'What's the weird bit?' Denning asked.

He removed his helmet and rubbed soot from the corner of his eye. 'Looks like there were at least two smoke alarms in the house. Assuming one of them worked, there should have been enough warning to give everyone time to get out the house, or at least to try and find an escape route. Judging by where the bodies were found, it doesn't look like any of them even tried to get out.'

'Maybe the smoke got to them before they had a chance,' Denning said. 'Or they panicked?'

'Yeah, but it's instinct, isn't it? The minute you're aware of danger, you look for the quickest way out. Usually when we find bodies, they're by a window, or at the top of a staircase.'

Denning thought about this. 'Did you examine the bodies?' he asked.

'That's your job, mate,' Keeble replied. 'Yours, and that lot in there.' He jerked his head towards the house, where the SOCOs could still be seen filing into the building, like a white-suited conga line.

'I don't mean "forensically" examine, but did you have a look at any of them?'

Beck shrugged. 'Our job is to ensure safety. If there was anyone alive in there when we pitched up, we would have got them out. As it is, they were all dead when our guys arrived on the scene.'

'What time was that?'

'The shout came in shortly after midnight,' Keeble said. 'We were here by quarter past.'

Denning looked around him. This was a quiet residential street. There was no public CCTV, and it was likely most of the neighbours would have been safely tucked up in bed when the house went up. His team would speak to neighbours, check any household CCTV that might exist, and put out a general appeal for witnesses. However, it was just possible whoever was responsible had taken care to cover their tracks.

'By the time we got here,' Keeble continued, 'it was already an inferno. Probably been going for around half an hour or so, maybe longer.' He told the younger fireman to start clearing up. Their shift would be finishing soon, and then the day shift would be taking over. Keeble waited until his colleague was out of earshot, then turned to Denning. He shook his head slowly. 'I've been in this job over twenty years, and it still gets me any time there's a kiddie involved.'

Denning nodded sympathetically. This was his first arson case where there had been fatalities. He wasn't looking forward to it. 'Do we have a name for the family?'

Keeble wiped his brow again. 'Galloway, according to the neighbours. A Brian and Ellie Galloway. Their daughter and grandson lived with them. They have a son, too, which would account for the fifth body. Apparently it was a family get-together for the old man's sixtieth birthday.' He pulled a face. 'Not much of a celebration in the end, was it?'

Denning agreed, adding that it was a shitty thing to happen at any time, birthday or otherwise, but the name Brian Galloway didn't strike any bells with him. He'd been involved in an investigation into an arson attack on a pub a few years ago while still a DS, but it had been a revenge attack by rival drug dealers. The landlord and his teenage girlfriend had managed to get out in time, so luckily no one was killed. If Brian Galloway had been a dealer his name would be in the system somewhere.

Keeble excused himself and headed back to join the other fire officers who were gathering by the fire appliances, packing away safety equipment and taking the odd swig from bottles of water, no doubt counting the minutes until they could return to the fire station and officially come off shift.

Denning dug into his jacket pocket and reached for his mobile. He was about to call his team and make a start on house-to-house inquiries when he spotted Sheila Gorton coming out of the house at some speed. She ducked under the inner cordon, pulling down her face mask as she approached him. He could see from the uneasy look on her face that something was wrong.

'They were right to call you in,' she said.

'It's definitely arson then?'

She shook her head. 'Too early to confirm that yet, but it's more than likely considering what we've just discovered.'

Denning tried to read her face. 'Which is?'

She lowered her voice until it was barely above a whisper. 'Preliminary examination of the bodies shows evidence of gunshot wounds.' She looked directly at Denning. 'The family was shot before the fire started.'

Chapter Two

Thirty-nine Gibney Road was one of the narrow terraced houses that ran along the north side of the street, almost directly opposite the Galloways' burnt-out home. The outside had recently been whitewashed, and the smart gravelled garden was dotted with brightly painted ceramic tubs overflowing with exotic-looking greenery.

Detective Sergeant Molly Fisher had already knocked on two doors but without much luck; there was no one in at the first house, and the second door she'd knocked on had been answered by a grumpy middle-aged man who told her he worked nights and only found out about the fire after he'd returned home that morning. He said he had nothing further to add and had politely but firmly shut the door on her. Molly was hopeful number thirty-nine would yield more productive fruit.

She gave the antique knocker a solid thud. A few moments later it was answered by a tall, young woman with flowing red hair and a slightly pained expression on her face.

'Yes?' she asked cautiously.

Molly flashed her ID and explained why she was there. She asked the woman's name.

'Marisa Powell,' she said after a pause. She had a vaguely bovine look about her, and Molly wondered if she'd just woken up.

'Could I come in?' she asked.

The bovine head nodded and the door opened fully to reveal a willowy woman in her early-to-mid thirties, wearing a black and white print dress and open-toed sandals. She smelled faintly of apple blossom hair conditioner and had a long, almost lugubrious face.

Marisa Powell showed Molly into a tidy sitting room off the hallway, the walls of which were painted a colour she was sure Farrow & Ball called 'Lulworth Blue'.

'Please sit down,' Marisa Powell said. There was a note of uncertainty in her voice, as though she was unsure as to the correct etiquette for entertaining a police officer in her own home.

Molly sat on one of the plump sofas and took her notebook and pen from her bag.

'Can I get you a cup of tea, or anything?'

'No. But thank you.' Molly had several more houses to cover after this, and if she accepted every offer of tea or coffee that came her way she'd be weeing for England before the morning was over. 'I'd like to ask you a few questions about the fire, if you don't mind.'

Marisa Powell sat on the other sofa and slipped off her sandals. She lifted her right foot and placed it on her knee. Molly noticed her face had a touch of sunburn but was bereft of make-up. Molly never left the house without at least a dab of eye-liner and a bit of lippy, but perhaps superficial appearances mattered less to Marisa Powell.

'My children are playing upstairs,' Marisa informed her, as though this was somehow relevant. 'I might have to go up to them if they call for me, but otherwise I'm happy to chat.' Molly spotted a wicker box filled with children's toys tucked neatly under a bookshelf in a discreet corner.

'How old are your children?' Molly asked, by way of conversation.

'Two and four,' she said. 'Thomas and Jasmine. Jasmine should be at nursery today, but we decided to keep her off after what happened last night.' She began picking at a painted toenail. 'Things like that just make you want to keep your family as close as possible.'

Molly nodded politely. 'We? I presume that means you have a partner?'

'My husband, Tim. He's just left for work. He's an accountant with JSP Broughton. He likes to get in early.' She said the name of the company as though Molly should have heard of it. 'I work from home,' she continued. 'A freelance translator. French and Italian mostly. It doesn't pay much, but it means we don't have to worry about childcare.'

'Could you take me through what happened last night?' Molly offered her a friendly smile. 'In your own time.'

She was sure Marisa Powell was sizing her up: looking at her and trying to guess how much her smart, but slightly frayed grey trouser suit had cost; clocking her red blouse that she hadn't had time to iron, and noting that a trip to the hairdresser's probably wouldn't go amiss.

'We were in bed,' she said. 'The noise woke us. There was a loud bang and what sounded like glass shattering. When we looked out the bedroom window, we could see the fire raging at the Galloways' house. There was smoke everywhere. It was horrible. Tim phoned the fire brigade. Luckily they got here quickly. We thought they might have to evacuate the street at one point, but it didn't take them long to get things under control.' She shook her head, wincing at the memory. 'Fortunately the children

13

slept through it all. Their bedrooms are at the back of the house.' She flinched. 'It's so awful. That poor family.'

Molly nodded again, then asked: 'Did you see anything unusual, or anyone acting suspiciously before the fire started?'

She shook her head. 'No, nothing. But we were in bed just after ten. We're neither of us night owls, and the children are in bed by eight most nights.' Molly watched as Marisa's forehead slowly creased into a frown. 'Are you saying the fire wasn't an accident?' She tucked a loose strand of hair behind her left ear. Molly thought there was something childishly endearing about the action.

'We can't confirm it one way or another at the moment,' she replied. 'But in the meantime it would be helpful to get some background information on the family. How well did you know the Galloways?'

Marisa gazed over at Molly, the strands of hair still hanging by the side of her face adding to the bovine look. 'Not well,' she said 'At least, not very well. We haven't lived here long. We were lucky to get this place, actually. It needed a lot of work when we bought it.' Molly smiled back at Marisa. 'About the Galloways,' she prompted. 'Is there anything you can tell me about them?'

'I knew Amber, their daughter. We used to meet up at the local park from time to time. I'd be there with my two and she'd often take Caleb, her son, there. She was friendly, and to be honest it was nice to have another woman my own age to talk to.'

'What did you talk about?'

Another slight shake of the bovine head. 'This and that. Our kids mostly. Amber usually did the talking. I would struggle to get a word in edgewise sometimes.' Marisa stared at her toenail as though it belonged to someone else.

'Actually, I did find Amber a bit strange sometimes. She kept asking questions about my relationship with Tim. And quite personal stuff too. I got the impression she was slightly immature, and perhaps a bit lonely.' She paused and pulled her knees up to her chin and hugged them. 'Caleb was a bit older than my two, but we all used the park quite a bit, especially this past summer when the weather was so nice. Caleb was such a lovely little lad. It's horrible to think…' She cut herself off mid-flow, unable to finish the thought. 'I would have said Amber was unhappy,' she continued, changing tack slightly. 'I mean, there was all the trouble she had with Caleb's dad. That must have got her down.'

'What kind of trouble?' Molly kept her voice light. This could have been two old friends gossiping about one of their mates; a harmless sharing of information prior to a leisurely lunch somewhere nice.

Marisa Powell hugged her knees even tighter. 'I'm not sure she'd be comfortable with me discussing her personal business like this.' She looked at Molly, another wrinkle creasing her forehead.

'We're looking at a possible murder inquiry, Mrs Powell, in which case anything you can tell me could be helpful.'

'*Murder?*' She couldn't keep the shock from her voice. 'So you really do think it was arson?' It was directed as a question, but it came across more like a statement. Marisa put her hand to her mouth and held it there for a moment, her eyes wide in her sun-blushed face.

'Like I say, we can't confirm anything right now, but it looks as though the fire might have been started deliberately.' Molly decided it was time for a more direct approach rather than risk their conversation turning into a merry-go-round of polite small-talk. 'If that turns out to be the case, we need to catch whoever was responsible, and quickly.' She flashed another smile at Marisa to both disarm and reassure. 'Anything you tell me will remain in the strictest confidence, Mrs Powell. And it may help us find the person or persons responsible.'

Marisa Powell sat back on the sofa, and picked some more at her toenail. 'It was Dan, Caleb's dad,' she said matter-of-factly. 'Amber told me he wanted custody of Caleb. He claimed Amber was a rubbish mother and that Caleb would be better off with him. He was talking about taking her to court to apply for a residency order. Amber was very upset about it all. Not that you'd blame her. I can't think of anything worse than having your child taken away.' She paused and considered what she was saying. 'Except losing your child altogether.' She shivered at the thought.

'Do you know Dan's surname?' Molly asked.

Marisa thought for a moment. Molly imagined cogs turning over and over in her head, until eventually something clicked. 'Hudson, I think. Not that I ever met him. I saw him in the street once or twice.' She lowered her voice, in case unseen ears should overhear what she was about to say. 'There was a big argument a while ago. He and Brian Galloway were having a massive ding-dong out there in the middle of the road. Right outside our house.' She pointed at the bay window. 'I heard Brian say he was going to call the police if Dan didn't calm down. I'm not sure he did though.' If he had, Molly thought, it will have been logged somewhere, and even if it hadn't, this was definitely something worth chasing up. 'It's not that Tim and I were being nosey,' Marisa continued, 'but when it's happening outside your front window, it's difficult to turn a deaf ear.'

'Do you know why Dan thought Amber wasn't a good mother?'

Another shake of the head. 'I don't know. She *was* a good mother. I mean, she loved Caleb, but I think things used to get on top of her. But that's how it is when you're a parent, isn't it?'

Molly nodded again. She had no idea what it was like to be a parent, and had no immediate plans to find out. 'When did this argument take place?'

'A couple of months ago.' Marisa shrugged. 'Late July, I think. It was definitely during the summer because the children had been playing out in the street shortly before it happened. It's a safe street,' she said, as though she felt the need to justify letting her children play in the road. 'Well, usually,' she added, throwing a glance at the bay window and the burnt-out house across the street.

'And it was to do with custody of Amber's son?' Molly asked, scribbling the details in her notebook. 'The argument between Dan Hudson and Brian Galloway? That was all it was about?'

Marisa stopped picking at her toenail and looked at Molly. 'We were trying to ignore it. It's not as though that kind of thing happens a lot round here. It's a very quiet street mostly; a nice mix of people. We did think it might be full of old folk when we first moved in, but there are a few young families. And professionals. We like it here.' She stopped looking at Molly and returned to her painted toenails. 'But yes, from what we could hear, it seemed to be to do with Dan wanting custody of Caleb.'

'Did Amber discuss the argument with you?'

'No. But she did tell me Dan was being difficult. She said he was controlling and manipulative. Between you and me, I think she might have been a bit scared of him.'

'Did he ever threaten her?'

She pulled a face. 'I don't think so, at least not physically. It was more that he could be unpredictable and she said he knew things about her. I've no idea what she meant by that, and to be honest with you Amber could be a bit of a drama queen sometimes. I suppose that's all par for the course for an actress.'

'Amber was an actress?'

Marisa Powell gave a light laugh. 'Well, that's what she called herself, but I'd never seen her in anything, and I don't think she ever did any acting work in all the time I knew her. I think she did a bit of modelling from time to time, but mostly she seemed to live off her parents.'

Molly made a note of this. 'What about Dan? Do you know where we might find him?'

'Well that was the tricky thing, wasn't it?' She looked at Molly as though about to tell her something that was blatantly obvious. 'He and Simon were business partners.'

'Simon?'

'Amber's brother. Simon and Dan ran some kind of promotions company. It had some stupid name: "Party Animals", or something like that. Dan and Simon were best friends. That's what caused all the problems. It seemed as though Simon had taken Dan's side in all this, or so Amber claimed.' She returned to her varnished toenail, rubbing the edge with the pad of her thumb. 'If you want my honest opinion I think, deep down, Amber wanted to get back with Dan. I think she still loved him. But her parents wouldn't have approved; I got the impression they didn't much like Dan.'

'How did Amber get on with her parents?'

Another wrinkling of the brow. 'She didn't get on well with her mum, but she was close to her dad. He used to spoil her. Brian Galloway was a nice man, but a soft-touch when it came to Amber.'

'Did you ever speak to him?'

'Occasionally we'd say hello if we saw him outside, or in his garden. He was a quiet man; kept himself to himself. It was a bit of a shock when he had that blazing row with Dan. It seemed totally out of character.'

'And Amber never spoke to you about the argument? She didn't say how it started?'

From somewhere upstairs the sound of a child crying could be heard. Marisa Powell glanced in the direction of the hallway and shouted, 'Mummy will be up in a minute, petal.' She turned to Molly. 'Look, I'm really sorry, but there's not much more I can tell you. I mean it's awful what's happened, but I still can't believe it was deliberate. I mean *murder*. That kind of thing just doesn't happen round here, especially not considering what house prices are.'

The hollering from above continued, louder now and in stereo, and with a determination that suggested it was only going to end when the individuals responsible were clutched to their mother's breast and eased with soothing words and kindness. Marisa Powell got to her feet. 'I really need to see to them. I'm sorry I can't be of more help.' She offered Molly an apologetic look. 'You don't mind showing yourself out, do you?' she said, heading into the hallway.

Molly followed her as the noise from upstairs continued. Molly thanked Marisa for her helpfulness, but

Maris Powell was already hurrying up the lightly carpeted staircase, informing her children that Mummy was on her way. Then, halfway up the stairs, she turned back to face Molly. 'There is something else.' She glanced up the stairs, making sure her children weren't within earshot, then looked back at Molly. 'It's probably nothing, but Amber told me once that Dan wasn't really Caleb's father. I mean, you had to take a lot of what Amber told you with a pinch of salt, but if Dan had found that out…' She let the words, and their implication, hang in the air before disappearing up the stairs to tend to her children.

Chapter Three

Back out on the street, Molly spotted Denning coming out of a house across the road. She waved, and waited until he crossed over to join her.

'Anything interesting?' he asked when he caught up with her. His ash-blond hair was slightly ruffled from where a breeze had brushed against it, but otherwise he looked as immaculately groomed as always. And was that another new suit...?

She glanced back at number thirty-nine and was sure she caught the briefest glimpse of Marisa Powell hastily ducking out of sight behind the curtain of an upstairs window. 'Seems Amber Galloway was in the midst of a nasty custody battle with her son's father,' she told Denning. 'Might be worth us having a word with him.'

Denning was staring at the burnt-out remains of number forty-two. The SOCOs were still toing and froing and carrying their bags and equipment between the house and their van. A solitary fire appliance stood guard outside the house as fire officers finished securing the building. But apart from the ghostly smoke patterns still lingering in the autumn air, the fire was now just a bad memory. She couldn't tell if the bodies had been removed from the property yet, or if they were still in there being examined by the SOCOs and a forensic pathologist. The whole grisly scene would be photographed and videoed and she would doubtless be a vicarious witness to the horrors of what lay inside the house at the first official team briefing later that day.

She wasn't looking forward to it.

After a moment or two Denning nodded. 'Sure,' he said, still gazing over at the fire-blackened mess across the road. 'Somebody wanted that family dead. In the absence of any immediately obvious motive, we need to speak to anyone and everyone who knew them.'

They were interrupted by the approach of DS Deepak Neeraj. Neeraj had pulled the collar of his leather jacket up around his neck, while his jet black hair had been sculpted into another trendy style. Neeraj was attractive, more so when he smiled, which was rare. He offered a half-friendly nod in Molly's direction then turned to Denning. 'Nothing happening, boss. Looks like nobody saw or heard anything until after the place went up. Even then folks were more concerned about trying to save the family than in looking for anything or anyone suspicious.' Neeraj jerked his head in the direction of number forty-two. 'Not that anyone could have done much for them. Poor sods.'

'What about any household CCTV?' Denning asked.

'One of the plods said there's a house further up the street with a camera that covers their garden and driveway, but I doubt it's captured anything useful.'

'We'll ask for any footage all the same,' said Denning. He was looking towards the far end of the street where Gibney Road ran into the busier Southgate Road. 'With a bit of luck the main roads round here will have street cameras. It's worth checking. In the meantime let's finish door-to-door. Just this street and only the immediate neighbours. Uniform can do the rest.' He turned to address Molly and Neeraj. 'Let's find out all we can about the Galloways. Try and build a clear picture of the family and then we can hopefully figure out why someone might want them dead. And, yes,' he said, turning to Molly, 'we'll definitely want to speak to the ex-son-in-law.'

'You think they were deliberately targeted, boss?' Neeraj asked.

'If I had to take a punt,' Denning said. 'I'd say this wasn't random. I'd put money on the family knowing their killer.'

Molly was still thinking about what Marisa Powell had said about the public argument between Brian Galloway and Dan Hudson. Family disputes were nothing unusual; her own family were no strangers to fights and squabbles, but to resort to murder...It seemed extreme, and yet when it came to murder, so often raw emotions took precedence over restraint, especially when children were involved. Something that should have blown over in a couple of weeks could so easily be allowed to fester and grow until eventually it erupted in an explosion of rage and unbridled hatred. She'd seen it happen too many times.

'How long until forensics finish in there?' she asked.

Denning nodded over at the house. 'They're working alongside fire investigators from the LFB, so it'll be a while before we get anything official from either of them. Then we'll have to wait for the post-mortems. Depending on the state of the bodies, that may take some time.'

A small group was beginning to gather by the outer police cordon. Most were either talking into mobile phones or whispering hushed conversations to one another. A uniformed officer was remonstrating with a couple of them who were trying to photograph the house. She recognised some of them as journalists.

'The vultures didn't waste much time,' said Denning coldly.

'I suppose they've got to get the story out there while it's still hot,' Neeraj added, with a notable lack of irony.

'We've got to make sure that lot don't backfoot us,' Denning said, looking over at the growing body of media hounds gathering across the road. An *ITV News* van had pulled up, and a camera crew were arranging themselves on the pavement outside number forty-two. Denning was right about the media not wasting time getting the story out, but Molly reminded herself news travelled at the speed of a mouse click these days.

'We'll need to issue a press statement as soon as possible,' Denning said. 'They'll want details of course, which are currently in short supply.'

The last comment felt more like a thought being voiced out loud rather than a statement directed at herself and Neeraj. Molly was about to say something when, out of the corner of her eye, she spotted a shiny black BMW parked further down the street. She was sure the driver was watching them. It was possible he was with the press pack and killing time before he joined the rest of his colleagues outside number forty-two. Or possibly he'd recognised her, Denning and Neeraj as detectives and was waiting for an opportunity to blag an exclusive ahead of his rivals. She was on the point of mentioning it to Denning when the driver suddenly started the engine and the BMW pulled out into the road. A moment later it drove off, carefully negotiating its way past the remaining fire appliance before speeding in the direction of Southgate Road. She'd tried to get a good look at the driver when the car passed them, but his face had been partly obscured by a baseball cap. This could have been entirely innocent, nothing more sinister than a neighbour heading off to work, or a curious onlooker come to gawk at someone else's tragedy.

But there had been something deliberate about the way he'd driven off the very moment she'd clocked him. If Molly had been a bit quicker she'd have taken a note of the number plate, but the BMW had already reached the end of Gibney Road and was turning left into Southgate Road. If there was any CCTV on Southgate Road it would pick up the car, assuming she wasn't just being paranoid. Yet somehow she had a feeling this couldn't be readily dismissed as paranoia on her part.

Chapter Four

He drove to the end of the street and checked the rear-view mirror. He was sure the group of people standing opposite number forty-two were police. Detectives. So by now they knew this was murder.

The young woman had looked directly at him as he'd driven past. But even if she'd clocked his face, there was a slim chance of them recognising him.

He glanced back at the burnt-out house and a wave of guilt swept through him like a burst of nausea.

Turning left onto the main road that ran towards Dalston, he pulled into an empty space in front of a bus stop and turned off the engine. He gripped the steering wheel and tried to stop shaking. A bead of sweat trickled down his forehead and ran down the side of his face. He hurriedly wiped it away and looked at himself in the rear-view mirror. He removed the baseball cap, the inside of which was damp with perspiration. He looked pale, his face tight. He was still shaking, either from adrenalin or fear, or both. He gripped the steering wheel even tighter and his hands trembled as his knuckles turned white.

His brain struggled to process what had happened; trying to make sense out of something that seemed too insane to comprehend.

He was responsible for the deaths of five people. He should have gone straight to the police and confessed, except that wouldn't have been an end to it, rather just the start of something messy and dangerous and bigger than he could handle.

How had it come to this? How had *he* come to this?

At first, he'd thought they were bluffing; idle threats intended simply to scare him, but the blackened house in the next street said otherwise.

There was no way he could risk hanging around. His luck would run out at some point. He could leave the country, but where would he go?

Even if he had somewhere to run to, he couldn't hide forever.

His options were narrowing by the minute.

Getting out of the car, he ran round to the pavement and threw up in the gutter.

Chapter Five

Denning sat opposite DCI McKenna in her cramped and stuffy office. He was sipping an Americano bought from the Costa across the road from the station, appreciating the slightly belated caffeine kick his system so desperately craved of a morning. It was slightly harsher than he liked, but still a considerable improvement on the liquid sludge that dribbled out of the coffee machine in the station canteen. He had briefly thought about buying one for McKenna, but decided it would feel too much like bringing in an apple for teacher.

The LFB's chief fire investigator had already emailed through his provisional report into the fire's cause. Denning had glanced over it before passing it on to McKenna. Most of it he already knew from his earlier conversation with Keeble, but it was sobering to see it confirmed in writing. The forensics report would follow, along with a more detailed report from the fire investigators. Until then, however, they had enough to convince them they were dealing with a murder enquiry.

McKenna was leaning back in her chair, leafing through the fire investigator's report, clutching a tuft of raven hair in her fist. She was dressed in her usual black Levi's and white blouse, her battered biker's jacket hanging on the back of her office door. Unlike Denning, who was a fast-tracked graduate, Liz McKenna had worked her way up through the ranks. Originally hailing from Motherwell, she had a reputation for straight-talking and a reluctance to suffer fools gladly. At some point in her career she'd earned the nickname Betty Taggart, a name generally uttered whenever she was out of earshot.

'Looks bad, doesn't it.' She made it sound more like a question than a statement.

'It's not good,' Denning agreed. 'Especially with a child involved.' He cleared his throat. 'I don't want to seem alarmist, but there was a bevy of journalists hanging around the scene earlier. The story's going to get out.'

McKenna threw the report on her desk and shook her head. 'We'll do a media statement this afternoon. We'll mention the arson, there's no point keeping quiet about that. But we should keep schtum about the shootings, at least for now. Let's wait until we have official confirmation from the post-mortems before we share that particular gem with the masses.' She leant forward, folding her arms on her desk and fixed him with a gimlet stare. 'Initial thoughts?'

Denning shuffled in his chair. He hated it when she put him on the spot like this. He preferred to chew things over in his mind and discuss the case with his team before offering up any tangible conclusions to his boss. But McKenna wasn't in a position to wait for the results of a team briefing. If she didn't issue a press release soon, social media would be awash with rumour and speculation which could so easily misdirect the investigation.

'We can't rule out the possibility this could have been a burglary gone wrong,' Denning said. He paused and rubbed a hand over his chin. 'However, I think we should consider other possibilities.'

'Such as?'

His focus briefly shifted to the desiccated cyclamen that sat yellowing and bare on top of the filing cabinet in a corner of McKenna's office. It had only just survived the recent torrid summer, but even Alan Titchmarsh couldn't save it now.

'DS Fisher mentioned something about Amber Galloway being involved in a custody battle with her ex-husband,' he said after a moment. 'We're still trying to get hold of him. Though I should stress we're not officially regarding him as a suspect at the moment.'

'We need to speak to him pronto, before he hears about what happened to his ex-wife and son second hand.'

'Uniform are onto it,' Denning replied. 'I asked DC Bell to accompany them. She's had experience in family liaison so she'll use kid gloves.'

'OK. Apart from the possible custody battle with Amber and her ex, what else do we know about the family?'

He shrugged. 'Very little at the moment. I spoke to some of the neighbours. Brian Galloway was a widower before he married Ellie. Seems they got together later in life. She was divorced. No one had nothing bad to say about them. Seems Ellie was a periodic churchgoer and Brian had been on the committee of the local neighbour-hood watch about five years ago. Weekends were spent washing the car or mowing the lawn. Occasional drinks parties with the neighbours at Christmas. Otherwise, it looks like they mainly kept themselves to themselves, rather like most of Gibney Road.' He gave another shrug. 'On the surface, they seemed like a pretty normal family.'

McKenna was leaning back in her chair again, tapping her chin with her steepled fingers. 'In my experience, there's no such thing. I can almost guarantee there will be skeletons hiding somewhere in the Galloway family closet. Let's make it our job to find them.' She stopped the chin-tapping and pointed her still-steepled fingers at Denning. 'In a way, I actually hope you're right, Matt, and this is something personal. I'd rather believe that than have to consider the possibility there's a nutter out there targeting households and willing to use significant violence to achieve their aims. But equally, I don't think we should be too hasty dismissing the whole burglary-gone-wrong theory. Sadly, violence isn't uncommon in domestic robberies these days, especially if the assailants go in tooled up. Someone waves a shotgun around, things get out of hand, or one of the householders tries to fight back, next thing you know we've got fatalities. The fire's an obvious way of covering their tracks.' She unsteepled her fingers and clutched at another tuft of hair. 'My gut instinct is to work on the assumption this *was* a botched robbery, but I'll be more than happy to be proved wrong on this.'

'Ma'am.' He watched McKenna wince. She hated being called 'ma'am', insisting it made her sound like Helen Mirren. Denning did it partially because it felt right and partially because he didn't know how else to address her.

'Did door-to-door throw up anything else?' she asked.

He shook his head. 'We've spoken to all the immediate neighbours. Uniform are finishing off the surrounding streets now. However, it doesn't look like anyone saw or heard anything prior to the fire, and certainly no gunshots, which is strange. We'll check any CCTV from the main streets around Gibney Road, but as we don't know what we're looking for at this stage, I'm not willing to spend too much time poring over endless hours of footage. It's not the most productive use of manpower at this point in the inquiry.' He looked at McKenna. 'No witnesses. And, at the moment, no motive.' His gaze briefly returned to the dead cyclamen. 'It's going to be a tough one. But I reckon as soon as we have a motive, we'll be a step closer to finding out who did this.'

'Let's hope you're right, Matt. Because if there is some psycho out there murdering people just to get his hands on their valuables, it's only a matter of time before he finds his next victims.'

–

Denning returned to his desk in the open-plan office that housed the MIT suite. The air conditioning had finally been fixed, just as the weather was turning cooler. Sod's law it hadn't been working during the recent hot, sticky summer, when his team had needed it most.

He sat at his desk and began checking his computer for emails.

Apart from a framed photograph of Sarah, his wife, his desk was clutter-free. Even his fellow detectives would struggle to discern anything useful about him from the impersonal state of his work space.

He looked up and saw Neeraj approaching. 'Boss...'

'Deep, I know. We were going to have a chat about your interview.'

Neeraj had gone after a DI's job at Hendon nick. He'd just been informed that he'd reached the inter-view stage and Denning had promised to help him prepare for it. This was the second DI's post Neeraj had gone after in recent months. The first one had gone to Denning. Neeraj's initial resentment had now subsided into begrudging acceptance, and even a sprinkling of admiration for Denning. 'We will find time to go over things before the interview, but it looks like today's going to be out.'

Neeraj nodded his acceptance. 'Cheers, boss. But I came over to tell you I've run the name Brian Galloway through the system and found out something interesting.'

'OK, Deep, do you want to share…?'

'Happened seven years ago.' Neeraj stood in front of Denning, arms folded. 'Cutting to the chase, it's a miracle the bloke wasn't banged up for what he did.'

Chapter Six

Denning had called a briefing for first thing that afternoon.

It was Molly's least favourite time of the day. Still sluggish from her hurried lunch, she would have preferred to spend the afternoon chasing up leads, or looking over any CCTV footage they had acquired. Having to stay alert and focussed on an information-heavy briefing was exactly what she didn't need. She was just grateful the air conditioning was now working.

She was still thinking about the black BMW that had sped past them on Gibney Road that morning. It could just have been a coincidence, and nothing to do with the fire. But she still wanted to speak to the driver; find out what he was doing in Gibney Road and why he drove off without speaking to them. She cursed herself for not getting a note of the registration number.

Denning was standing beside one of the mobile whiteboards at the front of the room next to the door to Betty Taggart's office. He was waiting for everyone to get back from lunch and switch their brains out of neutral so he could begin the briefing.

Ever since their return from Gibney Road, Denning had either been holed up with Betty Taggart in her pokey office, or sitting at his desk tapping away at his keyboard. There had been a brief confab with Deep Neeraj, which she'd tried to listen in to but had only managed to catch the odd word or two. She had clocked a look on Denning's face, though, and guessed Neeraj had told him something interesting.

Molly was still trying to figure Denning out. They hadn't worked together for long. He'd only arrived from another borough a few months ago, newly promoted to DI and thrust in at the deep end of a particularly nasty murder inquiry. Molly had been drafted in from CID to help with the investigation and had been offered a permanent position in MIT as her reward. She'd dreamed of joining MIT ever since she'd become a detective, but now she had, she wondered if it was what she really wanted. There were days when she felt like she was there on sufferance and it was only a matter of time before she was found out.

'OK,' Denning said once the room had quietened down, 'let's get this show on the road.'

Molly looked around the room and just caught sight of DC Trudi Bell sneaking into her seat at the back of the room, clearly making it back from a fag break in the nick of time. Molly had recently given up smoking, otherwise it would have likely been the two of them sneaking in at the last minute.

Molly watched as Denning scribbled notes onto one of the whiteboards. They'd found photos of the family from somewhere, which had been pinned to the board underneath a photo of the Galloway's burnt-out home. Luckily the only photos they had of the family were, as yet, all pre-mortem.

'Brian and Ellie Galloway,' Denning said to the room. 'Their children, Amber, thirty-three and Simon, thirty-six and Amber's son, Caleb, aged nine.' There was a general murmuring from the room at the mention of Caleb's age. 'Preliminary forensic investigations show that they were shot, after which the house was deliberately set alight. We're still awaiting the post-mortem results, but it's probably safe to assume shooting was the cause of death.'

Molly stared hard at the photos of the Galloway family. Brian Galloway looked what she could only call distinguished; a fine head of thick greying hair and a serious but not unfriendly face. Plenty of laughter lines around his mouth suggested he had been someone who had enjoyed life. Ellie Galloway looked younger than her husband, probably mid-to-late fifties, she guessed. She had a soft, kindly face; pale grey/green eyes and a shy smile for the camera. Her hair was cut in a chic chestnut bob that helped trim a few years off her age. Simon Galloway was undeniably handsome, with chiselled features and a floppy blond fringe that skirted his forehead, giving him a slightly boyish look. Amber was a year older than Molly. Her photo looked like it had been taken professionally: well-lit and highlighting her best features, which were all of them if Molly was honest. Amber looked impossibly beautiful in the photo, and Molly wondered if the picture had been digitally enhanced. But it was Caleb that was the hardest to look at. Dressed in his school uniform, his innocent eyes smiled from behind a pair of Harry Potter-style glasses. He looked so young. A child with his life snuffed out before it had had a proper chance to begin.

'Do we know what type of gun was used?' It was DC Ryan Cormack asking. Like Denning, Cormack was a university-educated, fast-tracked detective, likely destined for higher things, but unlike Denning he was always up for a laugh and happy to join the team for a few pints after work.

'We'll have a clearer idea when we hear back from forensics, Ryan. But I'd guess a shotgun of some variety,' Denning said.

'A sawn-off?' Neeraj asked. 'That would fit with the burglary theory.'

Denning nodded. 'We don't have any confirmation as to the make of weapon involved as yet, but as Deep has just highlighted, we're currently looking into the possibility this was a burglary that got out of control. We're checking details of any other burglaries in the borough and beyond for any similarities. We're also looking for any known criminals who have previous for this type of MO. However, at this stage it's impossible to say if anything was taken from the property.' There was a pause before Denning continued. 'So we have to explore the possibility this might be about something else. Something personal and specifically connected to a member of the Galloway family.'

'If it's not a burglary, then what?' DS Dave Kinsella asked. 'You're saying that someone could have deliberately targeted the family?'

Dave Kinsella was an old-school copper: gruff, thick-set with a moustache that wouldn't have looked out of place on a member of the Village People. He and Denning had something of a bruising relationship, and Molly was sure there was resentment towards Denning on Kinsella's part, and maybe just a little animosity going the other way too. She couldn't escape the feeling Kinsella resented his lot in life, and it rankled having to take orders from someone nearly twenty years his junior.

'We don't know, Dave,' Denning said. 'This is what we need to find out.'

'I knew a case similar to this, about ten years ago,' Kinsella continued. 'Drugs. Bloke was a dealer; not a big-time player, but he got greedy. Found himself on the wrong side of some nastier bastards and they torched his home. This has got a similar smell about it.'

'At the moment, it doesn't look like Galloway was party to any criminal activity, drugs-related or otherwise,' Denning replied. 'Having said that, there's still a lot we don't know about the family.'

Molly noticed that he didn't note Kinsella's comments on the whiteboard.

'We do know Brian Galloway used to own a hotel near Gatwick. He ran it with his late wife, Alison, and sold it about fifteen years ago, round about the same time he married Ellie. Seems he invested the profit in various business interests: part-ownership of a garage and car show-room in Muswell Hill; co-owns a bar in Majorca, and a string of rental properties in and around London. Nothing major league, but enough to give him a decent income. Ellie Galloway co-owned a fancy dress shop in Camden. Simon Galloway ran some kind of events company, which we're still checking out. Amber doesn't seem to have done much: one neighbour said she described herself as an actress, another said she was a full-time mum who was separated from Caleb's dad. There's nothing obvious that suggests the family was in any way connected with or involved in anything criminal.'

'Why do I sense a "but" coming?' Kinsella asked.

Denning ignored him and continued. 'About seven years ago, Brian Galloway was arrested for dangerous driving after he was involved in a hit and run that resulted in a child being seriously injured.' Molly watched as Denning's eyes turned towards Neeraj. She guessed this was what they'd been talking about earlier. 'Apparently, the kid was crossing the road when Galloway came out of nowhere and ploughed straight into him,' Denning continued. 'According to witnesses, he didn't even slow down; just drove off like he was oblivious to what had happened. Next day Brian Galloway hands himself in to his local nick. He claimed it was only after he got home that he realised he'd been involved in an accident. He insisted he hadn't seen the kid. The arresting officer suspected he'd been over the limit at the time, but the blood tests came back negative.'

'More than likely it was out his system by then,' Kinsella offered.

'Quite possibly, Dave. But without any evidence they couldn't charge him with drink driving.'

'What happened to Galloway?' Trudi asked.

Denning turned to Neeraj. 'Deep...'

Neeraj got to his feet and addressed the room. 'Galloway admitted his responsibility, offered his sincerest apologies to the kid's family and surrendered his licence like a good boy. It still went to court, though. Galloway was done for dangerous driving and failing to stop at the scene of an accident. But get this...' There was a pause before Neeraj delivered the punchline. 'All he ended up with was a suspended sentence and year's ban.'

'Talk about jammy,' Kinsella said.

'If they'd been able to prove the drink driving,' Neeraj continued, 'chances are it would have been a custodial sentence. Galloway was one very lucky sod.'

But his luck had eventually run out, Molly thought. Either that or someone had decided to take his fate into their own hands. 'What about the child he hit?' she asked.

'The kid was in intensive care for weeks: bleeding on the brain, broken ribs, broken arm, ruptured spleen. Pretty nasty.'

'Did he recover?' Ryan asked.

Neeraj shrugged. 'It doesn't say, but I guess he must have. I mean, we're not talking manslaughter.'

'What was the name of the victim's family?' It was Kinsella again.

'Chisholm,' Neeraj said. 'The boy was called Kyle Chisholm. The parents are David and Hester. We've got an address. Somewhere in Battersea.'

'Thanks, Deep,' Denning said. Neeraj sat back down.

'Suspended sentence,' said Kinsella, a sour note in his voice. 'He must have had a bloody good brief.'

'The guilty plea probably helped there,' Trudi added.

'Whatever the story,' Denning said coolly, 'it gives David Chisholm a motive.'

'But murder?' Kinsella said. 'A brick through the window maybe, or dog shit through the letterbox. But to slaughter an entire family just because some soft judge was playing silly beggars…'

'There's a bit more to it, Dave. David Chisholm sent Brian Galloway a threatening letter after the verdict. Understandable, perhaps, but it still resulted in him receiving a formal caution. Galloway insisted that no charges were brought against Chisholm, and nothing more came of it.'

'Until now?' Trudi said. 'But if this Chisholm bloke is responsible, why wait seven years?'

'Who knows? Circumstances could have changed. The child could have subsequently died. We'll have a clearer idea once we've spoken with them.' He wrote 'hit and run' on the board, then circled it, adding the names Kyle Chisholm and David Chisholm next to it.

'Does this bloke Chisholm have any previous?' Kinsella asked.

'Apart from the caution for sending the threatening letter, there's nothing on record.'

'What about Brian Galloway's first wife?' Trudi asked. 'Do we know what happened to her?'

'Nothing's been flagged up on the system, Trudi. But it's worth checking out on the off chance.'

Molly watched Trudi nod and write something on a notepad.

'However, there is another avenue worth looking into,' Denning said. He shot a look in Molly's direction. 'Molly, I believe one of the neighbours mentioned something about Amber Galloway being involved in a possible custody battle with her ex-husband.'

Molly cleared her throat. This was her time to shine. She repeated what Marisa Powell had told her, including the bit about Amber claiming Dan Hudson wasn't Caleb's father, even though Molly still wasn't sure if there was any truth in the claim given what Marisa Powell had said about Amber's drama queen tendencies.

Denning wrote the name Daniel Hudson on the whiteboard.

'Trudi, you went round there this morning to break the news. How did Hudson seem to you?'

Trudi looked sheepish. 'Well, that's the thing, boss. He wasn't there. There was no answer at his flat and his neighbours said they haven't seen him for a couple of days.'

'He's legged it,' Kinsella said, folding his arms across his barrel of a chest before casting a glance around the room. 'Well, come on, he's got as good a motive for doing the family in as this Chisholm geezer. And I bet *he's* got previous.'

'He's got a caution for assault,' Molly said, trying not to sound like the class swot, 'and another for possession of cocaine. Four years ago he got into a fight in a pub car park. He hit some bloke who ended up needing a trip to A&E to get his face patched up. Hudson claimed self-defence and the other bloke didn't want to press charges, so it never got as far as court. Then he was found in possession of a small amount of cocaine during a raid on Trailblazer's nightclub two years ago. The case went to the local magistrate's court. He pleaded guilty to possession, insisted it was for personal use and not for supply. It wasn't a significant amount, so the magistrate accepted that. Hudson was fined £1000.' She was reading from her scribbled notes. She'd looked Daniel Marcus Hudson up on the PNC when she'd got back from speaking to the neighbours. She thought the fight with Brian Galloway might have been entered on the system, but it looked like it was never reported. Perhaps Brian Galloway hadn't wanted the police involved in case his family problems became public knowledge. Or maybe it was at Amber's request, but whatever the case, there was no official record of the incident. All she had to go on was what Marisa Powell had told her that morning.

Denning smiled at her. 'Good work, Molly.' Then, turning to look at Dave Kinsella, he added, 'You have your answer there, Dave. Daniel Hudson has previous for assault. He may or may not have been involved in a potentially damaging custody battle and it now looks like he may have disappeared.' He looked round the room again. 'We need to find Daniel Hudson as a priority, to eliminate him as a suspect if nothing else. Molly, you said he and Simon Galloway had been business partners. Once you've got an address for this business, get round there and have a word with their work colleagues. Find out if anyone knows where Daniel Hudson might be hiding. And have another word with this neighbour: she seems to have had a good insight into the Galloway family's private dramas. Find out all you can about Amber's relationship with her ex.'

Molly nodded, and scribbled "Party Animals" on her notepad.

'Just one thing, boss,' Ryan Cormack had his hand in the air. 'Would Dan Hudson really murder his own son? Amber and the rest of them, maybe. But Caleb?'

'It's possible he didn't know Caleb and Amber were going to be there,' Molly said.

'Their bodies were found in an upstairs room,' Neeraj argued. 'Whoever did this went looking for them.'

'On the other hand,' Trudi said, 'it's not unheard of for fathers to kill their kids, especially when custody battles are involved.'

Kinsella shook his head. 'I know it happens, but it's a bit extreme, do you not think?'

'Until we find him and speak to him,' Denning said, 'we can only speculate. But he remains on the board. In the meantime, Dave, I want you and Ryan to go over Brian Galloway's business interests with a fine-toothed comb. If he was involved in anything dodgy, I want to know about it. I want everyone else to speak to any friends, acquaintances or business contacts who knew the family. We need to build up as clear a picture of the Galloways as we can, looking into every aspect of their lives, personal and professional. Hopefully this will give us some kind of clue as to why someone might want them dead.'

Denning brought the briefing to a close. He mentioned something about a media conference, but Molly wasn't listening. She was still staring at the photos of the Galloway family. Her eyes focussed specifically on Simon Galloway, not just because he was good-looking, but rather it was something else. She couldn't put her finger on it, but the more she looked at his photo, the more she felt there was something familiar about him.

Chapter Seven

'It was all a very long time ago. We've tried hard to put it out of our minds and move on.' David Chisholm looked at them as though resenting their right to be in his home, asking him questions he didn't want to answer. 'Kyle's fourteen now. He's doing well at school. There's no reason to be continually reminding him of what happened.'

They were sitting in the Chisholms' living room at the front of their modest terraced house, a few streets to the north of Clapham Common. The room was homely and unpretentious, with smudgy watercolours smothering every wall. It seemed Hester Chisholm was something of an artist, and even to Denning's uncritical eye it looked as though what she lacked in ability she more than made up for with enthusiasm.

Hester was the quieter of the two. In her late forties, she had nervous eyes and a thick mop of black hair. She sat blankly beside her husband on the sofa, while Denning and Neeraj occupied twin armchairs at opposite ends of the room. Under the circumstances he felt it would have been churlish to have declined the Chisholms' offer of tea, so dainty china cups in their matching saucers were now awkwardly balanced on their knees. Denning spotted a scattering of family photos on the mantelpiece, one of which was of a boy in his mid-teens dressed in a Chelsea top and wearing a baseball cap. He guessed this was Kyle.

David Chisholm was the same age as his wife. His thin hair was starting to grey around the temples and he had a narrow face, offset with a wide forehead. He was between jobs at the moment, he'd explained, hence he was at home during the day. Hester worked part-time in a local bakery.

'We're very sorry about what happened to Kyle,' Denning said. 'but I'm afraid that's not why we're here.' He told them about the Galloways and the arson attack on their home. He stuck to the official line as articulated by McKenna during her media briefing earlier that afternoon; they were still keeping quiet about the shootings, for now.

'I can't help you with that,' David Chisholm said coldly. 'It's a terrible thing to happen, but I can't honestly say I'm surprised. People like that so often attract trouble.'

'Can you explain what you mean by that?' Neeraj asked. Denning could tell he was trying his best to be tactful, something that didn't come naturally to him. At least he hadn't sounded too accusatory when he'd asked the question.

'He left our son lying in the road,' Chisholm said. 'I wouldn't do that to a dog.' He looked at Denning when he answered, even though it had been Neeraj who'd asked the question. 'The police reckoned he was drunk at the time, but they couldn't prove it. And I'm willing to bet it wasn't the first time he'd done something like that.' He sat back on the sofa and addressed both detectives this time. 'Call it karma, call it whatever you like. But people like that eventually come unstuck.'

Denning took a sip of tea, causing the cup to rattle when he placed it back in the saucer. He leant over and placed the cup and saucer onto the top of a smoked glass coffee table. 'I sympathise, Mr Chisholm. And I know it can't be easy having this brought up again, but you threatened Brian Galloway. I appreciate it was seven years ago, and more than likely done in the heat of the moment, but we can't overlook it.'

'Yes, I was angry,' Chisholm said. 'I was very angry at the time. You have no idea what it was like.'

Denning, who had a young son himself, had a pretty good idea of what it was like to fear you were going to lose your child. He thought it best to let David Chisholm get it off his chest if they were going to get anywhere. 'Tell me about it,' he said, his voice calm.

But it was Hester Chisholm who answered for them both. 'We got a call from the hospital saying Kyle had been involved in a road accident. We'd been slightly concerned when he hadn't come home when he said he would. But that was nothing too unusual with Kyle. He would often lose track of time, or go round to a friend's house and not think to tell us.' Her voice was quiet, with a slight catch to it. Denning thought he could detect the faintest trace of a Welsh lilt. He nodded and she continued. 'When we got to the hospital he was in intensive care, wired up to a load of machines. The doctors tried to explain what was wrong with him, but I couldn't take any of it in. They said his chances were sixty to forty against.' She looked at Denning, her face full of pain as the memories were rekindled. 'Do you know what I did? I prayed. I'm not religious, but I prayed. I prayed for my boy to survive.' A solitary tear made its way down her cheek. 'Oh, Brian Galloway was sorry enough for what happened. He even wrote to us to say how sorry he was. But we didn't want his apologies, we wanted him punished.'

'Kyle did recover, though?' Neeraj asked, holding a teacup in one hand and a saucer in the other. 'You said he's fourteen now.'

'Not a full recovery.' It was David Chisholm this time, taking over where his wife had left off. 'He was in a wheelchair for the best part of a year. His spleen had to be removed. He has to take antibiotics every day for the rest of his life as his body has no way of fighting infection. They thought he had a brain injury and might need round-the-clock care. And he missed so much school he had to be kept back a year. Away from all his friends. It was years before he got his confidence back. He was never the same boy after that accident. It was hell for my wife; well, for both of us. Not knowing if our son was going to be all right. And Brian Galloway, the man responsible, got clean away with it.' He looked at his wife, then turned back to face Denning, nodding slowly as he spoke. 'I'm sorry his family died in that fire, but if I'm honest, then no, I'm not sorry he's dead. I'd be a liar and a hypocrite if I said I was.'

There was a hint of ire in his voice. He was being forced to relive the pain and fury of seven years ago, and prod at wounds that had never fully healed.

'You want to know if we hate Brian Galloway enough to set fire to his house,' Chisholm continued, his domed forehead glistening with sweat, 'with his family inside. That's why you're here, isn't it?'

Denning could feel the muscle in his left temple start to throb. He felt like a bully, picking on a couple who had done nothing more than be the unfortunate victims of circumstance. There were some days he hated his job. 'We have to eliminate you from our enquiries. You have an obvious motive.'

'You did send him a threatening letter,' Neeraj said, taking a gulp of tea. 'We have that on record.'

Denning shot him a sharp look.

Chisholm glared at Neeraj for a moment. Neeraj glared back, waiting for Chisholm to respond. Eventually he spoke. 'I was furious. Galloway had a smart-talking lawyer. It was all a game to him. He'd got one up on the justice system, and wasn't he a clever dick. People like that make me sick.'

'Did you keep the letter he sent to you?' Denning asked. 'The one where he apologised for what he'd done.'

'We burned it,' Mrs Chisholm replied. 'I didn't want his empty words.'

'OK. Fair enough.' Denning felt sorry for the couple. Whichever way you dressed it up, they had been let down by the system. It was all very well people like him trying to uphold the laws of the land, but once a case went to court it was in the lap of the gods; sometimes justice was done, and sometimes, as in the Chisholms' case, it wasn't. This certainly gave the Chisholms a strong motive, but he was still to be convinced. He thought about something Samuel Johnson had said about vengeance being an act of justice, but was this about vengeance against Brian Galloway…? 'We have a copy of the letter you sent Brian Galloway. In it you stated you wanted to "make him pay for what he'd done". I believe those were your exact words, Mr Chisholm.'

'I wasn't thinking straight,' Chisholm said, his voice like broken glass. 'I wanted him to suffer for what he'd put us through and I just lashed out.'

'You need to understand,' Hester Chisholm said. 'Our boy was still in hospital when the case came to court. All right, he was out of intensive care and starting on his slow road to recovery, but we still didn't know what was going to happen to him in the long run. We needed someone to pay for what we were going through. We thought the law would give us the redress we needed, but when the judge handed down that sentence it was like a slap in the face for us.'

'Did you ever speak to Brian Galloway?' Denning asked.

'Or go to his house?' Neeraj asked. 'You would have known where he lived. I presume he put his address on the letter he sent you.'

A silence fell on the room. 'Why would I go to his house? Besides, as my wife just said, we burnt the letter.' He glared back at Neeraj. 'And I didn't make a note of his address before I burnt it,' he added.

'His address would have been in the papers,' Neeraj said, not letting the subject drop.

'Look, I didn't go near his house,' David Chisholm said, a brittleness creeping into his voice. 'Not then and not last night. OK, I tried to speak to him at the court, after the verdict, but I didn't get the chance. His son was acting like his personal bodyguard. He had a go at me, told me to leave his father alone. Hester persuaded me to let it drop, and I did. The letter was just me getting it out of my system.'

Denning could feel the temperature in the room begin to rise. He tried to calm things. It wouldn't help anyone if David Chisholm lost his temper. 'Mr Chisholm, I know how you feel. I have a child of my own. I know what it's like to feel helpless and angry whenever they're hurting. But it *was* an accident. The sentence wasn't his fault. Brian Galloway was genuinely remorseful. He handed himself in to the police and admitted his guilt. I know that's scant comfort to you. But I genuinely believe he meant it when he said he was sorry for what happened.'

'So that makes it all right?'

'No, of course it doesn't. And, if I were to speak off the record, then frankly, I think it's disgraceful that he received such a lenient sentence. But it happened and now the man's dead. Somebody killed him, and it's our job to find out who did it.'

David Chisholm shook his head and placed his hand in his wife's, giving it a gentle squeeze. 'Look, we had nothing to do with it. We were in bed last night. OK, we don't have an alibi, but we didn't go out, and we certainly didn't set fire to anybody's house. We're not savages, Inspector. I hated Brian Galloway for what he did, and I could never find it in myself to forgive him. But after years of resentment, I can see now that there's no point in wallowing in hatred and bitterness. It just eats you up. Kyle's what matters, at least as far as we're concerned.' He looked at his wife, squeezing her hand a little tighter. 'Kyle recovered. Yes, it took years, and he probably still bears scars, both physical and mental. But he's alive. He'll grow up and live as near a normal life as possible. That's what matters here, not what either of us felt for the man who nearly killed him.'

Denning sighed. 'All right, Mr Chisholm, I believe you.' He could sense they were telling the truth. They were just a normal couple who had been to hell and back. They weren't the sort of cold-blooded psychopaths who were capable of slaughtering an entire family out of some misguided sense of justice or a crazy desire for sick revenge. Sending a nasty letter was about as dangerous as this couple got.

David Chisholm nodded silently, while his wife blinked back another tear.

'We will need you to make a statement,' Neeraj said, placing his empty cup and saucer on the coffee table. 'Just so we have something in writing.'

Chapter Eight

Molly found the offices of Party Animals without too much difficulty. Whilst the company had an impressive and prolific online presence – a lively and picture-heavy website plus all the usual social media offerings – its offices were something of a let-down by comparison.

Party Animals was based in a couple of rooms above a second-hand clothes shop on the Mile End Road, a short hop from Whitechapel tube station. Molly had tried phoning ahead to say she was coming, but the number on their website was either incorrect or the phone had been cut off. All she heard when she rang was a dull whine.

There was an intercom next to a slightly faded green door with the name "Party Animals" written on a card above the button. Molly pressed the button. A moment later a slightly accented female voice answered. Molly announced who she was, then there was a brief pause before the door buzzed open.

A narrow staircase ran up to the first floor with a thin grey carpet that looked worn in places. At the top of the staircase she pushed open the door that led into a small but tidy office.

A young woman, Molly guessed the same one who'd buzzed her into the building, introduced herself as Natalya Koval, and said she was a partner in the company. Natalya was in her late twenties, slim, dark-haired and very attractive. She was wearing an Issey Miyake floral blouse and a pair of way-too-tight jeans, a look Molly wished she could pull off with as much conviction. She ushered Molly into another office, where two desks sat facing one another. The remaining space was dominated by a large, black leather sofa. They both sat on the sofa.

'It's Simon,' Natalya said, before Molly had a chance to speak. 'He's dead. That's what you've come to tell me.' Molly tried to place her accent. Eastern European, she thought, perhaps Russian.

'You were close? You and Simon?'

She gave an awkward smile. 'He was my boyfriend.' She shook her head sadly. 'I saw the story on the news today. About the fire at their house. The woman on the news said the fire was started deliberately. Is this true?'

Molly nodded. 'I'm afraid so.' She looked at Natalya, trying to appear sympathetic. 'I'm very sorry.'

Natalya flinched slightly and turned her head to one side. Molly thought Natalya was going to cry. She wondered if she should offer her a tissue, or place a hand reassuringly on her shoulder. But the young woman hurriedly regained her composure and looked at Molly, any suggestion of tears absent from her face.

'Did you come round here just to tell me that, or is there something else?' Natalya asked.

'You knew Simon, but you also knew Dan, his business partner,' Molly said, her voice friendly. Natalya nodded. 'Do you know where he is? We really need to speak to him.'

'Dan?' Natalya looked over at one of the two empty desks and twitched her shoulders in a shrug. 'He hasn't been in the office for some time. Not since the fight.' Molly assumed she meant the fight in Gibney Road that Marisa Powell had witnessed. She guessed it must have put a strain on the friendship and working relationship between Simon and his business partner. 'Has he been in touch with you since then?'

She shook her head. 'No. I've heard nothing. I tried to phone him but there's no answer from his phone.'

Molly took a card from her pocket and handed it to Natalya. 'If he gets in touch, please call me? It's very important that we speak to him.'

Natalya stared at the card before putting it on the arm of the sofa. 'If he calls, I let you know.'

Molly was about to leave and head back to the station when she thought of something else. 'You mentioned the argument with Simon's dad. Was this why Dan hasn't been in the office recently?'

'What are you talking about? What argument?'

'You said you hadn't seen Dan since the fight. I assumed you were referring to the argument between Dan and Brian Galloway a few weeks ago.'

She shrugged again. 'I dunno anything about that.' She gave a sharp toss of her head, her mane of hair brushing against Molly's cheek. 'I'm talking about the fight Dan had with Simon. Right here in this office. I had to stop them. They were like angry children.'

'When was this?'

'A couple of weeks ago. Maybe more. Dan was angry with Simon. He said their partnership was over and he wanted out of the business.'

'How did Simon take this?'

'It was nothing new. They were always arguing and threatening to end the company. Then the next day it would all be forgotten about. They were just boys really, playing at being big businessmen.'

'What was the fight about?'

'I dunno that either.' She turned her face away from Molly and shook her head. 'It could have been about Amber,' she said after a moment.

Molly was intrigued by this comment. 'Was it to do with the custody battle? Amber's son,' she said for clarity. 'Dan and Amber were fighting over who got to look after their son.'

Natalya tutted. 'I liked Amber. I liked her a lot, but she could be difficult. Dan and Amber used to argue almost as much as Dan and Simon.' She threw Molly a disdainful look. 'But I don't know anything about their child.'

'Could the fight have been to do with work?'

She gave a shrill laugh. 'They turn up, they talk to clients. They have expensive lunches, but actual work… That's what I'm here for.' Natalya gave another indifferent shrug. 'It was Dan's idea to set up Party Animals. He persuaded Simon to put a lot of money into it and work together as partners. They were friends from school. But I don't think either of them ever wanted to do any real work.'

'What exactly does Party Animals do?' Molly asked. She'd already checked out their website and Facebook page before she'd left the station. Lots of glitzy photos and testimonials from satisfied clients, but little in the way of actual content.

'We're an events company. We'll organise everything from corporate weekends to stag and hen parties. We specialise in high-end entertainment packages tailored to young professionals and people who just want to have a good time. We even provide extras for film companies and actors or models for promotions and adverts.' It sounded like a pre-rehearsed sales pitch that was dutifully trotted out whenever someone asked about the company.

'How many people work here?'

'Just Simon, Dan and myself.'

'And how was business?' Molly asked.

'Yes, good,' Natalya replied. 'We're very busy.'

Molly looked around the room. Apart from the leather sofa, the office furniture looked cheap, while there was tired woodchip on the walls. A couple of new-looking computers sat on the desks, but otherwise there was nothing about their surroundings that suggested the company was doing especially well. Equally, no ringing phones, or stack of work sitting on the desks waiting to be addressed. But perhaps most of their business came via the internet, and Party Animals' inbox was choc-a-block with requests to organise adventure weekends and children's parties...

'How will you manage now that Simon's gone and Dan's missing?' She realised it probably came over as a tactless question. At the end of the day, Simon Galloway had been more than just her business partner.

'I can manage.' She stood up, sweeping a hand through her dark hair and flashing an equally dark look at Molly. 'I am a partner in Party Animals, not just a fancy secretary. I know what I'm doing.' She'd perched a pert buttock on the edge of one of the desks now, and continued to fix Molly a disdainful look.

It was like she'd hit a nerve. She hadn't meant to imply anything. She was just curious as to how a company that had once consisted of three people would cope now that its personnel appeared to have been reduced to one. 'I just meant it will mean an increased workload for you.'

Natalya made a noise that sounded like 'pfftt' and tossed her hair over her shoulder again. 'I did most of the work when they were here. I don't imagine anything will change.'

Molly admired her spirit and her honesty. 'It must have been difficult for Simon,' she said.

'Difficult?'

'His sister and his best friend having had such a troubled relationship. He must have felt under pressure to take sides.'

'I suppose so.' She thought for a moment. 'Though Simon tried not to take sides. He knew what Amber was like, but she was his sister and there's an old English saying about blood being thicker than water.' She said it as though she didn't fully understand what it meant. She shrugged again. 'You know what, I liked Amber. I was always sad whenever she and Dan used to argue. It's terrible... her and her little boy...' She let the words trail away to silence.

'So you knew her then?' Molly asked, after a few seconds of silence had passed.

'She used to do some work for us sometimes. She would do hostess work for us whenever we were short of girls. She had a nice face and people liked her. *Men* liked her.'

It was almost said reproachfully, as though Amber's attractiveness to men was somehow responsible for what happened to her. Molly wondered if Natalya had secretly resented Amber; perhaps seeing her as some kind of threat to her relationship with Simon.

'So you have no idea where we can find Dan?' Molly asked, steering the conversation back to her reason for being there. 'His friends? Another girlfriend? Family?'

Natalya sighed and shook her head. 'Dan had no family. His father died when he was young and his mother remarried and moved away. I dunno where. He had a sister, but she lives in Scotland somewhere. Dan said they were never close. I dunno about his friends. Simon was his friend. He would know.' She flinched and gave a little shudder. 'Would *have known...*'

Molly was beginning to wonder if there was anyone Dan Hudson got on with. 'When was the last time you actually spoke to Dan?'

'I told you. When he and Simon had that fight. Dan punched Simon. He made his nose bleed. Then he marched out the office. That was two weeks ago. I haven't seen him since.' She stood and extended her hand in Molly's direction. 'It's been nice to talk to you, but I have a lot of work to do.' She looked at the card Molly had given her. 'I promise I'll call you if Dan gets in touch.' She stood defiantly by the door, making it clear their meeting was at an end.

—

Molly left the Party Animals office, and headed in the direction of the Tube station. She couldn't stop thinking about Natalya. There was something about her. A hardness. Perhaps that wasn't fair. Maybe the word she wanted was *toughness*. Molly got the impression Natalya was someone who was capable of coping with whatever life chucked at her, no matter how bad. But there was something else too. She had only just found out about Simon, presumably via Betty Taggart's press conference on the local lunchtime news, and yet she seemed remarkably composed. There had been the hint of a tear when she spoke about Simon and genuine sadness at the mention of Amber and Caleb, but her icy composure hinted at something else: a coldness. Yes, that was the word: *coldness.*

Natalya had been cagey at the mention of Dan, claiming he hadn't been in touch since he and Simon had had the fight in the office. But surely he would have been in touch with her by now, especially after he found out Simon was dead.

Molly had the feeling Natalya Koval had been lying to her. She suspected she knew where Dan was hiding, or at least had a good idea where they could find him.

She was about to cross the road at a set of traffic lights, when she spotted a black BMW Z4 parked in a side street. It was new and shiny and she was certain it was the same car she'd seen in Gibney Road that morning. She turned into the street and checked the car. There was no sign of the driver, but the engine was still warm.

First Gibney Road, then near the offices of Party Boys. This couldn't be a coincidence.

She took her phone from her bag, selected the camera app, and clicked a photo of the car's registration. She would check the number with the DVLA database, but she already had a good idea who the car belonged to.

Chapter Nine

Natalya watched from the window as Molly headed down the street towards the Tube station. She watched as the police officer suddenly stopped and disappeared down one of the little streets that ran off the main road. What was she doing, Natalya thought?

She'd liked Molly. In another life she reckoned they might have made good friends. But she also knew a visit from the police spelled danger. She had a feeling DS Molly Fisher would be back, asking more questions until she finally got the answers she wanted.

Dan and Simon had got them into this trouble. She had tried to warn them, but they didn't listen to Natalya. They only listened to themselves, and even then they only ever heard what they wanted to hear.

All the men in Natalya's life were wasters. She had somehow come to accept it over the years. Her father had walked out on her mother when they were all young. Her brothers were always in trouble with the police and all the time her mother tried to keep the family together, even though it had made her ill.

Natalya had learned from an early age never to put her trust in men. They would inevitably let you down. Despite that, she'd still lied to Molly.

She knew where Dan Hudson was. She knew exactly where he was. But she couldn't tell the policewoman. She had promised. Not that it would do much good if they did find him. It was already too late.

Chapter Ten

It hadn't been Denning's choice to live in trendy Shoreditch. However, his wife liked the location, specifically its proximity to the City, where she worked as head of investment portfolio for a merchant bank. As it was Sarah's salary that paid most of the extortionate rent on their warehouse apartment, Denning was in no position to argue.

Sarah was in the tiny study that doubled for a spare room now that his son was temporarily occupying the main guest room. Jake had moved in with them while Claire, his ex-wife, had gone down to Devon to look after her mother.

Not that Denning minded. Jake being there meant they could spend more quality father-and-son time together without Claire dictating the rules. Sarah, however, was yet to be persuaded. It wasn't that she disliked Jake, far from it, she just felt uncomfortable having a constant reminder of his previous life living under their roof. Not that she'd said anything. Sarah was far too subtle for that.

'You're back late,' she said. He brushed the top of her forehead with his lips and she gave him an affectionate pat on the arm. 'Busy day?' She was tapping away at her laptop, engaging in a frantic email exchange with her bank's New York office.

'Full-on, as always,' he said. 'Where's Jake?'

'Playing in his room, I expect.' She looked up from her inbox. 'There's some leftover chicken casserole in the top oven. It won't take long to reheat.' She returned to the emails. 'And I've fed Jake.'

She made his son sound like a dog. Though her tone was clear: *I've* fed *your* son. A not-so-subtle reminder that Jake was his responsibility rather than hers.

He headed into the vast, open-plan living room that occupied most of the flat's lower floor. French doors opened onto a small balcony at one end and a large oriel window overlooked a converted office block at the other. Jake's room was off the living room. He lightly tapped on the door and gently pushed it open.

Jake was sitting cross-legged on the floor, playing one of his computer games on the new telly they'd bought him. He glanced up from slaying aliens, gave his dad a half-smile, then returned to his game. Jake was small for his age, with an unruly mop of dark-blond hair and a button nose he'd inherited from his mother. He was wearing his favourite *Star Wars* t-shirt, down which he'd spilt some orange juice.

'Hey, little fella. How's it going?' Denning sat down beside his son, ruffling his hair, then putting his arm round his slender shoulders. Jake flinched slightly and jerked his body to one side. 'Who's winning?'

After a moment, Jake spoke, his eyes still on the TV screen in front of him. 'I've got to destroy another two Zodian battleships before I can capture the space captain,' he said. 'And the space captain has a robot army that can only be defeated by liquid gold.' Denning didn't understand a word, but it was enough to know that Jake seemed happy.

They'd tried to make the room comfortable for Jake by bringing over some of his toys and pinning his favourite posters on the walls. Yet he was slow to settle, and Denning knew he was going to struggle with a period of readjustment. Jake was like him. He was most comfortable with familiarity and routine. Living somewhere strange with people he didn't really know was always going to be a challenge for him. For all of them.

'Sarah says you've had your dinner. Would you like anything else? There's some ice-cream in the freezer.' He knew Sarah would disapprove. Claire too, if he was honest. If he was going to make any kind of progress with his son, he would have to stop trying to bribe him with treats every time he wanted a reaction. Jake shook his head and carried on firing lazar rays at CGI spaceships. 'OK. You take care, little fella.' He kissed Jake on the top of his blond mop, and slipped out of the room unnoticed.

Denning headed into the kitchen and went straight to the fridge. Suddenly, he felt like a stranger in his own home. Both his wife and his son seemed too preoccupied to fully acknowledge his presence. He took a cold beer from the fridge, prising open the cap with the novelty bottle-opener Jake had bought for him the Christmas before last.

He wandered back into the living room, sat on one of the linen sofas and took a welcome sip of cold beer. He turned on the music system, flicking the station over from Classic FM to Jazz FM, and rested his feet on the beechwood coffee table as the subtle tone of Stan Getz flowed over the speakers.

Jake was nine. The same age as Caleb Hudson.

He thought about Jake. His only son had already had to cope with a lot in his short life. He'd been diagnosed with ADHD and a mild form of ASD when he was five. This, combined with the recent traumatic events in his life, had meant that they'd had to handle him carefully. A child psychologist had advised a period of stability. He'd been signed off school for a few weeks, and long-term they were exploring the possibility of home-schooling. Denning had been opposed to the idea. He felt his son's needs would be better served in an environment where there were other children to interact with. Claire, however, had taken the opposite view, insisting it had been conventional schooling that had exacerbated Jake's problems in the first place.

Then, two months ago, their world had fallen apart. Denning had discovered Claire's partner was responsible for several murders stretching back more than a decade. It had culminated with the man holding them hostage in an abandoned church and threatening to kill them. Only good luck and good timing had saved them. He was currently on remand in Belmarsh awaiting trial but the memories of that day had been etched onto the minds of all concerned. Jake, in particular, was still having vivid nightmares.

Denning took another sip of beer. He looked up to see Sarah standing next to him. 'I forgot to tell you. Claire phoned earlier.' His ex-wife tended to use the home phone rather than his mobile when calling. She claimed it was because she didn't want to bother him with domestic matters when he was at work. In reality, he suspected she didn't feel comfortable talking to him at times. Whilst Claire and Sarah would never be bosom buddies, Claire seemed to find it easier to talk to another woman.

'What did she want?'

'Just checking everything was OK with Jake.' She perched on the edge of the sofa. 'And to say her mum might have to go back into hospital. Would we mind having Jake for a bit longer?'

Claire's mum was recovering from a stroke. Her recovery was taking its time. And taking its toll on Claire. 'Well, of course we won't mind,' Denning replied, then looked at Sarah. 'We don't mind, do we?'

'He's your son. Where else would he go?'

There was always his parents. They lived just outside Keele, working at the university there in different academic posts. Both looking forward to retirement, which wasn't too far in the future. But they wouldn't have time to look after their grandson. At least he was sure that's what they'd tell him. Might be a different story if it was his brother's kids though...

'If it's OK with you, then I'll tell her yes. Jake seems to be settling in now.'

'Yes,' Sarah replied coolly. 'He hasn't wet the bed again. So that has to be a positive sign.'

'It was just the once, Sarah. And after what he's been through, it's entirely understandable.'

She smiled. 'I know. It's just...' She grimaced. 'I might have to go over to New York. There are problems with one of the bank's investment portfolios and they want me to head up the team that sorts it out. Nothing's been decided yet, but if I have to go, it will be at short notice.'

He thought about this. Jake was still off school, but this state of play couldn't last indefinitely. Their neighbour's daughter Corrine had been looking after him during the day while he and Sarah were at work, but she'd be going back to uni soon. His irregular work patterns – especially with all the overtime that inevitably went with any major murder enquiry – meant he relied on Sarah to look after Jake when he wasn't around. Relied on her more than he would have liked. Perhaps he should be thinking about a nanny. But Jake would hate being looked after by a stranger. He was only just beginning to accept Sarah as a substitute mummy.

Sarah offered another smile. 'Don't worry, if it happens, I'm sure we'll sort something out.' She disappeared back into the office and her emails.

Denning took another drink of beer. He was surprised to feel the bottle was almost empty.

He thought about Jake playing his computer games in the spare room, and about Caleb Hudson lying dead in a mortuary.

His stomach knotted at the thought.

There was a ruthless killer out there; someone who was prepared to brutally murder a whole family without compunction. And then there was the fear they could strike again. McKenna would be on his back over this, wanting results.

He went to drink some more beer but realised the bottle was already empty.

Chapter Eleven

It took Molly some time to find the street she was looking for. Half-hidden in the shadows of Paddington station, the building she wanted looked like it had just managed to escape the developer's bulldozer by the skin of its teeth.

It had obviously been a grand house once upon a time. Its neighbours had long ago been converted into flats or bedsits, but this particular building now served a different purpose.

She rang the bell beside the battered front door and waited for an answer. Eventually a scruffy man with a straggly beard pulled open the door and stared at her with a quizzical expression on his face. 'Yes?' he asked after a few seconds of staring.

She explained who she was and who she was looking for. The quizzical expression was replaced with a nonchalant shrug. Then the owner of the straggly beard let her in.

The hostel was run by a homeless charity. Until a few years ago it had benefitted from a local authority grant that ensured the building was at least superficially maintained and had a basic staffing presence. Since then its future had been at the mercy and generosity of anonymous benefactors as the charity's coffers began to run dry. The peeling paint and cracked linoleum was testament to the hard times it, like most of its residents, had fallen on.

Straggly-beard man showed her along a dingy corridor until they reached a half-glazed door with a sign that said Common Room. The ceilings were high and the windows wide, and despite the shabby appearance, the building had a forgotten dignity about it. In another life this would have been a grand house.

As soon as she entered the common room, she spotted him sitting on an old brown sofa that was adorned with rips and fag burns. He was wearing a beanie hat and grey hoodie, and was chatting to a sallow-faced youth who couldn't have been more than a teenager. He shot her a brief glance, then continued chatting to the sallow-faced youth. Molly turned to thank straggly-beard man, but he'd already vanished.

The room was bare and shabby, with a scattering of tired, second-hand furniture and a carpet so worn that she could only guess what the pattern had once been. A large, plasma-screen telly sat incongruously on a seventies teak-veneered sideboard. Perhaps it had been donated by someone who thought television was more than just a luxury for people who had nowhere to live. Perhaps they were right.

She walked over to the sofa. 'Hello, Ben.'

He still didn't look up. There was a large piece of Elastoplast on the side of his neck. 'What do you want, Molly?'

'Can we go somewhere more private and talk?'

He seemed to think about this for a moment. The teenager sitting next to him gave Molly a curt glance, then looked back at Ben. Ben tapped the lad on the shoulder, said 'Laters', then got to his feet and ushered Molly towards a small kitchen area.

The kitchen was almost as scruffy as the common room, with a couple of grease-encrusted cookers in one corner and an ancient, noisy fridge in the other. At least the room was empty. She sat at a Formica-topped table, complete with nicks and scratches marks embedded in its surface. There was a faint smell of something putrid, like a blocked drain, or dead meat. She tried hard not to focus on it.

'Do you want anything to drink?' Ben was standing next to a kettle beside the sink.

'I'll have a cup of tea, thanks.'

He pottered round for a few seconds, getting tea out of a cupboard then rinsing a couple of mugs under the hot tap. 'We all have our own food, but there's a kitty for tea and coffee. Though I reckon the only one who puts any money in is Mack.' He caught her puzzled look. 'He's the bloke who showed you in. He runs the place. He's all right is Mack.'

Molly wasn't sure she would have trusted Mack to run a bath never mind a homeless hostel, but it wasn't fair to judge him. He likely did a near impossible job for, she suspected, very little thanks.

She looked around her as she waited for Ben to finish making their tea. She knew this wasn't an official bail hostel, though it did frequently take in ex-prisoners who were being slowly reintegrated into society. Ex-lifers mostly. Her brother was living amongst murderers, rapists and paedophiles. She reminded herself that everyone deserved a second chance, even after she'd done her best to get them off the streets in the first place.

Ben placed two chipped mugs filled with suspicious-looking brown liquid on the table, then took a carton of milk from the fridge, twisted open the top and gave the contents a sniff. Molly was tempted to say she'd take hers black, but before she had a chance, he'd tipped some milk into her mug, adding some to his own. 'I don't think there's any sugar,' he said.

'It's OK,' she replied, 'I'm cutting down.'

He put the carton of milk back in the fridge then sat down next to her. 'What's this all about, Molly? I ain't seen you for ages, then suddenly you pitch up here for no reason.'

She took a sip of tea. The milk tasted off, as she'd expected, but she tried not to grimace as she drank it. 'I wanted to see how you are. I know I should have been in touch before now, but things I've been busy at work.' She threw him a weak smile. It was an excuse and she knew he knew it. 'I've joined the Major Investigation Team,' she added almost by way of further explanation.

She could tell from the look of indifference on his face that this was of little interest to him, so she changed the subject. 'How long have you been staying here?'

He looked at her for a few moments, clasping his mug of tea in his right hand while unconsciously scratching on the Formica table top with his left. She wishes he'd take his silly hat off; it made him look a twat. 'About a month,' he said. 'It's like the Ritz compared with the last place I stayed.'

She knew he'd been homeless. She'd felt guilty about not offering him a place to stay, but there had been Jon to consider, her partner. Their relationship had been through tough times and things were still tricky between them. Inviting her troublesome brother to stay with them could well have been the final straw in their relationship.

'Where were you staying before?'

He continued to scratch at the Formica. 'A friend's sofa for a few weeks, then a couple of shop doorways. It wasn't so bad during the summer. At least it was warm. It was only after your lot picked me up that I was pointed in this direction.'

He'd been involved in a fight, during which he had been stabbed in the neck. Fortunately, it hadn't severed an artery. The staff at St Thomas' had told him he'd been lucky. A night in hospital, then a room in a hostel. According to the official crime report, Ben and another man named Colin Pyke claimed they had been attacked in the street by a group of men. One of the group had ended up in intensive care after allegedly being punched by either Ben or Pyke. Both had claimed they were acting in self-defence. CCTV hadn't been able to throw up anything useful, and Ben presented himself as having been nothing more than an innocent bystander who had been in the wrong place at the wrong time. It looked like his little-boy-lost act had found an appreciative audience and as things stood it was likely no further action would be taken. The individual who had been punched had a conviction going back years, and it was unlikely he'd press charges. If his condition deteriorated, however, it could well be a different story.

Details of Ben's arrest had appeared on the system a couple of days ago when Molly was looking for something unconnected to the assault. The name Ben Milne had jumped out at her. Ben had refused to take their step-father's name as she had done, though, to her knowledge, he'd had little contact with their natural father since they'd left Australia nearly twenty years ago. She'd clocked the address of where he'd been sent after being discharged from hospital, and her conscience had done the rest.

'What happened? The fight, I mean. What was it about?'

He just carried on looking at her, as though she was a stranger. 'It was something and nothing.'

Molly took another sip of the rancid tea. She glanced at the Elastoplast on her brother's neck; a reminder of both his vulnerability and his stupidity. 'Look, I'm not here in any official capacity. This isn't even my area anymore.'

'No,' he shot back at her, 'I don't reckon your brother being stabbed would rate all that highly with you.'

'I'm here now. And that's because I'm worried about you.'

He looked momentarily crestfallen, as though she'd clawed at a raw wound. When they'd been younger they had been so close; her kid brother who she'd always looked out for, especially when their parents had split up and they'd had to return to the UK. He'd taken it worse than she had. Unlike her, he'd been born in Australia, and being made to leave the sunny shores of Sydney and face the dank grey skies of a British winter had been a brutal wrench at an impossibly young age. He'd been forced to leave behind his friends, his school and his father without being allowed any say in the matter. Their mother had always claimed she'd had no choice: their father had left her – left them – for someone else, and she wasn't going to stick around where she wasn't wanted. At thirteen, Molly had been old enough to accept the inevitable, but Ben, eight years younger than her, couldn't understand why he wasn't allowed to stay with his daddy in a country he regarded as home.

'How long do you plan to stop here for?'

He shrugged. 'Until they chuck me out I suppose.'

She chose to ignore his flippant tone. 'And then what?'

He looked at her. 'Why are you pretending to care? You didn't care when I told you I was homeless. Just fobbed me off with some old guff about that twat of a boyfriend of yours not wanting me around. Why pretend to give a shit now?'

'We've been over that. It's Jon's house, not mine. And besides, if you really wanted a place to stay, you only had to apologise to mum and Pete. You know they would have let you move back in.'

He shook his head. 'You've no idea, have you? You're the big sister who never screws up. You get yourself a job with the plods to please Pete, settle down with a bloke. OK, he's a twat, but even so...'

It wasn't true. At least not entirely. She screwed up. She'd once screwed up big time, but Ben was either too young to remember, or conveniently chose not to. 'You deliberately wind Pete up. You know which buttons to press and then off you go.' Ben's relationship with their step-father had never been good. Molly knew how to smile and chat and play the dutiful step-daughter whenever she visited their mother and step-father, but Ben was too much like their dad: hot-headed, wilful and a natural piss-taker. A former neighbour who'd bred Spaniels once commented that Ben was like an awkward bitch he'd reared; whatever he asked it to do, it would always do the exact opposite.

'I can have a word, if you want me to. Try and calm the waters.' She tilted her head towards him, like she used to do when they were children. 'You know you were always Mum's favourite. She'd do anything for you.'

He didn't reply. He stared at his tea, refusing to drink it. Either because it tasted foul or because he simply didn't want it. 'You can't go on living like this,' she said, 'this chaotic existence, just drifting from one problem to the next.' She gave him a hard look. 'You need to sort yourself out, Ben. Before it's too late.'

She knew there would be more to Ben's story than he was willing to share. He was hiding something from her. She'd always been able to tell when he was lying, and he was lying now. She could ask around, find out the truth, but she wasn't sure she wanted to know.

–

Molly took the ninety-one bus to Crouch End. A five minute walk took her from the bus stop to the Victorian terraced house she shared with Jon. Autumn was only starting to make its presence felt with a crisp chill either first thing in the morning or last thing at night. In between times it was like summer had decided to stick around for a while, albeit without the same intensity as earlier in the year.

Jon was in the kitchen when she got in. He was frying something meatless on the hob, tossing it round the pan with a wooden spatula and stirring in some reddish sauce from a jar.

And the house was clean, or at least the carpet looked as though it had recently made contact with a Hoover and the sink wasn't full of dirty dishes. This was progress.

'Have a nice time with Trudi?' he asked.

She sat down at the kitchen table. Jon had already poured himself a beer, which sat half drunk in a glass beside the hob. He offered her one, but she shook her head. There was some sauvignon blanc in the fridge, which she'd have with dinner. 'Actually, I didn't go for a drink with Trudi after all,' she said. She told him about her decision to go and see Ben, and about his current situation, but omitted to mention the fight and its repercussions.

When she'd finished, Jon took a swig of beer and joined her at the table. 'He's having a tough time,' he said. 'I can sympathise. I've been through shit myself.'

It wasn't as though she needed reminding. A few months ago she'd left him, convincing herself it was over between them. Their relationship had always been rocky. Jon was twelve years her senior and four times divorced. He came with more baggage than Heathrow's left luggage department. She loved him, but sometimes that felt like it wasn't enough. Prone to depression, which had been exacerbated by unemployment, a recent visit from the black dog had almost driven them apart. She tried so hard to cope with Jon's mood swings and be the supportive partner he needed her to be, but so often her job exhausted whatever energy reserves she had and there was nothing to spare.

Then she'd found out he'd lied to her about a previous relationship and she'd struggled to accept his deceit.

Since then, however, they'd talked things through. She'd agreed to give their relationship another go. Jon had been to his GP, who'd prescribed a course of Fluoxetine and regular therapy sessions with a counsellor. He'd turned a corner in the past month, but it was still early days.

'If he needs a place to crash then there's a spare room here,' Jon said. She could hear the reluctance in his voice. 'You would need to make it clear it would only be temporary though.'

She shook her head. 'Except it wouldn't be. Temporary, I mean. Not with Ben. He'd move in and we'd never be shot of him. But thanks for offering.' She rubbed Jon's arm affectionately. 'What Ben needs is to remember that he's not still fourteen.' She sighed, feeling guilty for talking about her brother like this. 'All his life he's been indulged. Mum spoilt him from word go.' Her mother had been almost forty when she discovered she was expecting Ben. She'd thought it was an early menopause until her doctor did a pregnancy test. She had believed another baby might have helped cement her marriage to Molly's dad, stop him from playing around and focus on being a parent: give him reason to behave like a grown up. But by the time Ben was five, her parents' marriage was over.

Jon got back to his feet and stirred whatever was in the frying pan until it started to hiss and spit. 'If he needs space to get his head sorted, then the offer's there.'

She appreciated the gesture, but she knew that's all it was, a gesture. A nod from Jon to say he was serious when he'd said he'd change. Trying to turn back into the man she'd fallen for five years ago. 'He's got a room at my parents'. He needs to apologise to Mum and Pete for whatever he's done to piss them off this time, and beg them to let him back. But what's the point in even saying that? I know he won't. If being stabbed in the neck isn't enough to persuade him to sort his shit out, then I don't know what is.'

Molly stretched, easing the tightness from her shoulders. It had been a long day. 'Let's change the subject.' She massaged her left shoulder, where she was sure she could feel a knot of tension fighting back at her. 'Any luck on the job front?'

He turned to face her. 'Nothing much. I did speak to a bloke I used to work with who said there might be some teaching work going at a local colleges. Part-time and the money's crap, but it would be something to keep me going.'

She nodded and smiled. Until just over a year ago, Jon had been political editor with the *London Echo*. But since losing his job after the paper had folded, his purpose in life had been, if not exactly lost, then at least temporarily mislaid. He had been trying to write a book about political corruption, but that had been on the back burner for some time now. 'At least it would bring some money in,' she said, knowing that now his redundancy money had run out they were dependent on her salary to pay the bills and put wine in the fridge. Luckily, a timely inheritance had meant he'd been able to pay off the mortgage a few years back, so at least they would always have a roof over their heads.

'How was your day?'

She thought about it. She tried not to think about Ben and the wrong turns he'd taken in life which meant he was now sleeping in a homeless hostel. Instead she thought about work, and the Galloway family.

'Interesting,' she said, and her mind returned to Natalya Kovak, and why she'd felt the need to lie about not knowing Dan Hudson's whereabouts.

Chapter Twelve

The hospital's corridors stank of bleach. The long, grey walls seemed to stretch to infinity, while overhead signs pointed the way to various wards and departments.

The mortuary was in the basement of a new block that looked as though it had been built sometime in the last decade. Denning pushed open a pair of heavy glass doors and was met by a long corridor of whitewashed breezeblock. The curious smell that he had noticed the first time he'd visited a hospital mortuary was apparently called Formalin. It wasn't quite bleach and it wasn't anti-septic, rather it was closer to formaldehyde in a liquid form.

Denning found the room he wanted. He buzzed the door and waited to be let in. The door was opened by a young woman, black hair tied smartly behind her in a ponytail, a pale blue mask dangling by her chin.

'DI Denning,' he informed her. 'I'm here to see Dr Baker.' He showed her his ID and she held the door open to allow him in.

There were about half a dozen people in the autopsy suite, all wearing plastic aprons over their light blue cover-alls.

The bodies of the Galloway family would be in the mortuary freezers, except for whichever one was being examined at the time. Five bodies, all with a combination of gunshot wounds and burns. It would take time to get round all of them.

A man in his late fifties with a greying beard tucked neatly into a blue mask was in the examination suite. He was working on the blackened body of a youngish adult male: Simon Galloway, Denning guessed. There was nothing recognisably human about the burned corpse, though and Denning felt a shiver at the thought of the damage a fire could do to someone.

The man nodded an acknowledgement when he saw Denning, spoke to his two assistants and left the autopsy room.

'Dr Baker?' Denning asked.

The grey-haired man nodded, pulled down the mask and shook Denning by the hand. They'd met once before, briefly, when Baker had performed the post-mortem on a young woman whose body had been fished out of a canal. Denning returned the handshake. He hated attending post-mortems and usually waited until the pathologist had sent in his report before he took things any further. But they needed a quick result on this. McKenna had insisted he spoke directly to the pathologist.

Apart from the Formalin, there was an overriding smell of antiseptic and iodine.

Baker guided Denning to a quiet room away from the cold steel of the autopsy suite and led him into a windowless office at the end of the corridor.

The room was even smaller than McKenna's office, and almost as claustrophobic.

Denning sat opposite Baker and wished he was somewhere else.

'I've examined the two eldest adults,' Baker began. 'I'm working on the second adult male now.' He paused and scratched at his beard before continuing. 'I've decided to leave the young female and the child till last. I hope that won't be a problem for you.'

Denning said it wouldn't be. He wasn't about to tell the pathologist how he should do his job.

'My reasons aren't based on sentiment,' he said in a dry tone. 'It's just that I understand from the fire inspector's preliminary report that they were found on an upper floor and there was considerably less fire damage to the bodies. This will make any external examination easier.'

'OK,' Denning said. 'I really don't want to pressure you, but could you give me an approximation of when you think the full PM report might be ready?'

Baker sighed and continued to touch his beard, almost like a form of reassurance. 'A few years ago, a case like this would have seen two pathologists working in tandem. But the Home Office would demur at such a luxury in these impecunious times.'

Denning nodded sympathetically.

'I can confirm they were all shot at close range with a shotgun. I would guess something like a Browning A-500, though forensics will be able to confirm this. So far, I can tell you that each victim was shot once, with the exception of the oldest male. We found two bullets in him. One in the side of the skull and one in the chest. The other two bodies have bullet wounds in the head.' Baker spoke with a slight nasal whine. His head nodded slowly as he spoke. 'The only consolation, if you can call it that, is that they were all dead when the fire started. I will need to confirm that for the remaining two victims, but I would guess at that conclusion.' He paused and gave Denning a look. 'Most of the bodies were very badly burned, except for the young female, and the child. The others are, I would say, unrecognisable. We'll use dental records to confirm ID, but I believe you already have a good idea as to their identities.'

Denning nodded in agreement. 'I will need confirmation ASAP. And obviously we'd like to know when we can release what's left of the bodies.'

Baker continued looking at him for a moment. 'We should have finished our examinations by tomorrow, early afternoon at the latest.'

'Is there any way you can tell which of them was shot first?'

Baker shook his head. 'The fire didn't help matters, as you can probably imagine. But I would estimate that all the victims were shot at close range, judging by the size of the impact wounds and the amount of damage done to internal organs. As to which one was shot first, it's impossible to say at this stage, though we can obviously assume the young female and the child were the last to be shot.'

Denning tried to work it out in his head. Amber and Caleb were obviously hiding upstairs when it happened. The other adults were shot downstairs in the living room at kitchen. But who had been the main target? And why shoot the rest of the family? It didn't make any sense.

There was one more question Denning had to ask. 'You said the victims so far had been shot in the head. Judging by the point of contact made by the bullets, would you say this was someone who knew how to handle a gun?'

Baker gave a throaty chortle. 'Inspector Denning, I'm a pathologist, not a ballistics expert.' He scratched his beard again. 'But if I were to hazard a guess, I'd say whoever shot them knew what they were doing. Does that answer your question?'

Denning agreed that it did. It confirmed what he thought: whoever did this knew what they were doing. This hadn't been random. It had been deliberate.

Chapter Thirteen

Marisa Powell seemed slightly more awake when Molly called round to see her the next morning.

They were sitting in the kitchen this time. Modern white wooden units and apple green Farrow & Ball on the walls. A hessian bowl on the table was overflowing with fresh fruit.

Marisa was wearing a pair of trendy denim dungarees today, with a striped blue and white t-shirt underneath. She had offered to make them both a coffee and was currently fiddling with a sleek but complicated espresso machine that hissed steam and looked as though it would challenge the most skilled of baristas. Molly was beginning to wish she'd asked for a mug of tea instead.

'Do you take milk?' she asked Molly, having finally got the machine to produce some coffee.

'Just a drop, but no sugar, thanks.'

Marisa pulled open the door of a bulky, American-style fridge. 'I've only got soya, is that OK?'

Molly agreed it would be.

Marisa placed a tray with two oversized cups of glistening black liquid on the table, along with a white ceramic jug of soya milk. There was also a plate with what looked like homemade biscuits on it. Molly took one and nibbled the edges. It was crumbly and fruity and tastier than it looked.

'How are the children today?' she asked. She had yet to meet Marisa Powell's offspring, but the occasional thumps and bangs that came from the floor above suggested they were both in residence.

Marisa sat down opposite Molly. 'They're still upset. It frightens them anytime they look out the front window and see the burnt-out building opposite. They've convinced themselves there are monsters living in there.'

Molly smiled at the thought of children and their vivid imagination. She took a drink of coffee. It tasted better than the tea she'd had at Ben's hostel, even with the soya milk. 'I just wanted to follow up on something you said yesterday. About Amber.' She nibbled some more of the tasty biscuit, trying not to drop crumbs on the spotless tiled floor, and envying Marisa Powell for having the time and energy to bake delicious biscuits and keep her kitchen so clean. 'You said Amber told you Dan wasn't Caleb's father. Is it possible there could have been any truth in that?'

There was another thump from upstairs and Molly hoped Marisa wasn't going to have to abandon her to attend to her motherly duties again. But she either didn't hear or decided it was easier to ignore it.

'I do hope I didn't give you the wrong impression yesterday,' she said. 'Amber and I were friends, but it wasn't like I was prying into her private life. It's just that she liked to talk. I think she felt like she was unburdening herself onto me.'

Molly finished the biscuit and noticed Marisa hadn't helped herself to one. 'Marisa, this isn't about prying into somebody's private life for the sake of a bit of gossip. We're investigating a murder. Five people have been killed, including a child. Your neighbours. We need to examine every lead in the hope that something will point us in the direction of the killer. It could be that what happened has something to do with the family.' She paused and wondered if it would be rude to help herself to another biscuit. She decided to resist. 'As I said to you yesterday, anything you tell me will be treated in the strictest confidence.'

Marisa seemed to think the matter over before she spoke, lifting the massive cup to her mouth and taking a sip of coffee. 'It was after Dan had said he wanted custody of Caleb. We were chatting in the park one afternoon. My two were feeding the ducks, and Caleb was playing on the swings.' She stopped and dabbed a hand at the corner of her mouth where a tiny drop of coffee had dribbled down it. 'Amber just came out with it. She said something like, "Dan wants to take Caleb off me, but he hasn't got any rights. It's not as though he's Caleb's real dad". Or something like that.' She took another sip of coffee, then stared awkwardly at her cup. 'Although it was only just after lunch, I was sure Amber had been drinking. Her breath smelt strongly of mints. I think she'd had a glass or two of something with lunch. Personally, I never like to drink around the children. I think it sets a bad example.' She didn't sound judgemental when she said this, rather she was just stating a fact. 'To be honest with you, Amber used to make things up. I suspect a lot of what came out of her mouth was either said for attention, or for dramatic effect. Maybe even a bit of both. I got the impression Amber was an attention-seeker.'

'But there could have been some truth in her claim?'

She tilted her head to one side. 'I don't know. You could never tell if Amber was being entirely honest with you.'

Molly considered what she was saying. If Amber seriously believed there was a real danger she could lose custody of Caleb, then denying her ex-husband's claim to his paternity would certainly strengthen her case. But a simple DNA test, which any family court would insist on in such circumstances, would expose any lies on Amber's part. But what if she was telling the truth? It would certainly give Dan Hudson a good motive for wanting Amber dead. 'Did Amber think Dan was serious about wanting custody of Caleb?'

'I suppose so. I mean, I never heard Dan's side of the story, and that certainly seemed to be the gist of his argument with Brian that day in the street. But it's possible Amber was making that up too.'

'So Amber lied?'

Marisa seemed to ponder the question. She placed the oversized cup back on the saucer and decided to have a biscuit after all. 'I don't know that I would say she lied exactly... it was more that she liked to exaggerate. Well, maybe "overdramatise" would be a better word.' She sighed. 'But I honestly think she was genuinely concerned about the possibility of losing Caleb. I don't think that was a lie. Or if it was, then it was a convincing one.' She delicately broke the biscuit in two, then popped one of the halves into her mouth. When she'd finished it, she said: 'She'd started to believe that she was a bad mother. Apparently Ellie was always having a go at her. Little things, like how she dressed Caleb, or complaining about her staying out late. I got the impression Brian and Ellie were quite strict with her. She said they disapproved of her lifestyle. I expect they just wanted her to settle down.'

'When you say "settle down", did they want her and Dan to get back together?'

'God, no. I think they accepted the marriage was over. And from Amber said, I got the impression they weren't too keen on Dan, even before he and Amber split up.' She popped the final piece of biscuit in her mouth, munched it, then said: 'If I'm honest, I always thought Amber was a bit paranoid. I mean, we all fear people will judge us as being bad parents from time to time, don't we?' Molly nodded politely and urged Marisa to continue. 'Jasmine once had the most almighty tantrum in Sainsbury's, and I could just feel strangers' eyes burrowing into me. But it doesn't mean you're a bad parent just because your children can play up on occasions.'

'Did Caleb ever play up?'

She gave a light shrug. 'Well, no actually. He was quite a placid little thing.' She winced. 'He was a lovely kid actually, and always very polite, "please" and "thank-you", that kind of thing. Despite her misgivings, Amber did a good job bringing him up.' She paused. 'You know, Amber *was* a good mum, despite what she might have thought about herself.'

'Do you think Amber could have been a danger to herself? Or to Caleb?'

'No. Oh, no. She loved Caleb. Look, Amber wasn't a bad person. She just had problems.' She paused for a moment, then flashed her eyes at Molly. 'She did tell me once that she was seeing a therapist.'

Molly's curiosity was pricked. 'Did she say what for?'

A shake of the head. 'No, but my guess would be anxiety. Maybe depression. I'm no expert, but I suspected she may have had mental health issues.' She took a sip of coffee, though it must have been cold by now. 'She once told me she would kill herself if she ever lost Caleb. I don't know if she meant it. I mean it's the kind of thing you say, isn't it? I'd probably say it myself if I thought I was going to lose my two. But I don't know… That was the thing with Amber, you never could tell if she was exaggerating for effect or whether she really did mean it.'

'I don't suppose she told you the name of this therapist?'

'I think she said his name was Rolf or Ralf something. I know he had a practice in Bermondsey. But on the other hand, that could easily have been another of Amber's stories.'

Molly made a note to try and track down this therapist. 'Did she ever mention why she and Dan split up?'

'Apparently he was seeing other women. She thought he was having an affair with Simon's girlfriend at one point, but I don't know if there was any truth in that.'

'Natalya?'

She shook her head. 'Sorry, I don't know her name.' She looked into her almost-empty cup, and addressed her next comment to the coffee dregs rather than to Molly. 'Amber was a troubled soul. Despite the exaggerating and the tall tales, I felt sorry for her. I honestly think she was going through a difficult time. Even if only part of what she said was true, then she must have had a very unhappy life. I don't think she had any close friends. In fact, I don't think she was close to anyone, apart from Caleb.'

'She had you.' Molly meant it as a bland statement rather than a compliment, but the smile that flickered around Marisa Powell's mouth suggested that was how she took it.

'Yes,' she said, 'I was very fond of Amber. But she could be hard work. Every time we met up there would be another drama unfolding somewhere in her life.' She looked at Molly. 'Thinking back, even the last time we met, she was still coming out with her silly stories.'

'When was this?'

'Last week. I'd almost forgotten about it. I was pottering in the front garden and Amber suddenly appeared out of nowhere and started chatting. She didn't have Caleb with her, which I thought was strange. I wasn't really paying attention because I was waiting for the gasman to come round and fix the boiler. Amber was chatting away at me about her mum.'

'Her mum…?'

There was another loud thump from upstairs, but Marisa Powell was still oblivious to everything but her empty coffee cup. 'Some piece of nonsense about how she thought all her problems in life stemmed from being abandoned by her real mum. I expect she was after my sympathy and was hoping I'd ask her in for a chat.'

'Ellie was Amber's step-mum,' Molly said, trying to second-guess where Marisa was going with this. 'Her real mother died when she was young. That's probably what she meant.'

There was a moment's quiet. Marisa reached out for another biscuit before changing her mind. 'It wasn't that.' She looked uncomfortable. 'It wasn't that at all. I knew Ellie wasn't Amber's real mum. No, it was something quite different. Out of the blue, Amber told me she was adopted. Amber had told Brian and Ellie she wanted to find her real mother and find out why she'd had her adopted. She'd had a massive row with Ellie and Brian over it.' She looked at Molly, a sad, faraway look on her face. 'I expect it was another one of Amber's stories. You had to give her credit for having a vivid imagination.'

'What happened after she told you?'

Marisa Powell looked sheepish. 'Nothing. The gasman turned up to repair my boiler. I told Amber I was very sorry but I couldn't chat any more. Then a week later she was dead.'

Chapter Fourteen

Denning had just left the mortuary and was heading back to the station when the call came through on his mobile.

The voice on the other end of the phone was female and politely spoken. She gave her name as Ruth Forbes. 'I'm... I *was* Ellie Galloway's business partner,' she'd said. She gave him her business address – the fancy dress shop in Camden where Ellie had been a partner – and said she might have some information about Ellie Galloway. 'Or I can pop down to the station this afternoon, if that's convenient.'

Denning said he would come to her.

The fancy dress shop was called Alter Image. It was sandwiched between a trendy-looking barber's shop and a Japanese restaurant just off Camden High Street. The door gave a cheery ping when he pushed it open.

Ruth Forbes was standing behind the counter at the back of the shop. She was in her late forties, and dressed in baggy black cargo pants and a red t-shirt with a faded picture of Che Guevara on the front.

There were two young women at the counter who were asking about costumes for an upcoming thir- tieth birthday party. One of them was struggling to choose between a schoolgirl outfit and a Wonder Woman costume. In the end, they said they'd think about it and come back later. Once they'd left the shop, Denning introduced himself. 'Thank you for coming over,' she said. The shop wasn't very big. It was full to bursting with superhero costumes, nun's habits, scary clown outfits and various leather and latex get-ups. He even spotted a comedy police uniform, complete with rubber truncheon.

'I still can't believe it,' Ruth said. She took a box of novelty handcuffs from a shelf behind the counter and opened it. The handcuffs were adorned with a pink fluffy material and the box stated they were for adult use only. 'It's Godawful to think about it. Ellie, Brian and...' She shuddered. 'I did think about shutting the shop for a while out of respect for Ellie, but she would have told me I was being silly. Ellie and I were friends as well as business partners. In fact, she did me a huge favour when she bought into this place. I was struggling after the downturn and seriously thinking about selling up.' She reached for an old-fashioned pricing gun next to the till and started pricing the handcuffs. 'It was Ellie's cash that helped keep this place afloat.'

Denning looked around him. There was everything you could need for any type of party, from children's to adults'. It seemed the shop catered for a variety of disparate tastes. 'How come?'

She clocked him looking at the novelty handcuffs and smiled. 'They're only £5.99, a bargain.' Another smile. 'It was her step-son, Simon. He uses us for his company. They recommend us to a lot of their clients. He mentioned to Ellie that I was having money troubles, and she had some cash to invest.' She continued pricing the handcuffs. 'I have to admit, we didn't exactly get off to the best of starts.'

'No?'

She stopped pricing and sighed for a moment. 'I'd made it very clear I was looking for a sleeping partner: someone to put a lump sum into this place in return for a share of the profits. As far as I was concerned this was my business, it was going to be run my way. Ellie had other ideas. She came in that first day with lots of talk about how we could boost sales and expand our market. She started talking about diversifying and developing a social media presence, all sorts of bollocks like that. I told her if that was how she wanted to play things, she could take her money and shove it.' She picked up the pricing gun and resumed firing little white labels onto the handcuffs. 'At first I resented her being here. I'd run this place for years by myself, very successfully.' She put the gun back down and shot Denning a wry look. 'OK, fairly successfully. The last thing I wanted was a stranger coming in telling me what to do.'

'But things changed?'

'I had to hand it to Ellie, she knew her stuff. Turns out she'd worked in marketing before she was married. She really helped turn this place around, suggesting that we went after the more... novelty end of the market.' She nodded at the pink, fluffy handcuffs. 'We still do a lot of stag and hen parties, but we've also moved into more lucrative corporate stuff too. Simon's connections helped there.' She gave a distant smile. 'We ended up becoming good friends. The more we got to know each other, the more we realised we had quite a lot in common. Both divorced, both found happiness second time round.' She gave a light shake of her head. 'She never expected to find love again after she and James divorced.'

'James?'

'Ellie's first husband, James Metcalf. You did know she'd been married before?' *James Metcalf.* Denning knew that name from somewhere, but he couldn't quite place it...

'Ellie may have had her troubles in the past,' she continued, 'but she'd been given a second chance with Brian, especially as he came with a ready-made family. That's what makes this all so awful.'

Denning smiled at her. 'You said you had something to tell me that might be useful.'

She nodded. 'Sorry. You didn't come here to listen to me wittering on.' She pushed the box of novelty handcuffs to one side, like a child that had become bored with a toy. 'Ellie and I used to chat about things. Personal things.' She sighed. 'Amber. That girl meant well, but she could barely look after herself, never mind Caleb. You probably know that her ex-husband threatened to take Caleb off her? Ellie and Brian had to step in. They said if Amber didn't sort herself out, she would lose Caleb. They were terrified Dan would get custody. That poor child wouldn't have had a hope in hell if he'd ended up with Dan as his primary carer.'

Denning wanted to interject; point out that sometimes fathers could make excellent primary carers, then he remembered the assault charge against Dan Hudson. That would certainly have gone against him in any potential custody case, but it was still no guarantee he wouldn't have been given custody if it could be proved Amber wasn't capable of looking after her son.

'How did Amber take that?'

Ruth leant on the till, accidentally hitting a random button and causing the till to bleep loudly. She jabbed at another button – or possibly the same one, Denning couldn't tell – and the till was silenced. 'Not well,' she said. 'Even though it was for Amber's own good, she accused them of interfering.'

'Did she have a point?'

'Ellie and Brian could see that Amber was struggling to look after Caleb. Her relationship with Dan had broken down and she was having trouble coping. Nobody doubted Amber loved Caleb, but she was a mess. Ellie suggested to Amber that got a part-time job. It would give her something to do and stop her sitting round the house feeling sorry for herself. Ellie said she'd cut back her hours here and look after Caleb while Amber went out to work. But Amber wouldn't have it. There was yet another argument. She thought Ellie wanted to take Caleb off her.'

'So Amber over-reacted?'

'Not entirely.' She paused and looked over at the shop door, where someone hovered, as if weighing up whether to come in. After a second, they turned and walked away. Ruth continued: 'Things deteriorated. As Amber's behaviour became more erratic, Brian and Ellie felt they had no option but to be more proactive.'

'Proactive?'

'They decided to apply for custody of Caleb themselves, on account of the fact that neither Amber nor Dan was acting in the boy's best interests. Dan didn't want custody of Caleb, not really; he wouldn't have the first clue about bringing up a nine-year-old boy. He just didn't want Amber to have him. Their split was quite bitter, with plenty of unpleasant accusations on both sides. By the time their divorce came through they were barely on speaking terms. Ellie said they had no choice but to take the action they did. They didn't want the boy being used as some kind of pawn between two warring parents.

I mean, they supported Amber as best they could, both financially and emotionally, but at the end of the day it was Caleb's welfare that mattered.'

'So Ellie was the driving force behind the decision to apply for custody? Rather than Brian?'

Ruth glanced nervously in the direction of the shop door again, as though concerned someone might walk in and overhear their conversation. 'Ellie could see how things were with Amber. Brian was still trying to convince himself everything would work out OK in the end. He never liked facing up to trouble unless he had to. It was Ellie who pointed out the situation would only get worse if they didn't do something. She thought Amber might have been on the verge of some kind of breakdown. Plus there was a real worry that if it went to court, and it could be proved that Amber was an unfit mother, then Dan could be granted custody of Caleb over Amber or Brian and Ellie. He *was* the child's father, despite anything Amber might have said to the contrary. The final straw was when social services got involved.'

'Social services?' He failed to hide the surprise in his voice.

Ruth Forbes looked awkward, as though she'd said something she shouldn't have. 'I'm surprised you haven't already spoken to them.' Then she shrugged. 'Someone had contacted them. They suspected it might have been a neighbour. There was a young woman across the road who was quite pally with Amber. Amber used to fill her head with all sorts of nonsense, and it was just possible she believed some of it. The long and the short of it was that Ellie and Brian were paid a visit from children's services.'

'What happened?'

'They managed to fob them off. They put on a united front and insisted Amber was fine and was coping OK with Caleb. They told them how they pulled together as a family and all helped look after him. Social services seemed to buy it. Ellie and Brian persuaded them there was nothing to worry about. Privately though, it was a different matter. Ellie and Brian were worried that if they get the situation sorted, social services would be back, especially as the family was now on their system. They might not be able to persuade them everything was OK a second time. And there was a risk Dan could be awarded custody by default, or worse, that Caleb could be taken into care.'

A middle-class family in a nice home. Denning wasn't surprised they'd been successful at telling social services what they'd wanted to hear. Convincing them Caleb was safe. Which he probably would have been if fate hadn't so cruelly intervened.

'If social services were happy that Caleb was being adequately looked after, then that should have been an end to it.'

'Well, yes, you'd have thought so. Except Amber was still causing trouble. By now she'd convinced herself Ellie wanted to steal Caleb from her. She tried every trick in the book: threatening to top herself; saying she'd run away with Caleb and no one would ever find them.'

'Did her threats have any effect?'

She shook her head again. 'No. If anything, it made them more determined to go for custody. That was what made Amber bring out the big guns.'

There was an awkward pause. 'Go on,' Denning prompted.

'She said she would stop Brian and Ellie getting custody because they weren't Caleb's family. Well, not his *blood* family.'

'I know Ellie wasn't Amber's natural mother, but that shouldn't have made a difference if Brian supported her decision.'

'It wasn't just that though, was it?' She looked at him, hands on her hips, jerking her head at him as she spoke as though giving emphasis to her words. 'Amber was adopted. Neither Brian nor Ellie were related to Amber, or Caleb for that matter, by blood. That was the real problem. I mean legally, they were family, but then Amber suddenly announces that she's planning to find her birth parents and have a relationship with them. If that had happened, then Brian and Ellie's case would have been greatly weakened.'

Denning considered this. His knowledge of family law wasn't great, but he understood the basics. He doubted very much if a court would award custody to biological grandparents who had had no previous involvement in a child's upbringing. But nobody could be certain, and it could have potentially made the situation for Brian and Ellie more complicated.

'How did Brian and Ellie feel about Amber wanting to trace her real parents?'

'Ellie thought Amber was being ungrateful. OK, Alison was dead, but Brian was still her dad, and Ellie had been the closest thing Amber had had to a mother for nearly twenty years. But she was mostly angry on Brian's behalf. After all Brian had done for Amber, Ellie couldn't believe she was prepared to throw it back in his face to pursue some silly fantasy.'

Denning wasn't sure he agreed. 'I imagine it's quite common for adoptive children to try and trace their biological parents at some point in their lives. I'm not sure I would call it a fantasy.'

She huffed. 'But it wasn't really about that, was it? And that's certainly not how Brian and Ellie saw it. Of course, Brian gave in in the end. He was always far too soft with Amber. He said he'd support her decision if it was what she really wanted. Ellie wasn't happy. She thought he was indulging her.'

'That must have put a strain on their relationship?'

'Well, like I said to you earlier, Inspector, Ellie and Brian had a good relationship. Brian wasn't James. They discussed things like adults. They would have worked their way through these problems, given time.'

'One last question, Ms Forbes. Did Amber trace her real parents?'

She gave another shrug. 'I don't know, Inspector. If she did, Ellie never said.'

He thanked her and left the shop, the door pinging shut behind him. As he headed back to his car, the name James Metcalf was still bouncing around his skull. Suddenly his brain made the connection and he remembered where he'd heard the name, and in what context. And that was very interesting.

Chapter Fifteen

Molly saw that photographs of the crime scene had been added to one of the whiteboards at the far end of the room. Pictures of fire-scorched rooms and blackened corpses were pinned next to smiling photos of the family. Forensics must have finished in the Galloway's home. When she'd left Marisa Powell's house earlier that morning she recalled seeing a couple of white-clad SOCOs standing on the doorstep of number forty-two looking like they were finishing up inside the house.

Any time now the post-mortems would be complete and they would have to share the grisly mechanics of how the family's final moments had played out.

She knew she wouldn't be able to look at the post-mortem photos of Amber and Caleb. Instead she focused on the ones that had been taken when they were still alive: both young, smiling, everything to look forward to in life.

But she couldn't allow herself to wallow in sentiment. She had a lot to get through. She needed to track down Amber's therapist. If anyone was going to give them an insight into Amber's mental health, that would be the place to start. It would take time to go through every therapist operating in London, but at least she had a first name to work with. But there was something she had to do first.

'All right, Moll? How's it going?'

Startled, she looked up to see Trudi Bell waving a packet of B&H in Molly's direction. Molly had been trying to give up smoking for some time. She'd managed to go two whole weeks without a cigarette, but it had been hard going at times. Right now the prospect of a smoke and a gossip with Trudi was certainly tempting, but she reluctantly declined the offer. She gently shook her mouse, and her computer screen blinked into life.

Ignoring the dozen emails squatting in her inbox shouting for attention, she logged onto the Police National Computer database, typed in her password and accessed the DVLA records. She entered the registration number of the black BMW from the other day. It took a few seconds for the details to flash up on her screen, but when they did it confirmed what she already suspected: the car was registered to Daniel Marcus Hudson.

Chapter Sixteen

Denning wasn't the kind of detective who liked calling regular briefings. He preferred to let his team get on with the job of being detectives rather than trying to micro-manage everything to within a centimetre of its life. However, early on in an investigation, especially a complicated one like this was turning into, it was important to make sure everyone was up to speed with rapidly changing events.

'We've spoken to the Chisholms,' he said, once the team was paying attention and looking at either him or the grim photos on the whiteboard. 'We can rule them out of this. It was a longshot anyway, but it's safe to assume it wasn't them.' He thought back to David Chisholm, his anger at what Brian Galloway had done still lingering inside him, but not potent enough to murder the man's family and torch their house. 'Which means we have to look at the next name on our list of suspects.' He pointed at the whiteboard. 'Daniel Hudson. Are we any closer to tracing his whereabouts?'

Molly Fisher waved a biro at him. He gave her a nod. 'He's around. I've seen his car parked in a street near Party Animals offices.'

'It could have been there for ages,' Dave Kinsella said. 'Ever since he did his vanishing act.'

'The engine was warm,' Fisher said calmly. 'I think he's still in contact with Natalya Koval.' She looked at Denning. 'She was Simon Galloway's girlfriend, and a director with Party Animals. She claims she hadn't seen Dan since before the murders, but I'd say the car suggests otherwise.'

'Right. We need to find him and bring him in. Get onto Traffic. Give them the reg number and get them to alert us the minute it's flagged up on any cameras.' Denning thought about Dan Hudson. Whatever his guilt or innocence, he was a major part of this investigation and the longer he stayed off the radar the less convincing his innocence looked. 'This Natalya Koval: if she refuses to play ball, bring her in. Make it formal. If he's hanging around outside their office, then I'd say she's lying about not having seen him. It can't be coincidence, can it?'

Molly nodded. 'There was something else, boss.' She tapped the biro against her teeth as though she was trying to form the words in her head before sharing them with the rest of the team. 'She was upset about Simon Galloway, naturally. But I wouldn't exactly say she was distraught.' She pulled a face. 'On the other hand, maybe she's very good at keeping her emotions in check.'

'Who inherits Simon Galloway's share of the company?' Trudi asked.

'You think they were both in it together? Dan Hudson and this Natalya woman?' It was Kinsella again.

'I don't know,' Molly said, still tapping the pen against her teeth. 'There was just something about her. I couldn't put my finger on it, but I'm sure she was lying.'

'If she's lying about not knowing the whereabouts of Dan Hudson,' Denning said, 'then there's a strong chance she's hiding other stuff too. Find out what that is.'

'Hudson has a record for violence,' Neeraj said, 'and if he and Simon Galloway had fallen out, then he would have a pretty good reason for wanting him dead.'

'Plus, if you add in all the crap with Amber and the alleged custody case, then he would have strong motive for wanting rid of the rest of the family,' Trudi added.

'I'm not so sure.' It was Ryan Cormack again. 'I still can't believe he'd shoot his own son in cold blood.'

'We've already established that it's not uncommon for fathers to kill their kids because some court has taken the mother's side in a custody battle,' Trudi argued. 'That could have eaten away at Hudson until he eventually snapped.'

'But it hadn't gotten as far as court.' Cormack wasn't going to let it drop. 'And even if it had, there's every possibility Hudson could have been granted custody.'

'We don't even know for sure that Dan Hudson *did* want custody of Caleb,' Trudi stated. 'It depends how reliable you think Amber Galloway was.'

'According to her neighbour, Amber seems to have been a bit of a fantasist,' Molly agreed. 'She even told her neighbour she was adopted.'

'I think we have to give the adoption claim some credibility,' Denning said, remembering what Ruth Forbes had told him. He thought too about her other claim, that Dan Hudson wasn't serious about wanting custody of Caleb. If there was any truth in her suggestion, then did that give Hudson a stronger motive for killing them? 'It seems the family was visited by social services earlier in the year,' he said. 'Ryan, can you chase that up. Ideally, we'd like to get a look at their written report on the family, but if that's not possible, then at least let's hear what they thought about the Galloway family situation. There's also the added possibility that Brian and Ellie could have been planning to apply for custody of the boy. All this needs to be checked out.'

'That poor kid,' Kinsella said. 'Passed from one family member to another like a toy.'

'At least it shows he was loved,' Trudi offered.

Denning silenced them with a look. They were in danger of becoming distracted by the personal dramas within the Galloway family, and losing focus on finding their killer. 'In the meantime,' he continued, 'I've got the preliminary post-mortem report.' He held the folder aloft. 'They haven't finished down there, but they can confirm that, as we already believed, the family had been shot before the house was torched. And you should all have seen a copy of the forensic report by now. It confirms the whereabouts in the house of each family member when they were shot, so we now have a clearer picture of what happened, where it happened, and an approximation of when. Spent shell cartridges recovered from the house confirm the use of a Browning A-500 shotgun as being the murder weapon. More than likely it was used with a silencer attached, as this would explain why none of the neighbours heard any gunshots.' This backed up Baker's theory.

'A silencer suggests this was pre-planned,' Kinsella said.

Denning nodded. 'It's beginning to look like this was something more than just a random attack. We now have to assume the Galloways were deliberately targeted, although I seriously doubt burglars would bother with silencers on their weapons, so we probably want to think again about the burglary theory.' Denning continued to read from the report, which he paraphrased for his team. 'The fire was started in the hallway using an accelerant

– petrol – which the assailant had either brought with them or found in the house. Due to the location of the base of the fire and the use of accelerant, the fire had spread quickly, consuming the entire house in less than twenty minutes. Brian and Simon Galloway had been in the living room when they were killed; Ellie in the kitchen, and Amber and Caleb in an upstairs bedroom, probably Caleb's room. Ellie's proximity to the melted remains of a telephone suggested she was in the process of trying to call the emergency services when she was shot. As no call was ever received from the Galloway house on the night of the shooting, it's probable she was shot before she had a chance to make the call. The location of Amber and Caleb suggests they had been attempting to hide from the assailant.'

'Chances are Caleb was in bed when the shooting started,' Cormack said. 'Maybe she went up there to protect him.'

'Possibly,' Denning acknowledged. 'I suspect we'll never know.'

'Why didn't Amber call the police from a mobile?' Kinsella asked.

'Maybe she didn't have one to hand,' Cormack said.

'Or she was too shit-scared,' Trudi offered. 'Think about it: she's trying to protect her son and there's a maniac downstairs shooting dead members of her family. I expect she wanted to keep her head down and hope they wouldn't find her.'

'Better still,' suggested Neeraj, 'why didn't she just smash a window and jump to safety?'

'I refer you to my previous point, Deep,' Trudi said.

Neeraj opened his mouth to argue when Molly Fisher interrupted. 'There is another possibility.' Her eyes were fixed on Denning, but she addressed the room. 'This is just a wild theory, but how do we know we're not looking at a murder/suicide here?'

A general murmuring went round the MIT suite. Denning said: 'OK, Molly. Share your theory.'

'Amber. Her neighbour seemed to think she was suffering from mental health issues. Possibly depression. Apparently she was seeing a counsellor or therapist of some sort. I'm still trying to track him down. If, as the post-mortem suggests, she was the last person to be shot, is it possible she could have killed her family then turned the gun on herself? Especially if she was adopted. Maybe she didn't regard them as being her real family?'

Denning considered this. The post-mortem had shown that Amber had been killed by a single bullet fired at fairly close range, but there was nothing to suggest at this stage it hadn't been self-inflicted. Of course, Baker had still to complete the post-mortem on Amber, so nothing had yet been officially confirmed. It was certainly a possibility. And it would conveniently wrap the case up nice and neatly for them. Perhaps a bit too neatly...Baker said he would have completed the PM on Amber by the end of the day. Denning would get him to email it over as soon as he'd finished it. It sounded like a crazy theory, but at the moment, all options were on the table.

'That's nuts,' Kinsella barked. 'OK, maybe at a pinch I could buy the theory she killed the parents and her brother if they weren't blood related. But to kill her own son? Granted, I accept fathers have been known to...but a mother?'

'Again, it's not unheard of,' Molly insisted. 'There have been instances where mothers have killed their children...'

'Especially if she thought she was going to lose him.' Trudi added.

'Did she even know how to use a shotgun?' Neeraj asked. 'Let alone know how to get her hands on one.'

'This is London, Deep,' Trudi said drily, 'it's not difficult to come by a shooter, legal or otherwise.'

'Like I said,' Molly offered calmly, 'it's just a theory. But it isn't unheard of for mothers to kill their children when they're under duress, just as it isn't uncommon for fathers to do the same.' She looked at Kinsella when she made the last comment.

'So what are we saying?' Kinsella wasn't going to let it drop. 'She shot her family, set fire to the house, then ran upstairs and shot herself and her kid?' But Denning could tell from the look on his face that he didn't think it was as absurd as it first sounded.

'OK. As Molly says, it's just a theory. But one we should at least consider. We know Amber seems to have had her share of problems. We also know there was a real risk she might have been about to lose Caleb. Although this kind of thing is rare, it has happened before. Molly, you need to track down this counsellor of Amber's ASAP, and get an insight into her state of mind at the time of the murders. Find out if she was considered a risk to either herself or to anyone else.'

Denning turned back to the whiteboard. 'However, let's explore other possible motives. Dave, what did you find out about Brian Galloway's business activities?'

'Not much to report there, boss. I spoke to Galloway's accountant. Seems Galloway was a shrewd investor. He owns a couple of houses, which he rents out as student flats. All got their HMO certificates in order, and the properties are managed by a letting agency based in

Islington. They said Galloway was a good landlord, he would fix any problems quickly and ensured the places were all well maintained. We spoke to the other bloke who co-owned the garage and second-hand car dealership with Galloway. He had nothing bad to say about Galloway. Looks as though he was mostly hands-off and left the day-to-day running of the place to the manager. We're still waiting for the Spanish police to get back to us about the bar in Majorca, but so far there's nothing to suggest Brian Galloway was involved in anything shady. Ditto nothing to attract the attention of the boys at Revenue and Customs.'

'Trudi, anything on the first Mrs Galloway?' Denning asked.

She glanced at her notes. 'Apparently, she died from ovarian cancer when Simon and Amber were both young. A local hospice confirmed this. I spoke to a former employee at the hotel they ran together. Apparently Brian Galloway was devastated by her death.'

'Thanks, Trudi.' Apart from the hit and run, Brian Galloway seemed to be a man with a near blameless past. Perhaps Simon Galloway had some skeletons in his closet? 'Molly, what's your take on Party Animals?'

'I'm not sure yet.' She bit her lip. 'The business appears to be legit, but there's something not right about the place. Natalya does most of the work while Dan and Simon were happy to sit back and rake in the profits. But on first impression, I'm not sure there's all that much profit there. Certainly not enough to keep them in the lifestyle to which they'd grown accustomed.'

'Keep looking. And check out this Natalya, especially if she knows the whereabouts of Dan Hudson.'

Denning looked at what they had on the whiteboard. Next to the photographs of the victims and their burnt-out house he'd written, then scored out 'burglary' and 'business deal gone wrong'. That just left 'family dispute' and Molly's murder/suicide theory, however extreme it seemed. Whichever way he dressed it up, it now looked likely the answer to the murders lay somewhere within the dysfunctional dynamics of Galloway family. And that was exactly what he'd thought from the start.

Chapter Seventeen

Ralf Cavendish worked from home. Home was a large flat in Bermondsey, with a partial view of Southwark Cathedral, that could just be glimpsed from the living room window. The living room also served as his consulting room, and he'd agreed to see Molly during a gap between clients.

'Amber first came to see me about a year ago,' he told Molly. 'She was a very troubled soul.'

They were sitting in the book-lined living room, with Molly trying hard not to feel like she was undergoing a therapy session. Ralf Cavendish was in his early forties, with a neatly trimmed ginger beard and an irritatingly bouncy demeanour. He was dressed in a blue and grey open-necked shirt, out of the top of which poked tufts of wiry, gingery hair.

'Would you have said she posed a danger to anyone?' Molly asked. 'Either herself or her family?'

He nodded slowly as she spoke, fixing her with a warm smile that was presumably aimed at putting clients at their ease. It was having the opposite effect on Molly. 'If you're asking me if Amber was capable of harming herself, I would have to say yes.' He nodded at her. 'However, if you're asking if she was capable of harming anyone else, then I would have to say no. Especially Caleb. Caleb was her life.'

Molly was replaying Marisa Powell's conversation in her head. It was important for her to separate the facts from the fantasy as far as Amber was concerned. As Amber's therapist, Ralf Cavendish was best placed to do this.

'Can you be certain of that?'

He looked at Molly for a few seconds before he answered. She had the feeling he was analysing her. 'Amber resented her parents. There was certainly a degree of animosity there, but I wouldn't say that animosity was enough for Amber to wish harm on her family. And, as I say, certainly not against Caleb.'

'But if she wasn't thinking clearly? You said you thought she could have been suicidal. If she was thinking about taking her own life, then there's always a chance she could have decided to kill those closest to her as well. It does happen.'

'Sorry, Detective Sergeant Fisher, when I said there was a risk she could have harmed herself, that's a world away from saying she was suicidal. Amber certainly suffered from negative thought patterns and low self-esteem, both of which can manifest themselves in feelings of self-harm, but with the right support and behavioural programmes, depression of this kind can be managed.'

His mention of depression made her think of Jon and his own weekly therapy sessions with a counsellor, where he unburdened his soul and shared their secrets before a stranger.

'Are you saying she was cured?' she asked, still not entirely sure what the outcome of a therapy session was meant to achieve.

'I wouldn't go as far as that. Nobody is ever fully cured when it comes to depression.'

'So Amber was definitely suffering from depression?'

He nodded slowly. 'Not just depression, but that was her main concern when she first came to see me.' He tugged thoughtfully at his chin. 'Amber had a number of issues she wanted to address. Over the course of our time together, I managed to break down a lot of the barriers she'd become expert at putting up. I felt I was able to unearth the real Amber.'

Molly wasn't sure what he was driving at. 'Amber told a friend she was adopted. Was there any truth in that?'

'Oh yes. Initially she thought her problems were caused by the distance she felt existed between her and her parents. She believed that if she could find her birth parents she'd be much happier. It wasn't to be, unfortunately. She traced her parents. Her birth mother had been very young when she'd had Amber. She had remarried and didn't want to know her. Her father had died. He was a soldier and was killed in Iraq. To be honest, I think finding that out pushed her further over the edge. She felt abandoned all over again.'

'What did you advise?'

He smiled at her. 'I don't tend to offer advice, as such. Rather I encouraged Amber to consider what this inform-ation meant to her and how it affected her relationship with her adopted family. Brian and Alison clearly loved her, why else would they adopt her?'

'What about Ellie?'

'I'm not sure Ellie ever really entered into the equation much, at least as far as Amber was concerned. You see, she never fully accepted Ellie as a mother figure.'

'What about her relationship with Simon? Did she ever discuss that?'

His face remained impassive when he spoke, but she thought she saw something flicker in his eyes when she asked about Simon. 'Amber and Simon had what appeared to be a destructive relationship. She seemed to resent him. She felt he had things easier than she did. There was never any evidence to support this, and I suspect a lot of it was only in Amber's head.'

'So Amber lied?'

'I wouldn't exactly say "lied". It was more a case of her convincing herself of things that weren't true.'

'Isn't that the same thing?'

He gave a light laugh. 'Not really. I think Amber genuinely believed these things. She suffered from what psychiatrists call Borderline Personality Disorder. Another name for it is 'affective dysregulation'. The symptoms of BPD can be grouped into four main areas: emotional instability – the psychological term for this is affective dysregulation; disturbed patterns of thinking or perception – cognitive distortions or perceptual distortions; impulsive behaviour; intense but unstable relationships with others. The symptoms of a personality disorder may range from mild to severe and usually emerge in adolescence, persisting into adulthood. The causes vary, but in Amber's case it seemed to stem essentially from abandonment issues arising from being given up for adoption by her birth mother. She'd convinced herself that she wasn't loved.' He leaned in closer. Molly could smell the fruity aroma of herbal tea on his breath. 'This is why Amber could never have harmed Caleb. He was the focus of her life.'

'But if she thought she was going to lose him?'

'There was little chance of Caleb being taken from her. Ellie and Brian only wanted what was best for Caleb, but also for Amber too. Even if they had managed to win custody, it would only ever have been a temporary arrangement.'

'And Amber knew this?'

'Brian and Ellie had always made it clear this was never a long-term solution. Just a means to ensure Caleb stayed in the family should Amber's health deteriorate.'

This made sense. But had Amber really believed it? 'Did you ever speak to Brian and Ellie?'

'I would speak with her father on occasions. I made it clear I wasn't willing to disclose anything Amber and I discussed during our sessions, even though he paid for her therapy sessions. He accepted that and only ever wanted reassurance that she was getting better. He did, however, make me aware of her domestic situation, particularly with regard to Caleb.'

'And was she? Getting better?'

He thought carefully before answering. 'I believe she was turning a corner. She still had a long way to go, but I honestly think that in time she would have been better able to cope with life.'

Chapter Eighteen

Denning knocked on McKenna's office door. She was on the phone, but placed her hand over the mouthpiece and shouted at him to come in.

She jerked her chin at one of the two chairs facing her desk.

As he sat, he noticed the pained expression on McKenna's face. She wasn't someone who was known for her patience, and whoever was on the other end of the phone seemed to be seriously trying whatever was left of it. Her eyes were pointing towards the ceiling as she spoke; her contribution to the conversation being mostly a series of 'yes' and 'no' responses.

He was sitting opposite her, trying not to make it too obvious he was doing his best to listen in to what was being said. After a while McKenna ended the phone conversation with a curt 'OK', and replaced the receiver with a heavy thud.

'The Chief Superintendent. Wants to know why we don't have Dan Hudson in custody. He is still our prime suspect, isn't he? Nothing's come to light to challenge that?'

Denning shook his head. 'I'm not saying he actually pulled the trigger, but he's connected to all this somehow. Granted, there are questions that need to be addressed regarding motive, etc, but this is why we need to speak to Hudson as a matter of urgency.'

'Oh I agree with that sentiment, but do we have a plan? Hudson's done a pretty effective job at staying below the radar so far. What's next?'

'Natalya Koval,' Denning said matter-of-factly. 'She was Simon Galloway's girlfriend. She's also a partner with Party Animals. Molly Fisher reckons she knows more than she's telling us.'

'Including the current whereabouts of Hudson?'

'More than likely.'

'Well, either she tells us, or we bring her in.'

Denning smiled at her. 'It's all in hand.'

McKenna looked at him as though she was about to do some serious worrying, but then just shrugged. 'OK. Let me know as soon as he's in custody. It would be good to wrap this up sooner rather than later.'

'Assuming he's guilty,' Denning added.

She shot him a disgruntled look. 'Is that what you came in to tell me?'

'Actually, no.' He sat up in the chair. He was aware of a sudden dryness in his mouth. 'Ellie Galloway,' he said. 'Before she married Brian, she was married to James Metcalf.'

McKenna looked blank. 'OK. That's interesting, and thanks for telling me, but…?'

'I'm guessing Ellie is short for Eleanor.'

McKenna was being uncharacteristically slow; probably still chewing over her terse conversation with the Chief Super and its possible implications for her pension. After a moment it seemed as though the synapses finally kicked into life and she gave a knowing smile. 'James and Eleanor Metcalf. Well, bugger me!' She clutched at a clump of her hair and pulled it tightly, fronds of black hair poking out the top of her clenched fist like a burnt fern. 'Martin Metcalf.'

She repeated the name as though, like Denning, she couldn't quite believe it.

'It must be nearly twenty years ago.' She nodded again. 'My ex worked the case when he was a DS. It was all he could talk about for months.' She unclenched her fist and the black fern disappeared, leaving just a slight tuft sticking up. 'Martin Metcalf.'

'It was obviously before I joined the police,' Denning said, 'but I remember the story. It was all over the news at the time.'

'Indeed,' McKenna said. 'Martin Metcalf was, what, twelve years old? Disappeared on his way home from school one day. We never did get to the bottom of what happened.'

Denning had been a year older than Martin Metcalf when the boy had gone missing. He remembered his parents lecturing him on personal safety and clearly nervous about him doing a paper round by himself, and his school headmaster offering words of caution to anyone walking to or from school alone. And then suddenly it wasn't news any more.

'It was in the papers and on the TV news for weeks, then it all just seemed to grind to a halt. I remember there was a massive public appeal for witnesses, but without success.'

McKenna nodded. 'There was nothing. No body ever turned up, and no one ever copped for it.' She stared into space for a moment, thinking back to the events of twenty years ago. 'There was a suggestion that he'd run away from home. A couple of school friends said they thought he was unhappy and he was being bullied at school, but nothing was ever found to suggest he'd run away. CCTV at rail and bus stations was checked thoroughly, and drivers were asked if they'd seen anyone fitting his description. There was one reported sighting of him getting into a car, but that turned out to be a false lead.' She looked at Denning. 'It was a real mystery as to what happened to him.'

'What did the parents say?'

'He'd failed to return home from school. They phoned the school, his friends, but he was a no show. Eventually they contacted us to report him missing.'

'Didn't he have a mobile?'

'Apparently they wouldn't let him have one. They thought he was too young. Shame as it would have helped when it came to tracing him.'

'And nobody saw anything?'

'It was early January, so it was dark from about four. Plus it was a shitty day: rain, sleet, so it wasn't like there were many people out and about. The journey from school to his house took around half an hour. He walked it every day and there had never been any problems. Everyone who knew him was spoken to: family, friends, neighbours, teachers. A re-enaction was staged a week later in the hope of jogging memories, but again, nothing. Plus they had the media breathing down their necks too, which never helps.'

'He was never found?'

'The whole area was searched for days. Richmond Park and a couple of nearby golf courses were combed using specialist tracking dogs. They spoke to any drivers who had been in the area, and any CCTV that covered his route was checked, but there was no sign of him anywhere. One theory was that he'd got chatting to someone online and had agreed to meet up with them. His computer was checked over, but apart from an obsession with Dungeons & Dragons, there was nothing out of the ordinary. Naturally all the local nonces were rounded up, but even that was a dead end.'

'What was the official conclusion?'

'Technically the case was never closed. It's still open, though not active. According to my ex, his DCI reckoned the lad had been snatched by a paedo. And for a while that particular avenue was explored in detail. There had been an incident a few months before where someone had tried to snatch an eight-year-old girl from a children's play park not far from where the Metcalfs lived. But they got someone for that and he had a rock solid alibi the night Martin Metcalf went missing.'

'How solid?'

'He was banged up in Pentonville at the time.'

'OK.' Denning was turning this over in his brain. 'I take it there's been no reported sightings of him since?'

She shook her head. 'Nothing. And no one has come forward in the past two decades claiming to be him.'

'What was your ex's theory?'

He knew McKenna well enough to know there would have been talk between officers, theories shared, motives discussed. He'd never met McKenna's ex, but he'd heard people in the nick talking about him: a big bruiser of a bastard who liked a drink and a sentimental reminisce about the 'good old days' before political correctness had turned policing into glorified social work. He'd retired to Majorca a few years back with his new wife, who was rumoured to be around half his age. McKenna rarely spoke about him, and from what he'd heard about the man, Denning was glad their paths had never crossed.

McKenna tugged at her hair again. 'He never said. It was generally believed the lad had been snatched, taken somewhere, then murdered and the body disposed of. But there was never any proof, so we can only speculate. Over the years I half expected someone to 'fess up': a deathbed confession, or some rumour that leaked its way out of a prison. But nothing's ever been flagged up on the radar.' She leant her elbows on the desk. 'The lad just vanished.'

Denning scratched his head. He remembered at the time thinking it was strange that someone could just disappear without a trace. Even then he had thought it seemed suspicious. He thought carefully before asking the next question. 'Were the parents ever under suspicion?'

'They were on the list of possibles, at least initially. It's standard procedure in these kind of cases, isn't it? But they were clean. Both respectable members of the community. He was a solicitor with a blue chip firm in London, she worked part-time as a secretary for a local FE college. He'd been at work until gone six that day and Eleanor had been out with a friend: lunch, then a shopping trip in London.'

Denning thought to himself. A child disappears, then almost two decades later his mother is found murdered along with her new family. It seemed unlikely that the two incidents could be connected, but that was assuming Ellie Galloway hadn't been the intended target all along. They'd all been working on the assumption that this was to do with Brian Galloway, or one of the children. But now it seemed there were skeletons in Ellie Galloway's cupboard that had just rattled their bones.

'But it was possible people believed they might have had something do with his disappearance?'

McKenna shrugged. 'There are always sickos out there who want to believe in conspiracies. The parents were never on the official list of suspects, and our lot certainly never said anything to suggest otherwise.'

Denning was thinking this over in his head. It was rotten luck: Ellie Galloway losing her son, then dying in tragic circumstances. To experience one piece of bad luck in your life was unfortunate, two, whilst not exactly careless, was certainly unfair. 'We should speak to James Metcalf,' he said. 'He was once a big part of Ellie Galloway's life. And at the very least, he should probably be officially informed about what happened to his ex-wife.' He could tell from the expression on McKenna's face that she wasn't buying it. 'He had a raw deal from us twenty years ago,' he continued. 'His son disappeared and we failed to find him, or bring anyone to justice for what happened. If nothing else, it would be a common courtesy.'

'I'm not convinced. Granted it's possible he *might* know something about Ellie Galloway that could prove useful, but I wouldn't hold your breath. The family were living in Mortlake at the time of Martin's disappearance. I can get you the address.' She banged a fist against her forehead. 'I should have recognised Ellie Galloway from the pictures we had of her. I should have made the connection with Eleanor Metcalf.'

'Different times, different crime,' Denning said. 'I would never have made the connection. It was nearly twenty years ago. And you said it yourself, it doesn't have any bearing on the Galloway murders.'

McKenna sat back on her chair and folded her arms across her chest. 'OK, speak to James Metcalf. But tread carefully. He's a solicitor, and a shit hot one at that. And as you yourself pointed out, he got a raw deal from us twenty years ago. He could have given us a hard time over that. I don't want to give him any excuse to come after us now.'

'I promise I'll be tact itself,' Denning said, as he left the office.

Chapter Nineteen

Molly decided to swing round via Dan Hudson's flat before returning to the station.

The flat was in a luxury apartment block next to the DLR station in Limehouse. When she got there, she spotted a squad car parked outside the building and a uniformed officer standing by the entrance door to the flats. 'What happened?' she asked, flashing her ID.

'We got a report of a break-in about twenty minutes ago,' the officer informed her. 'One of the neighbours reported hearing crashing from the property.'

Molly entered the building and headed up to Dan Hudson's flat on the second floor. It looked like a large studio flat with wide windows at the far end and polished wooden floors. But the place was a mess. A shelving unit had been overturned and a sideboard had its contents spilling over the painted wooden floor like a sea of personal debris.

There was another uniformed officer in the living room. 'Bit of a mess,' he said. 'We're waiting on Scene of Crime to get here, and I'm trying to contact the owner.'

Aren't we all, thought Molly. 'And there was no one here when you arrived?'

He shook his head. 'The door to the flat had been forced, as had the entry door downstairs. Probably a crowbar. But the place was empty. According to the neighbours, the bloke who lives here hasn't been seen for a few days.'

'What do we reckon? Burglary?'

The officer glanced around the room. 'Telly's still there,' he said, jerking his head in the direction of a large, flat-screen TV sitting on the wooden floor by the window. 'I'd say it was more like someone was looking for something.'

Molly thought out loud: 'Or someone?'

There was greater incentive than ever to find Dan Hudson now. At the very least he could be in danger. From who and why she had yet to figure out, but this had to be something other than a coincidence.

'Did any of the neighbours see anything suspicious?' she asked.

'Apparently a woman downstairs said she saw a couple of blokes hanging round outside the flat earlier this morning, but didn't think anything of it. We didn't get a good description: dark-haired, thick-set. Said they looked Eastern European, but that means nothing. There's CCTV at the entrance to the flats, so with a bit of luck it will have picked something up.'

She glanced round the room again. It was a nice flat. She suspected Dan Hudson lived alone, at least since the split with Amber. Something caught her eye, glinting in a corner by the window. She went over to pick it up, after taking a plastic glove from her pocket. It was a framed photo of Dan, Amber and Caleb. There was no way of knowing when the picture was taken, but all three of them were smiling. Caleb was squeezed between his parents, wearing a red bobble hat and his Harry Potter glasses. Dan and Amber were smiling too. She placed the photo on a table. A reminder of happier times since gone.

Was someone else looking for Dan Hudson? If so, she thought, looking round the state of his trashed flat, it was vital she and Denning got to him first.

Chapter Twenty

The offices of Woodeson, Madeley & Metcalf Solicitors were based in a stucco-fronted building in Dorset Square, Marylebone.

According to the efficient-looking receptionist, James Metcalf was in a meeting but he wouldn't be long. Would Denning like to wait? As he didn't have much choice, Denning took a seat on one of the Chesterfield sofas in the wooden-floored reception area.

After a few minutes a door opened and a group of smartly dressed men and women filed out one after the other. He watched as the receptionist stopped one of the group, a tall, broad-shouldered man in his early sixties, and pointed over at Denning. A moment later, the man approached him, his brow wrinkling ever so slightly. 'Inspector Denning, I'm James Metcalf. Harriet said you wanted to speak to me.'

Denning explained why he was there and asked if there was somewhere private where they could talk.

Metcalf indicated for Denning to follow him. They headed up the stairs and into a large, comfortable office that overlooked the leafy gardens at the front of the building.

Metcalf's office was clean and uncluttered. A solid mahogany desk dominated the room, while gilt-framed portraits adorned the walls. Denning sat on one of the deep leather armchairs in front of the polished desk.

'Firstly, I'd like to say how sorry I am about what's happened,' Denning said. 'And I'd like to assure you that we're doing everything we can to find whoever was responsible for your ex-wife's death.'

Metcalf eyed Denning from behind his oversized desk. His face was impassive, so it was impossible to read him. He was well-groomed, and distinguished rather than handsome, smartly dressed in an expensive pale grey suit, with a pink silk tie.

'Thank you for your sentiments, Inspector, but wouldn't a phone call have sufficed?'

If he was honest, Denning wasn't entirely sure why he was there. Professional courtesy, of course. James and Eleanor Metcalf had been let down by the police twenty years ago when they failed to find his son, the least he could do was inform the man of his former wife's death in person. But there was an element of curiosity too. Ellie Galloway had had another life before she'd married Brian. One she'd seemed keen to put behind her, if Ruth Forbes was to be believed. Understandable, considering what had happened, but somehow Denning felt there might be more to it. 'I appreciate you're a busy man, Mr Metcalf, and I really don't want to take up too much of your time. I just have a few questions you might be able to help with.'

Metcalf nodded politely. 'I was very sorry when I heard what had happened. Naturally I was shocked, even though I hadn't seen Eleanor since our divorce. I knew she'd remarried, of course, but I can't say I knew much about her new family. I'm afraid I don't think I'm going to be much help to you.'

Denning carefully framed the next sentence in his head before he uttered it aloud. 'I'm sorry to have to bring it up, but is it possible that what happened to Ellie may, even indirectly, have something to do with your son's disappearance?'

Metcalf was silent for a moment. His gaze fell to the polished desk top. Then he said: 'I was wondering when you were going to get around to that.' He sighed. The elephant in the room had made its presence felt. 'It was nearly twenty years ago, Inspector,' Metcalf said. 'I'm sure you don't seriously think someone somehow blamed my ex-wife for whatever happened to Martin and then waited until now to exact their revenge? That's a bit fanciful to say the least.' He looked up at Denning, as though resenting the impertinence of the question. The mention of his son's name clearly still rubbed at a raw wound.

'I appreciate that, Mr Metcalf, but we have to consider every possible motive when it comes to murder. There are some very disturbed individuals out there, and when a child goes missing, people can often leap to conclusions that aren't always right or fair. I understand it's difficult for you, but thinking back, did you or Ellie ever receive any threats of any kind at the time of Martin's disappearance?'

Metcalf didn't need to think before he answered. 'No. People may have whispered things behind our backs, but nobody seriously believed we had anything to do with Martin's disappearance. Why would they? We were never under any suspicion. The police believed he'd been snatched by a pervert, and eventually we came to believe that ourselves.'

Denning tried to read Metcalf's face. His expression seemed to speak of anger more than sorrow. Perhaps he still blamed the police for failing to find his child. Perhaps he blamed himself for moving on with his life. Whatever the case, Denning felt there was something he had to say: 'I'm sorry we weren't able to find your son, Mr Metcalf. It must have been a very difficult time for you and your wife. All that I can say is that I'm sure the detectives working the case did everything they could. Every effort would have been made to find Martin. However, I can sympathise with any frustration you may feel about the way things turned out.' Although he hadn't been involved in the case, Denning was still a representative of the Met Police; the same police force that had let James and Eleanor Metcalf down when they'd depended on them. Irrespective of how thorough the investigation had been, James Metcalf's son was officially still missing. 'I'm sorry I had to ask, but it's important that we look into every aspect of Ellie's life.'

The expression on Metcalf's face told Denning all he needed to know. This was a wound that was never going to heal, no matter how much time passed.

Metcalf nodded slowly. 'I think it's highly unlikely that Martin's disappearance had any bearing on what happened to Eleanor. If I were you, I'd look into Brian Galloway's life for any possible motive. I'm willing to bet there were quite a few skeletons in his past.'

'Did you ever meet Brian?'

He gave a deep, gravelly laugh. 'Why would I have anything to do with Brian Galloway? The man ran a hotel, didn't he? Though he could well have been involved in other business dealings for all I know. But whatever the case, we hardly moved in the same circles.' He frowned and pursed his lips. 'He might have married my ex-wife, Inspector, but that's all we had in common.' He clasped his hands together and leant on the polished desk. 'I appreciate you taking time out from what I'm sure must be a busy murder investigation to officially inform me of my ex-wife's death, but I really am unable to provide you with any information relating to why someone would want to kill her, or her family. I'm sorry I can't be of more help. I'm sure you wouldn't want me to waste any more of your time.'

He was still being professionally polite, but the inference was clear: their time was up.

As he left the plush offices, Denning wondered just how much Metcalf's time would have cost him if he'd been paying for it.

Chapter Twenty-One

Molly hadn't seen Susan Gorman since they'd last worked together nearly five years ago.

They'd been good friends back then but had somehow managed to drift apart in recent years. Sue had transferred to Hammersmith now, where she'd been promoted to DI. Molly thought it would be nice to have a catch up.

'Been a while,' Sue said over a pint at a trendy gastropub in the slightly less trendy part of Chelsea. 'Heard you'd joined MIT.'

Molly had only just sat down. Sue already had a pint of Kronenbourg waiting for her on her arrival. Sue hadn't changed much in five years; still the same sharp features and even sharper sense of humour. She'd changed her hairstyle and now sported a softer, feathery cut, which Molly had to admit, suited her.

'Still a DS though. You're one up on me there.'

Sue laughed and knocked back her pint. 'So, Betty Taggart's your boss. What's she like? I've only ever heard the rumours.'

'Yeah, well the rumours are probably not too far removed from the truth. But she's OK.'

'And what about Jon?'

'Jon's fine, thanks.'

'Still together...?'

Molly drank her pint and they chatted for a while, catching up on old times and filling in the blanks of the past five years. Sue was still single, claiming she found relationships to be more hassle than they were worth, and always difficult to fit in around a DI's job. Molly nodded and smiled. Then, when a natural gap in the conversation had formed, she turned to address the real reason she was there.

'You arrested some men a few days ago. A fight behind a pub not far from the Lyric Hammersmith. One man was stabbed. Another was badly assaulted. What was the story?'

Molly watched as Sue arched her eyebrows. 'I take it you're not asking in any official capacity?'

'One of the men, Ben Milne... I know him. He's a friend of a friend. I promised my friend I'd try and find out what happened. She's worried sick.' Not for the first time in her life, she was glad she and Ben didn't share the same surname.

Sue continued to look at her. Molly guessed she was trying to figure out the real reason Molly was asking about Ben. If she was as good a detective as Molly knew she was, she wouldn't find it too much of a challenge to discover her connection to Ben.

'Just what it says on the tin,' Sue said. She was sipping her pint but still looking over at Molly. 'You can tell your "friend" there's nothing to get herself alarmed about. Mr Milne was stabbed during an altercation between two groups of young men. One of the other group came off worse. According to the paramedics who treated him, the other gentleman hit his head on the kerb after being punched. Mr Milne and his friend claim it was self-defence.' She kept looking at Molly. 'But I imagine you know all that already.'

'Is there enough for this to go to court?'

Sue stopped looking at Molly and took another sip of her pint. 'That's up to the CPS. The gentleman who was injured has previous for GBH, theft, fraud and a zillion other things. In fact his record's that would take the best part of a working day to read from start to finish. The other two characters, including your Mr Milne, don't have any previous convictions. If it were to go to court, it's likely a jury would buy the self-defence argument. But if the injured gentleman wants to press charges after he recovers, or if he doesn't recover, then know knows?'

'But there's nothing more? This was just a fight that got out of hand?'

'Officially, yes.'

'But unofficially…?'

Sue lowered her voice. 'Let's just say, the twat who wound up in intensive care is part of a gang that's known to us. There are rumours they're involved in something. We don't know what at this stage, and obviously the only gang member we have is currently unconscious with a load of wires stuck to him. We don't have anything to directly link him with the stabbing; the weapon was never recovered, and technically we should be treating him as a victim. But when and if he's in the mood for talking, we're going to have a nice long chat with him.'

'What about Ben? Mr Milne? Is it possible he could be mixed up in whatever this gang is alleged to have been involved with?'

Sue just shrugged. 'Until we know the facts, I can't say one way or the other. But I can tell you something off the record: I don't think this fight was entirely out of the blue. I'm pretty sure they all knew one another, and I think they'd arranged to meet. Whatever the plan had been, something went wrong and two people ended up injured.' She offered Molly a knowing smile. 'I don't know what Ben's told you, but I'd take it a lot of it with a pinch of salt. He's more involved in this than he's letting on.'

Chapter Twenty-Two

It was a warm evening, so Denning decided to go for a run.

The flat had been empty when he'd got back. Sarah had said she'd take Jake to an autism-friendly screening at the cinema as a treat as she'd planned to finish work early. Jake could find the whole surround-sound experience overwhelming, and would occasionally shout things out if he got over-excited part-way through a film, or scream if he saw something he didn't like. It didn't bother most people, who just accepted he was a child enjoying a film. But sometimes other cinema-goers would take umbrage and make their unhappiness known with a succession of tutting or a lengthy stare that made their displeasure all too obvious.

He ran along Shoreditch High Street, listening to his iPod and weaving his way through mothers with buggies, elderly pedestrians who neither saw nor heard him approach, office workers returning home late, even the odd cyclist who thought cycling on the pavements was a safer bet than cycling on the roads, albeit not for pedestrians.

It gave him the chance to think. To think about the case, and how they seemed to be so far from getting the break they needed. To think about Jake and Claire, and him and Sarah, and how they all fitted together. A disparate group of individuals calling themselves a family, much as the Galloways had done.

He passed the imposing red-brick edifice that had housed the Wells & Co Commercial Ironworks back in Victorian times, the ground floor of which was now taken up with a couple of trendy eateries. The building stood as a signifier of how London's industrial past and commercial present had seamlessly welded themselves together. He ran under the bridge carrying the Overground line north to Dalston and Islington, where Shoreditch High Street ran into Kingsland Road, dodging a man so engrossed on his mobile phone that they nearly collided beside a bus stop.

The Galloways: a seemingly normal family on the outside, but so clearly something more once the flimsy veneer was scraped away. Someone had wanted that family dead.

The pavement began to thin out now, though he had to swerve to avoid a man on a mobility scooter coming out of a mini supermarket. The man waved a hand by way of apology.

He tried to clear his mind so that it would be free to focus on finding the answers that seemed to elude him. Work. Family...

Sarah had told him over breakfast that she was going to have to go to New York after all. The bank's US office was having, according to Sarah, 'a minor meltdown'. She would be flying out that weekend. She'd tried to get out of going, she'd insisted, citing domestic issues as her excuse. But her employers hadn't bought it; she was paid a substantial salary, they argued, to ensure work took priority over domestic matters. She'd said she hoped to be back within a week, two at the most.

Jake had overheard them talking and insisted he wanted to go to New York too, thinking that's where Disneyland was. They'd spent the best part of twenty minutes trying to calm him down and convince him that Disneyland wasn't in New York, and even if it was, he still couldn't go; Sarah would be there to work and not for a holiday. They'd promised him they would all go away somewhere later in the year, when Daddy and Sarah weren't so busy. Jake had seemed to accept this, but as soon as Corrine had turned up, Denning overheard his son telling their neighbour's daughter that he was going to Disneyland.

Corrine had laughed and said that would be lovely. Then she'd informed Denning that she and her boyfriend would be going to France for a couple of weeks before they started back at uni next month. Denning would have to make alternative childcare arrangements. There was always the possibility he might have to bite the bullet and ask his parents for their help, but that would be an absolutely last resort…

He'd reached the bridge over Regent's Canal, and stopped to catch his breath. He looked down at the canal, a breeze rippling its surface. Only a few months ago the body of a young woman had been fished out of the water not far from here. It had been his first murder investigation as an SIO. He shuddered at the memory and the implications it had meant for him and his family.

Snapping the memory out of his mind, he turned left and followed the towpath that ran along the canal bank.

Brightly painted barges were moored next to the towpath, overlooked by luxury flats and abandoned buildings. Random graffiti artists didn't seem to discriminate between old or new, lived-in or empty, and colourful artwork adorned many walls. Now he was dodging cyclists and dog walkers, as well as other runners. A couple of young women raced past him as he reached the bridge over the entrance to Kingsland Basin, both dressed in tight-fitting Lycra and so tuned into their iPods that they barely noticed him. A man was fishing by the side of the canal, though Denning suspected he was doing so more out of hope than expectation. Everyone seemed so preoccupied with whatever they were doing, all oblivious to the ever-changing urban landscape around them. But perhaps that was a London thing.

London was such a strange city, disparate and disconnected; old and young, rich and poor living side by side, each seemingly impervious to the existence of the other. At best, Londoners were tolerant and understanding of one another; at worst, they were parochial and insecure. Somebody had once said London was just a series of joined-up villages. But a village suggested intimacy and belonging, and London certainly didn't offer that.

Although it was still early days, the case was making slow progress. It wouldn't be long before McKenna would be on his back, pushing for results. His team were good, but they couldn't work miracles. They needed to speak to Dan Hudson and they needed to find him soon. It was possible he'd already left the country, in which case tracking him down would take time and resources, both of which were in short supply.

And then there was James Metcalf... Denning had studied psychology at university. It meant he was good at reading people. But Metcalf had been something of a closed book. Perhaps he was just good at keeping his emotions in check...?

He glanced at his watch and realised it was later than he'd thought. He would run as far as the next bridge, then up onto Whitmore Street, down Pitfield Street, and then head for home. The run had done him good, shaking off the excess baggage of the day, and freeing up space in his brain to think clearly.

–

It was quiet in the flat when he got in. Jake and Sarah weren't back from their cinema trip, and the flat felt strange and empty. He missed the gentle thrum of white noise that filled the space whenever Jake and Sarah were around; Sarah tapping on her laptop, interspersed by her occasional chatter on the phone, or the techno soundtrack that accompanied Jake's computer games.

He showered and changed into a pair of jeans and a rugby top, shoving his running gear into the washing machine. Rummaging in the fridge he found some leftover mince and some tomatoes that were still in date. He could reheat the mince, add the tomatoes, find an onion and make a pasta dish for dinner. With a bit of luck, it would be ready by the time Sarah and Jake got back from the cinema.

Sarah had been on at him for some time to buy a house somewhere. However, Denning was reluctant to move. Shoreditch may not have been his first choice of location, but they were settled now. Jake was happy staying there, and it was handy for both their jobs. But a house with a garden would be beneficial for Jake. He knew if he turned on the laptop in the study it would be bookmarked at a property page, probably some over-priced abode some-where in north London that they would struggle to pay the mortgage on. It was a conversation that had been endlessly deferred but would have to be addressed at some stage in the near future.

Denning was chopping an onion when he heard the front door open. A moment later Jake came running in, spotted him in the kitchen and ran up to him, throwing his arms round Denning's waist. 'We saw *Sherlock Gnomes*, Daddy. It was brilliant.' He smiled and ruffled Jake's hair. 'Hey, that's great, little fella.'

A couple of seconds later, Sarah appeared. 'How was he?' Denning mouthed at her.

She smiled. 'He was fine,' she said. 'He enjoyed the film.' She put her arm round Denning's shoulder and kissed him. 'Everything will work out OK. You and Jake will be great together when I'm away.'

Denning nodded. He didn't doubt they'd be great together. In fact, if it wasn't for an ongoing murder investigation getting in the way, he would be looking forward to it.

Chapter Twenty-Three

McKenna sat grim-faced behind her desk. 'Dan Hudson. Where is he?'

It was first thing. Denning wanted to call another briefing, find out where they were all up to with the case so far, but McKenna was unwilling to wait. The story was still featuring on the daily news bulletins, which meant the Chief Super would be kicking her arse. She, in turn, needed an arse to kick, and his was about to experience the blunt end of her boot.

'Apparently there was a break-in at his flat yesterday. Doesn't look like anything was actually taken, but until we speak to Hudson himself, we can't confirm that.'

'Well let's hope that glorious moment isn't deferred for too much longer.' She raised an eyebrow. 'Anything else?'

There was something Denning had been chewing over ever since he'd arrived at the station that morning. 'I spoke to James Metcalf.' He waited for her response, keen to gauge her reaction before he continued.

'And?'

She wasn't giving much away, so he continued. 'I don't know. There was something about his attitude. It was like Ellie was already dead to him.' He searched for the right words. 'It was almost as if he'd blanked her out of his life completely.'

McKenna wasn't convinced. 'He's moved on. It happens: wife leaves him, he remarries. He hasn't seen her for years. What did you expect him to do? Break down and weep on your shoulder?'

'No, of course not. It's just… well, strange, I suppose.' He still couldn't put a finger on what it was that rankled with him. At the moment, it was little more than a gut feeling…'They shared a life together. Their child goes missing and then years later, his ex-wife is murdered. You'd think he'd feel something.'

'I really don't see that there's any connection between the two. Sometimes shitty things happen to people more than once in their lives.'

'But we're assuming his son was killed?'

She sighed. 'We don't know that for certain. Like I said the other day, the case is officially still open. Should any new evidence come to light, then we'll look into it again.' She folded her arms across her chest. 'But we can't rule out the possibility Martin Metcalf simply ran away from home. It does happen.'

'I accept that. But I can't help feeling there's something about James Metcalf.'

Her eyes flashed something between a gimlet stare and a withering look. 'Whatever it is, Matt, drop it and focus on finding Dan Hudson.'

Chapter Twenty-Four

There was no sign of the BMW when Molly pressed the buzzer at the Party Animals office later that morning. Natalya reluctantly let her in. She didn't seem especially pleased to see Molly, and she got the impression she had arrived at a bad time.

'I said everything to you yesterday,' Natalya insisted, tossing her head back, and throwing her mane of black hair over her shoulder. 'I have nothing more to tell you.'

They were in the outer office this time. Cramped, with most of the space taken up with Natalya's desk and a couple of chairs, it reminded Molly of Betty Taggart's office, except minus a dead house plant.

Molly tried her winning smile. 'Natalya, it's vital we speak to Dan Hudson. If you have any idea where he is, then you have to tell me.'

Natalya was sitting behind her desk. She was wearing another Issey Miyake top today – Kermit-green with a diamond pattern – and a pair of sprayed-on Levi's. 'Like I have already told you, I haven't seen Dan for two weeks and I have no clue where he is.' She stared directly at Molly, holding her gaze and willing Molly to prove her wrong.

Molly stared back at her, refusing to drop eye contact until Natalya dropped hers, like this was some unspoken personal battle between them. 'I'm sorry, Natalya, but I don't believe you. You told me Dan Hudson hadn't been to the office since he and Simon had that fight, but I know that's not true. He has been here, and recently.' Then Natalya shifted her gaze to the floor, and Molly took that as a minor victory.

'We need to speak to Dan,' she repeated. 'I know you know where he is because I saw his car parked in a street round the corner from this office yesterday. I also saw his car in Gibney Road the morning of the fire, so that suggests that he's still around and knows what's happened.' Molly felt bad bullying the girl like this – whatever the case, she was still grieving for her boyfriend – but she knew if she went back to Denning without Dan Hudson's head in her handbag then her own would be on a meat skewer in Betty Taggart's office before the day was out. 'Natalya.' She perched on the edge of the desk, close enough to smell the other woman's perfume: expensive, like the top. Something told her Natalya Koval liked the nicer things in life. 'Simon was your boyfriend. You must want to find out who was responsible for his death as much as we do. And we'll get there a lot faster if you tell us where Dan Hudson is.' But that didn't work. Natalya stared at the floor, her face tight, creases flitting across her otherwise smooth forehead.

'You're wasting your time asking me these questions.'

Molly tried a different approach. 'Did you lie to me about the fight between Dan and Simon?'

Natalya shook her head. 'No. It's true that they had a fight.' She paused. 'But they made it up the next day. Dan came round here and apologised to Simon.' She looked at Molly. 'So you see, they were friends. Dan would have no reason to kill Simon. Or his family.'

'So why won't you tell me where he is?'

Another shake of the head. 'I keep telling you: I don't know.'

Molly felt deflated. Time was against her. She just wasn't getting through to the girl. She had clearly lied about not having seen Dan for the past two weeks. Was she protecting him? If so, why? 'Natalya, you do know it's against the law to withhold information from the police? I could make this official. I could arrest you for withholding information, take you down to the police station and make you tell us where he is. I don't want to do that, but if I'm left without a choice then I will.'

Natalya continued to stare at the carpet, probably chewing her options over in her head. 'You have to believe me when I say that Dan didn't do it.' Her face lifted and she met Molly's gaze full on, suddenly finding confidence from somewhere. Molly reckoned Natalya wasn't someone who was easily intimidated. 'You need to look somewhere else for your killer.'

'OK, if it wasn't Dan, let's hear him tell us that.' Molly wanted to push this. 'If you know something about what happened to the Galloways, you have to tell me.'

Natalya continued to look at Molly, dark eyes smouldering with defiance. Like the last time she visited, Molly was struck by her – at least outwardly – calm composure. She suspected Natalya was someone useful to have around in a crisis. But there was something else there today: a hint of anxiety just discernible in her voice, a wrinkle of worry about her face.

'Natalya, has someone threatened you? Has Dan threatened you? If so, then tell me.' She got off the desk, stood there with her arms folded, patience wearing thinner by the minute. 'I'm not leaving here until you tell me what's going on.'

There was still no response.

She sighed. 'OK, you haven't left me with any choice. Natalya Koval, you are under arrest on suspicion of withholding...'

But before she had a chance to finish there was a noise from the other office. Natalya looked up, her eyes darting quickly to the door then back to Molly.

A second later the door opened.

Molly felt a momentary dryness in her throat. There was a man standing there. Tall and broad-shouldered, with a few days' worth of stubble round his chin and ash-blond hair half flopping over his eyes. At first, she thought it was Dan Hudson. She was about to speak to him, when she realised she recognised him from the photo on the whiteboard back in the MIT suite.

It wasn't Dan Hudson.

Standing in the doorway to the other office, looking like a child who had been caught with his hand in a sweetie jar, was Simon Galloway.

Chapter Twenty-Five

'Back again, Inspector. I had a feeling you wouldn't be able to resist the novelty handcuffs.' Ruth Forbes looked up from the counter and smiled when Denning entered the shop. She nodded at the box of pink, fluffy handcuffs still sitting on the counter.

He returned the smile. 'Tempting as that is, I'm afraid I'm only here to ask some more questions.'

She was wearing a blue-striped man's shirt this time, and a pair of oversized novelty earrings. There was a mug of coffee cooling beside the till and half a chocolate Hobnob on the shelf behind the counter, which she'd obviously forgotten was there.

'You couldn't do me a huge favour,' she said. 'Mind the shop for two minutes whilst I nip to the loo?'

Before he had a chance to argue and tell her he was there on police business, she'd disappeared behind a curtain that separated the main shop from whatever lay out the back. He heard a door close, followed a few minutes later by the sound of a toilet flushing.

'Thanks for that,' she said, reappearing in the shop. 'I haven't had a moment to myself this morning.'

He told her it was no trouble, even though he didn't mean it. 'It's just a follow up query about Ellie.'

'Ask away.'

'You mentioned her marriage to James Metcalf? Did she ever talk about him?' It was a niggle that kept refusing to go away, despite Betty Taggart's insistence that he dropped the matter. If James Metcalf really had deleted Ellie from his life, had the feeling been mutual? Ruth Forbes had mentioned his name at least twice the other day. That suggested he still had a presence in Ellie's life, even indirectly.

'Oh, yes. I mean there was no animosity between them. The divorce was a bit messy, but then they always are, aren't they? They ended up on good terms though.' She paused for a moment before continuing. 'Obviously you know about Martin?'

Denning nodded.

'As you can probably imagine, something like that can break up even the strongest of marriages.'

Or bring them closer together, Denning thought. But clearly not in this case. 'That was the reason the marriage ended?' he asked.

'Ellie never went into detail, but I would have assumed so.' She looked at Denning. 'I'm not a mother, but the very thought of losing a child like that...' She gave a little shudder. 'I don't mean dying, though that's horrendous. I mean to never know what happened. To always be wondering...'

Denning preferred not to think about it. If anything were ever to happen to Jake he didn't know how he'd cope. 'You said there was no animosity between James and Ellie, but they didn't have any contact with each another after the divorce. That would suggest relations between them weren't all that great?'

She shot him a quizzical look. 'What makes you think they had no contact? She was still in touch with James. In fact she met up with him not all that long ago.'

Denning tried not to let his surprise show. 'Are you sure about that?' If this was true, then James Metcalf had deliberately misled him. But why?

'Yes. They met up at least once. There was certainly no suggestion of any animosity between them.'

'Did Ellie say why they met?'

'No. I know it was the first time she'd seen him in a while, but they'd kept in touch over the years. She knew he'd remarried and he seemed to be happy with his new wife. Ellie was relieved. She didn't want James to be lonely.'

'That was very generous of her,' Denning said. He thought it was especially generous considering her ex-husband appeared to have no discernible feelings for her as far as Denning could make out. Or had that just been down to some kind of macho bravado as McKenna had suggested?

Ruth nodded. He thought he could see a prickling of sadness in her face. 'She was one of the most generous people I'd ever met. As I told you the other day, I couldn't have survived if she hadn't put money into this place. And then there was Simon.'

'Simon?'

'She loaned him some money earlier a few months back. I don't know how much but it seems he was desperate. He couldn't ask Brian, so Ellie helped him out.'

'Why couldn't he ask Brian?'

She sighed. 'He'd already asked his dad for money and it had been the cause of more than a few arguments in the past. You see, Brian lent Simon money to help set up the business in the first place. And I think on another couple of occasions too.'

'Why did Simon still need money once the business was up and running?' He remembered what Molly Fisher had said about Party Animals being light on profits, but it must have brought in some money.

'Simon was in debt. He was always in debt. He owed people money, according to Ellie. And they weren't the sort who were happy to take I.O.U.s. She was genuinely concerned they might do something to harm him.'

'Money lenders?'

'Ellie didn't say. She just said that he'd told her if she didn't give him the money they'd put him in hospital. Or worse.'

Chapter Twenty-Six

Natalya had made them some coffee. She placed a cafetière on the table and waited a few moments before pressing the plunger, then poured the steaming black liquid into three mugs. 'Help yourselves to milk and sugar,' she said. Natalya took her coffee black. She lifted the mug to her lips, took a long sip and sat back on the leather sofa, leaning a slender elbow against the arm, letting Molly and Simon do the talking. She seemed more relaxed now that things were out in the open and she no longer had to keep up the pretence of mourning a boyfriend who was very much alive.

They were in the other office now, the one Simon had, until recently, shared with his business partner. Unlike Natalya, Simon Galloway seemed anxious and twitchy. He kept rubbing a hand through his thick wavy hair and glancing at Natalya, as though hoping she would provide the answers to the awkward questions he knew Molly was about to ask.

He added some milk to his coffee, and then stirred in a lump of sugar, but pushed the mug away after a couple of seconds, deciding he didn't want it after all.

Molly knew she should phone this one in. The whole course of the investigation had suddenly lurched down a different route. Someone who had previously been presumed dead was now alive, and quite possibly a suspect.

But he was also a victim. His family was dead; murdered in the most appalling circumstances and he should really be speaking to someone from Family Liaison right now. Instead he was talking to her.

Only he wasn't.

In the few minutes since he'd made his presence known, he'd so far confirmed his identity, ushered her through to the other office, and promised to speak to her as long as she didn't call anyone. Natalya had offered to make some coffee.

Simon Galloway was sitting opposite Molly on one of the padded chairs beside the two desks. She sat next to Natalya on the sofa.

'This must be a difficult time for you,' she offered. She wasn't entirely sure what she should be saying. Her condolences seemed inconsequential, while any serious questions should be coming from Denning as the Senior Investigating Officer. But Denning wasn't here and she was.

She really should phone this in…

'I haven't spoken to anyone apart from Natalya since it happened,' he said. His voice was rich and clear; she would have said posh, but there was just a faint suggestion of estuary English in the slightly elongated vowels. 'There's part of me that still can't process what's happened.' He looked over at Natalya, his eyes reddening as he spoke. 'It feels like a bad dream.'

Molly had seen the photos of him back in the incident room, and one or two she'd checked out online. In the flesh, he was certainly as handsome as the photographs implied, with boyish features and a rugged tan that had survived beyond the summer months. The designer stubble had grown into a full-on beard, and he looked at her with deep blue eyes that reminded Molly of her grandmother's Siamese cat. Except he looked haggard, like he hadn't slept, which he probably hadn't. But was that down to the stress of what had happened to his family? Or was it down to guilt?

'Why didn't you come forward?' she asked. 'At the very least, we needed to know you were still alive.'

He didn't answer her.

'There's an unidentified body in the mortuary that everybody thinks is you.'

Unidentified, but judging by the looks that passed between Simon and Natalya, and if she were to put two and two together herself, they had a pretty shrewd idea of who that body belonged to. It certainly answered the immediate question of where Dan Hudson had disappeared to.

'You might as well tell her,' Natalya said. 'She's not going to go away until you talk to her.' She drank her coffee and watched them like a spider in the middle of its web. Molly wondered just how much Natalya knew. She got the impression she was the dominant one in the relationship, pulling the strings and keeping Simon on just the right side of self-destruction.

'I was in shock,' he said, but she knew it was a lie. And not even a convincing one. Shock didn't last forever. And at the very least he would have needed to speak to them as the next of kin. They would require an alibi from him if nothing else.

'I understand that, but we have a lot of questions that need answering and I think you may be able to help with that.'

Simon Galloway looked at Natalya, but she just shook her head.

'I don't know what happened. Why would I know? I wasn't even there.'

But why wasn't he there? It was a family gathering and he was family... Molly took another sip of coffee. She really wanted a cigarette, but she knew if she gave in now, then it was the beginning of the end as far as giving up smoking went.

She was already regretting not phoning this in the second she recognised Simon Galloway standing in the doorway to the inner office. Denning wouldn't be happy. And as for Betty Taggart... At least a bollocking from Denning would be mostly toothless, and he'd probably apologise for it afterwards when no one else was around to hear. Betty Taggart, on the other hand, would drag her through the MIT suite by her roots and lambast her in front of every single detective present. And that was if she caught her on a good day...

'So where were you?'

It wasn't an unreasonable question, but again he didn't answer; just looked over at Natalya, hoping she would speak for him.

Eventually he accepted Natalya's silence as confirmation that only he could answer Molly's questions. He rubbed his hand through his hair again and spoke. 'We were at home. Natalya and myself. The first I knew about the fire was when I tried to phone Dad the next morning. There was no answer, which was strange. I'd tried both his home phone and the mobile. I thought something might have happened to him, but I never imagined...' His voice trailed away and his eyes began to redden again. She thought she could see tears glistening on his lashes. Was he a good actor, or was the emotion real?

'I drove round to Gibney Road straight away. Dan had let me borrow his car as mine was getting repaired. I saw the fire engines and police cars in the street. And then the house. It just wasn't there anymore.'

He gave an audible sob. Natalya reached over and placed a hand on his arm, rubbing it gently like someone would do to a child.

Molly waited a moment until he seemed more composed. 'I saw you,' she said. 'You drove past me in Gibney Road. I thought you were a journalist.'

He nodded. 'You were with two blokes. I guessed you were coppers. I thought it must be serious if the plain clothes mob were involved. Then it said on the news that it was arson. I thought it must have been a mistake.'

Natalya stopped rubbing his arm, sat back on the leather sofa and drank her coffee. She was watching Molly, waiting to gauge her reaction.

'Why didn't you say something? Tell us who you were?'

'Like I said, I was in shock.'

She didn't believe him. There was more to it than that, there had to be. But she would have to play this cool. Now they had Simon Galloway alive and chatting, and not chilling in a mortuary fridge, they would have to make sure he was comfortable enough to tell them everything he knew without fear of being treated like a potential criminal.

'Then why not come forward today? I know it's not easy for you, and I accept shock doesn't disappear at the flick of a switch, but you must have known we'd want to talk to you.'

He looked from Molly to Natalya, both sitting on the sofa looking back at him, waiting for him to give them some clue as to what was going on inside his head.

'Let's just say it might be best if some people think I'm dead.'

'What people? The people who did this?' She glanced at Natalya to see if her reaction could throw any light on what he was saying, but there was nothing. 'Are you saying you think you were the intended victim?'

There was a pause and another exchange of glances between Simon and Natalya. But she remained impassive. She just sat there, elbow on the sofa, hand on her head, drinking her coffee. After a moment, she finished it and placed the empty mug on the low table in front of the leather sofa.

'I don't know,' he said. 'I don't know why anyone would want to do this to me or my family.'

Molly could feel her patience beginning to wane. She felt sorry for him, but that sympathy would only go so far. 'It wasn't just the arson attack, Simon,' she said quietly. 'They were shot before the fire was started.' She hated being so blunt with him, but she had to get through to him somehow. There was a real danger he was playing games with her. She could sense he was holding back because there was something he and Natalya didn't want her to know. But what secret could be worth five people losing their lives?

He stared at her, shaking his head in disbelief at her words. 'Shot...? Why?'

'We're still trying to work that one out. It would help if you spoke to us. Tell us what you know about this.' She looked at him sympathetically. 'Simon, I suspect you know more than you're letting on.' It felt strange calling him Simon. For the past two days he'd been little more than a name on a whiteboard; a victim of a brutal crime that she had to help solve. And now he was sitting in front of her, real and vivid and consumed with grief for his lost family. If Natalya hadn't been there, she might have reached over and placed a hand on his arm too, but it would be unprofessional, and Natalya could so easily misinterpret the gesture.

'I told you,' he said, a hardness in his voice now. 'I don't know who killed my family and I don't know why they were killed. I'm sorry. I can't help you.'

'Who was the intended target, Simon? Was it you?'

'How the hell would I know?'

'Then why do you want people to think you're dead?'

He didn't answer this. He looked at Molly and just shook his head.

'Whatever the story, you need to come down to the station and make a formal statement to my DI. And I am going to have to insist on that.'

'He's not ready,' Natalya argued, jumping into the conversation unprompted. 'Can you not see he is still very upset? You just told him his family were shot dead and now you want him to go to a police station and answer more questions?' It was like watching a mother fighting to protect her child. Molly waited for Natalya to touch him on the arm again; reassuring him she was on his side.

'Look, you can't stay in hiding forever. You have responsibilities. For a start, you may have to formally identify the bodies.' Although from what she knew about the state of the victims, there probably wouldn't be much left to identify. 'And you'll have to make arrangements for their funerals at some point.'

'The coroner won't release the bodies for a while. And I don't plan on laying low forever,' he said. 'Just until I've got my head sorted, then I'll talk to you officially.'

Molly sighed. She couldn't force Simon Galloway to come down to the station with her, unless she arrested him. He certainly had questions to answer, and she was as yet unpersuaded by his alibi. But could she justify arresting someone who'd just been told his family and best friend had been shot dead prior to their house being set on fire? And then there was Natalya. Molly was willing to bet Natalya could fight dirty when it came to protecting her man.

'And when will that be, Simon? We need to find the person or people who killed your parents, your sister, your nephew and your best friend. It's just possible they could kill again. Time is never on our side in these situations.'

Again, it was Natalya who answered for him. 'As he has already told you, he's in shock. You can't make him talk to you if he doesn't want to. We're not living in a police state in this country.'

Molly ignored her. She was beginning to tire of Natalya's interference. Simon was an adult; he wasn't in need of a nanny to wipe his nose for him. 'If you think your life is in danger, we can offer you protection,' she said, taking a punt that Simon's reluctance to talk was down to fear and not guilt.

He laughed. 'It's a bit late for offers of police protection, don't you think? My family's dead. How do I know I won't be next?'

'Then talk to us. Tell us what you know and help us find whoever's responsible.'

He just gave a shrug. 'I will. I promise I'll come down to the station and talk to you. But not today. Not now. I need time to get my head round all this.' He looked imploringly at Molly, his blue eyes wide like a puppy's.

'Thank you for being so understanding,' he said, throwing her a smile. It was a warm and winning smile, that under different circumstances she might have found endearing.

Chapter Twenty-Seven

'Still alive? You're shitting me!'

They were in Betty Taggart's office: Molly, Denning and McKenna. A faint taste of Glenmorangie lingering in the air.

The expression on McKenna's face had said 'gobsmacked' when Denning had told her about Simon Galloway, but the look of shock had quickly been replaced by one of nodding acceptance.

The minute Molly had informed him that Simon Galloway was alive and well and not dead in a deep freeze, he'd gone straight to McKenna. Molly had insisted on joining him to explain why she hadn't brought Simon Galloway in for questioning straightaway. Denning was happy to let Molly talk her way out of that one.

McKenna had been studying the contents of a manila folder when he'd knocked on her door a few moments ago. She'd hurriedly closed the folder as soon as Denning and Molly had entered the office. However, he recognised the logo on the sticker at the top right-hand corner of the folder and realised it had come from the pathologist's office.

'We can confirm that the body of the male in his late thirties that was recovered from the house in Gibney Road is not that of Simon Galloway.' Denning kept to the facts, only mentioning Molly's meeting with Galloway when he had to.

McKenna sat back in her chair and eyed Denning and Molly. It wasn't quite her usual gimlet stare, but it was a look that said she wasn't in the mood for taking prisoners.

'OK, well, perhaps that shouldn't have come as too much of a surprise considering.' She threw the manila folder across the desk, where Denning caught it just in time. 'This would tie in with what the pathologist has just informed me. The dental records of the male victim don't match those of Simon Galloway. They initially thought Galloway's dentist had made a mistake, but in light of what you've now said, it looks like they were right. In hindsight, we all simply assumed the fifth body was that of Simon Galloway.'

Denning flicked through the report. At first glance it seemed to confirm what McKenna was telling them. They would now be asking the mortuary to track down Dan Hudson's dentist for confirmation of ID as a matter of urgency. His next of kin would need to be traced and informed before they made anything public.

'We'll have to wait for it to be officially confirmed,' Denning said. 'But I take it we're assuming victim number five is Daniel Hudson.'

'Would be a bloody strange coincidence if it wasn't,' McKenna agreed. 'Though you're right, we don't make any media statements until we know for certain. No more cock-ups.'

McKenna turned to Molly, throwing her a tight-lipped smile. 'So what does Simon Galloway have to say about this?'

Molly had been quiet up until now. She shuffled awkwardly in her chair. 'Not much,' she offered. 'In fact he didn't say a great deal.' A leaden silence descended on the room. McKenna leaned forward and placed her elbows on her desk. She looked like she was about to say something when Molly jumped in to fill the void.

'Look, I know I should have phoned DI Denning the moment I realised what was going on. I should have made this official, or at the very least, dragged Simon Galloway kicking and screaming down to the station to tell us what the hell he's playing at. But I didn't.' She looked at her two senior detectives, flicking a loose strand of hair behind her ear before continuing. 'He was upset. And he was scared. I don't know what of, but something has spooked him. I didn't want to add to his problems by suggesting that we're now considering him a suspect.'

'But he *is* a suspect,' McKenna said dryly. 'I mean I haven't seen the contents of Brian Galloway's will, but I imagine Simon Galloway stands to inherit a tidy sum.' The gimlet stare was back and now fixed on Molly. 'That gives him a very good motive for wanting his parents dead, and us a good reason to officially question him, especially in light of the fact that he's been off the scene since it happened.'

But Molly was quick to jump to Simon Galloway's defence, perhaps too quick. 'He seemed genuinely upset when I spoke with him. I'm sure he wasn't putting it on.' She looked at Denning when she spoke, assuming if she had him on side, then McKenna would be less likely to rip her throat out. 'He didn't know they'd been shot. When I told him…' She paused. 'Well, let's just say, I don't think he did it. Granted, he has a strong motive and a weak alibi, but I believe his grief was genuine. If you saw him, you'd understand.'

'None of which is a reason to not question him,' McKenna said dryly.

Molly was looking at McKenna now, meeting the gimlet stare full on. 'I think he's scared of something.'

'His whole family has just been murdered,' McKenna said sharply. 'And now he's on our radar as a possible suspect. I'm not surprised he's shit-scared.'

'It's not that,' Molly said. 'At least not just that. There was something else. I think he's trying to avoid some people, that's why he hasn't come forward until now. He wants them to think he's dead.'

'Only he hasn't exactly "come forward", has he?' McKenna said. 'You chanced upon him. And credit to you for that much, detective; it's just a pity you didn't think to bring him in.'

'He's promised to come down to the station first thing tomorrow.'

'Well that's very magnanimous of him,' McKenna said. 'Let's hope he does, because at the moment, I'd say he's looking pretty tasty for this.' McKenna's voice was even, but Denning sensed it wouldn't take much for her to turn feral and the decibel levels to rise along with the temperature in the office. For Fisher's sake, he decided to calm the conversation down, as well as the heat. 'Ruth Forbes said Ellie believed Simon Galloway was in debt. If that's true, then we can't rule out the possibility that whoever was after him could have had something to do with what happened to the family. In which case, it could well be that he thinks they're coming for him next.' He turned to Molly. 'But we *do* need to speak to Simon Galloway, whatever the case. If he's not here first thing tomorrow morning then we go and get him.'

Molly nodded. 'I'll drag him down here by the gonads if I have to.'

Denning tried to suppress a smile, while McKenna drummed her fingers on the desk. The look on her face told Denning she was willing to buy this for the time being. 'OK. Let's assume he's innocent, at least until we get a whiff of anything that suggests otherwise. But we go over his alibi, irrespective. If it's not watertight, then we start asking some difficult questions. Agreed?'

'Agreed,' said Denning. Then turning back to Molly, 'What was his alibi, exactly?'

'Nothing original,' she answered. 'At home with his rather over-protective girlfriend. She'll back him up. In fact, I reckon she'd back him to the hilt no matter what.'

'What do we know about this girlfriend?' McKenna asked.

Molly shrugged. 'Name's Natalya Koval. I've run her name through the PNC, but nothing's come up. She's registered with Companies House as a director and secretary of Party Animals. Home address given is the same as Simon Galloway. Some trendy pad in Docklands.'

Denning was impressed. Molly had certainly been doing her homework.

'So,' McKenna said, 'she checks out.'

'For now,' said Molly.

McKenna asked Molly to leave the office; she wanted a word with Denning. Molly pulled a face as she left the room, which he was sure McKenna didn't clock, or if she did, she said nothing.

As soon as the office door closed behind Molly, McKenna turned to Denning. 'She's a good officer, despite her shortcomings. You were right to take a punt on her joining MIT.'

'Do I sense a "but"…?'

McKenna placed her elbows on her desk again. 'I think she's letting Simon Galloway play her.'

'Really?'

McKenna was quiet for a moment. She was turning something over in her brain, which Denning never took to be a good sign. 'She's taking it as read that he's a victim in all this.'

'And, to be fair,' said Denning, 'it's entirely possible he is.'

'Hmm…'

'You think otherwise?'

'Admit it, Matt. If it hadn't been for Fisher's single-minded assurance that we treat Simon Galloway like a vulnerable adult, you would be thinking the same as me. He's the obvious choice for this.'

'I certainly think he's got a motive. But until I speak to him, I'm reluctant to make any broad assumptions. And if he is guilty, finding the evidence is going to take time.'

'Oh, I agree. We should definitely keep an open mind.' She waved a finger at him. 'But something has just occurred to me.' She pursed her lips and sat back in her chair, folding her arms across her chest. 'Let me chew over this and get back to you. I've got an idea, which might help us cut to the chase here.'

Denning returned to his desk with an apprehensive feeling hanging over him. McKenna was planning something, and he wasn't going to feel comfortable until he knew what it was.

Chapter Twenty-Eight

Denning tried to hide his surprise the following morning when the front desk phoned through to inform him that Simon Galloway was downstairs waiting to see him.

He gave instructions for Galloway to be shown into Interview Room B, and phoned McKenna to let her know what was happening. He had a feeling she'd want to take the lead on this particular interview, and he didn't have the energy to argue with her.

Simon Galloway was dressed in an old rugby top and faded designer jeans. There was a fuzz of stubble round his chin. He nodded at each officer when they entered the interview room. They introduced themselves in turn: McKenna first and then Denning. Galloway appeared cool and unflustered. He had declined any offer of tea or coffee, and hadn't requested a solicitor. He just wanted to get straight down to business, and that suited Denning.

Denning decided to adopt the kid gloves approach. He was sure McKenna would more than likely end up playing Bad Cop to his Good Cop. He could tell that she'd already marked Simon Galloway down as guilty, even before they'd walked through the interview room door. Denning was determined to keep an open mind. Yes, Simon Galloway had the strongest of motives and the weakest of alibis, but he'd also just lost his entire family as well as his best friend. A bit of compassion wouldn't go amiss.

'We're sorry about your family,' Denning said as they started the interview. They were recording it, but had reassured Simon Galloway that he was neither under arrest. He was merely answering some questions and was free to leave at any time. 'We will get the person or people responsible,' Denning reassured him, 'but we need your help to do that.'

He nodded his acknowledgement. Whilst Interview Room B was the more comfortable of the two interview rooms, it still had a claustrophobic feel about it, and a slightly stale smell that seemed to emanate from nowhere.

'Can you tell us where you were on the evening of Monday 24th into the early hours of Tuesday 25th?'

'I was at home with my girlfriend. Natalya Koval. In bed, asleep.'

'And she'll confirm this?' It was McKenna. She was sitting on Denning's right, directly opposite Simon Galloway trying her best to fix him with her gimlet stare. He flashed her a cheeky smile, which bounced off her like sunlight off broken glass.

'Yes,' he said after a moment. 'She'll confirm it.'

'You didn't go to your father's birthday party on the Monday?' Denning asked. 'It was quite a family gathering by all accounts.'

'Natalya wasn't feeling well, and neither of us were in the mood for a fight.'

'What do you mean by that?' McKenna's voice was calm, non-threatening, but there was the very real possibility that could change in a moment's notice.

'Ellie had invited Dan round. They wanted to talk about the on-going custody drama involving Caleb. It was inevitably going to end in a fight.' He looked at the two of them. 'I don't mean a physical fight, but certainly a heated argument. *Another* heated argument. Neither Natalya or myself could face it. That's why we stayed away.'

'So why not come forward as soon as you heard what happened? You must have known we'd want to speak to you?' McKenna wasn't going to let it drop. 'You've got to admit, Simon, that looks suspicious.'

He shook his head, then looked at Denning. 'I panicked.'

'Really?' McKenna's eyebrows arched towards the ceiling.

'I knew you lot would think I had something to do with it. Then it said on the news that I was dead. It was easier just to go along with it.'

Denning didn't believe him. And judging by the look on her face, neither did McKenna.

'You can see how this looks to us,' Denning said. 'You led us to believe you were dead. As DCI McKenna says, that looks suspicious.'

'I told you, I panicked. My family and my best mate had just been killed. I needed time to get my head sorted before I spoke to you lot.' He sighed and rubbed a hand over tired eyes. 'Look, if you're going to charge me, then charge me. But I didn't do it. And whilst I'm sitting here chatting to you two, the real killer is out there.'

McKenna turned to Denning and suggested a break. She reached over and turned off the recorder.

Once they were outside in the corridor, she turned to Denning. 'I don't believe him. Panic's one thing, deliberately letting people think you were dead... He's lying to us, Matt. I can almost smell the lies coming off him.'

Denning nodded quietly, thinking to himself. 'I admit he's definitely hiding something.'

'His guilt?'

Denning shrugged. 'Maybe. But if he is guilty, we don't have anything like enough to charge him. What we have is, at best, circumstantial. And if he did do it, it doesn't look like he's about to confess. We could speak to the girlfriend, but I reckon all she'll do is corroborate his alibi. Unless DS Fisher can get anything out of her, but according to Fisher, she's a tough nut.' He looked at McKenna. 'What do you think?'

She tossed a glance back in the direction of Interview Room B. 'I say we let him go for now, but we keep tabs on him. And the girlfriend. If he did do it, hopefully he'll trip himself up at some point, and as soon as he does, we'll bring him in.'

'Do we have the manpower for that?'

McKenna was still staring at the door to the interview room. 'I wasn't thinking of manpower,' she said, then added: 'OK, thank him for coming in and tell him he can go, but we want to see him in here again Monday morning. Perhaps by then something will have come to light.'

Denning wasn't convinced. 'Over the weekend?'

'A weekend's a long time, Matt.' She turned on her heel and headed towards the lift and back to her office on the fourth floor. Denning took that as his cue to return to the interview room and give Simon Galloway the news that he was free to go, for now.

–

Natalya was sitting behind her desk, looking like she wanted to break something, quite possibly Molly's neck, going by the thunderous look on her face. She'd buzzed Molly into the office despite insisting she had nothing more to add beyond what she'd already told Molly.

There was something different about her today. The energy that she'd exuded the first time they'd met was missing this time round. She was wearing the same Issey Miyake top as yesterday, and it looked to Molly like she'd slept in it.

'Simon spoke to your lot this morning,' she said. 'Why do you need to bother me again?'

Molly had wanted to be there when they interviewed Simon Galloway that morning, but Denning had insisted he and Betty Taggart were going to handle it. They probably believed he was guilty, and for all she knew they might be right.

Denning wanted Molly to talk to Natalya again; find out all she could about Simon Galloway, especially anything he would rather the police didn't know about.

'Simon claimed he was with you the night of the fire,' Molly asked. 'Can you confirm this?'

She looked directly at Molly when she spoke as though daring her to catch her out. 'Yes. Like he said, we were at home, together.'

'You didn't go to the party?'

Natalya continued to stare at Molly, like a panther just before it eats its prey. 'No. We didn't want to go.'

'Why was that?'

She muttered something else in what Molly assumed was her native tongue, talking to herself but not making a lot of sense to Molly.

'This is all Amber's fault,' she said suddenly. 'Everything that's happened is because of Amber.'

Molly waited for her to continue. Christ, she could really do with a cigarette right now. When Natalya didn't speak, she said: 'What exactly has Amber got to do with all this?'

'Amber tells lies, and her lies get people into trouble.'

Molly didn't understand. 'Natalya, I can help you if you tell me the truth. What do you mean about Amber's lies getting people into trouble?' She knew from what Marisa Powell had told her that Amber's relationship with the truth could be fleeting, to put it mildly. She had assumed Amber's lies were mostly a form of self-protection. But was there malicious intent there too?

'She told people Dan was violent and he attacked her. This was a lie. She also told lies about Simon.'

'What were those lies?'

'She told people Simon wanted to sleep with her.'

Molly couldn't hide the shock from her voice. 'Amber and Simon? But they were brother and sister?'

'Not blood-related. But it was all lies anyway. OK, so Simon used to sleep around. Sometimes he and Dan would have competitions to see who could get the most women to go to bed with them.' She tossed her thick mane of hair over her shoulder. 'They were like boys. Always like boys. Whatever Simon had, Dan wanted and the other way round.'

Did that mean Amber? She couldn't see it somehow, but perhaps that was because she didn't want to see it. Did it mean Natalya too, she wondered? Were they all part of some sleazy sexual merry-go-round, swapping partners like it was a sordid barn dance?

'Why would Amber say that if it wasn't true?'

'Amber was unhappy. Unhappy about everything. She knew Dan used to sleep with other women and it upset her. I think she was jealous of me and Simon too. She never liked him being with me.'

'Did Dan believe Amber's lies?'

She shrugged. 'Only Dan can answer that.'

'How did Simon and Dan get on before they fell out?'

'Like I tell you the other day, they were always fighting and making up. Usually falling out about money. Sometimes girls, but mostly money.'

Or had they fallen out about Amber? Did Dan believe her story about Simon? Molly thought carefully before asking her next question.

'Natalya, is Simon in trouble?'

The look she gave Molly said she knew very well that Simon was in trouble, though with whom and why was information she was clearly not prepared to share.

'What's he scared of, Natalya? Who's after him?'

Natalya tossed her hair over her shoulder again. She had somehow regained some of the self-assurance she'd shown on previous occasions. 'No,' she said defiantly. 'He's not scared of anything. Except you lot and your stupid questions.' She looked around the office. 'This business is going down the drains. I've tried so hard to keep it going, but Dan and Simon, they don't care anymore. They just wanted easy money.' She threw her hands in the air. 'And look where it got them.'

Molly still wasn't sure where it had got them, apart from Dan dead and Simon now a possible suspect. She felt they were in danger of going round in circles here, with nothing at the end of it. She suspected Simon Galloway had a pretty good idea who killed his family, and was keeping quiet because he thought he might be next. Then there was Denning and Betty Taggart who clearly thought he was guilty. But if they were wrong, and Simon had

175

been the intended victim all along, there was a real chance that sooner or later Simon Galloway was going to turn up dead too.

Chapter Twenty-Nine

Denning had never been to Mortlake before. It was a pleasant part of leafy south west London, topped by the Thames to the north and tailed by the lush, green landscape of Richmond Park to the south. Apparently Mortlake had been part of Surrey until the mid-nineteen-sixties, and it still retained something of a villagey feel.

James Metcalf lived approximately halfway along a wide avenue of detached houses that overlooked Richmond Park. When Denning was reversing the Ford Focus into the only available space outside Metcalf's house, he was sure he spotted deer running wild in the park opposite.

According to the information McKenna had given him, Metcalf still lived in the house he'd shared with Ellie at the time of their son's disappearance. It was a substantial house: elegantly proportioned and white-washed, with an impressive view over the park. A wide driveway ran parallel to a neatly-manicured lawn, which was surrounded by attractive flower beds, trees and shrubs.

He rang the ornate doorbell beside the half-glazed front door and waited for an answer. He'd phoned ahead to make sure Metcalf would be in, guessing he'd probably finish work early on a Friday.

Denning still wasn't sure what, if anything, James Metcalf could add in the way of useful information to the investigation. He and Ellie had divorced years ago and seemingly on good terms. Plus he'd had little or no contact with Brian Galloway. But he'd lied about not having seen Ellie since the divorce, and that lie had rung alarm bells with Denning.

James Metcalf nodded a polite greeting when he answered the door. Denning asked if he could have a few words, as he had one or two follow-up questions from their meeting the other day. Metcalf sighed through his nose, then pulled the door back to let him in. He showed him into a large, but slightly clinical-looking sitting room. Denning estimated the house to be worth a couple of million at the very least. The kind of place Sarah would be happy to call home, should their collective salaries ever manage to stretch that far.

He looked around the sitting room: pale beige walls and a cream carpet gave it the look of a show house rather than a home. There were stylish pictures on the walls, but no photographs, certainly nothing to remind James Metcalf of his ex-wife and son. In fact, there was nothing to suggest they'd ever lived there.

Metcalf sat on an armchair beside the fireplace; Denning opted for the sofa. There was no offer of tea or coffee, just straight down to business.

'There's just a couple of follow-up questions I need to ask you. About Ellie.' He fixed Metcalf with a convincing smile. 'About you and Ellie.'

'I believe I said everything there was to say when you came to my office the other day,' Metcalf said coolly. He was still adopting a tone of professional politeness, but Denning could sense a chilly note in his voice. Bearing McKenna's words in mind, he knew he was going to have to tread carefully.

'My apologies for disturbing you at home, Mr Metcalf, but when we spoke the other day, you told me you hadn't seen Ellie since your divorce. Is that true?'

'I wouldn't have said it if it wasn't.'

'It's just that I understand from Ellie's business partner that you had been in contact with her recently.'

If his question threw Metcalf, he certainly hid it well. There wasn't a flicker of emotion. He looked at Denning, then calmly said, 'We met up during the summer to discuss a private matter. It wasn't a social occasion, so I didn't consider it relevant.'

'What was the purpose of this meeting?'

A moment's silence, then he said, 'It was a private matter and in no way relevant to your current investigation into my ex-wife's murder.'

'I'd say I was better placed to judge what is and isn't relevant in this investigation, Mr Metcalf. As I'm sure you're aware, withholding information from the police is an offence.'

Metcalf continued to stare at Denning with cold, penetrating eyes, not unlike a watered-down version of McKenna's gimlet stare. But Denning wasn't to be swayed. 'This is a murder investigation, Mr Metcalf.'

He sighed and drummed his fingers on the arm of the chair. 'Eleanor contacted me because she wanted some legal advice about applying for custody of her husband's grandson. My firm specialises in family law, amongst other things.'

'What exactly was that advice?'

'Advice to a client is always in the strictest confidence,' he said, but quickly judged from the expression on Denning's face that he was going to have to share it with him anyway. 'My advice was to drop the matter. It would be costly, with no guarantee of a successful conclusion at the end of it. Plus there would be the emotional cost; such cases often result in families being torn apart, or at the very least put under considerable strain.' He paused and pressed his hands together, rubbing at a fingernail. 'There was also a risk that Eleanor's personal life would be put under the microscope in a very public way. I'm not sure she would have been able to cope with such scrutiny.'

Denning suspected he was referring to one specific aspect of Ellie's personal life. Something neither she nor James would feel comfortable having to revisit in private let alone in public. 'Did Ellie accept this advice?'

'No. No, she didn't. She said she'd talked things over with her husband and they both felt this was a course of action they were willing to pursue irrespective of the cost, both financial and emotional.'

'Would you have said this was driven more by Ellie than by Brian?'

He shook his head. 'As I told you the other day, I never met Brian Galloway. I told Eleanor that if she was serious about this, then I would need to meet with both of them to discuss how best we should pursue matters. Eleanor never got back to me. I assumed she'd reconsidered, or the matter of the boy's custody had been resolved through mediation. Very often that's the best course of action in these kind of situations.'

'That was very generous of you. I imagine a case like that could have potentially been very lucrative for your firm.'

He offered Denning a withering look. 'We're a blue chip firm, Mr Denning. We don't need to go chasing ambulances in order to get business.'

Denning ignored the barb. 'When, exactly, did the two of you meet?'

Metcalf made a great show of puffing out his cheeks and sighing heavily. 'I can't remember the exact date. It was late August sometime. I'd have to consult my diary, but it was lunchtime on a Saturday.'

'Lunchtime? So you met for lunch? I thought you said it wasn't social?'

'It wasn't. It just seemed logical to meet for lunch. I need to eat, Inspector, as did my late ex-wife. It wasn't as if we were strangers to one another, even if we hadn't spoken to each other for some time. There was no animosity between Eleanor and myself, despite our divorce. We'd both subsequently remarried and were both happy in our new relationships. We were perfectly capable of being civilized about things.' He looked at Denning. 'You must appreciate that yourself, Inspector. You clearly manage to have a good relationship with your ex-wife.'

If the intention had been to try and catch Denning off guard, then it almost worked. Did this mean Metcalf had been poking into his private life? Or had he read about the incident with Claire's ex-partner, which had appeared in the press not so long ago? But why did he feel the need to mention it? Denning refused to rise to the comment. 'And this was the only time the two of you met? To discuss the custody of Caleb?'

Metcalf didn't respond. He looked like he was about to say something when Denning heard the front door open and close. A couple of seconds later a smartly dressed woman in her late forties appeared. She looked slightly startled to see Denning sitting there.

'Oh, hello,' she said, looking at Denning, before turning to Metcalf.

'My wife, Karen,' Metcalf said. 'Karen, this is a detective asking me questions about Eleanor.'

Karen Metcalf was not only younger than her husband, but friendlier too. She smiled at Denning, walked over to where he was sitting and shook his hand. 'I see he hasn't offered you anything to drink. Would you like something?'

Denning shook his head, but thanked her anyway. Karen Metcalf was slender and immaculately groomed, just like the house. She was wearing a smart trouser suit and looked like she'd recently had her hair done. Polished and unfussy. Denning imagined the house was testament to her ideas on interior design rather than her husband's. Compensation, no doubt, for having to live in a house that had previously been home to her husband's former family, any reminders of whom seemed to have been expunged from every surface.

'You don't mind if I do?' she asked, and headed to a glass and chrome drinks cabinet in a corner of the room. Denning watched as she poured herself a generous helping of gin before adding a splash of tonic to taste.

'Oh yes,' she said. 'We saw that on the news. Terrible. That poor family. And that kiddie too.' She closed the drinks cabinet and wandered over to join her husband, perching a buttock on the arm of the chair. He seemed oblivious to her, however, and Denning wondered why she hadn't offered James a drink. *Did Metcalf have a problem with booze.* 'Though I'm not sure how we can help you. James hasn't seen Eleanor for years, and I've never even met her.' She knocked back her G&T and flashed her husband an affectionate look. 'But I understand she was a lovely lady.'

Metcalf didn't respond to this. His attitude towards his late first wife, combined with the noticeable lack of pictures of either Ellie or Martin Metcalf, led Denning to think that he had blanked them out of his life altogether. Perhaps this was how he coped with loss and grief: shut it away and put it in the box labelled 'past'. People worked through their grief in different ways; there was no instruction manual that showed how best to handle sorrow. He'd learned that much since he'd joined the police.

Metcalf looked at Denning. 'I believe I've now answered all your questions, Inspector. So unless there's anything else you need to ask…'

Karen Metcalf showed Denning out. When they were in the hallway, and out of earshot of the clinical sitting room, she said, 'He blamed himself, for years, for what had happened to Martin. And then Ellie leaving him. He blamed himself for that too.' She lowered her voice so it was barely above a whisper. 'He became quite ill for a time. In fact, I was worried all this would bring things back.'

She smiled as she opened the front door for Denning. 'It might be best if you let the dust settle a bit before you ask him any more questions.'

Chapter Thirty

Molly was sifting through some emails when her mobile rang later that day. She didn't recognise the number on the screen and was momentarily taken aback to hear Simon Galloway's voice when she answered it. Then she remembered she'd given Natalya her card with her phone number on it.

'Can we meet?' he asked 'I want to talk, off the record.'

He gave her an address and she agreed to meet him after work.

The address turned out to be a small hotel in Ebury Street, not far from Victoria Station. Molly gave her name to a bored-looking receptionist, and told him she'd wait for Simon in the bar just off the reception area. The hotel had been converted from a couple of former townhouses knocked into one, and had a slightly down-on-its-luck feel about it, as though the designer had aimed for shabby chic, but had forgotten to add the chic.

She had only been waiting for a couple of minutes when Simon appeared. He looked tired; the heavy bags under his eyes hinting at a lack of sleep. But even in a tired state he still looked handsome.

'DS Fisher.' He smiled at her. A warm, boyish smile that showed even white teeth. She could see why Natalya had fallen for him. He had an easy charm. She suspected some of that charm was about to be used on her.

A voice in the back of her head whispered caution.

'Are you staying here?' she asked.

He nodded. 'For now.'

'Why?'

They sat at a table beside the window. The metal shutter in front of the bar telling them there was no possibility of a drink. Perhaps this was just as well.

'Let's just say, I want to keep a low profile.'

She remembered Dan Hudson's wrecked flat. Whoever was responsible hadn't been messing about. If Simon was next on their list then keeping a low profile was probably a wise move.

'What's going on, Simon?'

He toyed with a beer mat, turning it over and over in his hand like a card trick. 'Your DI seems to think I topped my family.'

'Did you…?'

He smiled at her again, slightly less endearing than before, but still with a hint of the previous charm. 'Is that what you think?'

She wasn't sure. A part of her wanted to believe he was really the victim in this and not the perpetrator. But the cold, logical part of her brain said it would be dangerous to trust him. As Dave Kinsella had so acutely pointed out, he had a lot to gain from his family's death. 'OK. Maybe I'm willing to accept you didn't do it. But I think you have a good idea who did, and for some reason, you're refusing to say.'

'And can you blame me?' He twisted his face as he looked at her. 'Whoever killed my family is probably going to come after me next. That's if they can find me. As long as I'm lying low I have a good chance of remaining alive, especially after you lot went public and told the world it was Dan who died in that fire and not me.'

'That's because it's the truth, Simon. We had no choice but to issues a press release, now that Dan's next of kin has been informed of his death. We can't be expected to lie to the media just because it's convenient for you.'

'It's more than convenience. It might just have stopped me from going the same way as Dan and my family.'

'Then tell me what's going on. Who are these men who are after you?'

He shook his head. 'I can't tell you that.'

'If it's got something to do with what happened then you have to tell us. Whoever did it is obviously dangerous. If they do decide to come looking for you, then who's to say they won't find you? Or go after Natalya?'

He shook his head again. 'They won't go after her. It's me they want. Me and Dan.' His face fell. 'Well, they got Dan.'

She nodded sympathetically, wanting to believe he was telling the truth, even though doubts lingered. 'You can't hide here forever.'

'I can go abroad,' he said. 'I've got mates in Majorca.'

'And then what? Spend the rest of your life looking over your shoulder? Jumping every time your phone rings or you see a strange face in the crowd?'

He looked like a child lost in a grown-up's world. He was clearly frightened of someone or something, but until she found out what, there was little she could do.

'You need to come back to the station and make a full statement. Tell us who's responsible and we can protect you. It's the only way this is going to end.'

'Like I said, your governor wants to pin this on me. I could tell that from the off.'

'Then tell us the truth. DI Denning's a decent bloke. If you're straight with him, then he'll play fair with you.'

She tried to make eye contact, but he was still playing with the beer mat, twisting it round and round the table now. Then he looked up at her and smiled again. 'Why did you become a cop? You're attractive, though you could make more of yourself. I reckon that, buried under all that Cagney & Lacey bravado, you're quite sweet.'

Sweet. She wanted to kick him in the bollocks. Instead she said: 'This isn't about me, Simon. I'm here because I've got a job to do, and I'm not going to fall for your bullshit.'

He took a pen from his jacket pocket and scribbled something on the beer mat he'd been playing with, then pushed it across the table to Molly. 'Meet me here, tomorrow.'

She looked at what he'd written: *The Riverview Inn, Maidenhead – 12.30pm.*

'They do great food and a half-decent pint.' He smiled again, and his eyes lit up. 'I reckon you're a lager girl, am I right?'

'I told you: I'm not playing games.'

'See you there tomorrow. I'll tell you everything.'

'Simon…'

But he was already heading out of the bar and back into the reception area.

She stared at the beer mat. She had an aunt who lived in Maidenhead. It had been years since she'd seen her… But this was insane. She opened her mouth to shout after him, tell him to stop being a dickhead. But when she looked towards the reception area, he'd already disappeared. She could walk over to the desk, flash her warrant card and demand that the bored-looking receptionist tell her which room Simon Galloway was staying in.

On the other hand, what would be the point in bringing him down to the station now? There would be no one in the MIT suite at this time on a Friday. Even Denning had mentioned something about having to be somewhere, and Betty Taggart rarely worked late if she didn't have to.

She looked at the beer mat again: *The Riverview Inn, Maidenhead.*

She hadn't been in Maidenhead for ages. She could catch up with Aunt Mary, and then have lunch by the river… He'd promised to tell her everything, and that would be easier on his terms.

Chapter Thirty-One

Denning was tired when he opened the door to the flat. He'd collected Jake from the neighbouring flat where Corrine had been looking after him. She'd reminded him that she was off to Paris that weekend and then university on her return.

Denning had already begun to look up the details of local childminders. He worried about how Jake would cope in an environment where he wasn't the only child. Sometimes Jake was great with other kids and sometimes he just didn't take to them at all. There was never any rhyme or reason as to why he'd decide they were friend or foe; a wrong word maybe, or a look misinterpreted, or simply because they were wearing a colour he didn't like. If he didn't like someone, he didn't hide it, and it could occasionally lead to tricky situations that took deft and careful handling.

He'd already promised Jake he could play on his game before dinner, and no sooner were the two of them in the flat and the door closed behind them, than Jake made a beeline for his bedroom. A few seconds later the sound effects came booming into life.

In the main bedroom, Denning changed out of his work suit and into a pair of chinos and a rugby top. He couldn't stop thinking about James Metcalf. He *should* feel sorry for him; pity the man for having lost two people he'd once loved. And yet, something about Metcalf just didn't feel right.

He headed down to the kitchen and began to prepare dinner. Sarah was working late, so he'd agreed to cook. He could hear Jake's computer game blasting out from his bedroom. There was something reassuring about having him there. Sarah was off to New York the next day. Jake would be his sole responsibility until Claire finally returned from her mother's, assuming she did eventually return.

He could hear Jake in his room, playing his computer game, happy and oblivious to the world around him. And right now that was something Denning envied. Ordinarily this would have been Denning's weekend for having Jake, and they would have enjoyed some quality father/son time together. But with a murder enquiry hanging over him, and the killer still out there, it was difficult to pretend this was going to be a normal weekend.

Denning was already regretting the decision to let Simon Galloway go. Granted they had no evidence to hold him, but there was something about the man he didn't trust. Despite the lack of evidence, he was sure Galloway had been lying to them. And then there was Molly Fisher. She'd been quick to defend Galloway, painting him as the victim in all this. Granted, she might have a point, but Denning wasn't convinced. Simon Galloway was more involved in this than he'd admitted to. He was sure of it.

–

Molly waited in a quiet corner of the pub. It wasn't a bar she'd been in before. Loud music blasted out from hidden speakers and scruffy student types had eyed her warily as soon as she'd walked in, perhaps sensing she was a cop.

After about ten minutes of sitting by herself, sipping her pint of Kronenburg, Ben appeared. He looked unhappy about something, and she got the impression he didn't want to be there. She waved over to him. He pushed his way past a noisy group of youths standing by the entrance to the toilets, and sat down at the table next to her. She'd already bought him a pint, which she pushed across the table towards him. He stared at it for a moment, then took a drink and smiled at his sister. 'Cheers, sis. This is the first booze I've had in weeks. There's a no alcohol rule at the hostel.'

'How long will they let you stay for?'

He shrugged. 'Dunno. Someone said they chuck you out after six months, but I don't plan stopping that long.'

He was dressed in a pair of scruffy trackie bottoms and an old t-shirt with a stain obscuring the words on the front. He seemed shifty; his gaze jumping from Molly to the bar to the group of noisy students, and then back to Molly. 'What do you want, Moll? If it's another lecture about going back to Mum and Pete's then save your breath. I told you the last time we met, I don't want to know.'

She took another sip of her Kronenbourg, then said, 'I just want to make sure you're OK.' She tried to relax. There was no point in being edgy with him. She knew if she said the wrong thing he would get up and walk out of the pub, and possibly out of her life for good. 'It was... seeing you in that place. How can you live somewhere like that when you've got a decent home? Something I reckon most of the sad bastards in that hostel will probably never have.' She reached out to touch his arm reassuringly, but quickly withdrew it, thinking back to Natalya caressing her boyfriend in the Party Animals offices the previous day, treating him more like a child than her lover. 'Mum and Pete would take you back, you know they would.'

He sipped his pint, his vague eyes staring at nothing. She wondered if he was stoned. Or depressed. She should have been able to recognise the signs of both having lived with Jon for so long. But her relationship with her brother had deteriorated over the past few years to the point where she now barely knew him at all. She would struggle to second-guess what was going on in his head.

'It's only temporary, Moll. I've got a mate who knows about a squat going in Balham.' He looked at her, clearly reading the look of disapproval she was trying so hard to conceal. 'It's a hell of a lot better than being on the streets.' He gave a dry laugh. 'You really have no idea, have you? You've never had to fight for anything in your life. That's why you're able to sit there and judge me.'

She knew he was trying to wind her up. Pressing her buttons to get a reaction. She wanted to shout at him, tell him to stop wallowing in self-pity and sort his life out. Instead, she said, 'I've had a hard day and I'm not in the mood to be lectured either, so why don't we just try and make an effort.' She smiled at him, like she used to do when they were kids and he'd made some witty rejoinder that their parents just hadn't got, or had played some silly practical joke on someone who had failed to see the funny side. 'I'm not judging you. I would never judge you. What would be the point? I only want to make sure you're OK. And you're not OK, are you?' Despite the olive branch, mutual unease radiated off them like BO. 'Ben, a squat isn't the answer.' She knew what that would involve: half a dozen dopeheads, living in squalor and stoned out of

192

their brains on Christ knows what, waiting for the next police raid. Her brother was in danger of screwing up his life by making an endless series of poor decisions, and it looked like there was nothing she could do to stop it.

'If you really want to help, you could lend me a few quid,' he said.

'I could. And you could tell me the truth about what happened in the fight.'

He looked at her, trying to win her round with his puppy-dog expression. But she'd had years to develop immunity from that.

'I know there's more to it than what you've told me. I know because I've checked.'

Ben shook his head and stared hard at the table top. 'What are you accusing me of here, sis?'

'He claims there were a few of you. You lay in wait for him and his mates, and he claims there were more than just two of you. I think the exact word he used was "ambushed".' Sue had been in touch. They had arrested two members of the gang that had been involved in the altercation with Ben. They were telling a very different story to Ben's version of events.

He took another drink of his pint, looked at her, then let his eyes drop. 'Don't know what you're on about, sis.'

'I think you do. I think you know exactly what I'm talking about.' She waited for him to say something. It was only fair she gave him a chance to offer up his defence first. But he just looked at her with a silly, slightly vacuous look on his face that told her all she needed to know. 'This fight you were involved in. You didn't tell me it was to do with stolen credit cards.'

She looked over at him, waiting for a response.

'Who told you this? One of your copper friends, I suppose? Well it's bullshit.'

'They don't, as yet, have any proof you were directly involved, but once the rest of this gang are rounded up it's only a matter of time before your name is mentioned.'

'This has got nothing to do with me. *I* was the one who was stabbed. But instead of giving me any kind of sympathy, you accuse me of being involved in something I wasn't. Col just asked me to go along with him that night for company.'

'Ben, you're coming up with excuses, and not very good ones at that. A man's seriously ill in hospital. If he dies, we're talking manslaughter at the very least, possibly a murder charge. And for all I know you might be involved in that. *Directly* involved I mean.'

'Are you saying you think I hit that bloke?'

'I'm saying I think there's a lot you're not telling me.'

He drank his pint, eyes fixed on the table top.

The noisy crowd standing by the toilets were getting louder now, pushing each other and shouting rather than talking.

'I want the truth,' Molly said, after Ben's silence was in danger of growing. 'What really happened the night you were stabbed?'

He looked up at her, finally. 'Some guys I know… one of them said he knew where there was easy money going. He asked if I wanted to be part of it. I needed the cash. I was skint. I was on the bones of my arse. It was easy money.'

'So what went wrong?'

He glanced over at the noisy group standing by the toilets. The barman was arguing with one of them. Molly couldn't hear what they were saying, but the barman was pointing in the direction of the door and shaking his head.

'The geezers who were running the scam accused us of creaming off more than our share. They got nasty with us. We arranged to meet them one night and that's when the fight broke out.'

'And had you ripped them off?'

He didn't answer. The commotion at the bar had died down now and the group had moved to a vacant table.

'I'll take that as a yes.'

'It wasn't my idea. I said we shouldn't mess them around, but Col got greedy. He said it wasn't as if they'd go to the Bill about it. In the end they didn't need to. They arranged to meet us, like I said. Only thing was, they'd turned up mob-handed. Six of them against two of us. There was a bit of a scuffle, one of them got hit, next thing I've got a blade sticking out my neck.' His eyes met hers. 'They ran off after that. Col phoned for an ambulance – only after I'd yelled at him, mind.'

'So it was Col who punched the other guy?'

After a moment he nodded. She wasn't sure if she believed him. Perhaps it was easier just to accept his version of events rather than push him for the truth. This wasn't her case. She wasn't CID anymore, this was Sue Gorman's problem. But she couldn't just let this drop.

'Then he's guilty of serious assault. The guy could have died. You need to tell the police.'

'No way, sis. I'm not grassing Col up. Besides, it was self-defence. They attacked us first.'

'Only because you'd conned them. Why did you get involved in this in the first place? There must have been another way.'

Ben shook his head. 'I said you wouldn't understand and you don't. You just don't get it, do you?'

'I don't think I recognise you anymore, Ben. You always used to push your luck, but this is something else. What have you got yourself into?'

He shrugged again and finished his pint. 'Look, it's over. They'll leave us alone now, and we're not involved in that racket any more. Anyway, I haven't seen Col since it all kicked off. So you've got no worries there.'

But Molly was worried. She was worried about what was happening to her brother and what he'd got himself involved in. And, if she was totally honest with herself, she was worried about how it could potentially impact on her. Having a criminal for a brother was unlikely to do her career prospects much good, and she was sure she was hanging onto her job in MIT by a wing and a prayer as it was.

'Ben, promise me you'll sort yourself out. Stop hanging round with dodgy people and don't get involved with anything illegal. You've got to give me your word.'

Ben played with a beer mat, twisting it round and round like a magician practicing a card trick. 'How's the ape?'

She sighed, still refusing to let him press her buttons. 'Jon's fine. He's got the possibility of a job, which is great. He needs a purpose in life.'

'He'll still be a wanker though.'

She took another sip of her Kronenbourg. 'What happened with your music?' she asked Ben. 'You were in a band not that long ago? What happened to it?'

He snorted. 'We fell out. The lead guitarist was a twat with an ego problem. Then we found a producer who promised to make us famous, but only if he could get into our pants first.' He yawned. 'It was all too much hassle. We went our separate ways in the end. Best all round probably.'

'That's a shame. You were really good.'

'You never heard us play.'

'Jon and I went to see you at a pub in Camden a few years back. Don't you remember?'

He played some more with the beer mat. 'Oh yeah. You'd just started going out with the ape.' He gave a wry grin. 'I thought he was all right then.'

'He *is* all right, Ben. And we're good for each other.'

'Sounds like you're trying to convince yourself of that more than me.'

The youths standing by the toilets were hassling some student types who had invaded their space.

She decided it was time to play her ace. 'Ben, I've had a word with Mum. She says you can move back anytime. Pete's OK with it.'

He didn't answer. After a few seconds he stood up. 'I need a slash.' She watched him head off in the direction of the gents' in the far corner beside the bar. She considered buying another pint, but realised she still hadn't eaten. Maybe she would suggest going somewhere for food once Ben returned from the gents'. Perhaps it would be easier to talk in a restaurant. On the other hand, perhaps she was wasting her time with him.

She waited for him to return. After ten minutes, she realised he probably wasn't going to come back. From somewhere above the racket of the noisy youths and the tinny din of the music she could hear what sounded like the beeping noise a fire door makes when it's been opened.

Chapter Thirty-Two

The Riverview Inn overlooked the Thames in Maidenhead, slightly downstream of Brunel's famous bridge. The weather forecasters had accurately predicted a warm sunny day, and the pub was busy with families and couples making the most of the mild autumn weather.

Simon Galloway had found them a table in the terraced beer garden, overlooking the river. There were people boating on the Thames, and judging by the shouting and general revelry, Molly guessed there was some kind of competition going on.

They drank their pints and perused the menu. The restaurant specialised in Mediterranean cuisine, with a heavy emphasis on salads. Simon had insisted lunch was on him; generous, she thought, considering his current financial predicament.

'I'm not going to call you DS Fisher,' he said. 'What's your first name?'

She told him.

'Your parents christened you Molly?' he asked, and she wasn't sure if he was taking the piss.

'Actually, no.' She blushed slightly. 'Firstly, I was never christened, and secondly, my name is actually Margaret. My brother couldn't say Maggie when he was little, it came out as Molly, so I've been Molly ever since.'

He laughed when she told him this. He looked different when he laughed, less stressed, more like someone who was simply enjoying lunch with a friend rather than someone whose family had just been brutally murdered.

Molly was still unsure that she'd done the right thing in agreeing to join Simon Galloway for lunch. But he'd dictated his terms and she'd felt obliged to accept them. 'I really shouldn't be doing this,' she said, voicing her thoughts aloud. 'It could be deemed unprofessional.'

He smiled at her. 'So I *am* a suspect then?'

She sipped her Kronenbourg. 'You tell me...'

They both laughed this time. Under different circumstances, she would have considered this an enjoyable way of spending a weekend. Jon wasn't really a pub-lunches kind of guy, and would certainly never countenance abandoning London unless it was for work.

Simon seemed more relaxed today. Getting out of London probably helped. Somehow the pace of life seemed slower away from the city. Although London was only a few miles to the east of where they were sitting, it felt like another world. Yet the pace of life seemed not only slower, but less frantic. She gazed out at the river: a small yacht cruised past; a couple sitting at the stern, sipping drinks and ignoring the envious looks from passers-by. It all felt so civilised and a million miles removed from her everyday life of murder and mayhem.

A waitress came over to take their order. Molly opted for an apple and walnut quiche with a beetroot and watercress salad, Simon for grilled sardines and a tomato salad. She'd clocked the prices on the menu: not cheap, but not exorbitantly expensive either.

'How was your aunt?' he asked, once the waitress had left.

She'd told him she'd been planning to meet up with her Great Aunt Mary, and he'd even suggested bringing her along for lunch. But, despite the mellow atmosphere and easy chat, she still classed this as work.

'She's great.' She smiled at the recent memory of visiting her eccentric aunt. Although technically her step-father's aunt, she was someone Molly had always been close to for as long as she'd been in her life, and had been something of a surrogate granny when she'd been growing up. 'She's in her eighties, now. And still writing. She's just finished her forty-second novel.'

He looked impressed. 'Is she famous then?'

'Only if you read a lot of romantic fiction.'

He laughed. But she noticed the laughter did not quite reach his eyes.

He was gazing out at the river, taking in the scene. 'We used to come here as kids. Me and Amber. With our parents. When Mum was still alive.' He flicked his hand through his hair. 'My *real* mum, I mean, not Ellie.'

'You must miss her,' Molly said.

The laughter had now faded from his face, and was replaced with a melancholy, soulful look, his sharp blue eyes slightly dulled and sorrowful. 'Things changed after she died.'

'In what way?'

He was still staring at the boats on the river; canoeists in bright-coloured life jackets and matching caps splashing around without a care in the word. A couple of ducks, suddenly roused from their slumber, flew into the air, then landed a few feet away amidst a cacophony of fervid quacking. 'Dad became a different person after Mum died.

It can't have been easy for him; two teenage kids to bring up by himself. And Amber was never the easiest of people to get along with, even at the best of times.'

'Was she close to your mum?'

'No. But then, I don't think Amber was ever really close to anyone, except maybe me once, and even then not always.'

'Because she was adopted?'

His face wrinkled with a momentary confusion. 'How did you know about that?' Then he looked at her and shrugged. 'I was forgetting: you're a cop.'

She ignored the comment and continued. 'Did Amber always know she was adopted?'

'My parents never hid it from her. They told her from the off that it was because she was special.' He was still looking at Molly. 'It was OK when she was younger. She just accepted it. I was her brother and Mum and Dad were Mum and Dad. It was only when she became a teenager that things started to get difficult. When Mum died, she argued that she still had a mummy out there somewhere, so she was all right. It resulted in one of our biggest fallings out. I told her that her real mum didn't want her, so there was no point pretending she was any better off. She sulked for days. She even threatened to run away from home, find her real mum and prove me wrong. Things calmed down a bit after Dad married Ellie. But I think that was when things really changed between me and Amber. Well, Amber and all of us really. It was almost like she resented us. She argued that I got preferential treatment, claiming it was because I was their proper son. It was rubbish though. OK, I had a bit more freedom, but that was because I was older and Dad felt less protective of me. She resented this too. There were times when I think she resented me full stop.'

Molly glanced over to a table in the far corner of the beer garden, not far from the entrance to the conservatory restaurant. A couple of men had grabbed the table shortly after she and Simon had sat down. They were both thick-set, with short dark hair and neat beards. She was sure they were looking over at her and Simon. At first she'd thought they were a gay couple out for a bite of lunch like themselves, but judging by the unfriendly looks on their faces, she was beginning to think otherwise. She was sure she was being paranoid, and they were simply miffed because she and Simon had nabbed the last available table that directly overlooked the river. 'How did Amber get on with Ellie?' she asked.

'Brilliant at first. Ellie was lovely. She was brilliant at settling arguments and never treated Amber and me any differently. She was ever so patient with us. Ellie may not have been our natural mother, but at least we felt like a proper family again.'

He was staring back out at the river again, lost in thought, his memory more than likely returning to a time when life was simpler and he was happier. Before things started to go wrong for him. A time when he still had a family.

'Why did Amber want to start looking for her birth parents again? I can understand why she might have wanted to as a teenager, but she must have got over that by the time she was in her thirties.'

'She got it into her head that we didn't want her. After she and Dan split up she became obsessed with finding what she kept calling her "real family". It caused terrible ructions with Dad and Ellie, especially Ellie. That was partly what Dad's birthday dinner was about. It was supposed to try and bring the family together again. Ellie had asked Dan along as a kind of reconciliation. She thought that if Amber and he could get back together again then Amber might drop the talk about looking for her birth parents and settle down for Caleb's sake. They were getting desperate. Amber's behaviour was becoming more and more erratic. She was drinking too much; even back on the white powder, which she'd sworn she'd given up. Social services were sniffing around. I was supposed to go to the party that night but I couldn't face it. I knew it would have ended in another massive family bust-up.'

'So you made an excuse and didn't go?'

'That's about the size of it. Truth be told, I couldn't face any of them: Dad or Ellie, but especially Dan and Amber. I might have gone for Caleb's sake, though. I loved that kid. He deserved so much better than being a pawn in the middle of all the silly games Dan and Amber played.' He turned his head away, and she thought she saw him blinking back a tear. He was clearly very fond of his nephew. Perhaps losing him had been the hardest to bear.

'Were you and Amber close?' She remembered what Ralf Cavendish had said about their relationship, but he had only ever seen things from Amber's perspective.

'We were. Most of the time. But when she was playing up she could be hard work. And I knew she'd be playing up that night. If I turned up I'd just get dragged into the various fights.' He sighed. 'I was in an impossible situation. Whatever I said or did I'd be hung out to dry for it. I couldn't win, and frankly, I didn't need the aggro.'

'Amber claimed you wanted to sleep with her.'

He shot her a wary look. 'Amber lied. And not for the first time. She thought I was on Dad's side about the custody battle, and on Ellie's side about trying to stop her looking for her birth parents. She just wanted to make me look bad in front of the family. Luckily no one believed her. They were used to Amber's behaviour by that stage.'

But Molly wondered about this. She sensed that Natalya hadn't been entirely convinced by his denial. Molly didn't want to believe it, but like Natalya she would be unwilling to stake her life on it.

'Why did your parents adopt Amber?' she asked, partly out of curiosity and partly to keep the conversation going. 'You're not adopted, are you?'

'No.' He sighed. 'Mum had a miscarriage about a year after she had me. There were some complications and she developed a nasty infection. In the end she had to have an emergency hysterectomy.' He shook his head and looked back at the frolics on the river. 'It would have been a little girl. Mum had always wanted a girl, so they adopted Amber. It was all done through an agency. They never met her real parents, and all they knew about her was what little information her birth mother had left with the agency, which wasn't much.'

'How did you feel at the time?'

'I was too young to understand it. I was just told I was getting a little sister, and then before I knew it, Amber had appeared. I was only three years old. I didn't know where babies came from.' He looked over at her, his eyes looking bluer now the sadness had left them.

Molly glanced over at the men at the far table. They were drinking a couple of pints now and deep in conversation. Not paying any attention to Simon and her.

She relaxed. 'You got on with your dad and Ellie?' she asked.

He smiled. 'Very much. That's the worst thing about all this shit. It feels like I've lost two mums. And my dad… OK, we could argue, but he was a good man.' His face dropped. 'You probably know my dad was charged with dangerous driving after he knocked down a kiddie on a crossing. Well, he was covering for me. I'd been driving his car that night. I might have been slightly over the limit, I can't remember. I panicked. I told Dad what I'd done and he took the rap for it. He said he was doing it to protect me. He kept telling me my life would be over if I ended up going down for what happened. I was shit scared, so I went along with it. But I kept thinking about that poor kid. There was no way I'd have been able to live with myself if he'd died. In the end I agreed to let Dad take the blame for it, partly to get him off my back, but yes, partly because I was frightened I could have gone to jail for what I'd done.' He looked at the table cloth, fluttering very slightly in a cool breeze. 'I don't know, maybe a short spell in jail would have done me some good.'

Molly was only half surprised. From what she knew of Simon and Brian Galloway, it made perfect sense that Brian had covered for his son. It was still a criminal offence though, perjury and covering up a crime, and she was angry at how his sense of entitlement had allowed him to get away with something, even though he knew he'd done wrong. But she felt some sympathy for him. Young and stupid, he'd taken the easy option, and who could blame him. Everyone did something they regretted at some point in their lives. She was no exception to that. Rather than anger, she just felt sorry for him. 'I can sympathise with your plight,' she told him. 'After my mum remarried, it might have taken me a while before I accepted my step-dad was part of our lives, but I realised he was on my side.

My brother... well, he's a different matter entirely.' She thought about Ben; wondered where he was and what he was doing. She wanted to think he was managing to dodge trouble, but wasn't holding out a lot of hope. 'My own dad didn't want to know us after he'd remarried.'

'Do you still see him?'

'No. He lives in Australia and we don't have any contact. Not for some years.' The last time she'd seen her dad was just over ten years ago, during a dark phase in her life. He'd made it clear, without actually saying it, that Molly no longer fitted into his new life.

The waitress arrived with their food. She handed them each some cutlery and asked if they'd like anything else. Simon said, 'I wouldn't mind another beer,' then looked over at Molly and added, 'but as I'm driving, I'll have a mineral water instead.'

She smiled at him. 'You're learning.'

They ate their lunch in silence for a few minutes, then Simon said, 'You never did tell me why you joined the police?'

She poked a piece of beetroot with her fork. She told him the story of how and why she'd joined the police; about how her best friend from school had been murdered; how she'd then gone off the rails completely, drifting from job to job without a sense of purpose until her step-father had persuaded her to apply to the Met. How she'd worked her way up, and had earlier this year achieved her dream of joining the Major Investigation Team.

'Do you enjoy it?' he asked.

'Most of the time.'

'But not all.'

She ate some more food, enjoying the sharp tanginess of the salad and the tartness of the quiche. 'Sometimes I find myself in difficult situations, where things aren't clearcut. And when I find myself having to make compromises.' She took another bite of quiche. 'Like when I know I should have made something official rather than having allowed my emotions to overrule my judgement.'

He looked over at her. 'Like now, you mean?'

There was an awkward pause. They'd almost finished eating. Simon had left most of his salad, pushing it to one side of his plate uneaten. Molly's mother never allowed her to leave food uneaten, especially salad, insisting there were too many hungry people in the world, and salad was good for you. But perhaps his mother hadn't bothered, and his step-mother had found it easier to indulge him and his sister in return for them accepting her as part of their lives.

'We shouldn't forget why we're here.'

'Aren't you having a good time? I said I'd buy you lunch, and I have.'

'I'm not talking about lunch, Simon. I'm talking about you telling me who's after you and why. And more importantly, why you think they might be responsible for murdering your family.'

He winced, and pushed his plate of uneaten salad away from him, like a spoilt child who expected it to be taken away immediately he had finished eating it. 'Dan and I borrowed money to put into the business. At first we did OK. We kept things low-key: parties and promotions; gigs with small set-up costs and big profit margins. Then Dan got ambitious. Some people he knew asked us to invest in a nightclub. They'd found a venue: an old theatre in Hackney. The place had been derelict for years. Turned out it was riddled with dry rot. It was going to cost a fortune to get it converted, assuming they could even get planning permission to convert it. We lost thousands on it. It's still standing derelict on Dalston High Road.' He paused, glancing over at the river again. 'There were other problems too. But the long and the short of it was that we needed a major cash injection to keep us going. The bank just laughed at us; my dad had already poured a load of money into the business, which he had still to get back. Ellie's ex-husband gave us some money, but Ellie asked that we didn't tell Dad. In the end, even that wasn't enough to cover what we owed.'

'You borrowed money from loan sharks?'

He stared at the leftover salad on his plate. 'Something like that.'

The waitress came over and took their plates away. She asked if they wanted to see the dessert menu. Simon shook his head and asked for the bill. A couple of clouds had scudded over the sky, concealing the sun behind a blanket of grey. The mood had changed. A pleasant lunch by the river had turned into something heavy.

'How much do you owe?'

He shook his head. 'It's not just about the money. It's not *even* about the money...'

'Simon?'

'Can we talk about something else?'

'What do you suggest?'

He shrugged. 'You asked Natalya if she thought Amber could have done it. Do you still think that?'

She raised her hands in a gesture of surrender. 'I don't know. Do you?'

He stared at her for a few seconds, his boyish looks incongruous in a serious face. 'You never knew Amber.

She was confused and unhappy, but she wasn't capable of killing anyone. Especially not Caleb.'

'But if she thought she was going to lose him…?'

'She still wouldn't kill him. Nor dad and Ellie for that matter, even if she knew how to use a gun. No. You need to look somewhere else for your killer.'

The waitress returned with the bill on a small plate and a credit card machine tucked under her arm. She handed both to Simon. He glanced at the bill and tapped his card against the machine. For a few seconds nothing happened, and Molly thought the card was going to be rejected and she would end up paying for lunch after all. Then the machine bleeped and a couple of receipts poured out. The waitress handed one to Simon and kept the other.

'It must be tough,' she said. 'Have you considered grief counselling? Or at the very least, victim support. We'll appoint a Family Liaison Officer at some point, but to be honest, since the cuts the whole process isn't as slick as it should be.'

'I don't need counselling. And I don't need Family Liaison Officers. I just need to be allowed to get over this. I need you to catch the people who killed my family.'

'We will. But only if you help us, Simon.'

He sighed and rubbed his hand through his hair again. It was almost like a nervous tic; something he did when he was anxious, or faced with questions he didn't want to answer. 'I've promised you I'll come down to the station on Monday morning and make a formal statement. I'll tell you everything.'

He'd promised this before and failed to do so. She strongly suspected there was more to this than an unpaid debt, however large. She reached across the table and placed her hand on his, not caring how he chose to interpret the gesture. 'Whatever the story, we'll offer you protection. You have my word on that, Simon. We'll make sure the men responsible can't get to you.'

'Will you be able to protect me when I'm banged up?' He looked at her, trying to smile, but not succeeding. 'When the truth finally comes out the shit really is going to hit the fan. You won't see me as the innocent victim in all this after all.'

She quickly removed her hand from his. 'What do you mean? Simon?'

'I can't tell you. Not here. It wouldn't be fair on you.' He rubbed a hand over his face. He looked like he was about to burst into tears. 'God, it's such a bloody mess. I've fucked up. I've fucked up big time. It's all Dan's fault. Dan and Natalya. I curse them. I absolutely *curse* them.' He wasn't shouting, but his voice was loud enough for heads to turn in their direction.

'What have they done? Simon, what's this really all about?'

He suddenly stood up, digging in his pocket for loose change, which he threw onto the table. Three pound coins and some silver. 'Tip,' he said. 'I always prefer to leave cash.' He turned and headed towards the exit. Molly grabbed her bag and followed him. Out of the corner of her eye she noticed the table where the two unfriendly-looking men had been sitting was now empty. She hadn't remembered seeing them leave.

She followed Simon through the restaurant and out into the car park. Dan's BWM was parked next to a lilac tree. Some of its petals had landed on the roof, making a pretty pattern. She caught up with him just as he was unlocking the car.

'Do you want a lift back to London?' he asked abruptly.

She'd come to Maidenhead by train. She had a return ticket, but he was already climbing into the driver's seat. Without thinking, she opened the passenger door and climbed in just as he started the engine. Before she'd even had a chance to fully close the door, he was reversing the BMW out of the parking space and turning the car in the direction of the exit. A few seconds later he pulled onto the main road and was heading for the A4 and London.

Chapter Thirty-Three

There was a tailback on the A4 just before Burnham station, which meant they couldn't join the M4 to get back into London.

He turned left and followed a sign to Beaconsfield. 'We can join the M40 just outside Beaconsfield, it'll be quicker than queuing here.'

It was the most he'd said to her since they'd left Maidenhead ten minutes ago.

Simon drove like a man possessed. He'd clearly not learned from his previous accident. He was the exact opposite of Denning, she thought, who drove like he had his granny's best china on the back seat. They skirted Burnham village, some distance from the station of the same name. It looked like a typical English village from the brief glimpse Molly caught of it: cricket pitch and an ancient church in the distance. He then turned up a narrow road that was signposted 'Burnham Beeches'.

Molly had tried to talk to him ever since they'd left the hotel in Maidenhead, but he'd just stared straight ahead, cursing when they'd hit the tailback.

She'd glanced briefly in the wing mirror and was sure there had been a 4x4 following them since Maidenhead. She tried to tell herself she was letting her imagination get the better of her. The 4x4 had turned off the A4 at Burnham Station too, but had disappeared from view by the time they'd sped past Burnham village. Probably taking the same short cut they were using to get to the M40, only via a different route.

They were out in lush green countryside now; large, detached houses set well back from the road and wallowing in their own extensive grounds. An equestrian centre and a golf course sped past. She marvelled at how pretty it all was. How it was so close to London, but so obviously separate from it. No inner-city knife and gun crime out here, she thought. She suspected only those with bulging wallets could afford to call this home.

'These men,' she said, finally breaking the silence that hung in the car like a bad fart, 'the ones who are after you. What do they have to do with Dan and Natalya?'

He didn't reply. He just stared at the road ahead, turning onto another narrow road without indicating, but with a slight screech of rubber on tarmac. Maybe this was his thing, not talking whilst he was driving, but it was twisting her shit.

'Simon. You can't just ignore me. You've practically told me everything already.'

'It's her brother,' he said eventually. 'Dan and Natalya's brother did a deal. It was supposed to make us all rich.' He slowed down slightly to pass a van, but as soon as it was past he pressed his foot to the accelerator again. 'But in the end they screwed us over. They screwed us over and now they're after us.' He flicked a look in the rear view mirror. 'After me.'

She was on the point of asking him what he meant by that when she spotted the 4x4 coming round a bend behind them. She studied the number plate to make sure it was definitely the same one as before, but there was no mistaking it. Were they following them? It seemed unlikely, but why else would they be on the same road in the middle of nowhere? They passed a sign saying 'Burnham Beeches Nature Reserve'. She glanced out of the window to see an expanse of woodland that seemed to stretch for miles.

'Is this the only way to get to the M40?' she asked.

'Why?'

'If someone else were taking a shortcut to get to it, is this the only way they'd come?' She was trying to keep any note of panic from her voice.

A car passed them: a Honda Jazz driven by an elderly couple. The 4x4 seemed to be hanging back now, and she was still trying to convince herself this was nothing more than rampant paranoia inflamed by all his talk of threatening moneylenders.

'It's not the only route,' he said. 'I haven't been out this way for years, so I'm not one hundred percent sure of the roads. But I know we're heading in the right general direction.'

'Dan and Natalya…' she said, but the 4x4 was speeding up now, looming larger in the rear-view mirror. She hoped it was because it was about to overtake, but something told her that wasn't what they were planning.

She checked their speed. Despite the narrowness and twistiness of the road, Simon was doing well over forty, jumping to over fifty whenever they reached a rare straight section.

The 4x4 was almost on top of them now; its grill filled the rear-view mirror, blocking out anything else from sight.

They turned a tight corner and a straight section of road opened out in front of them. The 4x4 pulled out to overtake and Molly felt her heartbeat return to near normal.

The 4x4 was alongside them now, racing ahead to pass. 'Simon…?'

He didn't seem to be showing too much concern. He slowed slightly to let it overtake, which it did. As it passed them, Molly tried to get a look at the driver. There were two of them in the front of the vehicle: driver and passenger. She was sure she recognised the man in the passenger seat as one of the two men who had been watching them in the beer garden.

She had a bad feeling about this.

Seconds after passing them, the 4x4 spun sharply left, swerving into their path. Simon turned the car and hit the brakes, but they were travelling too fast. Another bend appeared in the road. The car spun wildly, clipping the rear of the 4x4 at speed, then skidding across the road. The sound of tyres screeching and the smell of rubber burning hit her like a punch in the face. Simon tried to keep control of the car, but it spun violently, swerving off the road and careering down a short embankment, heading straight for a tree.

The last thing Molly remembered was the windscreen imploding, then everything went black.

Chapter Thirty-Four

Denning was at home with Jake. They'd already waved their goodbyes to Sarah at Heathrow that morning; Jake still wondering why they weren't all going to Disneyland, just Sarah.

She'd told Denning she'd get back as soon as she could, but she couldn't be sure when that would be.

He and Jake were back in the flat now. Denning wanted some serious daddy/son time, which meant Jake would have to forgo his computer games for a while. He'd pulled a face when Denning had mentioned this, but then just shrugged and asked what Denning wanted to do.

But he didn't know, truth be told. He was only just beginning to realise how little time he'd actually spent with Jake over the past few years. Usually they would spend every other weekend together, visiting everything from the Planetarium to London Zoo; endless trips to bowling allies or the cinema, or sometimes just sitting in fast-food places chatting about nothing in particular. Jake had been very young when he and Claire had split up, and his son was growing up fast. There was a part of Denning that worried he had already missed out on too much of Jake's development, and there was a fear deep inside him that they could grow up to become total strangers if he wasn't careful.

So they now found themselves sitting on the living room floor, building a model of the *Mary Rose* together. It was something Denning had enjoyed doing when he was a boy, and as he lacked even a basic knowledge of computer games, this was something they could do together. He'd pushed the rug out of the way in case they got any glue or paint or anything else nasty on it, and were presently trying to understand which bits of the miniature *Mary Rose* went where. The picture on the front of the box didn't give much of a clue, and the instructions were in such tiny print that they might as well have not bothered putting any in the box at all.

Jake seemed to be enjoying himself. Denning had discovered that he was fine, as long as his mind was occupied with something. It didn't matter how complex or how fiddly, Jake enjoyed the challenge of focusing on something tricky and working at it until it was finished. Denning realised this was probably a characteristic he shared with his son.

'Daddy, what's a "gunwale"?' He pronounced it phonetically, which made Denning smile.

'It's pronounced "gunnel",' Denning said.

'But it's spelled "gunwale",' Jake argued, and Denning couldn't fault his logic.

Corrine had left for France with her boyfriend, so Denning was left chewing over the quandary of what to do about Jake while he was at work.

He'd phoned Claire, on the pretext of asking about her mother, but really wanting to have at least some indication of when she might be returning. Her mother was no better, he'd been informed, and therefore she couldn't say when she'd be back in London. She would be in touch nearer the time.

They would need to have a conversation sometime soon about finding a suitable school for Jake. The longer he stayed away from school the harder it would be for him to integrate when he did finally go back. Not to mention the effect this disruption was having on his education.

But that was a long-term issue. He still had to find a solution to the problem of short-term child care.

Despite its boasts about being a modern employer, the Met still had a long way to go when it came to addressing childcare issues. He had already made tentative approaches to various agencies about providing someone to look after Jake during the day, but had baulked at the cost. He and Sarah both had good incomes, and if they would struggle to meet childcare costs, he dreaded to think what it would be like for most working families.

It had been different when he was growing up. His mother worked part-time until he and his brother were old enough to be trusted alone in the house, and academics' holidays had always neatly coincided with school holidays. But things were different nowadays. He couldn't expect Sarah to go part-time at work, even if she wanted to, and it just wasn't practical for a detective inspector to investigate murders on a part-time basis, not that the Met was ever likely to allow such luxuries.

'Are you helping me, Daddy?' Jake asked. He'd somehow managed to get glue in his hair. It had already hardened, and Denning suspected the only way to remove it would involve getting the scissors from the kitchen drawer.

'OK, little fella, how's it coming along?'

As he helped his son build the model boat, he thought about James Metcalf in his pristine home, the memories of his missing son erased from every surface. He looked around the flat. There were numerous photos of Jake dotted about the place, not to mention the ones on his phone, and even the screensaver on his laptop featured himself and Jake at Alton Towers a few years back.

He felt a cold shiver trill his spine. If, God help them, anything ever happened to Jake, he'd want permanent reminders everywhere. He couldn't imagine not having Jake in his life.

Then there were the arguments the Galloway family had had over custody of Caleb. All wanting the same thing, but failing to agree on how best to achieve it. He dreaded to think what would happen if he ever had to fight Claire for custody of Jake.

Thinking about Caleb made him want to hold Jake tighter. He put his arm round the boy and kissed his head, trying to avoid the bit with the congealed glue.

Jake pushed him away, still unsure about his daddy, and never one for too much physical attention at the best of times. 'You know Daddy loves you,' he told the boy.

Jake nodded and said 'yes' in a bored voice.

Denning helped him assemble the gunwale and rummaged in the box for what looked like it could be a mast. He was about to unscrew the lid of the superglue, when his mobile rang. It was DS Neeraj.

'Boss, it's Molly Fisher. There's been an accident...'

Chapter Thirty-Five

There were already a couple of squad cars and an ambulance at the scene when Denning arrived. He parked the Focus on a grassy verge behind the second squad car. In the absence of any available grown-ups, he'd had no option but to take Jake with him. He'd knocked on a couple of neighbours' doors to ask if anyone would mind Jake for a bit, but there was either no one in, or they weren't answering.

He told Jake to wait in the car and play on his tablet; that Daddy wouldn't be long. Jake thought this was all part of some big adventure.

It had taken Denning less time to drive there than he'd expected. The nearest place of any civilisation was a tiny hamlet called Dorney Wood, after which point the SatNav had left him to get on with it.

He spotted Neeraj talking to a couple of uniformed officers who were standing by the ambulance, its back doors open. One was talking into a radio and trying hard to look like he was in charge. As the area was outside the Met's jurisdiction, it would be an officer from Thames Valley Police who would be calling the shots out here.

Denning got out of the car. There were tyre marks on the road, but little else to indicate what had happened. It looked like they were in the middle of nowhere, with nothing on the horizon except trees. Lots of them. And wrapped around one of them was a smashed-up BMW. Neeraj nodded an acknowledgement when he spotted Denning getting out of his car.

The uniformed officer who looked like he was in charge had just finished chatting into his radio. Denning managed to catch the words 'recovery vehicle' when the officer saw him approach. Neeraj greeted him with an attempt at a smile and introduced him to the officer in charge, Sergeant Nick Reamy.

'Bit far from home, aren't we sir?' Reamy asked, with a cheeky grin. He explained he was a sergeant with the local traffic police. 'Your colleague was just explaining how it was one of your officers in the car at the time. Not often we yokels find ourselves dealing with the big boys from MIT.' Reamy looked like he'd just left school, and Denning was sure he could see acne scars round the officer's chin but in all fairness he reckoned he was probably only a few years younger than Denning himself. The other officer was of a similar age to Reamy, but without the air of confidence that suggested he was of senior rank.

The BMW lay at the bottom of a short embankment with a wide expanse of woodland beyond. Its windscreen had been shattered and the passenger door was open, the wing mirror hanging limp and broken by the side of the door. The front of the car had buckled inwards where it had hit the tree – a substantial looking oak – head on, with the car bonnet forming an inverted v shape and bits of the engine poking through the metalwork. Steam was hissing from the damaged engine, but Sergeant Nick Reamy assured him there was no danger of the car bursting into flames. 'There's no indication the fuel tank has been ruptured,' he said, 'so I think we're safe.'

Reamy then turned to chat to his colleague, while Denning and Neeraj addressed the patient in the back of the ambulance. A couple of paramedics were fussing round Molly, who had a cut on her cheek and was wearing a neck brace. She had been wrapped in a silver blanket, and looked like she was recovering from shock. But otherwise she didn't appear to be too badly hurt.

'What happened?' he asked.

As well as the cut on her cheek, he spotted a nasty bruise on her forehead. 'We were forced off the road. A 4x4. I'm pretty sure it had been following us since Maidenhead.'

'Us?'

'I was with Simon Galloway. We were having lunch at a place by the river.' She paused to catch her breath. It was all coming out like a bit of a mad burble, and Denning had trouble keeping up. 'A couple of scary-looking blokes had been watching us during lunch. I didn't think too much of it at the time, but I'm absolutely certain they were the ones in the 4x4.'

Denning was aware of Neeraj looking at him. He gave a slight shake of the head. 'Sorry,' Denning said. 'Could we just rewind a second? Did you say you were having lunch with Simon Galloway?'

'Yes. At a restaurant in Maidenhead.'

'That's the same Simon Galloway who's a suspect in an ongoing murder enquiry?'

She offered him a doleful look. 'He asked me if I wanted to go for lunch with him. It seemed like an obvious way of getting him to open up.' She was still looking at Denning. 'There's something going on. With Party Animals. I think that might be the key to all this. He and Dan were involved with something dodgy. It's to do with Natalya's brother. I don't have any more details at the moment. He was about to tell me everything when this happened.' She pointed at the crash scene.

'How bad is it?' He was asking Molly, but looking at the paramedics.

'Nothing serious. They want me to go to A&E to be checked out. This is just a precaution,' she said, lightly touching the neck brace.

One of the paramedics nodded. 'We don't think there are any bones broken, or any internal damage, but it's best to be on the safe side.' She smiled at Molly. 'I don't think you need to hang up your dancing shoes just yet, love.'

Molly just looked at her. 'I'm fine,' she said to Denning. 'I really don't need all this fussing.'

'And how's Galloway?'

'According to the paramedics he'll live. He was unconscious when they got here. Apparently he's got mild concussion and a dislocated shoulder. They said something about taking him to Stoke Mandeville. It's the closest hospital with an A&E department.'

'We'll need to make sure there's an officer with him at all times.'

'Good. These men may try again.'

Denning considered her, wondering how she'd managed to get herself into this mess in the first place. 'I was thinking more to make sure he doesn't go anywhere before we have a chance to formally question him.'

Molly looked like she was about to argue, when Sgt Reamy popped his head round the side of the ambulance. He smiled at Molly. 'You up for answering some questions now?'

She nodded, though the look on her face said otherwise.

'Can you talk me through what happened?'

She repeated what she'd just told Denning about the 4x4 forcing them off the road.

'And it definitely wasn't an accident?' Reamy asked.

She shook her head. 'No way. It was deliberate. They swerved in front of us and forced the car off the road. Luckily the airbags deployed in time. Otherwise God knows what would have happened.' She rubbed a hand over her forehead and winced when it made contact with the bruise. 'I managed to get out of the car. I phoned 999, and asked them to notify the station, then my battery died. I could barely get a signal out here as it was.'

Unless their particular MIT was unlucky enough to be on twenty-four-hour call, there was usually just a skeleton crew staffing the MIT suite at the weekends, in case someone needed to contact them with any urgent information. It had been Deepak Neeraj's turn to draw the short straw this Saturday. He'd phoned Denning as soon as the call had come in.

'Did you get a note of the number plate?' Reamy asked.

'CUU569F,' she said, and Denning was impressed by her recall.

Reamy wrote it down. Denning made a mental note too. 'How fast was he going?'

'I'm not sure. About fifty, maybe fifty-five. Simon slowed when he overtook us, but I'd say it could have been closer to sixty when he swerved.'

'Simon? I take it he was the driver of the BMW?'

'Yes. Simon Galloway.' She shot an awkward look in Denning's direction. If Reamy recognised the name, he didn't let on.

'And this Simon Galloway, is he your boyfriend?'

The look on Molly's face turned from awkwardness to embarrassment. 'No,' she replied. 'He's just... a friend.'

'How fast was he going?'

'About forty-five, fifty, tops.' Denning thought she was lying, but Reamy seemed happy to buy this.

'Had he been drinking?'

'He'd only had one pint.'

'You sure?' Reamy asked, leaning against the side of the ambulance and looking even more than ever like someone who had only recently started shaving. 'A boozy lunch, speeding back to London. Shortcutting along here because of a hold-up on the M4?'

'He had one pint,' Molly repeated. 'He knew I wouldn't let him drive if he was over the limit.'

Reamy made a noise that sounded like 'hmmm'. 'What about these men who were in the 4x4? Did you get a good look at them?'

'Not really. Like I said, I'm pretty sure it was the same men who were at the Riverview Inn in Maidenhead when we were having lunch there. Maybe the restaurant's CCTV picked them up.'

Reamy nodded. 'We'll check it out.' He scribbled in his notepad. 'And neither yourself nor Simon Galloway spoke to either of these two men whilst they were at the restaurant? There was no altercation or anything?'

'No. I saw them looking over at our table a couple of times, but that was all.'

'And you didn't recognise them?'

She sighed. 'I've never seen them before today. Except...' She stopped. 'No. Like I said, I've never seen them before.'

'What about Simon?' Denning asked. 'Did he recognise them?'

'No. I mean I don't think so. He certainly never said if he did.'

'Do you think they knew you were a police officer?' It was Reamy again.

She looked at Denning before she answered. 'I don't know. But I don't think I was the intended target.'

Reamy stopped writing. He turned to Denning and Neeraj. 'We don't know for certain this was deliberate. It is possible it could have been an accident. If you don't know these roads...'

'Look. It wasn't an accident,' Molly said, the tension in her voice clear. 'They drove us off the road. Deliberately.'

'You should get forensics out here to look at the scene,' Denning said. 'We could be talking attempted murder.' He had to tread carefully. He had no jurisdiction out here in the sticks. Despite his relative youth, Reamy was the one in charge.

Reamy glanced over at the scene of the crash, then looked at Denning and Molly. 'OK,' he said, flipping shut his notepad and slipping it back into the top pocket of his shirt followed by the pen. 'We'll cancel the recovery vehicle for now, and get SOCO to examine the scene. We'll also have a look at the CCTV from the Riverview. See if anyone else saw anything suspicious. We'll be in touch when we have something.' He smiled at Molly and nodded at Denning and Neeraj before heading back to his patrol car, presumably to phone this in. Denning turned to Neeraj. 'Deep, go with him. Make sure he knows what he's doing.'

Neeraj opened his mouth to argue, but clocked the look on Denning's face and headed off in Reamy's wake.

As soon as Neeraj was out of earshot, Denning said, 'I hope you know what you're doing, Molly. If McKenna hears about this, I'm not sure I'll be able to save your arse.'

She tried to avoid eye contact with him, her face flushing slightly crimson. 'McKenna knows about me and Simon.'

'Sorry?'

She sighed, and touched the bruise on her forehead again, this time without wincing. 'This was McKenna's idea. She suggested that I should – to use her words – "cosy up" to Simon and see if he lets anything slip about what happened. I only went along with it because I was determined to prove Simon had nothing to do with his parents' murder. And this proves I'm right.' She nodded in the direction of the mangled BMW still lying bent and bashed and half-embedded in an oak tree. 'Whoever did this, that's who we should be going after, not Simon.'

Denning couldn't believe what he was hearing. McKenna's behaviour was not only irresponsible, it was bloody crazy. He couldn't believe Molly had been naïve enough to have gone along with it. 'McKenna should never have put you in that situation. What if he's guilty? Anything he'd told you would have been inadmissible in court. The whole case could have been jeopardised. What the hell was McKenna thinking?'

She opened her mouth to say something, then turned and glanced over his shoulder, her forehead wrinkling in bemusement. 'There's a child heading this way.'

He spun round to see Jake walking towards the ambulance, Reamy looking at him like an alien had landed.

'Jake, mate. I told you to stay in the car.'

'I was bored, Daddy.'

Jake stared at Molly as though he'd never seen a badly bruised women wrapped in a silver blanket sitting in the back of an ambulance before. 'Who's she?' Jake asked, pointing at Molly.

'Daddy?' Molly asked, the bemused look now turning into a full-on grin.

Denning explained about Jake, mentioning the fact that he was facing a temporary lack of childcare. He introduced Jake to Molly, telling him she was a lady Daddy worked with who had been in an accident. Jake seemed to accept this explanation, and continued to stare at Molly.

'None of this takes away from the fact that McKenna has been totally unreasonable placing you in danger like this,' Denning said. 'But this probably isn't the time or the place for a lecture.' He'd grabbed hold of Jake now, trying to stop him climbing into the back of the ambulance with Molly. 'I think you should get to A&E and get yourself checked over.' He nodded at the paramedics. 'I'll arrange for someone to keep an eye on Simon Galloway, for his own protection if nothing else.'

Molly was still grinning like an imbecile. 'I only have one thing to add to that.' She looked over at Jake. 'Why's he got glue in his hair?'

Chapter Thirty-Six

'What's your point?'

It was Monday morning and Denning was in McKenna's office. The dead cyclamen still sat on top of the filing cabinet like a memento mori of his own mortality.

McKenna was sitting behind her desk, looking less than happy. Denning was sitting opposite, determined not to back down. He was just managing to keep a lid on his anger, though it was simmering a fraction beneath the surface, at risk of bubbling over any second.

'My point is this,' he said. 'You put one of my officers in danger by asking her to do something foolhardy and reckless, and you didn't even have the good grace to consult me about it first.'

'I accept that it was high risk, but it paid off in the end. There was no point in running it by you beforehand; you would never have sanctioned it. And I would have been disappointed if you had. I know how...' she searched for the right word, '*cautious* you are. Don't get me wrong, I admire that, it makes for a sound detective. But, Matt, sometimes you've got to take a bit of a punt, especially if progress on a case is too slow. I've got the Chief Super breathing fire up my arse. He's not happy with balls-up over Dan Hudson, though I did try to punt much of the shit over to the coroner's office. Technically – and I'm not entirely convinced he bought this – identification of bodies is their responsibility, so we may have dodged some of the flak.' She sat back in her chair, folded her arms and looked directly at Denning. Not yet the gimlet stare, but he could sense one wasn't too far away.

She wasn't convincing him. 'Apart from the fact that Molly Fisher could have been killed, there's the whole morally questionable matter of you encouraging her to associate with a suspect in an ongoing murder enquiry. It could have compromised the whole investigation. Honey-traps are notoriously dodgy. They have a proven track record of failure, not to mention the dubious legality of the whole thing.' Judges, in his experience, took a dim view of any kind of entrapment.

McKenna gave a throaty laugh. 'I don't think anyone actually mentioned the word "honey-trap".' She reclined in her chair and steepled her fingers. 'But I fully take on board your concerns, and I admit I should probably have at least run the idea by you first. But whichever way you dress it up, this is my shout; my name's on the door and my arse is in the frying pan if this investigation goes tits-up. We need results and I saw a way of getting them.' She offered Denning what he took to be a propitiatory smile, though with McKenna it was always hard to tell. 'Look, I simply had a word with Molly on the QT. I knew she'd convinced herself Galloway was innocent. He had a reputation as a bit of a lady's man. I just put two and two together and saw a convenient way of cutting to the chase. If he did it and let something slip to Molly, then we'd have him. If not, then no harm done. At the end of the day, she got a free lunch out of it.'

'She nearly got a hell of a lot more besides.'

McKenna looked across the desk at Denning; eyes hovering on the brink of another gimlet stare, but aware she was treading on dodgy ground so holding back on her usual pugnacity. 'I've spoken to Molly and she's fine. A few bruises and a bit of a fright, but that's par for the course with the job these day. And more to the point, we've got a bit of chatter from Galloway. OK, we're still light on details, but we know this is down to Natalya Koval's brother and Dan Hudson. Though I still think Galloway's underplaying his own part in this particular shitshow, but if he helps us put away the men who are directly responsible for what happened in Gibney Road, then I'm prepared to overlook that in return for his cooperation.'

'None of that justifies placing an officer in danger. And what if he had confessed to killing his family? We could never have used that in court.'

'Then we'd have got proof some other way. At least we would have known we were going after the right man rather than wasting valuable resources chasing false leads. You know the pressure we're under. And you know that means sometimes we have to take shortcuts. Nothing that Simon Galloway said would have been evidential, it would simply have guided the direction this investigation needs to take to help it reach a swift conclusion. Or, as it happened in this instance, give us a possible lead.'

Denning still wasn't happy. Molly Fisher's safety was his responsibility and the direction the case took was down to him and not McKenna, even if she did ultimately carry the can. As long as he was SIO, he should be the one making the decisions. 'I'd like to have been consulted in advance, rather than having to find out about it by chance afterwards.'

There was a hint of a smile on McKenna's face. 'This wasn't an operational decision, Matt. This was nothing more than me asking an officer on this team if she was prepared to put in a bit of unpaid overtime to help the case along. Strictly off the record. If DS Fisher had said no, or shown any reluctance to go along with my suggestion, then the whole thing would have been dead in the water. Trust me, I'm not in the habit of placing my officers in situations that make them feel uncomfortable, or asking them to do anything I wouldn't be willing to do myself.'

Denning tried to imagine McKenna offering herself up as bait in a honey-trap, but he just couldn't see it somehow. It would involve tact, charm and empathy: three qualities Betty Taggart had in desperately short supply.

'I've told Molly to take today off,' he said. 'She said she was all right and wanted to come in, but I insisted. I fed her some crap about her not being covered by the Met's insurance. I don't think she bought it, but she's agreed to stay at home anyway. I'll give her a call later, see how she is.' He knew that McKenna had been in touch, but suspected that was mostly to ensure her own backside was being covered. He wanted to check on Molly's wellbeing; tell her she was to worry about something other than the job for a while.

'Any word on Simon Galloway?' McKenna asked.

'I phoned the hospital yesterday afternoon and again first thing this morning. He's regained consciousness and is being looked after in a private ward. Doctors seem to think he's dislocated his shoulder, but as I'm not family, they're unwilling to share too much information. There's an officer outside his room at all times. He claims to have no memory of the crash and isn't up to being questioned yet, but we are going to speak to him. He's wriggled his way off the hook for long enough.'

'What about Natalya Koval and her mysterious brother? What do we know about them?'

He scratched his chin. 'About the brother, not much. We don't even have a name yet. She's clean. Been in the country some time, no convictions, either here or her native Ukraine. But there's no mention of a brother anywhere.'

'Could he be here illegally?'

'It's possible. It would help if we had a name.'

McKenna thought. 'Speak to Natalya. Bring her in if you have to, but get her talking. We want the name and whereabouts of her brother and any known associates. Particularly anyone who drives a 4x4. Any news on that, by the way?'

'Thames Valley Police are going over all the relevant CCTV, but there's no trace of it. My best guess is that it's being stashed, probably stabled in a lock-up somewhere, either awaiting a respray and some new plates, or it'll be found torched in the middle of a field in a few weeks' time. The plates were fakes, unsurprisingly. They came from a Renault Clio that was stolen about six weeks ago. With a bit of luck the CCTV will lead us somewhere. We're liaising with Thames Valley Police over this. Obviously the crash took place in their jurisdiction, so one of their DIs is handling things their end.' Denning had been told the DI's name, but it was currently swimming around somewhere in his brain lost amongst a dozen other bits of information.

'What about these two blokes from the restaurant? The ones Molly claims were in the 4x4? Any luck tracing them?'

'The restaurant's handed over their CCTV, but we're still looking over it.'

'And we're sure one of them was definitely at the wheel of the 4x4?'

He shrugged. 'Molly seems convinced she saw one of the men in the passenger seat before the 4x4 hit them. It would be too much of a coincidence otherwise.'

'You reckon one of them could be Natalya Koval's brother?'

'It's possible. I mean we don't even have a name, let alone a description of her brother, so we're in the dark here.'

McKenna nodded quietly to herself, clearly thinking something over in her devious mind. 'Molly has built up a relationship with Natalya. It would be helpful to go over what she's managed to find out about her so far. From what I know of Molly, she's pretty thorough when it comes to keeping her notes up to date. It might be worth your while skimming through them to see if anything useful jumps out.'

He nodded at her and was about to head back to his desk when McKenna said, 'How are things on the domestic front, Matt? I hear you've had some childcare problems.'

He wondered how she'd heard about his situation with Jake. But then the whole nick thrived on gossip. If Molly had told someone, who'd told someone else, then it would inevitably reach McKenna's ears at some point.

'I've found a reliable childminder in Hackney Road,' he told her. 'She comes highly recommended, and it's only until my wife gets back from New York.'

'If you need any time off, I'm sure something can be worked out. It looks like we'll be rounding off the

Galloway investigation fairly soon, so, with a bit of luck, things will quieten down for a while.'

'Thanks, but everything's sorted now.' He had a hand on the door handle and was about to open it when she added, 'Matt, let me give you a piece of advice for free. Learn to trust people more. You've been here nearly six months; you should know by now that we don't bite. It never pays to bottle things up. You might be a copper, but you're human too. Sometimes we lose track of that.' She threw him another tight smile. 'You are allowed to have personal problems.'

'Thanks, but I've found it's generally easier to focus on the job while I'm at work and worry about my personal life in my own time.'

'Matt. Sit down.' She pointed at one of the two empty chairs opposite her. Reluctantly he pulled one away from the desk and sat. He wasn't sure if this was leading up to a bollocking or a pep talk. He wasn't in the mood for either.

McKenna smiled and laid her hands on her desk, palms uppermost. 'Matt. Let me give you a bit of advice, strictly off the record. When you've been playing this game as long as I have you learn that the boundaries between work life and personal life can quickly become blurred. Sometimes they can end up being one and the same. Keeping your work self and your home self separate can sometimes become an impossible juggling act. You're a good detective and a solid member of this MIT. But it's a team. I think sometimes you forget that.'

'Ma'am, I...'

'I'm just gently reminding you that sometimes it pays to give the team a little more of yourself. Behave less like a boss and more like one of the gang. Take your tights off now and again, and have some fun with the team.'

'Is that all?'

She nodded. 'For now.'

He left the office and returned to his desk.

–

Back in the MIT suite, he bumped into Trudi Bell. 'How's Molly?' she asked.

He knew Trudi and Molly were good friends and often socialised together. It was rumoured Molly had even stayed with Trudi and her partner when she'd been having some domestic problems recently.

'She's OK. Hopefully over the shock. She should be at home today, resting. But give her a call. She'll appreciate that.'

Once he was sitting at his desk, he checked his inbox. There was one from the coroner's office containing an attachment with the post-mortem report in full. It confirmed the earlier findings about the order in which the family had been shot, and established that Amber Galloway hadn't shot herself. The impact of the bullet suggested she'd been shot from at least a distance of two feet. So much for Molly's theory about a murder suicide. It was looking more and more likely that Natalya Koval's brother was their best option. The only problem was nobody knew where to find him.

Chapter Thirty-Seven

Jon was fussing round Molly like a shaven-headed Florence Nightingale in a Led Zeppelin t-shirt.

She preferred it when he was being morose and moody, and spending his time drinking cans of Stella whilst watching football on the telly. She wasn't used to being fussed over, or treated like a sick child, although she had to accept that he was trying his best to look after her.

The hospital had told her she was OK, but she had to rest and take it easy. Some industrial-strength paracetamol and good strong tea seemed to be aiding the recovery process. The hospital had patched up her torn cheek, and the bruise on her forehead was only sore when she forgot it was there and accidentally touched it. Thankfully, she'd been allowed to dispense with the neck brace. She'd spent most of the previous day taking it easy. But now she just wanted to get back to work. Denning had phoned, twice yesterday and once that morning, ostensibly to see how she was, though she reckoned he really just wanted to make sure she kept away from the investigation until they knew for sure Simon Galloway was a victim and not a player in the drama that had unfolded on Saturday. Even Betty Taggart had been in touch, saying she was glad Molly was OK and how it was great they had finally made some kind of breakthrough with the investigation. Like Denning, Molly suspected Betty Taggart had an agenda too, probably hoping she wasn't going to drop her in the shit by telling everyone she had suggested Molly get to know Simon Galloway better in the first place.

Molly was in the living room, lying on the rickety chaise longue and watching television, though she wasn't taking much of it in: some documentary on Discovery with Bear Grylls teaching a forgotten celebrity how to live like their ancestors. The celebrity was clearly hating every minute, which at least made the programme marginally entertaining.

Jon was in the kitchen, clattering around, making a mess that she would more than likely have to clean up later. He said he'd make them something to eat, though her appetite was still too subdued to think about food.

The celebrity was now arguing with Bear Grylls, insisting she couldn't skin and eat a rabbit. Molly muted the sound and gazed half-heartedly at the silent images on the screen. Her mind returned to the conversation she'd had with Simon in the car, just before the 4x4 had forced them off the road. Natalya's brother. Natalya had mentioned something about seeing her brother the other day, so they were obviously still in contact with each other. She wondered what the dodgy deal was between her brother and Dan Hudson, and how it had impacted on Simon. Perhaps Natalya too? Maybe she was as scared as he was, though Molly doubted it somehow. Her gut was telling her Natalya was more involved with this than she was likely to let on.

Brothers and sisters… A complicated relationship at the best of times. Even when it worked, it could be fraught. Natalya and her brother… Simon and Amber. And then there was her and Ben…

She thought about Ben. She'd phoned and texted him a couple of times since Saturday, but had heard nothing back. Not even a text to say he was OK. But she knew her brother; he would get in touch when he felt like it. Or when he needed money. He'd be skint. Skint and desperate, and that was when he made poor decisions. It was also likely he'd left the hostel and was staying god-knows where. She should try not to worry. Jon had told her to focus on herself for the time being: work, Ben, everything else should be kicked into the long grass until she was feeling better.

But she couldn't entirely forget about work. She'd briefly popped in to see Simon before she left the hospital on Saturday. He was still unconscious but apart from the dislocated shoulder, there didn't appear to be any serious injuries. She'd tried to speak to a doctor, but not being a relative, there was little information she was willing to share with Molly. She had momentarily thought about saying she was his girlfriend, then realised that had the potential to over-complicate things, especially if Natalya were to put in an appearance. There was a uniformed officer outside his room, and she'd nodded her acknow-ledgement when Molly had flashed her ID. It was unlikely that whoever had been driving the car would come after him at the hospital but they had to be careful. She suspected the crash had been intended to scare them rather than kill them. Miles from anywhere with no one around, it wouldn't have been difficult to have finished them off without much effort. Or perhaps they'd sussed she was a cop and hadn't wanted to risk making things worse for themselves.

She wanted to go back into work now. Follow up the lead Simon had given them. The only reason they had this lead was because she'd literally risked her life to get Simon to talk. Denning would go after Natalya, but he didn't know how to handle her. She suspected he didn't have too much of a clue how to handle women at the best of times. But she knew how to get through to Natalya; make her tell them what they needed to know.

Jon appeared in the living room, his bear-like frame filling the doorway. 'I've made us something to eat. Just a stew cobbled together from leftovers with some mashed potato on top.'

Molly suspected it would be inedible. 'Sounds lovely,' she said. 'I'm not sure I'm hungry though.'

'It won't go to waste,' he said, then added, 'Do you want another mug of tea?'

She nodded and smiled, and passed him her mug. He disappeared again in the direction of the kitchen. A few moments later she heard the kettle being filled and Jon rummaging around in the cupboards searching for the teabags.

Jon was being so patient and supportive with her. He'd driven straight to the hospital as soon as she'd phoned him on Saturday to tell him what had happened. She hadn't gone into detail about whose car she'd been in and why; just stuck to the bare facts. She'd told him it had been police work, which wasn't a lie. Jon was still coping with his own demons; still getting used to the anti-depressants and the counselling sessions where he was being forced to talk about issues he would rather keep buried.

But she couldn't stop thinking about Simon Galloway. He must be awake by now. Awake and frightened that the men who'd tried to kill him were still out there and possibly biding their time until they could have another go. One solitary police officer sitting outside his room wouldn't be enough to stop someone if they were determined enough to go after him.

She reached for her bag, which was beside the three house bricks that stood in for one of the chaise longue's missing legs, and dug out her phone. The hospital had given her a card before she'd been discharged on Saturday, in case she needed to contact them. She keyed in the number and when it was answered, she asked to be put through to the nursing station outside Simon Galloway's room. She said who she was, making this sound like an official request, and waited while someone went to check on Simon. A couple of minutes later the same voice was back on the phone, this time with a slight note of panic. 'I'm sorry,' the voice on the other end of the phone said, 'he's not there.'

Molly assumed whoever had answered the phone must have misunderstood her request, assuming, perhaps, that she'd wanted to speak to one of his doctors. 'Simon Galloway,' she said clearly. 'He's a patient in Room 306. He was brought in on Saturday afternoon with concussion and a dislocated shoulder.'

'I know,' the voice said. 'We're just looked in his room and it's empty.'

'Have you checked the toilet?'

There was a pause from the other end of the line. 'His clothes have gone.'

Chapter Thirty-Eight

'Deep, good luck with the interview this afternoon.' Denning patted Neeraj awkwardly on the shoulder. The DS deserved a lucky break, and with a bit of luck his interview later that day would give him the chance to finally make it to detective inspector.

'Cheers, boss. I'll let you know how it goes.'

Denning headed to the front of the office and waited until there was quiet before starting the briefing. He glanced at the whiteboard on which were photos of the Galloway family along with the burnt-out remains of their home. He'd added a photo of Natalya Koval taken from the Party Animals website, and a blank square next to her that simply said 'Koval's brother'.

He began the briefing by filling the team in on the events of the weekend, without going into too much detail. However, most of them already knew the story and Molly's part in it. He reassured them Molly was OK and she expected to be back at her desk the next day.

'Simon Galloway has gone walkabout,' he told them, moving on to the main point of the briefing. 'The PC who was supposed to be outside his room had nipped to the loo, by all accounts. It was then that Galloway slipped out. He was spotted on hospital CCTV leaving by the main entrance. After that there are no further sightings of him. I'm guessing he headed to the nearest railway station and legged it back to London, but there are no reported sightings of him at Stoke Mandeville station, or anywhere else in the immediate area.'

'Bit of a fuck–up,' Kinsella said.

'Thames Valley Police provided the officer,' Denning said. 'And strictly speaking, they were doing us a favour.'

Kinsella shook his head, but didn't add anything further.

'I thought Simon Galloway had concussion,' Trudi said.

'I guess he made a quick recovery,' Denning added. 'But he may still be confused or disorientated.'

'If he had concussion, it's just possible he could have passed out,' Trudi offered. 'He could be lying unconscious somewhere.'

'Despite the concussion, his injuries weren't considered serious. The hospital had been planning to discharge him in a couple of days anyway. Looks like he just made the decision for them.'

'He could have hitched a lift somewhere,' Neeraj said.

'Again, that's a possibility.'

'What about his girlfriend?' Ryan Cormack asked.

'Who, Molly?' Kinsella said, earning ribald laughter from the team and a stern look from Denning.

'We're trying to get hold of Natalya Koval. Deep, you went round to the flat she and Simon Galloway share this morning. Any luck there?'

'Nothing, boss. None of the neighbours have seen either her or Galloway for a couple of days. One of the neighbours has a spare key for the place. She let us in to have a look around, but it doesn't look as though anyone's been there for a while, which backs up the neighbours' story about not seeing either of them.' He looked around the room, before adding: 'Nice gaff though. I bet it cost a few quid.'

'No doubt Daddy paid for that,' Trudi said.

'I suppose we've checked the hotel he was holed up in last time?' Ryan asked.

'Uniform have been round there,' Denning said. 'According to the receptionist, neither Simon nor Natalya have been near the place since Saturday. Apparently Simon had booked the room until the end of the week, so he was obviously planning on heading back there at some point.'

'He still might,' said Trudi. 'Now that we've checked it out, he probably thinks it's a safe bet to lie low there. Unless we plan on placing the hotel under twenty-four-hour surveillance.'

'I doubt he'll head back there if those two blokes are after him,' Kinsella said. 'Though I still think that story's a load of old pony.'

'What about the crash?' Trudi looked over at him, shaking her head. 'Someone forced them off the road.'

'Still could have been an accident. Roads like that; boy racers driving like madmen.' Kinsella was refusing to let it drop.

'According to Molly, it was deliberate,' Denning said firmly. 'And forensics confirm that the tyre marks on the road suggest a vehicle swerved into the path of another at some speed. Plus CCTV from the Riverview Inn shows the two men Molly described getting into a 4x4 that matches the description of the vehicle used to force them off the road. We also now know that the same 4x4 followed Simon Galloway. Apparently he'd been staying at a hotel on Ebury Street.'

'So they'd been keeping an eye on him?' Trudi said.

'Then why wait until after lunch to have a go at him? They must have had ample opportunity before Saturday afternoon,' Kinsella said.

'Simon Galloway drove to Maidenhead via the M4 then the A4; both are busy roads with plenty of cameras and plenty of witnesses,' Denning said. 'Plus we can't rule out the possibility they recognised Molly as being police and were worried Galloway was going to tell her something he shouldn't.'

'Which he did,' Neeraj said.

'So where is he?' Kinsella asked. 'He's just out of hospital, his car's been totalled, he's not been back to either his flat or the hotel he's been staying at. He's got to be hiding out somewhere.'

'There aren't too many places he could go,' Neeraj offered. 'It's not like he's got family he could call on.'

'That's why I think Natalya is the obvious choice,' Denning said, brushing off Neeraj's tactless comment. 'We find her, we find Galloway.'

'There is another possibility,' Kinsella said. He cast his gaze around the room, then focussed on Denning. 'He could be staying with Molly Fisher. She's obviously chummy with him.'

'Fuck off, Dave,' Trudi said quickly.

Denning calmed them down before things got too heated. 'He's not staying with Molly, Dave, so I'll forget you said that.' He addressed the room. 'Wherever Simon Galloway is, he's either with Natalya, or she knows where he is. We go after her, we get Simon Galloway, and with a bit of luck, we can speak to this brother of hers.'

'About which we know Jack Shit,' Kinsella said.

'We suspect he may be in the country illegally, or at the very least living here under a different name. We've run the name Koval through the system and nothing's come up. We've also touted the name round Interpol, but we're still waiting for them to get back to us.'

'We still haven't established a credible motive for the Galloway murders,' Kinsella said. 'I mean, we're all buying the whole "Simon Galloway as victim" scenario but we can't ignore the fact that Simon Galloway stands to inherit a tidy sum from his parents.' He looked around the room at a sea of doubting faces. 'Well, come on, it's a pretty strong motive. We've conveniently chosen to ignore it, just because he managed to sweet-talk a gullible DS into buying his little-boy-lost act.'

'What's the matter, Dave,' Trudi responded, 'jealous because he didn't take you out for lunch?'

There was a general sniggering from the team. Dave Kinsella opened his mouth to say something further, but changed his mind, probably knowing when he was beaten.

'Simon Galloway *is* still a suspect, Dave,' Denning said, jerking his head at Galloway's photo on the whiteboard, and going some way to salve the grumbly DS's blushes. 'But we can't ignore what he told Molly.' He turned to DC Cormack. 'Ryan, any luck with social services?'

'They visited the Galloways on 27th July this year to check on Caleb's welfare. Whilst they had some concerns about Amber, they agreed the child was being well looked after and there were no signs of neglect or abuse. Any concerns they had about Amber's ability to cope were mitigated by the fact the child was living with his extended family and Amber had access to a strong support network.' Cormack looked up and addressed his next comment to the room. 'A follow-up visit was due to take place after six months.'

'But there were no immediate concerns for Caleb's welfare,' Denning confirmed. If Caleb wasn't at risk, then Ellie and Brian's case for custody would have been weakened. 'We can now assume it's unlikely Amber was responsible. Irrespective of whatever was going on inside her head, there was no immediate risk of Caleb being taken off her.'

'So if we rule out Amber, and we accept Simon Galloway is telling the truth, do we then assume that whoever's after him is the same person who killed his family?' Neeraj asked. 'It seems a bit much to murder an entire family over some dodgy deal.'

'I suspect there's likely to be more to it than that, Deep. This is why we need to find both Simon Galloway and Natalya Koval, and as a matter of some urgency,' Denning said. He pointed at their photos pinned to the whiteboard. 'Whatever lies at the heart of the Galloway family murders, these are the two who know where we can find the answers. We need to find them, and quickly.'

'Assuming they're not already dead,' Kinsella added coldly.

–

'You shouldn't have gone round to his house. At the end of the day, the man is guilty of nothing more than being the parent of a child that went missing.' McKenna was sitting behind her desk, arms folded, fixing Denning with her gimlet stare.

Denning reckoned James Metcalf must have been on the phone to the Chief Super the moment he'd left the nice house overlooking Richmond Park. But if he'd done so as some kind of warning to Denning, all he'd succeeded in doing was raising his suspicions about the man even further.

'He lied about seeing his ex-wife. I would have thought that was reason enough to speak to him again. And it wasn't as though he was being formally questioned or anything. I simply wanted to tidy up a few loose ends.' He told her about James Metcalf giving Ellie money, and the fact that he'd kept this from Denning.

'So Metcalf lied about seeing Ellie and didn't mention the money?' She steepled her fingers under her chin. 'Neither of which is against the law.' She dropped the gimlet stare and threw a half-smile in Denning's direction. 'All I'm saying is, be careful. James Metcalf is a solicitor. He knows the law. And I get the distinct impression he won't be shy when it comes to putting in an official complaint.'

Which reminded Denning of something that had been bugging him ever since his first meeting with Metcalf. 'What about during the investigation into his son's disappearance? Did he put in any official complaints then?'

She gave a slight shrug. 'I don't know. Would he have had reason to?'

'We failed to find his son. He can't have been happy about that. Was there any threat of litigation at the Met's handling of the matter?'

She thought for a moment. 'Not as far as I'm aware. I don't know that there were any grounds for complaint. To my knowledge, Martin Metcalf's disappearance was thoroughly investigated; there were no corners cut. OK, there wasn't a satisfactory conclusion, but, to quote my charming ex, "you can't hit a coconut every time".'

'What about since? You said yourself, the case is still open, officially? Has he ever been on our backs to get out there and keep looking for Martin?'

Another shrug. 'I don't know that one either. The case is nothing to do with us. It might still be open, but that isn't the same as it being actively pursued. There are dozens of unsolved cases over the past few decades that have never been officially closed. However, that doesn't mean to say there are detectives with the time and resources to look into them.'

'Not even at the ten-year point? Isn't it normal to have some kind of collective memory jog on particular anniversaries?'

The gimlet stare made a brief return, meaning McKenna was uncomfortable about something. 'What are you getting at, Matt?'

'There's been no mention of Martin Metcalf for almost twenty years?'

She pulled a face. 'Not as far as I know, and I think we would have heard. I mean, the story was all over the news at the time.'

Denning thought about this. 'Did your ex ever share any theories with you? Beyond the official line about the child having been snatched off the street? The two of you must have discussed it at the time.'

She shot him a puzzled look. 'To be honest we didn't tend to talk about work much. Too busy getting pissed and fighting.' She smiled at the memory. 'But I don't see any reason to challenge the official theory. It makes sense.'

'But no one was ever caught over this. There was no one in the frame. And the body never turned up.' He looked at her. 'It's strange, that's all.'

She gave a raucous laugh. 'You're not telling me you think Martin Metcalf is still alive and living a secret life somewhere? Granted, it's possible. But let's face facts, children do go missing. No matter how careful parents are or how aware we try to make them, it happens.' She sighed. 'It's coincidence, that's all, Matt. Let it drop. It's all just an unfortunate, shitty coincidence.' She steepled her fingers together again and tapped her chin. 'Matt, we're in the middle of a murder investigation. Hopefully one that's about to reach its conclusion as soon we get hold of this elusive brother of Natalya Koval. We have neither the time nor the authority to investigate a twenty-year-old missing child case. I'm asking you to leave James Metcalf alone. You're chasing shadows.'

'Maybe. There's something about him that doesn't add up here.' He paused, briefly glancing at the dead cyclamen, and suppressing a smile. 'You couldn't do me a massive favour? Then I promise you I'll let the whole James Metcalf situation drop.'

The gimlet stare was still fixed on her face. 'Why do I have a feeling I'm going to regret this?'

'Could you speak to your ex? Ask him what he remembers about the case. About James Metcalf in particular.'

The gimlet stare had now become a filthy glare. 'I haven't spoken to him for years. I doubt very much if he'd welcome a call from me of all people.' But she seemed to chew over this in her head. 'If I do speak to him, you promise me you'll stop hassling James Metcalf?'

'You have my word,' he said, but McKenna was looking at him as though she very much doubted his word.

Chapter Thirty-Nine

Molly was sitting in a café opposite the Party Animals office. The café was what she could only describe as 'ungentrified': plastic banquettes and faded lino. When she'd asked the purpled-haired girl behind the counter for a cappuccino, she'd looked at Molly like she'd just asked for a trip to Venus. In the end she settled for a mug of slightly stewed tea.

She'd been there for almost an hour. She was on her second mug of tea, which had been joined at some point by a doughnut, whose sell-by date had long since come and gone.

She'd already been over to the Party Animals office, pressing her finger against the buzzer for so long that the buzzing noise had changed pitch. She'd also left a couple of heated phone messages telling Natalya she was coming round to the office to see her and wasn't going to leave until Natalya had told her what she needed to know.

'Can I get you anything else?' The purple-haired girl had moved out from behind the counter and was standing next to Molly's banquette, noticing that her mug was almost empty. As well as purple hair, she had piercings all along her left ear, in her nose and, when she spoke, Molly noticed there was one in her tongue. She wore a t-shirt that said 'Bitch with Attitude' on the front, along with a picture of the Queen Mother wearing a Mohican.

'Another tea?' Molly made it sound like a question rather than a request, unsure as to how many mugs of tea she was allowed to drink before being asked to either buy something more substantial, or leave the premises. The girl grabbed her mug from the Formica table and dawdled back to the counter humming some indiscernible tune as she went.

Molly glanced out of the window again. She had the perfect spot to watch the entrance to Party Animals. If and when Natalya appeared, there was no way she'd miss her. She flicked another look at her watch. She'd now been there for just over an hour and there was still no sign of Natalya.

She'd told Jon she had to get out and get some fresh air. He'd wanted to come with her, but she'd persuaded him that she also needed some space. He'd taken the hint and she'd felt guilty.

The girl brought Molly's tea. She placed it on the table, offered her hand palm up and asked Molly for another two pounds.

As Molly dropped two pound coins in the girl's hand, she glanced out of the window and caught sight of Natalya climbing out of the back of a taxi. As she paid the driver, she looked directly over at the café and Molly was sure their eyes met, just for a brief second. But if Natalya spotted Molly sitting in the café window, there was no flicker of recognition.

Molly raced out of the café and made her way across the road, deftly negotiating a bus as she did so. She just reached the other side of the road in time to see Natalya disappearing behind the faded green door of the Party Animals offices. With seconds to spare, she dashed across the pavement and jammed her foot in the doorway just as

Natalya was closing the door. The door bounced off her boot and was quickly opened again. Natalya stood there, glowering at Molly.

'Get to hell.'

'I'm not going anywhere, Natalya. You're going to let me in and we're going to talk.'

She continued to glower at Molly. But Molly's boot remained stubbornly stuck in the doorway: it was going nowhere and neither was the rest of her. If Natalya wanted her to budge, she was going to have to find an axe and chop Molly's foot off.

'I told you to get to hell!' There was greater force to her threat this time, but they both knew it was meaningless. One phone call and Molly could have a team down here if need be, complete with an enforcer to batter down the scabby green door – not that it looked as though it would take too much battering to open anyway.

Natalya looked at her, then looked down at her foot; a tan-coloured Chelsea boot with a four-inch heel. Not Molly's favourite pair but one which was going to ensure Natalya had no option but to let her in, whether she wanted to or not.

Natalya thought for a moment. She peered past the door and seemed to scan the street outside before jerking her head over her left shoulder and opening the door wide enough to let Molly enter.

Natalya shot up the narrow staircase and hurriedly unlocked the door to the office. Molly followed her inside.

'Where is he?' she asked as soon as she was in the outer office. 'And don't twat me around this time, Natalya. Just tell me where Simon is.' She was shouting at her without realising she was doing it. But there was now so much at stake, she couldn't afford the luxury of letting Natalya mess her around again.

Natalya was behind her desk, playing messages back on the messaging service. There were a couple of enquiries about corporate events, Molly's own snappy message, which Natalya fast-forwarded, but nothing from Simon. Natalya said, 'Shit,' and started punching her forehead with her fist.

'There are people after Simon,' Molly continued. 'He told me Dan did some kind of deal with your brother. He didn't have a chance to go into detail as some men tried to kill us, one of whom may have been your brother. So I need to know three things from you: where is your brother; what was this deal; and where's Simon?'

'Why don't *you* tell *me* where Simon is? I know about you and him. Lunch. You think it means something? He's just after a shag, that's all. Simon and Dan… they're like little boys.' She was rambling; eyes wide and damp with tears. 'You're nothing special. He just likes the challenge of screwing a cop. It's one of his fantasies.' There was spittle flying from her mouth as she spoke. 'I do not know where Simon is. I don't even know if he's still alive.'

Molly waited until Natalya had paused for breath and then dived in. 'Natalya, I need you to calm down and tell me what's going on here. There was nothing between me and Simon. He took me out to lunch, and in return I hoped he would give me some information about what connects Party Animals with his parents' murder. That was all.' She offered her a tissue from her bag so she could dab her eyes. 'In Simon's absence, I now need you to help me fill in the blanks.'

Natalya grabbed the tissue and used it to blow her nose. When she'd finished, she threw it in the wastepaper bin beside her desk. 'I can't tell you anything. I don't *know* anything.'

'I told you not to twat me around, Natalya. We both know you're the person who runs this company. OK, Simon and Dan may have made all the decisions and pocketed whatever profit there was, but you're the one who really pulls the strings here. So let's not waste anymore time; just tell me the truth.'

She'd knuckled her eyes dry now, and had regained some of the composure she'd displayed when she and Molly had first crossed swords. 'My brother, Artem. He knew people who could help Simon and Dan. Provide them with whatever they need for parties.'

'What are we talking here? Drugs?'

'Sometimes.' She looked at Molly, sadness and regret filling her eyes. 'And girls.'

'Girls? What are you saying? Your brother provided Party Animals with models?'

Natalya looked at Molly like she was too innocent to be a real police officer. 'Use your brains, Molly. Most of our business comes from either corporate gigs or stag parties. These men are rich and they like to think they are important. If we provide them with what they want, we can charge them big bucks.' She flicked her hair over her shoulder, her dark eyes fixed on Molly. 'These men, they like to have attractive women around to entertain them. It's good for their egos. They were paying us a lot of money. We had to make sure they got their money's worth.'

'Entertain?' Molly's brain made the connection. 'So these girls were expected to sleep with the clients?'

'If that's what the client wanted, then yes, that's what the girls would do.'

'And if the girls didn't want to?'

She couldn't look Molly in the eye any more. Instead she stared at the phone on the desk. 'They didn't have any choice. Not if they wanted to eat.'

It was all starting to make sense now. This was something far bigger than she'd initially thought. 'These girls,' Molly said, 'they were in the country illegally?'

Natalya didn't answer. She kept staring at the phone, probably willing it to ring with news of Simon. But it stubbornly refused. After a while, she looked at Molly. 'My brother and his friends bring them to the UK with a promise of a better life. Women and children mostly, but men too. They find them work but they keep their money.'

'Why are they after Simon?'

'He and Dan owe them money. To begin with, Artem's friends agreed to provide the girls in return for a share of the profits. But then they wanted more. They told Dan the price had gone up and they were to pay.'

'And Simon knew about this?'

She nodded. 'He knew, but he wasn't happy about it. That's the real reason he and Dan had the fight that day. Simon wanted out. He told Artem he would tell the police what they were doing if they didn't call off the debt. They threatened Simon. They said they would harm Amber and her child if either he or Dan went to the police.'

Molly was still trying to take all this in. It was too big for her to handle by herself. She needed to make it official. 'I want you to come down to the station with me and give us a full statement. My boss needs to hear about this. Your brother made threats against Dan and Simon, not to mention Amber and Caleb. Three of them are now dead and Simon's life's been threatened. It's all pointing in one direction.'

Natalya shook her head. 'No. Artem and his gang, they had nothing to do with what happened to Simon's family. He swore to me it wasn't them.'

'I'm sorry, Natalya, but I don't believe that. We need to speak to your brother right now. Tell me where he is.'

She wouldn't say. She shook her head and repeated what she'd just told Molly about her brother not being responsible for killing the Galloways. 'These are dangerous men.' She looked at Molly. 'My brother only got mixed up with them because they threatened him.'

Molly doubted this. She suspected Artem Koval was more than just a bit-part player in this whole sordid scenario. In fact, she reckoned he was probably up to his neck in it.

'Give me his address, Natalya.'

She shook her head again.

'I'm prepared to accept you don't know where Simon is, but I'm not leaving here until you tell me how we can get hold of your brother. I also need you to come down to the station and make a formal statement about his gang and what they've been up to.'

'I have told you…'

But Molly wasn't listening. She knew how this was going to pan out. She'd known since the first day she'd met Natalya that the only way to get her to talk was to *make* her talk. There was a certain inevitability about what was coming next, combined with a feeling of déjà vu.

'Natalya Koval, you are under arrest on suspicion of withholding information…'

Chapter Forty

'Artem Koval,' Denning said. 'Interpol's confirmed he's on their most wanted list. Nasty bastard by the sounds of it. He's wanted for a string of offences back in Ukraine: everything from drug dealing to GBH and plenty in between. He was even rumoured to have been involved in a couple of murders. There had been some talk that he'd been a hitman for the Russian Mafia at some point in his career, but there was never any proof. It's possible he started that rumour himself to big himself up. According to Interpol, he dropped off the radar about a year ago. That's when they suspect he entered the UK. Illegally.'

McKenna was scratching her chin. 'And to listen to his sister, you'd think he was the victim of bigger, badder boys who made him do it all against his will.'

'She came good in the end,' Denning said. 'Thanks to Natalya we might be about to break up a very unpleasant people-trafficking racket.'

McKenna looked over to Denning, tapping her chin with her steepled fingers. 'Hudson and Galloway were involved in all this?'

'Yes, but in all fairness, I think they found themselves in way above their heads. Once they realised the implications, they wanted out.'

'Paid a very high price for their consciences,' McKenna added. 'And only after Koval put the screws on them.'

They'd formally questioned Natalya in Interview Room B, the one interview room that didn't smell of stale vomit and piss. They felt, under the circumstances, that was the very least they could offer her. A duty solicitor had accompanied her throughout, urging her to answer their questions as fully as possible. Molly Fisher had warned them Natalya Koval would be a tough nut to crack. She had wanted to be part of the interview team until Denning had reminded her that she was officially still on sick leave. He'd sent her home with her tail between her legs. She'd done well bringing them Natalya Koval, and possibly more besides, however, he didn't want her hanging round the MIT suite, especially when one or two people were still jumping to their own conclusions about her involvement with Simon Galloway.

Natalya Koval had been released on bail pending further questions, but she'd given them an address for her brother; Denning and McKenna just had to work out what their plan of action should be for going after him. McKenna had arranged for Natalya to be kept under observation, as much for her own safety as out of concern that she might tip off her brother.

'We need to get onto SCD9,' Denning said. 'This is their territory.' SCD9, otherwise known as Human Exploitation and Organised Crime Command, was part of the Met's Specialist Crime Directorate. Denning didn't want to tread on any toes.

McKenna agreed, before adding a note of caution. 'On the other hand, these individuals are suspects in a multiple murder inquiry. That falls within the remit of MIT.'

Denning wasn't so sure. 'People-smuggling. You'd want to keep a low profile if that's your game. Not run the risk of drawing attention to yourselves by murdering a family then setting fire to their house.'

This earned a shrug from McKenna. 'Maybe. Or maybe they didn't have much choice. If what Molly told us is accurate, then it looks like they wanted to put the frighteners on Simon Galloway. It's just possible things got a little out of hand.'

'More than a little,' Denning said. 'It's pretty extreme lengths to go to just to stop someone grassing up their operation.'

'I'm not so sure. From what I know about these gangs, they're pretty ruthless, Matt. Murdering an entire family just to prove a point is small beer to them.'

Denning knew something about gangs and how they worked. He knew it was all about profit; lives, humanity, none of it mattered at the end of the day, just as long as there was a quick buck to be made. 'OK. Let's speak to SCD9. Maybe we can work together on this, some kind of joint operation. But the Galloway family murders remain our primary concern.'

McKenna nodded. 'I'll get onto the Chief Super. Make this official. He can liaise with SCD9 and head up any joint op.'

Denning smiled. 'Changing the subject slightly, I don't suppose you've had a chance to talk to your ex about the Martin Metcalf case?'

She pulled a face. 'I didn't think you were going to let that drop.' She sighed. 'Despite my better judgement, I Skyped him during lunch.' She unsteepled her fingers and stared at a coffee stain on her desk. 'He lives in Majorca these days. Runs a beach bar with his latest wife. Ironic really as he's teetotal now. Had to give up the booze on health grounds.' Her focus suddenly shifted back to

Denning. 'None of which, I'm sure, is of any interest to you.' The steepled fingers were again tapping her chin. 'He backed up what we already knew. The Metcalfs played it by the book. As soon as they realised the lad was missing, they contacted us. Nothing suspicious. Friends and neighbours vouched for the Metcalfs being a normal, happy family. A neighbour said there was the occasional row, and someone else mentioned James Metcalf being a bit of a disciplinarian, but nothing out of the ordinary.'

'So the Metcalfs were never under suspicion? Not even initially?' He'd been looking into the background to Martin Metcalf's disappearance. The PNC presented him with the bare facts of the case. He'd even gone as far as to Google press coverage at the time. There was nothing to suggest the investigation hadn't been thorough, and no one had ever officially pointed the finger at either James or Eleanor Metcalf, but something didn't sit right. Even after almost twenty years there were no new theories or even speculation as to what had happened. He couldn't believe people just vanished without leaving some sort of footprint, however small.

'Well, the couple were questioned. Which, let's be fair, is standard procedure in those circumstances. How often has a child gone missing only for it to be discovered hiding in a wardrobe, or a relative has taken it off somewhere as part of some family feud? It was generally believed at the time – and is still the case today – that Martin Metcalf was snatched by a paedophile and murdered, then his body buried somewhere. Nothing has come up in the past two decades to suggest otherwise. However, nor has anything come up to confirm that theory. The family was never in the frame. Not seriously.'

'But…?'

She sighed. 'Apparently, and this is according to my ex – never the most reliable of individuals at the best of times – there were some questions that were never satisfactorily answered.'

'What kind of questions?'

'There was a witness, a neighbour, who came forward and claimed she saw Martin Metcalf in the street at around the time he was supposed to have gone missing. She later claimed she was mistaken. It was dark, it was raining and she couldn't be one hundred percent sure it was Martin she'd spotted: just some kid in a school uniform. There were no other sightings of him, and what CCTV there was in the vicinity failed to reveal anything useful.'

'OK, but why do I get the impression there's more?'

McKenna scratched her chin with her steepled fingers and her mouth gave a little twitch. 'Metcalf had form. Well, not form, exactly. I mean he was never arrested or charged, or anything, but just over a year before Martin Metcalf disappeared, a couple of uniforms were called to the house after a report of a possible domestic incident.'

'A domestic?'

'It turned out to be something and nothing. A neighbour reported overhearing them arguing. She thought Metcalf might have hit his wife. However, when the uniforms got there, Eleanor Metcalf insisted everything was fine and she didn't want the matter taken any further. The officers in question spoke to James Metcalf and nothing more came of it.'

'How come none of this is on the PNC?'

'Like I said, no charges were ever brought.'

'A neighbour overhears what they think is an incident of domestic abuse, the police are called and no charges are brought?' He was struggling to accept what he was hearing.

McKenna just looked at him. 'It has been known, Matt. Particularly if the individual in question is wealthy and has influence. And this was twenty years ago. Rules have been tightened since then. In most cases.'

'James Metcalf was influential?' Denning wasn't totally surprised to hear this. There was something about Metcalf's imperious attitude that suggested he was someone used to being taken seriously.

'He was a member of a government-appointed committee that advised the Police Advisory Board at the time,' McKenna said. 'He was also friends with their local MP, who just happened to be a junior minister at the Home Office. You know how it goes.'

Denning took a punt. 'But your ex wasn't entirely convinced by Metcalf?'

She fumbled awkwardly. 'Gav was an old-school copper. Not like you bright boys today with your flashy degrees and people-management skills. He worked off gut instinct half the time. He said there was something about Metcalf he didn't like. Well, no, not *didn't like...*' She searched for the right word. 'Didn't trust. There was something he didn't trust about James Metcalf.'

'Specifically...?'

'This was all twenty years ago, Matt. Ancient history.'

'Humour me.'

'It was to do with his whole attitude during the investigation. Gav said they got the distinct impression he resented them being there. It was almost as though they were made to feel like they were intruding on his privacy. He seemed more concerned with what people were saying about him rather than what had potentially happened to his son. But, and I do stress this, at that particular stage in the investigation it was still felt that Martin had simply run away from home of his own free will. There was nothing to suggest he'd been snatched, at least not initially.'

'Was there any reason to support the theory he'd run away?'

'There were rumours he was unhappy at school. A couple of school friends said he was being bullied. The teachers disputed this, however, claiming there was no evidence of bullying. The longer he stayed away the more they realised it was likely he'd been the victim of something sinister.'

'Would you say your ex was a shrewd judge of character?'

She thought about this, tapping her steepled fingers against her chin, her face tensing into a tight knot. Then she said, 'No. I'd say he's a crap judge of character. Which is why I would dismiss anything he had to say about James Metcalf with a massive pinch of salt.'

She looked at him as if to say their conversation was now at an end.

But Denning wasn't so sure. There was something about James Metcalf that he just hadn't liked. And McKenna's ex-husband had clearly felt it too. That couldn't simply be dismissed as a coincidence.

Chapter Forty-One

There was no answer at the Metcalf's front door when Denning knocked on it later that afternoon. He was aware that he was breaking his promise to McKenna, but James Metcalf was an itch that just wouldn't go away. Perhaps he was guilty of nothing more than being a bad parent. But something just didn't fit. The more he looked into James Metcalf, the more questions remained unanswered; specifically why he'd lied so readily to Denning. It was now clear that his relationship with his ex-wife was closer than he'd wanted them to think, and Denning was curious as to why.

He was about to return to his car and wait when Karen Metcalf appeared at the top of the path. If she was surprised to see Denning standing on her threshold, she didn't let on; she just tilted her head in his direction and tried her best to smile.

'Inspector,' she said drily, 'if nobody's answered the door, then my husband must still be at work. He won't be back until later.'

Denning returned the smile. 'That's OK. I can talk to you.' There was something he wanted to do; well, not so much do, as see.

She sighed and dug in her bag for her door keys, finding them with a rattle before opening the heavy, part-glazed front door. She let Denning follow her into the house and then showed him into the kitchen. It was a large, airy room at the back of the house, which opened into a vast conservatory extension. The floor was covered in expensive-looking slate tiles that ran from one room to the other, so it was hard to see where the kitchen ended and the conservatory began. There was a six-seater table in the conservatory extension, along with a profusion of potted plants. He guessed this was where the Metcalfs had breakfast. The kitchen area itself contained slick, clean units that ran along three walls. There was a solid-looking Aga where a fireplace had once been, and an island unit in the middle of the room with a couple of stools beside it. As with the clinical sitting room, the kitchen was spotless; it looked like nobody had ever eaten in it, let alone cooked in it.

Karen Metcalf took a bottle of fruit juice from the fridge and poured herself a glass. She offered Denning something to drink, but he politely declined. She perched on one of the stools beside the island unit and nodded for Denning to take the other one.

'I was curious about why your husband lied to me,' he said once they were both seated. 'He claimed he'd had no contact with Ellie since their divorce, but that's clearly not true.'

She sipped her chilled fruit juice, tracing her tongue over her lips. 'You really would need to speak to James about that.'

'Well I can certainly put the question to him when he gets back, but I thought perhaps you might have something to say on the matter. This is your husband and his ex-wife, after all. How did you feel about them meeting up?'

'I…' She started to speak but then closed her mouth. 'Yes, OK, so he did meet up with Ellie to discuss a private family matter. He told me about it and I was fine with that. Why shouldn't I be? They were married for a long time. They shared certain… They shared a life together.'

'It's not just that, though.' He watched her, trying to read her; the tight body language wasn't giving anything away. 'He gave her money. Did you know about that?'

She sipped some more of her drink. Denning was sure she'd have added gin to it given a choice. He sensed the other day that Karen Metcalf was someone who enjoyed a drop of the hard stuff to help soften life's sharper edges.

'These really are questions you should be directing to my husband, Inspector. I'm afraid I can't help you.'

'Can I guess from that, you didn't know about the money?'

But her face gave nothing away. Karen Metcalf may enjoy a drink now and again, but he reckoned she'd still make an ace poker player.

'What James does with his money is up to him. He never questions how I spend mine. Or his, come to that.' She'd tried to make a joke of it, but the humour didn't reach her eyes.

'Did you ever meet Ellie?'

'No, I've never met her. James has told me all about her, but I've never met her.' Denning noticed she wasn't being as friendly as she had been the other day. Perhaps Metcalf had warned her to treat him with caution should he ever call round again.

'Not even when they met for lunch a few weeks before the murders?'

She shook her head and stared at the glass of juice. She lifted it to her lips as if to take another sip, then changed her mind. 'I don't know why you're asking me all these questions, Inspector. James is a solicitor. Ellie was his ex-wife. She approached him about a legal matter and they met to discuss it. There's nothing strange about that.'

Denning smiled at her. He thought it might be good to try a different approach. 'Actually, maybe I will have something to drink. That looks nice.' He nodded at her half-empty glass of fruit juice.

She got off the stool, headed over to a glass-fronted cupboard, and removed a chunky glass tumbler. Then she took the bottle of juice from the fridge, poured some into the glass, and then topped up her own. She placed the other glass of juice on the granite-topped surface of the island unit in front of Denning.

He thanked her, and then said: 'I meant it the other day, when I apologised to James for the way the invest-igation into Martin's disappearance was handled. Don't misunderstand me, I'm not admitting any kind of liability on behalf of the Met. It was twenty years ago now, and I imagine the majority of the detectives who handled the case will have retired by now.' He thought about McKenna's ex, living it up in Spain with a younger wife. Would such opportunities or pensions exist for him when he retired, he wondered? 'I have a great deal of sympathy for what James and Ellie went through at the time. I only wish things had turned out differently.'

'That's very kind of you,' she said. She smiled, perhaps sensing his sincerity. 'James never talks about Martin, but I know he took it very hard. He became quite ill after-wards. Well, after Ellie left him.' She lowered her voice and looked around the sparkling kitchen in case there was someone hiding in a corner ready to eavesdrop. 'James had a breakdown after he and Ellie split. It was only really after he met me that he began to get his life back together. His work were very understanding: they let him take a leave of absence until he was better. He wasn't a partner then though, so it was very good of them.'

'Things must have been difficult between James and Ellie after Martin disappeared. It's understandable the marriage ended. I don't think there are many relationships that could have gone through what they went through and survived.'

'It was worse for Ellie, I suppose, with her being a mother.' She looked at Denning. 'I'm not a mother, so I can only imagine what it must be like. To not know where your child is. It would haunt you every day for the rest of your life.'

'I can understand.' He drank some of the fruit drink. It was orange and mango and something else, possibly lime. 'There must have been arguments.'

She looked at him again, as though she was unsure where he was heading with his questions. 'I suppose there must have been. Like I told you, James has never really spoken about it.'

'Karen, I have to ask you: do you think James was ever violent towards Ellie?'

'Of course not! James isn't violent. All I meant was that things were likely to have been fraught between them. It would have been a challenging time for any couple.'

It was clear to Denning that she was uncomfortable talking about this; sharing family business with a stranger, and discussing matters that were over and done with. He decided to cut to the chase. 'Could I ask you something? I realise it's a bit unorthodox, but could I have a look in Martin's old room?'

She seemed taken aback by the unusual request. 'Why? He's not been hiding up there for the past two decades, if that's what you think.'

'Could I just have a quick look, please?'

He had no right to ask and she would have been within her rights to tell him to piss off, or to come back with a warrant, not that he would have a hope in hell of getting one. However, after a moment, she reluctantly nodded. She gave him directions: Martin's room was the first door on the left at the top of the stairs, opposite the bathroom.

Denning climbed the stairs, still not sure what he was looking for, or even what he expected to see. At the top of the stairs, he turned to his left, and opened the door to the room Karen said had belonged to Martin. His first thought was that he'd misheard her directions and had got the wrong room. It was laid out exactly like a spare bedroom: a double bed, a large oak-style wardrobe and a couple of chests of drawers. There were bland prints of nothing special on the walls, and a pair of floor-length linen drapes at the window. There was no sign that a child had ever lived in the room. He opened another couple of doors, just in case he had gone into the wrong room. A master bedroom and a small study at the front of the house. All pristine and clinical like the kitchen and the sitting room downstairs.

Then he realised what it was that had first provoked a strange feeling within him: the house felt cold. Tidy and clean, but not a home where a child had once lived. It was as though Martin Metcalf had been expunged from their lives; his memory obliterated, his very essence erased. It would explain the lack of photos of him in the sitting room, and the general absence of anything that even hinted at a child's presence about the house. He thought about Jake; how his personality had already taken over his and Sarah's flat in a short space of time, and would linger on long after he'd gone back to stay with Claire.

But there was no given rule as to how a family should behave when a child had gone missing. Perhaps this was how James Metcalf coped with the fact that his son had vanished and his wife had left him. If the pain was too great to bear, then maybe it was easier to pretend he'd never existed.

But it felt wrong.

To have no reference, nothing tangible or real that said Martin Metcalf had been part of this household didn't feel right. In fact, it felt very, very wrong.

He was roused from his thoughts by the sound of James Metcalf arriving back from work. He heard him in the hallway announcing to Karen that he was home, followed by her saying she was in the kitchen. This was Denning's cue to head back downstairs.

Karen Metcalf was in the process of explaining to her husband that Denning had called round to ask some more questions, when Metcalf suddenly spun round to see Denning standing in the kitchen doorway.

'What the hell do you think you're doing?' he shouted. 'It's not enough for you to harass me at work. I now find you hassling my wife in my own home, again. If this is still to do with my ex-wife's murder, we've told you everything we know, which is very little.'

Karen Metcalf opened her mouth to speak, but Denning jumped in before she had a chance to explain. 'I wanted to speak to you, Mr Metcalf. Maybe we could go into the sitting room and talk in there.'

Metcalf was shooting icy daggers in Denning's direction and kneading his hands together in agitation. 'What were you doing upstairs?'

'What really happened to Martin, Mr Metcalf? Did he run away, or was it something else?'

'I asked you what you were doing upstairs?'

Denning could sense Karen Metcalf was starting to feel uncomfortable with the increasing levels of animosity emanating from her husband.

'I wanted to see Martin's room, Mr Metcalf. You remember: Martin, your son? Because looking around me, it looks like you've forgotten you ever had a son.'

There was a sudden chill in the already frigid house. 'Get out of my house now, Denning. I'm not going to ask you again.'

Denning turned to leave. 'Just one last question, Mr Metcalf. Why exactly did Ellie leave you? Was it because you were violent to her?' He was speaking to Metcalf but looking at Karen, trying to gauge her reaction, but she just drank her glass of fruit juice as though she were somewhere else entirely.

Metcalf's face had now turned puce. Denning couldn't help thinking that if Metcalf had been a cartoon character, there would have been steam coming out of his ears at this point. 'Goodbye, Mr Denning. And you can look forward to enjoying a heavy conversation with your chief superintendent first thing tomorrow morning.'

Chapter Forty-Two

Molly was tired. She had a throb in her temple that was usually the precursor to a headache. She just wanted to go home and open a nice bottle of shiraz. Instead, she found herself back at the homeless hostel in Paddington. Ben was sitting opposite her in the communal living room. He was trying to avoid eye contact.

'Ben, Colin Pyke has been arrested. He's admitted the assault on Thomas Ferrier. He's also admitted to his involvement in a number of cases of fraud by deception, including credit card cloning.' She waited for her words to sink in. 'He hasn't mentioned your name. So far.'

Her brother looked over at her. He had the same sad, puppy-dog expression in his eyes that she remembered from when they were children. Anytime he'd been chastised, or had been caught doing something he knew he shouldn't, he would adopt that look. It was his way of managing to look guilty and yet innocent at the same time.

'So I'm in the clear?'

'I wouldn't quite put it like that. But if he doesn't say anything, and there's no evidence to link you to any of this, then there's a strong chance you'll get away with it. This time, Ben. You might not be so lucky if you fuck up again.'

If she was fair, then she was bailing herself out as much as she was her little brother. If she totted it all up, then she probably had more to lose than he had, and unlike him, she actually gave a shit about her future.

'What do I do now?' he asked, still looking like a little lost puppy.

'That's up to you. But if it were me, I'd try and sort myself out before it's too late.'

Ben finally met her gaze. 'I suppose I should say thanks. I'm still not sure what for, though.'

She got to her feet. 'If you don't know, then there's not much point in saying it, is there, Ben?' She turned to leave, still unsure as to whether she was doing the right thing. Ben was her brother: flesh and blood; a part of her. But in the end, it was his life and his choices, and all she could do was watch from the sidelines and try and catch him when he fell.

—

Denning had collected Jake from the childminder's. He'd found someone who came with impeccable references and didn't cost the earth. And she was located roughly halfway between the flat and the station in Stoke Newington.

Jake was unusually quiet and sullen on the journey back to the flat. Denning had asked him if he was alright and Jake had merely nodded. The childminder had insisted everything had been fine and Jake was making friends. Denning hadn't been convinced of this. Jake never really made friends in a conventional sense. It took time for him to break down barriers, and to let down his own carefully constructed defences.

Denning let the silence grow between them. Jake would talk when he was ready. There was never any point in trying to make him do something he didn't want to. That would only lead to tears and further silence, only heavier and more immutable.

The silence continued in the lift up to the flat. As soon as the front door was unlocked and opened, Jake ran straight into his room and switched on his telly.

'You can have an hour on your game, then it's dinner time,' Denning said through the bedroom door. There was no response, but he knew Jake would surface when he was hungry.

Denning closed Jake's bedroom door and headed upstairs to his and Sarah's bedroom on the mezzanine level and changed out of his work suit. He wanted to go for a run; use exercise as a catharsis for dealing with the slings and arrows of a stressful day, but he could hardly leave Jake home alone.

As he hung his suit on a coathanger and placed it in the wardrobe, he thought about James Metcalf and his threat to report him to the Chief Super. Any official reprimand would come courtesy of McKenna, as she was technically his line manager, or the closest thing he had to one. She would roll her eyes and shout, but little else would come of it. At least that's what he hoped. It all depended just how cosy Metcalf was with the Chief Super. Or anyone else in the Met for that matter.

He slipped on a pair of jeans, not the expensive pair Sarah had bought him last Christmas, but an old, slightly faded pair that he wore to slob around the flat when there was no one else around. Technically, he had been out of order going round to the Metcalf house without good reason, or, indeed, a warrant. Metcalf, being a solicitor, would have been fully aware of any legal shortcomings on Denning's part. There was nothing to suggest Metcalf had been in any way involved with his son's disappearance, and certainly nothing to suggest he had any potential connection to his ex-wife's murder. But there were too many unanswered questions hanging in the air. The fact McKenna's ex had had a similar hunch about Metcalf reinforced his concerns about the solicitor. Metcalf was hiding something, he just wasn't sure if it was in any way relevant.

Denning pulled on a long-sleeved t-shirt and a pair of trainers and headed back down to the main part of the flat. Jake would be happy with something simple for dinner: pizza, probably. He found one in the freezer and preheated the oven to the correct temperature.

He headed back into the living room and flicked on the telly, hoping to catch the early evening news. He could hear Jake playing in his room, the noise of exploding spaceships and exterminated aliens loud enough to pass through a closed door.

He was pleased to know that Jake had been OK at the childminder's, but he reminded himself that tomorrow would be a different day. The two things Jake needed most to ensure he could function were stability and security, and they were the two things that were lacking in his life right now. He thought about phoning Claire again, even though there would be no point. She would let him know when she was ready to return. *If* she was going to return. During their last serious phone conversation, she had hinted that she might move to Devon permanently to be closer to her mum. It made sense, she'd argued. Although her mum was better, and still young enough to make a full recovery according to the doctors, there was her long-term prognosis to think about. She was still in her sixties, but another ten years and health issues would become a regular concern. Claire was an only child; there was no one else to share the responsibility. And Devon, she'd argued, would offer a much better quality of life than London ever could. She would take Jake, naturally; she could provide the security and stability he had proved he couldn't. That would mean he would see his son less and less. And what if she met someone else? Her last relationship had been a disaster, but there was always the chance she would date someone who turned out not to be a serial killer, and they would settle down. Jake would have someone else to call Daddy, and Denning would become someone he visited from time to time, until eventually he didn't, and then he'd be just a memory.

He thought about how the custody battle for Caleb Galloway had seen the child being fought over as though he were a prize calf in a cattle show. Jake deserved better. But Denning was starting to ask himself whether he was the best person to provide it.

–

Jon wasn't at home when Molly returned later that evening.

There was no note, no message scribbled on a Post-it Note and left on the fridge door, just an eerie quiet about the place. But she was secretly quite glad. It would give her space and time to do some thinking. She sat down at the kitchen table, having made herself a mug of tea. She was awash with tea today. She'd probably be up half the night running to the loo.

She'd wanted to be part of the team that interviewed Natalya. After all, she was the one who'd brought Natalya in. Denning had texted to say that Natalya had talked: they now knew where her brother was staying and were planning to raid his address the following morning. It was some consolation. She was relieved that the case was drawing to a close. If they could find enough evidence to pin the Galloway family murders on Artem Koval and his gang, then that would be some kind of closure for Simon. She'd tried phoning him, but there was no answer from his phone, and no voicemail to leave a message. She hoped that meant he was lying low until Koval was under arrest and his gang was off the streets, but she had never really managed to figure Simon out. He remained something of an enigma.

Then there was Ben.

She knew there was no point worrying about Ben. He had proved to her over and over that he would do whatever he thought was right rather than what she or anyone else advised. And in so many ways she admired him for that. He was an independent spirit, and so had she been, once upon a time. She'd sent him a final text message, wishing him well, and asking him to get in touch if he needed anything, but otherwise he was on his own as far as she was concerned. She wasn't going to waste any more time running round after him.

From now on, she told herself, she should focus on her relationship with Jon. Ben was an adult, she had to keep reminding herself, and as such, would be capable of fending for himself in the big bad world.

She heard the front door click open and watched as Jon arrived carrying a couple of bags of shopping. He smiled when he saw her. 'Everything all right?'

She nodded and returned the smile.

Jon pulled a bottle of Prosecco from one of the bags. 'I thought we could celebrate. I got that teaching job. It's only sixteen hours a week and the money really is crap, but, who knows, it might lead to better things.'

'It's been a good day all round for results,' she said.

Chapter Forty-Three

They were outside a three-story terraced house in Walthamstow that looked like it hadn't seen a lick of paint this side of the millennium. Denning and McKenna, dressed in flak jackets, were waiting in the back of a police van, trying hard to look like they didn't feel slightly out of place. They had insisted on joining the raid, as this was technically their shout. Sergeant Rob Nicholls from SCD9's Trafficking and Prostitution Unit, had disagreed, insisting they would simply be getting in the way of a carefully planned operation that relied on people who knew what they were doing. SCD9 were not used to having their authority questioned, but Nicholls had been overruled by both their own Chief Superintendent and the Met's Deputy Commissioner. People trafficking was a serious offence, they'd agreed, but a multiple murder investigation took priority.

They were being assisted by armed officers from Specialist Firearms Command, otherwise known as SCO19, just in case there were any weapons in the property that could potentially be deployed during the raid.

According to land registry, the house was owned by an Italian couple, but none of the neighbours who'd been spoken to had ever seen them there. Council tax records said the property was rented by a Jamal Kumar, but despite the recent change in the law, which had tightened the rules around property letting, they suspected this was a false name.

Sergeant Nicholls had ordered Denning and McKenna to stay in the van whilst his team conducted the actual raid. From the intelligence they had managed to gather about the property, they knew that at least seven adults lived at the address, possibly more. There was no indication as to how many, if any, children were inside the property, but the Child Protection Unit had been notified as a precaution. Neighbours had reported seeing different people coming and going at different times of the day and night, but had thought nothing of it. This was London; people saw no reason to ask too many questions of their neighbours.

In the east, a horizontal band of amber slowly filtered through the cloud as the chirruping of the dawn chorus made its presence heard. It was early. So early, Denning had had to pay the childminder twice her usual rate before she would even consider taking Jake at that time of the day. He'd still been half-asleep when Denning had dropped him off at some ungodly hour.

The air in the van was growing tighter and space was limited. They were sitting on a cold, hard bench in the back, where the smell of sweat and adrenalin threatened to over-power them. They were waiting for the say-so from Nicholls to go in.

Nicholls was chatting on his radio; liaising with another section of his team waiting in a van parked in a nearby side street. A couple of officers had already conducted a recce of the house, and confirmed there were at least three adult males present in the property and a couple of women. They couldn't tell if anyone was armed, but Nicholls had decided they'd hung around for long enough. 'Another minute, and then we're going in,' he muttered into the radio.

Denning looked at McKenna. She was chewing her thumbnail. He wondered if she was nervous, but suspected she was probably just keen to get on with it. The sooner Artem Koval was in custody, the sooner they could start questioning him about his possible involvement in the murders of Dan Hudson and the Galloway family. He glanced at his watch, wondering why a minute suddenly seemed like a long time.

He looked out of the grubby window of the van and spotted movement at the house: a thick net curtain twitched at a downstairs window and a dark figure peered out for a brief second. That was enough for Nicholls who had also noticed it. He barked an order into the radio for his team to go in.

Everything then happened at great speed.

Denning and McKenna watched in silence as a dozen officers jumped out of the van and charged up to the front door of the terraced house: a rippling tide of black gilets and blue helmets. The officer at the front of the phalanx was carrying an enforcer, known colloquially as the 'big red key': a hand–held tubular steel battering ram that quickly reduced the front door to a curtain of splintered wood.

Denning realised he was holding his breath; McKenna was staring directly ahead, eyes darting from the officers to the front of the house, scanning the scene and taking everything in. She'd told him earlier that she'd been on similar raids before, but not for a long time. They rarely fucked up, she'd reassured him, but there was always a danger something could go wrong.

The armed officers from SCO19 piled into the house first, followed by Nicholls's team, bellowing instructions at the confused inhabitants. After a few minutes, a group of terrified-looking men and women, most of whom were still in their night clothes, were led out of the building. Mercifully, Denning couldn't see any children amongst the melee.

Denning and McKenna were out of the van now, hurrying over to Nicholls, who was talking to one of the armed officers from SCO19. As soon as Denning and McKenna were within earshot, Nicholls turned to speak to them. 'We found nine young women and three young men living in the house. All of them appear to be either Eastern European or Russian natives; some speak little or no English. But we suspect there are more staying there, or have been housed there at some point before being dispersed around the country. They'll be taken to a place of safety in the short term. After that, they're at the mercy of the Home Office.' He glanced over his shoulder at the house they'd just raided. 'It was disgusting in there. I wouldn't keep a dog in those conditions.'

'We need to speak to Artem Koval,' McKenna said. 'Have you identified which one he is?'

'Probably still inside,' one of the armed officers said.

'Is it safe to go in?' McKenna asked.

The officer gave a sharp nod. 'They're unarmed, so it should be safe.'

Denning and McKenna headed into the building. The main living room at the front of the house contained a couple of stained mattresses and a battered sofa. The scrappy detritus of sandwich containers and empty cartons of shop's own brand orange juice littered the bare floor. The house stank of piss.

There were still some people being led outside by specialist officers: they looked frightened, as though they had no idea what was going on. Denning felt for them. Promised a new life away from the poverty they'd known back home, they'd been exploited and manipulated in return for a quick profit. He caught the look on one young woman's face: she must have been in her late teens. Her face pleaded with Denning, but there was little he could do; her fate would be in the hands of the Home Office.

'If Koval's the ringleader of a people smuggling racket, why's he living in a shit hole like this?' Denning asked.

McKenna shrugged. 'I suspect in reality he's no more than a bit part player. More than likely his job is to keep an eye on this lot. Make sure they don't leg it and alert the authorities. But I'm willing to bet he knows who the big boys are.'

They found Nicholls in a dirty room at the back of the house.

'Which one's Koval?' McKenna barked.

Nicholls gestured towards one of the four men sitting with their hands on their heads looking both defiant and nervous, their eyes darting from McKenna to Denning and then back to Nicholls. Koval looked like he was the eldest of the men: tall, broadly built and with a manner about him that said he was just itching to break the neck of anyone who looked at him the wrong way.

'We need him to answer some questions about a recent murder and attempted murder of a police officer,' McKenna said. 'The others are all yours.'

Nicholls nodded. 'Fair enough. I've been told your mob get to play with him first. We'll take over as soon as you've finished with him.'

'As soon as he's told us what we want to hear,' McKenna growled, 'he's yours to do with as you please.'

–

So far Natalya's brother was refusing to speak. At first he claimed he couldn't understand English and considerable time was wasted trying to track down an interpreter. Then he revealed he could speak English; he just wasn't going to. At least, he wasn't saying anything that was of much use.

He'd been appointed a duty solicitor who tried his best to understand what was happening, but his heart didn't seem to be in it.

Koval was sitting opposite Denning and McKenna in Interview Room A, seemingly oblivious to the stench of spilled bodily fluids, and staring a hard stare at both detectives. McKenna stared back at him, offering the same gimlet glare that could probably bore a hole in solid metal if she let it. If this was going to be a staring contest to judge who was the toughest bastard in the room, Denning would put money on Koval blinking first.

Denning had adopted the role of good cop by at least trying to toss him a lifeline, which he had so far refused to grab.

'We've spoken to your sister, Artem, and Natalya has told us all about the girls you provide and how they arrive in the country. Now, that's not our concern. Other police officers will speak to you about that in due course. We need to know about Simon Galloway and what happened to his parents at number forty-two Gibney Road in the early hours of last Tuesday morning. We think you can help us with that.'

Koval just stared back at them, dark eyes locked on McKenna, clearly refusing to allow himself to be intimidated by a woman. He was a big man, more than filling the space around him, forcing his slender solicitor to sit uncomfortably close to the edge of the table. Denning reckoned Koval was no stranger to a gym; biceps straining to stay contained within his grubby t-shirt; his shaven head looking like a bearded bowling ball that had been welded straight onto his shoulders. 'I don't know anything about no women, or any murders. Natalya has a strong imagination.' He muttered something in his native Ukrainian and kept his eyes fixed on McKenna.

McKenna continued to stare at him, until she suddenly banged the metal table with the palm of her hand causing some papers to jump and nearly fall on the floor, and signalling that the staring competition was now at an end. Denning had felt his shoulder give an involuntary shudder, while the duty solicitor, who had just taken a sip of tea from a paper cup, managed to spill some of the tea down the front of his shirt. He shot McKenna a filthy look which she failed to register.

'Don't waste our time, Artem. We know what that house was used for, and we know you're up to your thick little neck in it. What we want to know is who murdered the Galloway family. And then there's the matter of nearly killing Simon Galloway and one of my officers in Berkshire last Saturday. You bear an uncanny resemblance to one of the two men in the CCTV footage taken at the Riverview Inn on Saturday, and seen getting into the vehicle that was used to drive them off the road.'

Koval flinched when McKenna mentioned this fact, and stole a brief look in his solicitor's direction. He then fixed McKenna with another steely glare. 'No comment.'

After an hour and a half of game-playing, Denning and McKenna took a break. They'd just stepped into the corridor outside the interview room when Neeraj came over to them. He was clearly unsure which senior officer he should be addressing, so his eyes flicked from one to the other in quick succession.

'SCD9 are chomping at the bit to speak to him once we're done,' he said. 'Apparently the others have named Koval as the ringleader.'

McKenna made a noise like a disdainful snort. 'That doesn't surprise me. But the fucker's going nowhere until he's confessed to the Galloway murders and attempted murder of Molly and Simon Galloway. We can apply to hold him for another twenty-four hours if need be.'

Denning wasn't so sure. 'He doesn't look like he's about to talk any time soon. We don't have much to threaten him with. Natalya's confession connects him directly to the people-smuggling, and the CCTV from Maidenhead, combined with any ID Molly Fisher gives us, will tie him to the incident on Saturday. But let's be honest here, there's bugger all to connect him to the Galloway murders. What we have is, at best, circumstantial.' He looked at McKenna. 'I can't see the CPS buying this. Not unless he confesses, which at the moment is looking about as likely as him singing an aria from *La Bohème*.'

'He's an obvious choice for the murders. He's got a motive and he's clearly not encumbered with a conscience.'

'Agreed. But that doesn't mean he did it.'

Neeraj was looking at them, boredom beginning to creep onto his face. 'So what do I tell the bloke from SCD9?'

McKenna looked at her watch then looked at Denning. 'Give us another half hour, Deep. Then we throw him to the wolves at SCD9 and hope they hang him up by the bollocks and beat him with a shitty stick.'

Chapter Forty-Four

They had almost been up to the wire with Koval, but in the end he'd confessed. Not to the Galloway murders – his denials on that score had grown ever more insistent as the interview progressed – but he admitted being in the 4x4 that had driven Simon Galloway and Molly off the road. He said they had only intended to scare him; there had been no intention to kill anyone, and he was very sorry that people had been hurt. Simon Galloway. Denning had noticed McKenna's eyes jumping towards the clock on the wall from time to time, both aware that Koval's presence was required elsewhere, and SCD9's patience would only stretch so far...

It gave them some satisfaction charging Koval with the attempted murders of Simon Galloway and Molly, though it was likely they would have to eventually settle for a lesser charge of dangerous driving. But there was no way he could ever hope to dodge what SCD9 were about to throw at him.

'We're handing him over to SCD9,' McKenna said. 'They'll do him for trafficking, drug dealing, anything else they can throw at him and make stick,' McKenna said. 'But we can't pin the Galloway family murders on him.' Koval was already being transported to a police station in west London, ready for his next round of interrogation.

'We're back at square one,' Denning said.

'You seemed convinced he didn't kill the Galloways,' McKenna said. 'How can you be certain?'

'I can't be certain, but whoever did it was clever, and that rules out Artem Koval. The man's little more than a hired thug. I don't think he's got the bottle for anything bigger.'

'I hope you're right, Matt. Because I wouldn't want to think we've just let the person responsible walk out of this nick.'

'We've taken a dangerous psychopath off the streets, and freed a bunch of women from a life of Christ alone knows what. That's a result.' It would have been so easy, so *convenient* to blame Natalya's brother for the Galloway family's murder, but it would have been wrong. 'We're going to have to look elsewhere for our killer.'

'Where do you suggest?'

'Let's go back to Gibney Road, speak to the neighbours again. There has to be something we've missed.'

'We've been over everything: witness statements; whatever CCTV we could get hold of. Nothing's come up.' McKenna was tugging at her hair again. 'If something's been missed then I think our chances of finding it now aren't looking great.'

'Then we keep looking until we find it,' Denning said, though he was starting to wonder if whoever had killed the Galloways had covered their tracks so well there was nothing left to find. 'Like I said at the start of this investigation, I believe the answer lies close to home. It's got something to do with the Galloways themselves.' But it was more than that. He couldn't explain it because the answer wasn't obvious as yet, or he was just too muddle-headed right now to spot it, but he was sure the whole thing was somehow connected to Martin Metcalf's disappearance.

Chapter Forty-Five

Molly pored over the PNC. James Metcalf's name hadn't appeared once. She wasn't even sure what she was trying to find. Denning had asked her to look into James Metcalf, and find anything that might have been overlooked during the investigation into Martin Metcalf's disappearance. Anything that was suspicious, or simply didn't fit, he wanted it flagged up.

Artem Koval was being questioned downstairs, and the word in the MIT suite was that they had their man. Denning said he wanted a few straggly loose ends tidied up before they officially closed the case. Part of her was grumbling about why she'd been asked to look into a cold case, especially as it didn't look like any new evidence had come to light, and any connection with the Galloway case was at best tenuous. But Denning had told her she was the best person for the job, having already proved her skills at searching through old cases when she'd found a link between a decade-old murder investigation and a more recent killing spree earlier in the year. Molly was sure there was a compliment buried in there somewhere.

Abandoning the PNC, she turned instead to the original case files for the investigation into Martin Metcalf's disappearance. They'd been sent over from Wandsworth CID who had inherited the case at some point in the past two decades for reasons that had never been made clear. The case was still active, so the files were 'on loan' and would have to be returned eventually.

There were pages of transcripts of interviews, witness statements and photographs of Martin Metcalf, his bedroom and his journey to and from school. But there was nothing that told her much about Martin Metcalf himself. It seemed he was a bit of a loner: an only child with few school friends, he'd kept himself very much to himself. So much so, that one or two of the investigating officers had wondered if he'd led a double life. All of this had been looked into, but there had been nothing to suggest he was anything other than a twelve-year-old schoolboy who liked books and dogs and playing computer games in the privacy of his own bedroom. This was in the days before the explosion in social media that dominated the lives of teenagers – and quite a few adults – today. The internet was still something of a novelty and mobile phones couldn't offer much beyond phoning or texting. She wondered for a moment at just how so much had changed so quickly and how technology, in it all its deviant forms, had allowed itself to become so ingrained in the lives of teenagers. In her youth, an iPod was a novelty: a mobile phone a luxury you didn't take for granted. These days teenagers couldn't function without instant access to everything and each other; every aspect of their lives lived out for others to see and comment on.

But none of this helped with Martin Metcalf. She reckoned even if Instagram and Snapchat had existed twenty years ago, he would probably have let most of it pass him by.

There were plenty of statements from what few friends he had, but no one had reported anything strange in the days leading up to his disappearance. Additionally, there had been no reports of any strangers hanging around either the school, or the immediate vicinity.

She looked at the photographs, all carefully preserved in a series of polythene pockets. There was nothing out of the ordinary about his bedroom, except she was struck by how tidy it was. A single bed in one corner, with a pale blue and grey duvet. A desk beside the bed with a home computer on it. A shelving unit laden with books and a miniature globe of the world. No toys, but weren't twelve-year-old boys past the toy stage by then? There were no posters of footballers or pop stars on the wall, or anything that hinted the room was occupied by someone who was about to start his hormone-crazy teenage years. She thought about what Ben's room had been like at that age and there was no comparison. Ben liked mess and clutter: clothes lying on the floor; CDs and DVDs scattered everywhere, minus their covers, and usually a plate of half-eaten food next to or under his bed. Their mum used to complain until eventually she realised there was no point in wasting her breath. But at least the room told you something about the person who lived in it. Martin Metcalf's room was so anonymous it could have belonged to anyone.

And then there were the photographs of Martin Metcalf himself. There were four: three of them taken at around the time he'd gone missing – including a school photo that had been used in the Missing posters and TV appeals – and a CGI mock-up of how he might have looked at the ten-year anniversary stage.

Like the room he slept in, Martin Metcalf looked unre-markable: short for his age and slight, he looked younger than his twelve years. A pale, freckled face was framed by a pair of metal-framed glasses. His light brown hair had been mussed with a bit of gel; the only feature about his appearance that even hinted at a note of individuality. The school uniform he was wearing in the 'official' photograph consisted of a smart blue blazer and a red pullover underneath. Every bit of Martin Metcalf looked like it had been ironed to perfection. He looked like the kind of child whose mother had lavished a lot of love and attention on him, perhaps almost suffocatingly so. Had Eleanor Metcalf then transferred all that love onto Simon and Amber when she'd become Ellie Galloway, and then lavished what was left on little Caleb when he'd finally come into her life?

She rubbed a hand over her forehead, unconsciously touching the bruise that reminded her of the recent car crash. Yet again, she wondered about Simon and where he was. She thought it would be ironic if he'd disappeared too; the children in Ellie Galloway's life either dead, or vanished without a trace. But she knew that at some point Simon would reappear. Once word got out that Natalya's brother was locked up, likely for a long time, he would feel safe to emerge from hiding.

Unlike Martin Metcalf. His disappearance had been a mystery, and it wasn't one she thought she was going to solve by poring over dusty paperwork from two decades ago.

She slid the photos back into their cellophane pockets and started leafing through the witness statements. One in particular jumped out at her: the only known sighting of Martin the afternoon he vanished. An elderly neighbour, a Mrs Joyce Levisham, had stated she thought she'd seen the boy walking along the road at around four forty p.m. the day he went missing. She had been sure he was heading in the direction of home. But it had been dark, her eyesight wasn't as good as it had once been and she'd only glanced out of her living room window for the briefest of seconds to see if it was raining. But she was sure it was him. However, when she'd later been asked to confirm this, she'd changed her mind, saying she couldn't have been certain it was Martin as it was so dark, and perhaps she'd been thinking of the previous day. Her statement was vague and slightly disjointed. Clearly she was an unreliable witness but that shouldn't have automatically discounted what she'd said. Had someone persuaded her to change her mind about what she thought she'd seen that evening?

She looked up from her desk to see Denning returning to the MIT suite. He'd been downstairs interviewing Natalya's brother but judging by the look on his face, he hadn't got the outcome he'd been hoping for.

'Did he confess?' she asked, half joking.

Denning shook his head. 'He admitted driving you and Simon Galloway off the road on Saturday, so we'll get him for that. But he's denying having anything to do with the Galloway murders.'

'You've let him go?'

'Only as far as Paddington Green and the electrodes and shackles of SCD9. They'll get him for the trafficking, but that doesn't help us.'

'Shit.'

'It's not the result we were after.' He looked annoyed rather than deflated, which suggested to Molly he had a Plan B up his sleeve.

'What does Betty Taggart say about it?'

'She's in a meeting with the Chief Super as we speak, trying to underplay the whole scenario with Koval. The main ace up her sleeve is the fact that he'll go down for something, so it's not been a waste of time. Plus there's the Brownie points from SCD9.'

'So where do we go from here?' she asked.

'I'm going to call a briefing this afternoon. Go over everything again. Let's try and find a motive and then hopefully that will point us in the direction of possible suspects.' He smiled at her. 'In the meantime, have you managed to find Martin Metcalf yet?'

She pulled a face at him. 'Despite the disappointing outcome there too, the investigation was pretty thorough. There are dozens of witness statements that all say there was nothing to suggest he ran away from home.' She gestured at the stack of paperwork on her desk. 'Despite the lack of evidence, it looks like he was snatched off the street somewhere between school and home.'

'Nothing that would make you question that?'

She thought about this. She was reluctant to stick her neck out when there was very little to suggest there was anything *to* question. Even so, she felt she had to say something to justify the time she'd spent wading through the endless paperwork. She told him about the elderly neighbour and how it was strange that she'd retracted her statement.

'But,' she added, 'it's possible she was spoken to a second time by detectives rather than uniform, once it had been established his disappearance was potentially sinister. Maybe she didn't feel confident enough to stick by her original statement. If Martin had been snatched, then her first witness statement would contradict that.'

'You think, maybe, one of the investigating officers put pressure on her?'

'There's nothing to say that was the case. In all likelihood, she probably just wasn't sure she had actually seen the boy on the day in question.'

'Maybe…'

Denning had the pensive look he always adopted when he was clearly mulling something over in his head. She noticed the vein on his right temple had started to throb, which meant he was slightly agitated. 'It might be worth speaking to her again,' he said.

She glanced back at the original statement. 'Says here she was in her eighties at the time, so probably not with us anymore.'

'OK.' The vein continued to pulse. 'What about the other neighbours? The ones who lived next door to the Metcalfs. Are they still around?'

She hurriedly shuffled through the papers. 'A Mr and Mrs Welland lived next door to them twenty years ago. I've got no idea if they're still there.'

'Could you find out for me?'

'I suppose… why?'

But Denning was already heading back to his desk without offering her an answer. Packing the paperwork back into its various box files, she prepared to do a Google search on Richard and Annabelle Welland, convinced that Denning might be on the point of completely losing the plot.

Chapter Forty-Six

The Wellands were no longer living in the same street as the Metcalfs, but they had been easy enough to trace. Denning had dispatched Molly with instructions to find out everything she could about an incident they'd reported to the local police about a year before Martin Metcalf's disappearance. For reasons he hadn't explained, there was no record of the incident on the PNC.

Molly knocked on their door and explained who she was. Mr Welland showed her into the living room, where Mrs Welland was sitting in a comfy armchair positioned towards an uninterrupted view of the river. Molly tried not to think about Maidenhead and her lunch date with Simon Metcalf.

'We lived next door to the Metcalfs for nearly twenty years,' Mrs Welland told Molly over a cup of tea and a slice of homemade banana cake. 'And we were friends for most of them.'

The Wellands were retired, but looked like they were still relatively active. Molly placed their ages at either late sixties or very early seventies. They were sitting in the living room of their pleasant flat overlooking the Thames in Twickenham, though Mr Welland had given their address as St Margarets, which sounded slightly grander. There had been a set of golf clubs in the hallway when she arrived, and she wondered which of the Wellands played. Possibly both.

'After our children left home,' Mrs Welland continued, 'we thought it made sense to move somewhere smaller.' Molly looked around the decent-sized living room. There was a nice balcony beyond the sliding doors on which sat a table and chairs and a small gas-powered barbeque. Not somewhere that Molly would ever have described as small, but she supposed it depended on what you were used to. 'I kept in touch with Eleanor for a while, but we lost touch eventually. Apart from the odd Christmas card.' She looked at Molly. 'I saw on the news what happened, though I must admit, it took me a moment or two to recognise her as it had been a few years. And, of course, she was no longer called Eleanor Metcalf.'

Molly nodded her agreement and ate some more cake. 'I'm actually here about something else,' she said. 'Back in the late 1990s, you contacted the police about a domestic disturbance at the Metcalfs' property. Do you remember the details?'

The Wellands exchanged looks with one another. After a moment, Mr Welland answered. 'Well, yes. Please don't think we were the kind of neighbours who ran to the police every time there was a problem in the street. Naturally, when you live next door to someone – even if your house is detached – you tend to overhear things that I'm sure they would rather were kept private.'

'It's worse here,' Mrs Welland interrupted. 'The walls are paper thin.' She nodded at Molly as she spoke, as though to emphasize her point.

'It was a summer's evening,' Mr Welland continued, as though his wife hadn't spoken. 'We were working in the garden. They had their patio doors open.'

'This was before they built that huge extension on the back of their kitchen,' Mrs Welland helpfully added, though Molly had never seen the house, except for random photographs of one of the bedrooms. She smiled at Mr Welland, urging him to continue. 'We overheard an argument between James and Eleanor. It was quite heated. I did wonder if I should pop round and check that everything was OK. We often used to hear arguments coming from next door. I mean nothing serious, just the usual bickering that families do. I mean all families argue and what goes on behind closed doors is private.' He paused and looked at his feet before continuing. 'But this was more than just bickering.'

Whilst he was thinking about how best to phrase what had happened, his wife jumped in again. 'Richard said he thought James had hit Eleanor. There was a smash, a terrible smash; it sounded like crockery breaking or glass being smashed, then what I thought was crying.'

'Eleanor?' asked Molly.

'Well it wasn't James,' Mrs Welland retorted.

'But could it have been Martin?' Molly asked.

The Wellands looked at each other again. 'Well, I suppose it could have been,' Richard Welland replied.

'Did you go round?'

'We thought carefully about whether we should go round,' Welland said. 'But when Anna said we were good friends with James and Eleanor, it would probably have been more accurate to say that Anna and Eleanor were friends. James and I tolerated one another for the sake of good neighbourly relations, but, truth be told, we didn't really get on.'

'There had been a couple of incidents over the years,' Annabelle Welland said, with a slight shake of her head.

'Oh, I mean nothing serious, you understand, just the usual minor neighbourly disputes.'

Molly finished her cake and waited for Annabelle Welland to continue, but she just sat there, drinking her tea and looking over at her husband, expecting him to finish the conversation.

'Could you give an example?' Molly asked eventually.

'A hedge in their garden was intruding into ours,' Richard Welland said. 'I asked James, very politely, if it would be OK for me to cut it back slightly.' He sighed before continuing. 'He told me quite abruptly that it was his hedge and that if I touched it, he would have me up in court.'

'And we don't think he was bluffing,' Annabelle Welland added. 'And then there was the incident with Helen.'

'Helen?'

'Our daughter,' offered Mr Welland. 'She and Martin were friends when they were children.'

'Helen was a year older than Martin,' Annabelle Welland explained. 'They used to play together when they were kids. One day James accused Helen of bullying Martin, then she wasn't allowed round there anymore.'

'It was all nonsense,' Welland said. 'Helen gave us her side of the story and she claimed Martin had gone running to his dad because Helen wouldn't let him play on her bike. She'd got the bike for her tenth birthday and didn't let anyone play on it, not even her big sister.'

'So relations between yourselves and the Metcalfs had deteriorated somewhat by the time you heard them arguing that summer?'

'Eleanor and I were still friendly,' Mrs Welland said, 'but Richard had decided he wanted little to do with

James. What was it you called him, darling? A "self-righteous prick", wasn't it? Or something like that.'

'I may have used intemperate language,' Richard Welland told Molly with the beginnings of a blush, 'but the man would have tried the patience of Mother Teresa.'

'So you called the police?' Molly prompted. 'About the argument.'

Both the Wellands looked sheepish. 'Anna thought it best,' Richard Welland said.

'You agreed,' his wife shot back. 'We were both concerned for Eleanor. She'd hinted to me before that James had an aggressive streak, though I don't think he'd ever hit her before.'

'We don't know that he hit her then, dear,' Welland added. He looked over at Molly. He finished his tea and cake, and placed the cup on the delicate saucer. 'In hindsight, I wish I'd never called the police. They made me feel like the villain of the piece, telling me that they'd spoken to James and Eleanor and everything was fine. They'd simply had a minor disagreement about dinner. They as good as suggested we were a pair of nosey busybodies.' He folded his arms across his chest and stared at Molly as though he expected an apology from her on behalf of the officers who'd investigated the complaint.

So nothing had become of what had potentially been an incident of domestic abuse. At least times had changed, Molly thought. These days the police were duty-bound to take all cases of possible domestic violence seriously, and rightfully so. It might be worth tracking down the officers who'd handled the call out, and hear what they had to say for themselves.

'Were you living next door to them when Martin went missing?' Molly asked.

Annabelle Welland sighed and nodded. 'Yes, it was an awful time. Police and newspaper people in the street. We were asked if we knew anything. We were even approached by a couple of journalists wanting information about James and Eleanor. It felt like we were living under siege.'

'Did you know anything?'

She shook her head. 'No. And we told the police that at the time.'

'What about your daughter? Did she not see Martin coming home from school?'

'Our daughter went to a different school to Martin. Our Lady of the Sorrow Convent School in Putney. Though it was no longer a convent school by this time. And I never let either of my daughters walk home from school in the dark,' Annabelle Welland said, as though any parent who did should have been reported to the appropriate authorities.

'So none of you saw Martin that day?' Molly asked.

They both shook their heads. 'If we had,' Annabelle Welland said coldly, 'we would certainly have told the police.'

Despite having been accused of being nosey busybodies last time, thought Molly.

'It was an awful time,' Annabelle Welland said. 'I really felt for Eleanor. Well, and James. Neither of them deserved that.'

'He was a nice lad,' Richard Welland offered. 'If perhaps a bit odd.'

'Odd?' Molly asked. 'In what way?'

'He was a very sensitive child. Gentle. He liked playing with our two daughters. But James was always pushing him to do the kind of things he felt boys should have been doing, like playing football and that kind of thing.'

'What about Eleanor? What was she like with Martin?'

'She was very overprotective of him,' Mrs Welland said. 'It's only natural, I know; I'm a mother myself, but this was something more. It was almost as though she suffocated him. That's never good for a child. They need to be allowed to take the knocks life throws at them. I mean, you can't mollycoddle people all their lives, can you?'

'Eleanor may have mollycoddled him,' Richard Welland argued, 'but James was a different story. Remember, he tried to make Martin join the junior cadets? He went once and hated it. He was a shy, sensitive child. God alone knows what James was thinking trying to get him to do something like that.'

Molly nodded her agreement. She would have quite liked another piece of banana cake, but it would have been highly inappropriate to ask. Instead, she asked the question Denning was so keen to hear answered. 'Is it right that a neighbour claimed they saw him the night he went missing?'

'Oh that.' Annabelle Welland gave the thinnest of smiles. 'Mrs Levisham at number twenty-nine. Bless her, she was always at that window of hers. I think she preferred looking out of the window to watching telly. She was our one-woman neighbourhood watch.'

'But she said she saw Martin? The afternoon he went missing?'

'So she said. She claimed she saw him walking up the street and into the house. The police spoke to her, but to be honest, I think by this stage she didn't know if it was Christmas or rice pudding half the time. She passed away about eight years ago now. Her son wrote to tell me.'

An unreliable witness. Was that why the police had been so quick to dismiss her at the time?

'Do you think it's possible?' Molly asked. '*Could* he have returned home that evening?'

The Wellands looked at each other again. 'If he had returned home, why would they call the police to say he was missing?'

'But is it possible he could have come back? Could Mrs Levisham have been right all along?'

'That's ridiculous,' Welland said. 'If he was there, the police would have found him. They searched the house and the garden. They even searched our garden.' He was looking over at his wife, who was nodding in agreement. 'No. Either he ran away, or a pervert took him.'

But Molly wondered. The police would have searched the house, but they wouldn't necessarily have conducted a forensic search, not unless they had suspected foul play. And nothing in the files had suggested the detectives at the time had seriously felt that was a possibility.

Then Annabelle Welland opened her mouth to say something, but looked at her husband and thought better of it. However, Molly urged her to speak. 'I've never said this to anyone, and I'm not sure I should say it now, but Eleanor told me that James once had a terrible row with Martin. She never said what it was about, but he was really going for the boy, screaming at him and calling him all sorts of things. She'd pleaded with James to leave him alone but he'd just continued to shout at him. It was only after she'd threatened to leave James that he stopped.' She looked at Molly, then her husband, probably wishing she'd kept her mouth shut. But Molly thanked her and said she'd been very helpful.

As soon as she left the apartment block, she took her phone from her bag and called Denning.

–

'Cadets?' Denning asked down the phone. 'Why the cadets? Why not the scouts, or the local chess club? Why specifically get him to join the cadets?'

'According to the ex-neighbour, Martin hated it,' she said. 'Do you think it could be significant?'

'Maybe… From what I've heard about Martin Metcalf, he wasn't the sort of child who was into shooting or *Boy's Own*-type adventures.'

'Perhaps it was more James Metcalf's thing,' Molly suggested. But there was no answer from Denning, and after a couple of seconds she realised he'd ended the call.

She was curious to know where Denning was heading with this. Had he discovered a new line of inquiry? Did he think James Metcalf was somehow involved in the Galloways' murder?

Chapter Forty-Seven

'Good timing. Another half an hour and I'd have closed up for the day.' If Ruth Forbes was surprised to see Denning back in her shop, she didn't let on.

He flicked the snip on the door's latch and turned the sign to Closed. 'I've saved you a job.'

She looked slightly taken aback, eyes wide with bemusement, then said, 'What's this about?'

'Some more questions, I'm afraid. About Ellie. Well, to be more specific, about Ellie and James.'

After he'd come off the phone from Molly, he'd done some checking. There had been something about James Metcalf that made him wary from the very start. McKenna's ex had clearly felt it too. He'd asked Neeraj to chase up a suspicion he had about Metcalf, but in the meantime it made sense to speak to the one person who seemed to be key to all this. The one person who had been given an insight into both the Galloway and Metcalf families: Ruth Forbes.

'I believe I've told you everything there is to tell, Mr Denning.'

'Except I don't think you have, Ruth. I think you know a lot more than you've told me.' He'd reached the counter now. He leant on it so that he could look her directly in the eye. 'In fact, I think you've always known the truth about who killed Ellie, Brian, Amber, Dan and Caleb, and why.'

If she felt awkward at this, she didn't let it show. She was tidying away some novelty face masks. 'I'm not sure there's anything else I can tell you. I think we've been over everything I know at least twice.'

'You said Ellie talked to you. I know you and she discussed what happened to Martin.' He leaned in closer. 'Did she ever say what she really thought happened to him?'

She began twitching. 'Like I told you before, she thought he'd been snatched by someone. Taken and god knows what done to him, then killed and dumped him somewhere.'

'But did she actually say that to you? Did she use those exact words?'

More twitching. 'Well, no. Not those words. She was never comfortable talking about it, and who can blame her.'

'But she did talk about it? On the anniversary of his disappearance for example?'

'No. Well, not really.'

'Which was it? No, or not really?'

She looked uncomfortable. 'Ellie was haunted by what happened. I don't think she ever came to terms with it. Yes, she would occasionally get emotional if the subject of children ever came up, or if a family with young children came into the shop. But I never pushed her on the subject. If she wanted to talk, I'd listen, try and be supportive, but there were times it felt like she was in danger of being overwhelmed by grief.'

'Did she ever blame James for what happened?'

She looked at him. 'No. Of course not. He wasn't to blame. Whoever took Martin, that's who was to blame. And you never found that person did you?'

'She said something though, didn't she? She blamed James. Am I right?'

She fidgeted, trying hard to avoid eye contact. 'It's just something somebody says, isn't it? You blame yourself, or you lash out at the people closest. It's only natural she'd blame James. He was her husband. Perhaps there are times he blames her.'

'But it was more than that. She specifically blamed James for what happened to Martin, didn't she? She actually named him as being the person responsible for what happened.'

She didn't answer. After a while, she nodded slowly. 'Yes. She blamed James. She didn't go into detail, and I didn't ask her, but she blamed him.'

'I thought so. That confirms what I've suspected, and I think you've suspected it too.'

She looked at him, probably already second guessing where he was going with this. 'What?'

'James Metcalf killed Martin.'

Ruth Forbes opened her mouth to say something, but nothing came out.

'Yes,' Denning said. 'I can tell from the look on your face you've put two and two together and come to the same conclusion. I don't know exactly how it played out, but I reckon it might have gone something like this: Martin came home that afternoon. A neighbour spotted him, but she later changed her story. I don't know exactly what happened, but I suspect James had a quiet word with her. Being a solicitor, he would be used to coaching people, questioning whether something they'd seen had actually happened. Perhaps he warned her that she would have to appear in court and say what she thought she'd seen in front of a judge and jury. It would be intimidating for a woman in her eighties who was already worried about the decline of her mental faculties. Did she really want to put herself through that? Could she be one hundred percent sure about what she thought she'd seen? It wouldn't have been difficult to persuade the one and only witness to change their statement. But let's assume she was right, and Martin did return home that evening. Then what happened to him? I think you might be able to fill in some of the blanks there, Ruth?'

She sighed. 'There had been some trouble at school. Some boys had stolen Martin's schoolbag and dumped it in the river. James was furious. He told Martin he needed to learn to stand up for himself. James was forever down that bloody school complaining about how Martin was being bullied and picked on. It was supposed to be a good school: it cost over three grand a term, but it seemed the school was in denial about any bullying that took place. It didn't look good for them, so they preferred to keep quiet about it.'

Denning could understand that. It might only have been twenty years ago, but it was a different era: bullying, like domestic violence and institutional child abuse, could be swept under the carpet if people on the receiving end didn't make too big a fuss.

'Let me guess what happened: they argued. Martin finally answered back. James hit him. OK, it's manslaughter, but he would still have gone down for it. Lost everything: job, pension, social standing. He convinced Ellie to keep quiet. Said that if they told anyone what had happened, the police would charge them both with manslaughter.'

Denning felt a wave of pity for Ellie Galloway. Bullied by her husband to go along with covering up their son's death, and not being allowed somewhere to grieve for him. It must have been a form of torture for her. No wonder she'd revelled in the happiness that her marriage to Brian had brought. But it was still hanging over her; *haunted* her, to use Ruth Forbes's own word. Until she'd finally decided she wanted some kind of absolution. She'd met up with James again after all those years, and realised she was no longer afraid of him…

'She finally found that courage, didn't she? She told him. She was going to go to the police, tell them the truth about what happened to Martin that night.'

Ruth Forbes looked at him. 'She'd invited James and Karen to Brian's birthday party that night. They were going to discuss everything as a family; find a way for the truth to come out with as little damage as possible.'

'So Metcalf knew about the party?' He was working things out in his head. Metcalf had been backed into a corner. Threatened. He would have more to lose than anyone. He thought about the pristine house overlooking the park; the smart office in central London with his name engraved on the brass plaque by the front door. It was a hell of a lot to give up.

His phone bleeped with a message. It was from Neeraj:

> Your hunch was right boss. Have spoken to them, and they confirm Metcalf had been a member.

Denning left the fancy dress shop, with Ruth Forbes shouting after him, 'Ellie was only doing what she thought was right.'

But he wasn't listening. He was already calling Neeraj's number. They needed to get round to Metcalf's house, and now.

Chapter Forty-Eight

Denning rang the doorbell with some force, but there was no answer. If James Metcalf was home, then he was refusing to answer the door. A neighbour had confirmed that she'd seen both James and Karen come home from work, so unless they'd sneaked of out the house unnoticed, they were in there and probably hoping the police would just go away.

'What next, boss?' Neeraj asked.

Denning pressed the doorbell again, then hammered on the door with his fist.

Neeraj had confirmed his suspicions about Metcalf having once belonged to a gun club and still holding a valid gun licence. It explained why he had wanted Martin to join the cadets: he wanted his own little mini me. But Martin wasn't interested in shooting. Something else that helped widen the gulf between father and son.

'Right. Let's try round the back.'

Neeraj had to kick open a locked garden gate to a gravel path skirting the west flank of the property.

The path led to a wide, stone-flagged patio that bordered the kitchen conservatory and the green lawn of the back garden. Denning ran up to the conservatory and peered through the glass. He was sure he could see a shape on the floor, partly obscured by the island unit. Cupping his hands round his eyes, he looked closer: it was

Karen Metcalf. She was lying on the floor; blood pooling on the clean, pale grey tiles. He looked around the patio and found a metal garden chair. Picking it up, he threw it against the conservatory doors, at the same time telling Neeraj to phone for an ambulance.

Denning carefully picked his way through the broken glass and ran over to Karen Metcalf. She wasn't conscious and there was a bloody wound on the side of her skull. The blood was already spreading over the otherwise spotless kitchen floor, turning dark and oily against the paleness of the tiles. He checked her pulse: at least she was alive. Neeraj said the ambulance was on its way: five minutes, ten at the most. Denning told him to phone the station; they needed to get a SOCO team there ASAP. Blood had matted against hair in Karen Metcalf's wound. He couldn't tell whether it was life-threatening, but the sooner the ambulance got there, the happier he'd be.

Neeraj told him McKenna was on her way, and had asked for uniform back-up. He told Neeraj to check the house to see if James Metcalf was still there, but Denning reckoned at some point between the neighbour spotting him coming back from work and their arrival, he'd attacked Karen and legged it. A few moments later, Neeraj confirmed that there was no sign of him.

Denning cradled Karen Metcalf's head in his hands. There was blood everywhere. She'd been hit with some kind of blunt instrument, he guessed, and looked around the kitchen to see if there was any sign of the weapon. Karen Metcalf suddenly opened her eyes. She groaned and it took a few seconds for her blurry vision to recognise him. She was trying to say something.

'Karen, there's an ambulance on its way,' he told her.

'James,' she said. Her voice was croaky.

'Don't try to speak. We'll find James, but we need to get you to hospital first.'

She was trying to talk, but her speech was incoherent. She was shaking, as though her body was going into shock.

'Simon...'

Denning thought he'd misheard her, but she repeated the name. 'What about Simon?'

He could feel some of the blood from her wound spilling onto his crisp new shirt.

'Simon Galloway. He was here when we came home, waiting for us. He and James...argued. He attacked James, then he hit me. I had my mobile phone but he hit me with...'

Her voice was faltering, more blood pouring from the wound on her head.

'Where's James?' Denning asked.

She was still shaking. 'I don't know.'

'Deep, find out how close that ambulance is.'

Simon was missing, as was Metcalf. Denning was thinking hard. The obvious assumption was that Simon had taken him somewhere. But where? And why?

The ambulance arrived, with a couple of uniformed officers hot on its heels. Another two arrived a few minutes later and started securing the scene and asking Denning and Neeraj for details about the attack.

He was answering their questions when he heard McKenna's voice in the hallway. She was brushing her way past a young PC who was trying in vain to stop her entering the house. She thrust her ID under his face, and he hurriedly backed off.

'What happened?' she asked, ignoring the paramedics and the uniformed officers who were talking to Denning.

McKenna was standing in the middle of the blood-splattered kitchen, hands on hips, looking like she was about to start shouting at someone.

He quickly filled her in on what had happened.

'Simon Galloway? Why would he go after Metcalf?'

'He may have put two and two together,' Denning said. 'Or someone's spoken to him, told him what we've been thinking.'

'What *you've* been thinking,' she was quick to say. 'Who could have told him?'

It was obvious the same name had entered both their heads, though there was no proof that Molly had known much beyond Denning's suspicions about James Metcalf's involvement in his son's disappearance.

'We don't know anyone who could have told him. We don't even know for certain this has anything to do with the Galloway murders.'

'But you've obviously convinced yourself there's a connection,' McKenna said, her voice just above a whisper.

Denning turned back to the paramedics. 'How is she?'

One of them looked up at Denning. He was dressing the bloodied wound, trying to stem the blood flow with a bandage. 'Blunt force trauma. I think her skull may be fractured. We'll know better when we get her patched up at A&E.'

He turned to McKenna. 'It looks like she'll live.'

One of the uniformed officers approached them holding a blood-stained hammer wrapped in a piece of kitchen roll. 'Found this in the bin,' she said. 'Looks like this is what he used to attack them.'

'In the bin?' McKenna said. 'Well, at least he's tidy.'

'Scene of Crime officers are on their way,' Denning told her. 'Keep it safe until they get here, then they'll bag it with any other evidence.'

McKenna jerked her head in the direction of the garden. They headed out through the conservatory and picked their way past the shards of broken glass that littered the floor. Once they were outside, standing on the patio, and making sure there was no one around who could overhear them, McKenna said: 'So where's Metcalf?'

'My best guess is that Simon Galloway's taken him.'

'You'd better be right about this. Because if Simon Galloway does anything to Metcalf, then it's on us.'

He told her what Ruth Forbes had said. 'She didn't dispute any of this. James Metcalf killed Martin, and I believe he killed the Galloway family because he knew they were going to spill the beans.'

McKenna digested this. 'That's quite a theory, Matt. I might buy it if it wasn't for the fact there's still no hard evidence Simon Galloway didn't do it. Thanks to him, we've already wasted considerable time running round after Artem Koval, and Christ knows how many other shadows we've been chasing. Maybe this whole thing's a ploy to ensure we go after everyone except the person who actually did it. The person who, let's not lose sight of it, has the most to gain from his family's death.'

But Denning didn't agree. 'My money's on James Metcalf. And I have a feeling Simon Galloway's thinking along the same lines.'

McKenna let go of her hair, and punched her chin with her fist. 'OK, if Metcalf was responsible, where would he have got his hands on a gun?'

He told her about Metcalf's membership of a local gun club. 'He was a solicitor. He was a criminal solicitor before moving into family law fifteen years ago. He wouldn't find it difficult to get his hands on an illegal firearm.'

He could see that McKenna was still sceptical. 'At this precise moment in time, these aren't the questions we should be asking. We should be focussing on where Simon Galloway and James Metcalf are,' Denning said.

'Which, let's face it,' McKenna said, 'could be anywhere.'

He looked back into the kitchen. The paramedics had left, taking Karen Metcalf to the nearest hospital. White-clad Scene Of Crime Officers were arriving in the kitchen now, talking to the uniformed officers, one of whom was pointing at Denning and McKenna. 'We should talk to whoever is Crime Scene Manager,' he said, just as his phone rang and Molly Fisher's name came up on the screen. McKenna was heading back into the kitchen as he answered the phone. She was just about to negotiate her way through the shattered conservatory doors when Denning shouted after her: 'That was Molly.' McKenna stopped and turned to look at him. 'She thinks she's found Simon Galloway.'

Chapter Forty-Nine

The house stood blackened and battle-scarred. The police tape had been removed, but barriers had been erected around the front of the building to keep out prying eyes and ghouls.

Tarpaulin covered what was left of the roof, and the downstairs windows had been boarded up.

A smell of burning still lingered in the air, now tinged with the clammy aroma of dampness.

Molly had received a call from Marisa Powell. Her eldest child had seen monsters in the burnt-out house across the road. Marisa had tried to humour her by showing her that there was no one there. But she'd spotted a figure at an upstairs window. Just for the briefest of seconds she couldn't even be sure that it was a figure and not just a dancing shadow. She'd phoned Molly rather than dialling 999 in case they thought she was being silly.

Molly had already received a text from Simon Galloway earlier in the day, telling her he was OK and she wasn't to worry about him. He wanted her to know he didn't blame her for anything. This had made her worry even more. She'd texted him back, asking where he was and what he was planning to do, but when no reply came she'd phoned and left yet another message on his voicemail, insisting he returned her call. When Marisa Powell's call came in,

Molly had put two and two together and headed round to Gibney Road.

The fire brigade had replaced the damaged front door of number forty-two with a temporary door. She pushed it open and entered the fire-blackened hallway. The stairs were still standing. They were burned and damaged, but they looked like they were still usable.

She tried to block the acrid smell from her sinuses. It made her think of burned flesh, and she had to suppress an urge to gag.

The fire had been started in the living room, where the first two victims had been shot. According to the forensic report, the upper floors weren't as badly damaged as the ground floor.

Everything was covered in a coating of black soot. It got onto her clothes and in her hair. She carefully made her way up the charred staircase, careful to ensure she neither made a noise nor put her foot through a damaged stair. At the top of the stairs she turned to her right. She could hear someone breathing: deep and choking and with a slight note of hysteria. She edged cautiously along the hallway. The ceiling was half hanging down in places and there were gaps where pockets of daylight could be glimpsed.

She passed the door to the rear bedroom, the one where Amber and Caleb had been found. She tried not to think of them in there, terrified at the thought of what was going to happen to them; panic rising inside Amber at the knowledge of what had already happened to the rest of her family.

The next room was what she guessed had been the master bedroom. This was where the noise was coming from: the frantic gulps of someone trying hard to breathe.

She carefully pushed open the door. Simon Galloway was sitting on his parents' bed. James Metcalf was sitting on the floor: an improvised gag in his mouth; a shotgun pointing at his head.

'This seemed the obvious place to finish it,' Simon Galloway said. He seemed unusually calm. It was as if he'd planned this from the start, but Molly suspected he was actually making it up as he went along. In which case he could be spooked at any moment. She needed to take control of this situation if anyone had any hope of getting out of there alive.

'Simon,' she said calmly. Her voice managed not to betray her fear. She'd been on a hostage negotiation course whilst she'd still been in CID. She'd never had to use the training, until now. 'Let him go. This is pointless. What do you think it will achieve?'

'If he tells the truth, I'll let him go. If he doesn't, I'll blow his fucking head off.'

Molly watched him. She was alone in a room with a dangerous man. Armed, and dangerous. She had to keep a level head for everyone's sake.

'Who told you about James?' she asked.

'I worked that one out for myself. As soon as I'd heard you'd let Natalya's meathead of a brother go, I sussed there must have been someone else who was responsible. I remembered something Ellie said about James. When she and my dad first got together, he'd threatened to shoot them. I always thought she was joking.'

Metcalf was trying to speak. Muffled noise was coming from behind the gag. He stared hard at Molly, his eyes wide and white with fear.

The fire hadn't done too much damage in this room. The wallpaper around the bedroom door had been reduced to charcoal and the room was covered in the same dusty film of black soot as the rest of the house. The room looked like it had been mostly affected by smoke damage, the ashen smell of which still penetrated every corner.

'I knew he'd been invited to Dad's birthday dinner. They wanted to "discuss" something important. Dad never told me, but he said it was something that might affect our whole family. I thought he meant Amber, and the hoary old chestnut about trying to take Caleb off her. It's only now I realise it must have been about something else. So I phoned Ruth at Alter Image. She told me you lot had been round asking questions about James and Ellie and what happened to that kid of theirs. I'd always suspected there was more to that story than we were all led to believe. Ellie would always act weird if you ever mentioned Martin. She once slapped Amber after she joked that Ellie and James had done him in and buried him under the patio.' He looked down at Metcalf, sitting on the floor, a faint smell of urine emanating from him. 'Perhaps that wasn't too far from the truth. I went round to confront him. He actually tried to threaten me. Would you believe the idiot still had the shotgun in the boot of his car?'

'Why come here?' Molly asked.

'I told you. It'll finish where it started. And this *is* my house now. What's left of it. I might not have a family any longer but at least I've got the burnt-out remains of a house.' He gave a dry, hard laugh, that seemed to die somewhere in the back of his throat.

'Simon, if that is the same gun that was used to murder your family, then we'll be able to test it. Gunshot residue, fingerprints. We'll be able to prove it was the gun that was used that night. He'll go down for it.' She nodded at

Metcalf. He was looking up at her, pleading at her with his terrified eyes.

'It wouldn't prove he was the one who pulled the trigger. And you've only got my word that it was in his car.' He looked at Molly with the ghost of a smile flickering around his lips. 'How do you know I'm not feeding you a load of bullshit? How do you know the gun doesn't belong to me and I was the one who did it?'

Molly had slowly edged her way into the room by now. She was standing only a few feet away from Simon. She took a punt that the same bloke who'd taken her out for lunch and chatted so openly about his family and his hopes and his love for his nephew wouldn't suddenly aim the shotgun at her. What if she'd been wrong about him all along? She'd been the one who'd worked at persuading the team Simon was innocent. But what if she'd made the wrong call?

Chapter Fifty

Denning and McKenna were outside forty-two Gibney Road now. An armed response unit was on its way along with more uniformed officers. They would have to evacuate the street as a precaution. The sound of approaching sirens suggested they weren't far away.

A couple of uniformed officers were already there when they'd pitched up five minutes ago, having left Neeraj in Mortlake to coordinate the SOCOs back at Metcalf's house. There was no sign of Molly.

Denning had instructed her to wait outside the house until they got there. It was possible she hadn't arrived yet, but Denning doubted it. Would she be foolhardy enough to have entered the building alone? Knowing Molly's impetuous streak that was a definite possibility.

The street had an eerie quiet about it, as if it sensed something was happening again. A breeze briefly rustled the branches on the tall, thin poplars that lined the grassy verge on either side of the wide street. Denning looked at the burnt-out wreck of the Galloways' former home, and wondered if it had ever been a happy house. Or had it, at some point in its history, been cursed: a hex placed on the building to ensure its residents could never enjoy a peaceful existence?

McKenna was talking to the two uniforms. They couldn't tell if there was anyone in the building and agreed no one would enter until the ARV got there and the building could be secured. A moment later a young woman came running across the road from the house opposite and began a conversation with them. She said her name was Marisa Powell and she'd phoned Molly about half an hour ago saying she thought there might be someone in the house.

'Should we try Molly's mobile again?' McKenna asked, once Mrs Powell had gone back inside.

'There's no point,' Denning said, 'she's got it turned off.'

He'd already left a message telling her to stay away from the house until they got there. He was now convinced she'd ignored him and was currently inside, possibly with Simon Galloway who may or may not be a killer.

Another two patrol cars had now pulled up, and at the top of the street he spotted the first of the ARV vans turning into Gibney Road. McKenna had already pulled a couple of flak jackets from the boot of her car and handed one to Denning whilst barking orders at the uniforms to start evacuating the street. She'd phoned the station and asked them to get on to the local authority and find a suitable venue to put the residents up in. Apparently a community centre two streets away was available, but only if they cancelled a Pilates class for the over-sixties.

Denning climbed into the protective jacket for the second time that week. The ARV had reached them now. Authorised firearms officers from SCO19 were exiting the van and heading towards them. McKenna flashed her warrant card at the man she assumed was the lead officer, only for a female AFO to state that she was the sergeant in charge. As they huddled together to discuss tactics, Denning watched as uniformed officers began evacuating the street. Neighbours were now hurrying along the road, a few glancing over at the police presence outside number forty-two. It must have brought back memories of the night of the fire: confusion and a mild sense of panic.

The AFO sergeant, a woman in her thirties with sharp eyes and hair tied back in a ponytail, addressed them: 'You reckon there are three adults in there, including one police officer with MIT and you suspect one of the adults may be armed?'

'We can't say for certain he's armed,' Denning told her, 'but there's a strong chance he is.'

'And you suspect the officer's life may be in danger?'

Denning looked at McKenna. She turned to the AFO sergeant. 'Yes. We believe an officer may be in danger.'

There was silence in the street now. Most of the residents had been evacuated; there were just one or two stragglers being led along the street as a police cordon was in the process of being set up around them.

McKenna came over to him. 'Sergeant McLeish suggests we have another go at communicating with Molly before they enter the house. They're nervous about going in there mob-handed in case the building isn't safe.'

He shrugged. 'It's worth a try. She must know by now that we're out here.'

'What the hell's happening in there?' McKenna clasped at a clump of hair in exasperation. 'I can't believe she was stupid enough to go in there when we specifically instructed her not to.'

'She probably thinks she's got some kind of connection with Simon Galloway. She's always believed he's innocent.'

'Christ. For her sake, let's hope she's right.'

Denning had his phone in his hand. He was on the point of selecting Molly's number when the near silence of Gibney Road was shattered by the sound of a gun going off somewhere from inside number forty-two.

Chapter Fifty-One

Molly had heard the commotion coming from the street outside and guessed it was Denning and probably Betty Taggart. The distant sound of sirens, which grew steadily nearer, confirmed her suspicions.

She wanted to go over to the window and look outside. Maybe even signal to her colleagues that she was OK and everything was under control.

Only she wasn't OK. Simon was rambling now. A semi-coherent rant about his family and how they'd never understood him. How he wished he was the one who'd been adopted and not Amber; then he would have a real family out there somewhere and not the bunch of nutters he'd been saddled with. Or at least it had been something along those lines. Molly hadn't been giving his little tirade too much heed. Her brain had been performing the mental equivalent of Olympic-style gymnastics trying to think up a practical way out of this situation. And preferably one that allowed everyone to walk out of what was left of number forty-two Gibney Road with their heads still attached.

James Metcalf was still sitting on the floor looking uncomfortable. She'd persuaded Simon to let her remove the gag: a dirty old handkerchief that was now damp with Metcalf's spittle. Metcalf had started jabbering nineteen to the dozen the moment she'd taken the gag out of his mouth: mostly garbled noise about him being innocent, Simon being mad and how she should do something as she was a police officer. He failed to ask how his wife was.

Suddenly Simon said: 'If he doesn't shut the fuck up, put the gag back on him.'

That did the trick. Metcalf was silent. Simon had stopped talking too. He was staring into space now, still with the gun directed at James Metcalf. She knew if she went for the gun he'd pull the trigger without hesitating. That was assuming he didn't point it at her first.

She tried to get him talking again. 'Simon, I never thought you did it. You know that. I've always fought your case with the rest of the murder squad. And they believe me now.' She edged slightly closer. 'If you stop this silly bollocks now, then he'll be arrested and you'll probably get off with all this on grounds of, I don't know, PTSD or something. But the longer it goes on, the less likely you are to be treated with any kind of leniency.' She tried to look into his eyes. She wanted to know if she was reaching him. 'It's likely that an armed response team will have been summoned by now. If they have to come in here, trust me, it won't be pretty and whatever kind of shit you think you're in now will be multiplied by ten when they come charging in.'

Simon stabbed the shotgun at Metcalf. 'Get him to tell you he did it. Get him to admit he killed my family: shot them one by one, then set fire to the house to destroy the evidence. Get him to say it.'

The focus was on Metcalf again. He looked from Molly to Simon, fear still flashing in his eyes. 'He's insane. He attacked me and my wife in our home. He's the maniac who killed his family. You only have to look at him to see he's mad.'

'If that is the case,' Molly said calmly, 'then why has he brought you here? Why does he want you to confess if he did it?'

'Are you stupid?' Metcalf barked, the fear diminishing enough for him to slip into professional solicitor mode for a moment. 'If he kills me, and then you, he can tell them that I confessed. He could say anything. He could say I shot you, then make it look like I killed myself. He'd walk. You said it yourself, he'll get off on some technicality: PTSD, or being mentally unhinged. Anything. You're enabling him to get away with murder here.'

Molly wanted to go over to the window and look outside; see what was happening with the Armed Response Team. If she could just persuade Simon to see sense and hand over the shotgun, there was a chance things wouldn't get too messy. But time wasn't on their side.

Simon and Metcalf had started goading each other again. An exchange of name-calling now: Metcalf accusing the Galloways of being dysfunctional; Simon saying the best thing Ellie did was to leave James. He was a bully and tyrant and he'd made her life a misery.

She was now roughly half-way between Simon and the window. She could try and grab the shotgun, hoping it wouldn't go off, or get to the window and indicate for the Armed Response Team to hang back. Or she could try and talk Simon into putting down the gun and she'd let Denning know everyone was going to be all right.

The decision was taken out of her hands. Metcalf was shouting at Simon now; calling him a mummy's boy; saying he was pathetic. Saying that if he'd been Metcalf's son then he wouldn't have been allowed to get away with half the things Brian had let him get away with. Cursing the day Ellie had ever got involved with the whole rotten lot of them. How his only regret was that Simon hadn't been in the house that night and burned with the rest of his scummy family.

Simon was agitated now; shaking and crying, but worryingly, still holding the gun.

Metcalf had got to his feet and was standing over Simon shouting at him.

Molly was close enough to both men now. She could hear herself telling Metcalf to be quiet; he was making things worse. But he was oblivious to Molly; it was as if she'd suddenly ceased to exist. As far as James Metcalf was concerned, it was just him and Simon in the room.

The goading continued. Molly was now close enough to reach for the gun and take it from Simon's hands. Metcalf was saying something about Simon's mother now; not Ellie, but his birth mother. Simon's face was tight with rage. He raised the gun, his finger on the trigger.

Molly dived for the gun just as it went off.

It was only when she hit the floor that she saw the blood. Lots of it.

Chapter Fifty-Two

Everything happened very quickly.

McLeish gave the order to go in. McKenna was arguing that she wanted to go in too as it was one of her officers in there. But this was McLeish's call. Denning suggested they held back until they knew what the situation was and McKenna reluctantly agreed.

A few moments later, Simon Galloway appeared. He was cuffed and looking sheepish. There was blood down his face and on his jacket. He was led to a waiting patrol car, glancing over at Denning just before a hand was placed on the top of his head and he was gently but firmly pushed into the back of the squad car. McKenna was shouting instructions that he was to be taken straight to the station and placed in Interview Room A. If he needed hospital treatment, it could wait. She wasn't going to let the slippery bastard go walkabout a second time, she told Denning.

An ambulance had been summoned as a precaution and now the paramedics were on standby. One of the paramedics jerked his head towards the front door and nodded at his colleague. Denning held his breath as Molly was led out of the front of the building by an Armed Response Officer; blood on her clothes and splattered against the side of her face. Behind her, two of the Armed Response team were leading James Metcalf out. There was a blood-stained wound on his shoulder, but it didn't look serious.

Denning and McKenna rushed over to Molly, while one of the paramedics asked if she was OK. She nodded that she was fine. The paramedics turned their attention on Metcalf who was muttering something about suing the police.

'What the fuck happened in there?' McKenna asked. They were standing in the middle of the road, out of the way of the paramedics and McLeish's team, but still within the police cordon.

'Simon. He fired at Metcalf. I only just managed to push Metcalf out of the way in time. The bullet must have grazed his shoulder. I'm not exactly sure what happened after that. I looked up; Simon was sitting on the bed in a state of shock. Metcalf was on the floor, whining. There was blood everywhere.' She looked at her hands, both of which were smeared with Metcalf's blood. 'The next thing I know the room was full of armed officers shouting at us. One of them took the gun off Simon and led him away.'

Denning could see that she was shaking. He guided her towards one of the squad cars, opened the back door and held her arm whilst she sat on the back seat. He handed Molly a clean handkerchief from his jacket pocket and suggested to McKenna that she head back to the station to formally interview Simon Galloway. She nodded her agreement and set off towards her car which was parked just beyond the perimeter of the cordon. Metcalf was currently being treated in the back of the ambulance. 'Are you sure you don't want one of the paramedics to check you over?' he asked Molly.

'God no! I've had enough of paramedics to last me a lifetime.' She laughed. Actually, it was more like a frantic giggling. She was wiping Metcalf's blood off her hands and face with the handkerchief and laughing. Denning shook his head.

'By rights, I should be chucking the book at you. Or threatening you with suspension at the very least. That was a crazy thing, that you did, Molly. Going into a situation like that alone and unarmed. Anything could have happened.'

'I didn't know Simon was armed, did I?'

Denning decided to let the matter drop. McKenna would be having words at some point. Molly would get an official roasting, but that could wait.

'What do you think Simon Galloway planned to do with Metcalf?'

She shook her head. 'I don't think he knew himself. Get him to confess to killing his family, then… I don't know. I don't believe he planned to kill him, if that's what you're thinking. But his head's so messed up at the moment, it's almost impossible to second-guess what he's thinking.'

Denning agreed. One of the uniformed officers came over to the car and opened the driver's door. He was a thickset man in his late forties, his mouth almost hidden by a bushy black beard. 'Ambulance is ready to take him in and get him looked over. They reckon it's just a graze, but there's the risk of infection, etcetera. We'll send a couple of guys over to keep an eye on Metcalf.' He looked at Denning. 'Nobody has formally arrested him yet and he's screaming blue murder about suing the backside off us.'

'OK. I suppose I'd better do the honours,' Denning said. He got out of the car and headed over to the ambulance. Metcalf was sitting in the back, arm in a sling, shoulder covered in a bandage. He looked daggers at

Denning when he saw him approach, opening his mouth to launch, no doubt, a tirade of abuse. But Denning was too quick for him. Before he'd even had a chance to speak, he'd read him his rights and formally arrested him with the murders of Brian Galloway, Ellie Galloway, Dan Hudson, Amber Galloway and Caleb Hudson. And, for good measure, the manslaughter of Martin Metcalf.

'I would advise you to contact a good solicitor, Mr Metcalf, because you really are going to need one.' Denning nodded at the paramedics to close the ambulance and proceed to the nearest A&E department. A few minutes later the ambulance moved off, blue lights flashing, but no siren. Gibney Road had had enough of sirens lately.

He glanced over at Molly, still sitting in the back of a squad car. She was chatting to the bearded officer, who was now sitting in the driver's seat. He would ask the officer to take them back to Stoke Newington nick as he'd just remembered they'd come out in McKenna's battered old Alfa Romeo, which she'd have driven back to the station by now.

He looked at number forty-two Gibney Road. An ordinary house in an ordinary street, lived in by an ordinary family. At least that had been his initial thought when he'd pitched up there a week ago to investigate a suspicious fire. But the family who'd lived there had turned out to be anything but ordinary in the end. Or were they? Were the dysfunctional Galloways any different to any other family living in Gibney Road, or any road in any town or city for that matter?

He climbed into the back of the squad car next to Molly. 'Are you sure you don't want to go to A&E? Make sure none of this blood belongs to you?'

'Like I said, I'm fine.' She handed him the bloodied handkerchief with a smile. 'All I need is a shower and a change of clothing.'

'OK,' he said to the bearded officer who was acting as their unofficial chauffeur. 'Drop me at the station, then take DS Fisher home.' He would square things with McKenna, as he so often did these days.

Chapter Fifty-Three

'James Metcalf is refusing to talk,' McKenna said. It was the day after he'd been arrested. His solicitor had argued that he wasn't well enough to be formally questioned straight after his arrest, citing blood loss and shock. The solicitor wasn't from Woodeson, Madeley & Metcalf, but another central London-based firm that charged by the hour.

McKenna had agreed that Metcalf could stay in hospital for one night, but due to the seriousness of the offences, she insisted they would be formally questioning him the next day.

He was currently sitting in Interview Room B, his solicitor sitting next to him, advising him to issue a string of 'no comments'.

Denning and McKenna were taking a break, recharging their batteries and trying to come up with a workable strategy that would offer them the best chances of getting a conviction.

'His prints aren't on the gun,' McKenna said. 'Simon Galloway's are, however, and Metcalf is still insisting that's because Galloway did it. I'll be honest, Matt, at the moment there's a strong chance Metcalf will walk and Simon Galloway will wind up in the frame for this.'

They were in McKenna's office. The cyclamen was no longer sitting dead and ignored on the top of the filing cabinet. Either McKenna had finally taken the decision to bin it, or one of the cleaners had made the decision for her. In a strange way, Denning missed it. It had become something of a focal point in McKenna's office.

'There's Ruth Forbes: she suspected Metcalf had killed Martin,' Denning said. 'It's a strong motive.'

'It was only a suspicion though: she had no real evidence he killed Martin.'

'As it stands there's very little evidence to prove he killed Martin. Though I am willing to accept it was manslaughter rather than murder,' Denning said, thinking aloud. 'We don't even know what he did with the boy's body.'

McKenna was sitting behind her desk, fingers steepling her chin again, a sure sign she was deep in thought. 'You don't think Ruth Forbes was stringing you along, do you? Inventing a story because she's some kind of deranged fantasist that gets off on wasting police time?'

He shook his head. 'She's not the sort. Besides, I had to practically force it out of her. It's not like she willingly offered this information.'

'Right,' said McKenna. 'We go after her. We find her, we bring her in, we threaten her with perverting the course of justice, wasting police time, lying to cover up a crime. Anything. We scare her into cooperating.'

But Denning wasn't so sure. 'At least let me talk to her. Try and persuade her. It's worth a go I'd rather have her onside than spitting venom in the witness box. The CPS are more likely to go for it if she's a willing participant.'

'What about Metcalf? How long are we going to hold him for without charging him?'

'That solicitor of his is shit hot. He's going to push for us to either charge him or release him. I'm just not confident we have enough to charge him.'

Denning was about to suggest calling it a day when there was a knock at the door. Neeraj stuck his head round the door. 'We've got him, boss.' His face beamed at them. 'Someone saw something the night in question.'

–

They were sitting opposite Metcalf again. His previously cool demeanour had given way to a look of cautious concern. He was looking slightly ruffled now, Denning noticed, as Metcalf looked at his solicitor, trying to gauge his reaction.

McKenna waited for a full minute before she spoke. 'You parked in a side street, just off Gibney Road. It was just after midnight.' Her voice was impassive, almost indifferent. They were on the home stretch now and she wanted to enjoy going in for the final kill. 'A neighbour glanced out of her window. She didn't think it was significant at the time. She only glimpsed you for a second, but I'd bet my pension she could pick you out in an identity parade if we arranged one. And then there's always CCTV. I imagine you probably stuck to side streets as much as possible, and I know you're not stupid. I suspect you used a hire car in a false name, or a stolen car for that matter. You must know enough dodgy people, which is how I imagine you got hold of a gun in the first place. But it's impossible to drive between Mortlake and Islington without passing at least a handful of CCTV cameras, and I'm positive that if we look hard enough – which we will – we'll find one that shows you driving that car. We've already got a team of forensic officers going over your home, Mr Metcalf, and they're very good. If there's something – anything – that links you to this crime, they will find it. You'll have been thorough because, as I said, you're not stupid, but I can guarantee there's something you'll have overlooked. Some tiny clue, or minute piece of DNA that will link you to these murders.' She waited for a moment, held her breath, then leaned over and said. 'And when we find it, then we'll have you.'

Denning had never seen McKenna in action before, but he'd heard that she was a ruthless operator. Now he'd seen it for himself, he was impressed.

Metcalf sat there saying nothing. He was no longer looking at his solicitor, but staring at the floor.

Then he spoke.

'I'd got hold of the gun from some bloke I knew from way back. I'd defended him years ago and knew he could get hold of guns easily.' He looked across the table at them. 'I was sorry about Amber's kid. I assumed the boy would have been in bed at the time. If Amber hadn't run upstairs…'

Denning might have believed that if it hadn't been for the fact he'd started the fire immediately afterwards: Caleb would have died anyway.

His solicitor was shooting stern looks at Metcalf. The interview room felt claustrophobic. The smell of BO wasn't yet overpowering but it was making its presence known. Metcalf had had an attack of conscience. Or he didn't know that Ruth Forbes was changing her story. Or his solicitor had made him realise he was screwed whichever way he looked at it. Whatever the case was, Metcalf clearly wanted to get the whole thing off his chest and out into the open. He looked tired. His right arm was still in a sling and the padding around the shoulder of his shirt suggested a bandage. There had been some blood loss from the bullet, but it wasn't significant. He would make a full recovery.

'I panicked,' Metcalf continued. 'At first I thought Eleanor was bluffing about telling you what happened with Martin. But then I realised she was actually serious. I suspect Brian had put her up to it. He never liked me.' He gave a light shrug. 'But whatever the case, she was going to confess: her conscience, she'd said. Which was fine, but why did she have to destroy my life as well? Mine and Karen's?'

'Oh, she's fine by the way,' McKenna interrupted. 'In case you'd forgotten. A fractured skull, and they're keeping her in for a few days for observation.' She gave Metcalf a withering smile. 'I don't think she'll be returning to the happy home though, not after all this gets out.'

Metcalf just blinked at her. He had the look of a defeated man: a boxer who had gone one round too many and was past the point of giving up. He shook his head. 'I'm sorry. I'm especially sorry about Amber and the kid. They never deserved that.'

Denning was sitting back in the uncomfortable plastic chair listening to all this. When Metcalf stopped talking, he leant on the table. 'About Martin, Mr Metcalf. Where is he?'

But the solicitor was quick. 'May I remind you that my client has agreed to answer questions on the Galloway murders only? He has nothing to say at this stage in relation to the allegations concerning Martin Metcalf.'

Denning looked at Metcalf. The Galloway murders he could just about understand. Metcalf had been desperate; backed into a corner and frightened of the outcome. But to go on covering up for what he'd done to his own son was something Denning was struggling to accept.

He glanced over at McKenna, who nodded. It was their pre-agreed code. They charged James Metcalf with the murder of the Galloway family and Dan Hudson. They would continue to search for evidence of Martin Metcalf's death, ideally by finding his body. But unless James Metcalf confessed, it was likely to be a long time before that went anywhere near a court.

Bail had been denied. Metcalf would be remanded in Brixton. His solicitor was not happy, citing personal circumstances, specifically Karen Metcalf, but McKenna hadn't bought that. He'd confessed, she'd said, and that was enough to prove he was a potential danger to the public and a flight risk.

Outside in the corridor, Denning turned his phone off silent. There was a voicemail message: *Mr Denning, it's Felicity from the childminders. Could you call me back, please? There's been an incident involving Jake.* He excused himself to McKenna, and headed outside to the car park where there was less chance of him being overheard. It seemed Jake had hit another child. There had been an incident involving a Lego model of a dinosaur. Denning sighed. Despite recent progress, he felt he was back at base camp with Jake. Sarah had already phoned to say that she wouldn't be back from New York for another week; Claire was refusing to return his calls.

He went through the list of options in his head. The only thing that was going to work was to ask McKenna for some time off. He had annual leave that still needed to be used up: he and Sarah had planned to use some of it for Jake's promised trip to Disneyland later in the autumn, but it looked like he was going to have to have a rethink.

Slipping his phone back into his pocket, he headed back up to the MIT suite with a heavy heart.

Chapter Fifty-Four

Molly was shattered by the time she returned home.

Jon was pottering around in the garden – something he rarely did. He'd mentioned something about clearing out the large and semi-derelict shed at the top of the garden and converting it into a writing room. He was beginning to feel better, he'd told her, and now that the fug was clearing from his mind he wanted to get back to writing his book.

She'd nodded and smiled and told him it was a good idea. The more he had occupying his brain the less likely he was to wallow in melancholia. At least, that was what she'd convinced herself.

She sat down at the kitchen table and poured herself a mug of stewed tea from the already cooling pot. Her mind turned to Simon. He and Natalya had been charged with their part in the people trafficking, though both had agreed to fully cooperate with the police. Their information had already led the police to Artem Koval, and with a bit of luck and a lot of pressure Koval would lead them to the main players: the bastards behind the operation, who had made so much from human misery. Simon had also been charged with shooting James Metcalf. She was a witness to that. She would argue in his defence that he was being goaded by the man who had murdered his family at the time; the balance of his mind clearly disturbed. A sympathetic judge might offer leniency under the circumstances. But there was the matter of Simon's confession about the hit and run that had almost killed Kyle Chisholm. Molly had kept this to herself for now, although she'd struggled with her conscience. On the one hand, Simon Galloway had admitted his responsibility for a serious crime. But on the other hand, he'd lost his entire family, including the father who'd lied to protect him. Was there any point in making him suffer further for a moment of stupidity that he clearly regretted?

There was a text from Ben. An ex-girlfriend had got in touch to tell him she'd got a job touring the pubs and clubs of south west England in a band and did he want to go with her? Molly hoped it would keep Ben out of trouble for a while, but she wasn't optimistic. Ben had a knack for attracting trouble and that was unlikely to ever change. At least out of London he would be someone else's problem.

There was a crash from the garden, and the sound of Jon cursing. She glanced out of the window and watched as he grappled with an ancient petrol lawnmower that was probably last used sometime during the previous century. She waved at him, letting him know she was home. He tapped his hand against his forehead in acknowledgement, then wandered back into the oversized shed. It would be worth it in the end, she thought. Jon needed a room of his own: a space to write and to think.

Molly had to do some thinking herself. Despite her reservations about her role in MIT, she was certain she wanted to be there.

Denning had told her what he thought: she took risks, which he didn't approve of, but she'd got results.

Betty Taggart however, had made her feelings very clear. Molly had pushed her luck. Twice. The third time would be the last. If she fucked up again, she would be off the team.

She wondered how things would have gone if neither Metcalf nor Simon had got out of there alive. Or if she'd called it wrongly and Simon wasn't innocent after all. At the very least they would be talking disciplinary action. At worst, she could have found herself out of a job.

It might still come to that. Perhaps there was going to come a time when she would have to ask herself where her future career lay.

—

Denning turned into the once-familiar street. Rows of neat, mellow-brick townhouses with their tidy gardens lined both sides of the road.

He hadn't called this home for a good few years now, but he still visited the street regularly.

As soon as he pulled up outside number eight, Jake opened the passenger door, climbed out of the car and raced up the short driveway to the front door. As soon as he reached it, he opened the door and ran inside. Denning followed, knocking lightly on the still open door and shouting hello.

Claire was in the kitchen, Jake clinging to her legs so tightly he was in danger of cutting off the circulation. She hugged him and told him she'd missed him. After a few moments, he untangled himself from her and headed into the back garden to play. Claire turned to Denning and said: 'I've only been back less than an hour. Are you so desperate to get rid of him?'

'I have to be somewhere,' he said. 'It's work related.' Neeraj had heard that he'd been turned down for the inspector's job at Hendon: lack of experience at senior level was the official reason, though Denning suspected he'd probably come across as a bit of a twat at the interview. Neeraj was a good officer, but tended to speak before he thought. Nerves would have compounded the situation and it was likely he'd said something he should probably have kept to himself. Denning had agreed to take him and the rest of the team out for a drink later, both to celebrate a good result with Metcalf, and to commiserate with Neeraj on not getting the job. It had been Betty Taggart's suggestion.

'How's your mum?' Denning asked, trying to defuse the situation before it had a chance to turn into an argument.

'She's better, thanks. Much better. She's got a carer going in every day to make sure she's OK, but I'll probably have to go back down in another couple of weeks.'

Claire was putting washing into the machine. She looked like she'd lost weight, either intentionally or due to the stress of recent events. Her face seemed narrower, but perhaps it was the light. 'How's Jake been?'

He'd already told her about the childminder and the problems they'd had with Jake. Her sympathy had been limited. 'We need to talk about where we go from here,' he said. 'I think we should look for a school that can cater for Jake's specific needs rather than trying to expect him to conform to something he's going to be uncomfortable with.'

She finished putting the washing into the machine, popped a capsule on top of the load and started the machine. 'Are you just saying this because you can't cope? Or is this something you and Sarah have discussed?'

He sat down at the kitchen table. 'You know I wouldn't discuss Jake's future with Sarah and not you. But we do need to discuss it, Claire. As Jake gets older his care needs will increase. I don't expect you to take on the care all by yourself, but Sarah and I both work full-time in demanding jobs. There's only so much we can do.'

Claire was standing by the table, half leaning against the kitchen worktop. 'You mean there's only so much you expect me to do. You've always been happy to leave Jake's care to me ever since you walked out on us. He doesn't fit in to your smart, comfortable life with Sarah. That's the truth, Matt.'

He wanted to argue with her but he was too tired. It had been a long day, coming at the end of a long and difficult week: the Galloway family; Martin Metcalf, it had all made him put things into perspective. He wanted Jake in his life, and maybe that meant having to make difficult choices. Perhaps it meant moving away, or changing job altogether.

Part of him wanted to turn the clock back and to keep things as they had been before he and Claire had split up. But it was no use wishing he could change things: what was done couldn't be undone.

He looked out of the window. Jake was running across the lawn, arms outstretched, pretending to be an aeroplane. Claire was still standing in the kitchen expecting him to say something. He stood to leave, tapping the kitchen window and waving goodbye to Jake. But Jake either didn't see him or was too wrapped up in whatever game he was playing in his head to notice.

Telling Claire he would be in touch to talk about making future arrangements, he headed down the hallway to the front door.

As he walked back to the car he spotted one of his former neighbours working on his motorbike in the driveway of the house opposite. He smiled and waved his hand in acknowledgement, the neighbour doing the same. He watched as the man's son came out of the front door and ran up to his daddy, tugging at his sleeve and showing him something in his hand. It all looked so normal: safe, happy. The perfect family.

It was only now that Denning realised the idea of the perfect family was nothing more than a fallacy.

As he got into the car, he thought about the Galloways. All Brian and Ellie Galloway were guilty of was trying to do the best for their children. Even Amber, when it came down to it, just wanted to be a good mum to Caleb. They might have failed. They might have got it wrong more often than not, as Denning himself probably did with Jake. His own parents had only ever wanted the best for him, even if they always made him feel like he'd let them down.

As he pulled away from the kerb, he glanced back at the house, half expecting to see Jake's face at the living room window, waving him goodbye. But there was no sign of Jake. He was probably still playing in the garden, happy to be home; his recent adventure with his daddy nothing more than a distraction.

A Letter From Graeme

Firstly, many thanks for reading *Blood Family*, and I hope you enjoyed the second outing for detectives Denning and Fisher.

I wanted to write about dysfunctional families and explore what happens when a family unit breaks down. When they work, families can be strong and loving and supportive, but when they don't, they can cause so much damage, often unintentionally. The Galloways may be fictional but I don't think they're untypical of families today. However, it's not just the Galloways' story: *Blood Family* sees Denning and Fisher having to face up to challenges in their own families, and ultimately they have to ask difficult questions of themselves.

I'm already planning the next book in the series, which will see Molly put through the emotional mangle as she has to face up to a traumatic event in her personal life that has implications for her job…

If you enjoyed *Blood Family*, please leave a review on Amazon or Goodreads, or even recommend it to your friends and family. I love hearing from readers, so please feel free to get in touch with me via my website: www.graemehampton.com, or follow me on Twitter at @GHam001.

Thank you,
Graeme

Acknowledgments

The second novel is no easier to write than the first. Fortunately, I already had an idea I wanted to explore, and *Blood Family* is the end result of that idea. As with my first novel, the final draft turned out to be quite some way removed from the initial concept.

As always, there are so many people whose help, advice and support have made the book possible, and I'd like to take this opportunity to thank them.

Firstly, Gary Metalle, Tracey Caswell and Jessica Dyson for their advice and continued support throughout the writing process. Thanks also to Sue Matthews, Jo Worthington Wilde and Ros Hooke who commented on an early draft and told me the story 'had legs', and to Christine Warrington for looking over the manuscript for me and flagging up the occasional error.

I'd like to thank Alyson Parker at the Met Police, and Denise Mubika and Stuart Drummond at The London Fire Brigade – your input is much appreciated and helped add credibility to the important early chapters.

Keshini Naidoo, Lindsey Mooney and everyone at Hera Books deserve thanks and my eternal gratitude, not just for their tireless contribution to the book, but for believing in me – for a writer, that means everything. And to Allie Spencer and the team at Jericho Writers, thank you for your helpful suggestions and feedback whilst I was writing an early draft of the book.

Finally, to everyone who read *Know No Evil* and was kind enough to leave a review, a massive thank you!